Jeff Abbott's novels are published in twenty languages around the world and include the massive international bestseller *Panic*. *The Last Minute* won the International Thriller Writers Award for best novel and Jeff is a three-time nominee for the Edgar Award. His novels *Panic* and *Run* have been optioned for film. Jeff lives in Austin, Texas with his family. Find out more at www.jeffabbott.com.

ALSO BY JEFF ABBOTT

Sam Capra Series

Adrenaline

The Last Minute

Downfall

Inside Man

The First Order

Whit Mosley series

A Kiss Gone Bad

Black Jack Point

Cut and Run

Other fiction

Panic

Fear

Run

Trust Me

Blame

THE THREE BETHS

JEFF ABBOTT

sphere

SPHERE

First published in the United States in 2018 by Grand Central,
a division of Hachette Book Group US
First published in Great Britain in 2018 by Sphere

1 3 5 7 9 10 8 6 4 2

A CIP catalogue record for this book
is available from the British Library.

ISBN 978-0-7515-7606-1

Printed and bound in Great Britain by Clays Ltd, Elcograf S.p.A.

Papers used by Sphere are from well-managed forests
and other responsible sources.

Sphere
An imprint of
Little, Brown Book Group
Carmelite House
50 Victoria Embankment
London EC4Y 0DZ

An Hachette UK Company
www.hachette.co.uk

www.littlebrown.co.uk

For Lindsey Rose, with gratitude and respect

1

MARIAH DUNNING SAW her missing mother standing on the other side of the crowd.

The food court at the mall—ugh—had been one of their mother-daughter hangouts. Mom endured the food court because Mariah liked it. Mom was particular about what she ate, while Mariah was not—chicken biscuits, Mongolian barbecue, pepperoni pizza, none of which Mom would touch and all of which Mariah would consume and then work off the calories playing basketball. And when Mariah got the summer job during her high school years selling tickets at the movie theater, a back corner booth at the food court was a place where they could meet and share a sacred hour between Mom's business trips, Mom saying, "Well it's better than airplane food—I think."

Mariah had not been to the food court since Mom disappeared. She had been careful to avoid it on the few outings she made to the mall. But she and her father had gone to the Apple Store to buy Mariah a new computer and a new iPhone; it made Dad happy to give her gifts even though she was an adult who could buy her own gear. His gifts were like a hug, sideways, when you didn't know the depth of the other person's feelings. The food court wasn't a place she wanted to be; it made the back of her brain itch, made her feel like she couldn't sit still. Dad had said, "Let's get a snack," and he was trying so hard to make today fun that Mariah didn't have the heart to say no. But in the middle of the music and the loud conversations Mariah glanced up from her pad thai and she saw her mother. Mariah froze, the chopsticks in her hand, the tangled noodles hanging like a noose.

Her mother had vanished nearly a year ago, and then there she stood, peeking out from behind a sunglasses display at the edge of the food court. Dark glasses, red lipstick, pale skin, even the distinctive twist of scar at the corner of her mouth that could only be Mom's. For five seconds Mariah couldn't move, couldn't make a noise; she felt like she might never speak again. They gazed at each other, like she was in a staring contest with a ghost. Mariah stood, dropping the chopsticks into the bowl.

Her mother retreated behind the display. Gone.

"Mariah?" Dad asked, glancing up at her. "What?"

"Mom is standing right over there." She pointed, her hand shaking. Dad stared for a moment and then turned.

"That can't be."

Mariah started to walk fast. Then to run, threading her way through the maze of tables and diners.

"Mariah?" Dad stood, craning his neck. "Where are you going?"

"I saw her." Mariah ran, heedless, toward the sunglasses display. She couldn't see Mom anymore. She shoved past two women, nearly knocking one's tray of Chinese food over and the other's milk shake to the floor. "Mom! Mom!"

"Mariah!" Dad calling, low and urgent. Like he didn't want people to notice. Hurrying in her wake, apologizing to the people Mariah collided with, apologizing to those she dodged. "Mariah, wait." He made his voice steel, trying to stop her.

"Mom!" she screamed, loud and long, like she could leash her mother with the sound of her voice. Like Mariah was still a child instead of twenty-two years old. She moved fast, but blindly, hardly seeing the people she pushed aside. She circled the sunglasses vendor. Mom was gone. She spoke to the clerk. "There was a woman just here: dark hair, dark coat, scarred mouth. Forties. Where did she go?"

The clerk shrugged. "I'm sorry, I didn't see her."

"She was just here!" Mariah's voice shook as she glanced around.

"I didn't see her," the clerk repeated. People were staring, watching. Mariah saw a girl aim a smartphone at her.

Mariah hurried beyond the display, past four other mall carts, out into the wide hub where two wings of the mall came together. Ahead of her was a two-story department store; to her left, a wing of the mall with a bunch of specialty shops; to her right, the ever-busy Apple Store and several smaller stores.

"You didn't see her," Dad said, touching her arm, and she flinched away. "Sweetie, if it was her, she wouldn't have run. You imagined it."

I didn't, Mariah thought. *She was here. I saw her.*

"You didn't," Dad said, as if Mariah's thoughts displayed on her forehead. "Mariah. Let's go." A tinge of embarrassment touched his voice. "We don't need this."

"What's your damn problem?" a woman demanded, a spilled chocolate milk shake running down the front of her white blouse. Her eyes were bright with anger.

"She's so sorry," Dad said, watching a mall security guard approach. "Please, let me take care of your cleaning bill for that." He opened his wallet, began to count out twenties. He seemed desperate for them not to be noticed.

"Hey. Haven't I seen you on TV?" the woman said.

"No," Dad said. "No."

Mariah ignored them both. *She wanted to see you. She came and looked right at you. No sign of her either to the left or right.* So Mariah ran, full tilt, for the department store ahead of her, Dad calling her name in a pitiful bleat.

Mariah tore through the department store, dodging around a woman spraying perfume samples then turning and grabbing her arm. The sample bottle fell and shattered, and the lavender aroma of the French perfume rose hard in the air.

"A woman, black hair, black coat, did you see her go past?"

"Um. I think so. She went out that exit." The woman pulled away, fright in her eyes.

Mariah ran to the nearby exit, jostling around a woman with a baby stroller, fury and impatience driving her out into a small side parking lot. She scanned the cars.

"*Mom!*" she screamed. But Mom was gone. She saw a car, the only one pulling out of the lot. Dark blue. Honda. And the car sped away, and was gone.

It must be her. It had to be her.

Mariah ran to her car. Thankful she'd driven, and not Dad, so she already had the keys. She got into the car, jabbing at the ignition, wheeling it backward before she could even get the door shut all the way. In the mirror she saw Dad running toward her, his expression frantic. She powered down the lane, racing out into traffic, narrowly missing an oncoming minivan loaded with a mother and kids. The mother honked and screamed at her, and Mariah screamed back "Sorry!" and pulled the car out of its swerve. The Honda turned and headed down the steep hill that led to the mall's exit onto a cross street.

She followed, blasting through a four-way stop and turning at the same hill. The blue Honda took a hard right, away from the highway, back toward the center of Lakehaven. Mariah accelerated; her old Ford sedan straining at the boost. She started to close the gap. She could see the driver was a dark-haired woman.

Get up next to her, she thought, *confirm that it's Mom. You're not crazy. It's Mom.*

She accelerated, drawing closer to the Honda, and then the Honda veered into a sharp turn. Mariah overcompensated, control drifting from the wheel, and she spun into the oncoming lanes. She saw the markings of a police sedan, the sirens atop the roof as she spun toward it and then the car hit her Ford's rear, spinning her again, and she came to a jarring halt. Shaking. Looking at the Lakehaven police car in her mirror. The Honda was gone.

"Get out of the car, now!" the officer's voice yelling at her sternly, and she trembled, because now people would have something else to talk about her family, a bright new flame of shame. She bit her lip.

Mariah Dunning got out of the car, hands up. "Hello, officer. I have a bunch of guns and gear in the trunk. And I've got a telescoping baton in my boot. Just so you know."

2

AN HOUR LATER, Mariah and her dad were dropped off by a rideshare service at the driveway of their modest house not far from Lakehaven High School. Home was a 1960s ranch-style house at the top of a hill, the type that had been torn down repeatedly in this Lakehaven neighborhood and replaced with a much larger, grander McMansion squeezed onto the lot. Sometimes when Mariah came home she'd see her father standing at the window, peering out to see if there was a for sale sign in a neighbor's yard on Bobtail Drive. There had been several in the past year. People were cashing in on the renovation craze. She wondered if her father was worrying about a teardown happening and hiking his property taxes or just hoping for new neighbors, ones who didn't know about his wife's disappearance. Neighbors who didn't look at him with thin smiles that seemed to whisper, *How'd you do it, Craig? How'd you get rid of the body?* The gossip always seemed to convey with the sale. The new neighbors never said hello when Mariah or her father were in the front yard or shooting baskets in the driveway.

She'd gotten him to venture out of the house today, for the first time in weeks, and it had all gone wrong.

Mariah had moved home right after her mother vanished, and she knew she should get her own apartment again, but she couldn't. She didn't feel ready to leave Dad quite yet…to leave him alone. She'd finished her degree in computer science at the University of Texas as fast as she could; she didn't like to leave Dad at loose ends for long, even for classes and labs. She got permission from her professors to do group assignments solo, even though it was harder, so she wouldn't have to let him dwell in his personal darkness.

It was the two of them against the police and against the world. Parties and service projects and all the other résumé padding and fun times of college had ceased to matter to her, gone on the wind of her mother's vanishing. It was too hard to explain to people with unsullied pasts and bright futures: *Well, you see, my mom disappeared without a trace and no we don't know if she was murdered or kidnapped or if she just walked away from her life and my dad was the prime suspect in her disappearance but nothing could be proven so we live in a limbo. What's your major?*

Now Mariah felt a hot embarrassment rise from the small of her back, spread through her chest, redden her face. She'd lost control. The control she kept in place for the world's eyes. And now Dad *knew*. The gear in the trunk, the file box with clippings about her mother, the guns and the police baton and the Taser, the laptop loaded with software designed to trace and find people. She'd had to explain it all to the police, in front of her father, when he'd been brought to the station. She could have argued she didn't have to explain anything. But telling them this had made them sympathetic, and they'd let her go without formal charge. One of the officers had stared at her father the whole time. Oh, they all knew Craig Dunning.

He was, in their eyes, guilty. The guy who got away with murder.

Her dad got a pitcher of iced tea from the refrigerator, shuffling, walking like a man carrying too heavy a burden. Craig Dunning had been a football player at Lakehaven High and then at Rhodes College up in Memphis on scholarship. He was a broad-shouldered blond with blue eyes and a strong jaw. In college he had done some modeling for a couple of Southern clothing catalog companies; Mom had kept a portfolio of his work, to his total embarrassment and Mariah's vast amusement. She liked to pretend to be horrified at him posing in modest swimwear and suits and cable-knit sweaters, and whenever she saw one of his modeling shots she'd make sure to say, "Ewww, I thought the point was to sell the clothes." Because he knew she was teasing him. Her handsome dad. There was no interest from the pro football scouts, so he'd put his trophies and disappointments on a shelf, and he'd gotten a master's in accounting and worked his way up to partner in one of the national firms. Now he "consulted," which meant he didn't go to the office in downtown Austin or wear a suit, and the firm sent him work he did mostly from home. Sometimes he rallied enough to go in for a meeting or a call; he no longer went to the firm's holiday party or the Fourth of July picnic. Now he was rail-thin and sunken-cheeked; ash-gray streaked his hair. He had loved just one woman in his life, and her loss was like a physical mark on him. He was still a handsome man, but the joy that once animated his best feature, his smile, was gone. To Mariah, he was like a painting you could look at and say, yes, the lines are all in proportion, the colors are right, but something is missing.

"You're lucky Broussard is not pressing charges," Craig said. Lakehaven's police chief, Dennis Broussard, had listened to Craig's account of Mariah's... confusion with a stony silence. *Yes, we're going to get her back into therapy. No, she has not imagined seeing her mother before. Just stress.* Ignoring the officers' stares at him because they thought he might be a murderer. And here was his daughter, with a car trunk full of weapons and gear, like she was planning a robbery or a heist.

"Do we have your consent to search the car?" the police had asked, and she had said yes. What else was she going to say? A towing service had already taken her car and the police cruiser both.

"You shouldn't have given your consent for them to search your car," Craig said, as if he knew her thoughts. "Why would they need to? They could plant drugs or something."

"Dad. They're not going to do that. Get real."

"They hate us. Or me, rather."

"I didn't have much choice. I was at fault, Dad."

"You don't...you don't need those weapons and gear. And saying it's to hunt down Mom's kidnappers. You can't say stuff like that to the police. They don't like people trying to do their job. It's dangerous, Mariah. I'm amazed they didn't arrest you."

"The police don't like us anyway."

"They don't like me," Craig said. "They feel sorry for you. Especially Broussard."

Sometimes Mariah had seen Broussard, in his own car, driving slowly past their home. Like he wanted to stop. Or simply put eyes on her father. It had been Broussard who, summoned to the scene by an officer because the Dunnings were involved and Mariah had claimed to be chasing her missing mother, had stopped to get the stranded Craig at the nearby mall and brought him back to the scene. Mariah imagined it had been an awkward few minutes together in the car for the two men. Her father had not shared any details.

Craig poured iced tea for them both, and Mariah took hers with a shaking hand. She had to ask. "Did you see her?" Mariah asked. She hoped he'd say, *Yes, she did look like Mom. I see how you thought what you thought.*

"No, honey, I did not." Craig sounded tired. Not angry. Not annoyed. Just exhausted.

"Did you see the blue Honda?"

"Well, the police saw it, but they didn't see the driver." Craig's voice went soft. "It was probably just an innocent woman who panicked when you chased after her."

It was Mom, Mariah wanted to say, but she didn't. He didn't believe her. No one did. They sat in silence for a minute.

"I wonder if the mall has parking lot security tapes." Mariah's tone had calmed, become thoughtful. "I could ask."

Craig took a deep breath. "Mariah, stop right now. You are not calling the mall and asking them to review security tapes. They will ban you from going back there. You drove recklessly, you damaged a police car, and the only reason the cops didn't arrest you and haul you off to jail is because they felt bad for you."

Mariah didn't like these words, so she ignored them. "I really thought it was Mom. I did."

"I know you think you did, sweetheart. I know. What I wouldn't give to see her..." His deep voice cracked, and he took a deep breath. "Can we please talk about what all you had in your car? Wrist ties and guns and a Taser? Who are you planning to kidnap?" His gaunt face was pale with worry.

Mariah set her tea down. "I told you, I legally bought the guns and the gear."

"Why would you have an armory in your car, sweetheart?"

"I have to be prepared for when I find Mom in case bad people have her. Dad, it's OK, I took classes on how to use this stuff."

He sat across from her, took her hands in his. "Classes?"

"And I watched online videos."

"Honey, you are not some sort of bounty hunter or movie detective. Mariah, this stops now. You can't do this to yourself. Or to me." His voice cracked.

"The police quit looking," she said. "Someone has to find Mom. Find out what happened to her."

"I love you so much. But you didn't see your mom today," he said. "Do you understand that, Mariah? That woman wasn't your mom. This is...this is your grief playing tricks on your mind."

Her voice shook. "Even if...I still have to know what happened to her. I have to know who took her from us." She fought to keep her voice steady. "I have to know."

"No, you don't! I mean...not like this. We just have to keep the faith the police will find her someday. But you, you stay out of it."

Mariah took a deep breath. "Dad, I never got the chance to fix things with her. I..."

"I don't know how to make this right for you. I wish I did. I wish I could make people understand how hard this is for us. More than anything."

Because of Lakehaven, Mariah thought. Because of so many people who had been sure her father had killed her mother, somehow made her body vanish. Although there was no evidence. No proof. And no other suspects in their circle of friends and acquaintances.

Only the low, ceaseless whisper of innuendo and hearsay against her father. But that constant drip was poison enough to nearly kill a man, leave him a shell. Beth Dunning had never reappeared—not on a credit history, not with a phone call, not on a security camera. She had stepped out of the world.

"Let me fix us a late lunch," Mariah said. They'd abandoned their meals at the food court. Craig usually cooked; he was much better at it than Mariah. But she wanted to do something nice for him.

"No, I'll fix it. You want a grilled cheese?"

She nodded and hugged him, and to Mariah he felt like skin and bones underneath the jeans and the Lakehaven basketball booster club shirt, faded in the years since she had played on the team. *I'm sorry, Dad*, she thought to herself.

Craig turned away and padded over to the refrigerator. He got out butter and sliced cheddar, set a pan on the stove, and began to assemble a cheese sandwich, melting butter in the skillet. "This feels like a point of no return. We can't do this again. You could have hurt yourself badly. You could have hurt a police officer. Or an innocent person. Do you think this town would ever forgive us for anything more? I'm not going back to people throwing rocks at the house or spray painted threats in the middle of the night. I'm not putting you through that again."

The phrases KILLER LIVES HERE and WHERE IS BETH, CRAIG? had been painted in bright red on their garage door. She would never forget. Some of the neighbors had helped them clean it up—but she could see the doubt in their faces. "Dad..."

"I think we need to have a service for your mom," he said. "We have to wait for her to be missing seven years to have her declared legally dead." Craig bit his lip. "But...maybe we go ahead and have a memorial of some sort. We let her go."

"No." She shook her head.

He met her gaze, and there was a steadiness there she hadn't seen from him in a long time. "This grief...Fine, it can ruin me. But it cannot ruin you. You have to move forward with your life. What if your clients hear about today?"

"How would anyone hear?" Mariah was a freelance web designer. She only had three steady clients, the largest one a hip clothing boutique, which did a high volume of online sales.

"People talk on social media. They're a damn lynch mob. Maybe someone recorded your scene at the mall on their phone. Or took a picture of you being put in the police cruiser. Maybe someone posts it. You think there wasn't someone from Lakehaven in that food court? And the police blotter, they post that in the town paper. It'll be on the Lakehaven news website." His voice cracked. "This can't happen. Not everyone looking at you this way..."

She had no answer to this. She thought of the teenager with a raised smartphone, aimed at her. People were so ready to record the awful moments for someone else. She could imagine the status posting: Girl hallucinates seeing missing mother in food court, ends up in car crash with cops. Surely no one would be that cruel. Then surely, she knew, they would.

"I could go see a therapist," she said quietly. "If you want me to. You said so to the cops."

"I don't think that's necessary." Craig eased the hot sandwich out of the pan, put it on a plate, and cut it into three equal strips, just how Mariah liked it. He handed her the plate and started making a sandwich for himself. Not looking at her, wanting, she thought, for the conversation to be over. Any time she'd mentioned talking to someone professional, a grief counselor, a psychiatrist, he'd resisted. Now he had lied to the police. She could go herself. She was an adult. But if he didn't like it, it felt like a betrayal. She thought he must worry about what she would say about him: *Everyone thinks my dad is guilty, and I don't, but... what if...*

She sat down with the sandwich, but it had no taste; the butter and cheese and soft bread just felt like grease in her mouth. "I mean, I'm surprised you don't want me to talk to a therapist."

"All it does is make people miserable. We have to learn how to deal with grief on our own," Craig said. "And I want you to stop this idea of finding whoever took your mom. The police, it's their job, leave it alone. Promise me you'll stop."

He waited. She wanted to say, *The idea of finding Mom is my therapy. It's the only thing that makes me feel better.* Instead she said, "I promise."

And then a vicious little voice, borne of hurt and pain and sadness, said in the back corner of her brain, *Why doesn't Dad want you to see a therapist or find out the truth? Why?*

And she strangled that little voice in her mind, quickly, before it could speak its poison again.

3

CRAIG CURLED UP into his leather recliner in front of a huge flat-screen television. He fired up one of the streaming services. He would binge through hours of shows, often mesmerized for most of the night. He slept very little, cocooned in the soft glow of the stories. Many nights he just slept in the recliner, which worried Mariah. It seemed unhealthy, but her attempts to get him to sleep normal hours all failed.

Mariah told him she was going to her room to read. She had stopped watching much TV: crime dramas made her edgy, and reality shows were full of people with invented problems. Books had been her refuge. She shut the bedroom door and leaned her head against the wood.

She hadn't come up here to read.

She locked the door, quietly. Dad could always seem to hear the lock clicking into place, and in those dark days after Mom disappeared he had been afraid Mariah would hurt herself. She had been afraid of the same with him. She dimmed the lights. She lit a candle her mother had given her on her fifteenth birthday. She thought candles made for crappy gifts, but this one she had liked. It smelled of vanilla and cinnamon, and she only lit it when it was time for her quiet secret ritual. It made her think of Mom, the warmth of her hugs, the smell of her skin, the strength of her.

They could laugh, even during the fights, the disagreements, the screaming matches of her teenage years. She loved her mother so much, and sometimes she'd acted like she hated her. She'd never told Mom how much she loved her. This failure seemed to widen the hole in her heart.

She stepped inside her small closet and reached behind her hanging clothes. She slowly eased out a large corkboard. Papers and photos were pinned to it. Pictures of Mom, printouts of news accounts when she vanished, sketches of men from around the country who were suspected in the disappearances of women. There were printouts of postings by a true-crime blogger and podcaster who wrote under the name "Reveal" and had taken an interest in her mother's case. A schedule of the day she'd last been seen: March fourth. The bits and pieces of her mother's case, and she'd mounted them like she was a detective on a TV show, or Claire Danes on *Homeland* hunting a terrorist, trying to see the data and the connections all at once, spot the unseen ties that would lead her to the truth. She used to sleep with the corkboard over her bed, as if the data would sift down into her mind and reveal the answers in her dreams. But she never remembered her dreams since Mom vanished, even if she awoke sweating and confused and near to tears. Her father had told her, in a quavering voice, to stop this foolishness and take the corkboard down. He told her this wasn't healthy. She thought it was all that was keeping her balanced. She told him she'd thrown it all away, but instead she'd just slid it into the closet behind her clothes.

She hadn't added anything to the board in a long while. There was nothing new to say.

She sat at her laptop and started to type in what she always did for the ritual: Beth Dunning disappearance Austin

The results appeared. The news stories from the time, both from the Austin and Lakehaven papers and from the local news stations. Her mother's story hadn't gotten much national coverage, a bit on CNN and some of the others, and then the world moved on. She knew most of them by heart. And the entries from Reveal's crime blog—but there was a new entry under Reveal's blog entries.

She clicked on it.

WHAT'S IN A NAME?

There are certain cases that I've written about numerous times. One of those is of Bethany "Beth" Blevins Curtis, who left Austin eighteen months ago in an apparent desertion of her husband. But since taking a flight to Houston she has made no subsequent contact with friends or family and has not left any kind of digital trail. No one has seen her. Six months later, Beth Dunning of Lakehaven, a suburb of Austin, also vanished, her car found at an empty lot in the hills above Lakehaven, where she and her husband were planning on building a home and where she often went for quiet time.

Two Beths, vanishing without a trace from the same city in less than a year.

A six-month interlude is consistent with certain serial killer cycles . . . but have you ever heard of a serial killer who chooses victims with a particular name? I haven't. And I haven't found a notice of another Beth disappearing this past year, though, for which we should be grateful there is not a name-obsessed serial killer lurking in our fair city (for a history of Austin and serial killers, see my earlier series of podcasts on America's first serial killer, who terrorized Austin in the 1880s, known as the Midnight Assassin, also known as the Servant Girl Annihilator). But wouldn't the psychology of someone who so hated a name that he had to kill victims bearing it be fascinating? Of course, neither woman's body has turned up to suggest a serial killer, so this is likely a coincidence, but an interesting one.

I noticed this unhappy coincidence when I was writing up my exciting new Calendar of Unsolved Cases, a new feature on the website that will link to my previous blogs and podcasts, tied to the major date of each case. These are two very different disappearances, but the names and the time frame struck me. I think it's always interesting to look for coincidences and see if they are something more.

Is it not the most human endeavor to seek the pattern of order in chaos?

If you agree, then hit up my PaySupport, so I can keep doing this podcast for you . . .

To seek the pattern of order in chaos. Yes. Mariah almost nodded at the screen. Patterns must be found. That was what she needed: a pattern, an explanation that made sense in a world that didn't.

She clicked on all the links to the Beth Curtis case.

The first was to an article from a tech news website on the disappearance. Bethany Blevins Curtis. Dark shoulder-length hair, wide mouth, cheekbones that Mariah envied, nice smile, age twenty-seven. She worked as an office manager for a transportation company in south Austin. She was married to a man who was a rising star in technology, CEO and founder of a small software company preparing for a public offering of its stock, valued at millions. Mariah tried to remember if she'd heard about this case, but she didn't watch the local news much before Mom vanished. And, as she read, she agreed with Reveal: this might not even have been a disappearance as much as an abandonment.

On September 4 eighteen months ago, Bethany Blevins Curtis had apparently left her home in north Austin, taken a few hundred dollars out of the joint banking account shared with her husband, boarded a Southwest Airlines flight, and flown the short jaunt to Houston. A security camera caught her walking alone through the Hobby Airport terminal. That security video was posted on a Faceplace page dedicated to her, apparently run by a friend: Bethany Curtis in a crowd, dark hair, floppy brown hat pulled low, a muted scarf tied around her throat, dark glasses. Glancing over her shoulder. Somehow, she had eluded the cameras in the airport; they'd lost her in the crowds. Did someone pick her up? Did she already arrange for a car to be there waiting? Did she shed her coat and scarf and hat and walk undetected? She was simply gone.

This case wasn't like her mother's. Mom had not made a withdrawal from a bank account or flown on a plane and been spotted in the airport security videos. Mom had gone to work at the software company where she was a sales rep, left for lunch, and had never been seen again. Beth Dunning's car had been found parked near some property in Lakehaven she and Dad owned and had been planning to build a house on. Mom had always liked being out on the property, a large empty lot with a stunning view. It was peaceful, and she liked to talk about the house they would build. It was a place she went for quiet, to escape the pressure and busyness of her job, imagining the house that would stand there one day, with its lovely views of the hills of Lakehaven.

Reveal was right: the only similarities were the name Beth, that the women's residences were separated by a matter of a few miles, and the short time frame between cases.

But...but...She went back to the links on the Curtis case. The other Beth left behind a husband, Jake, a software entrepreneur who steadfastly claimed he had nothing to do with her disappearance. He had a company that went public a few months after Bethany disappeared—apparently his investors stuck with him. He'd made millions. That got some press from both local media and the tech industry media, as if perhaps he'd gotten rid of his wife so as not to share his new wealth.

He'd been accused, just like her father.

Mariah read a follow-up article at the one-year anniversary...Bethany Curtis had still not left any kind of digital trail. No use of credit cards, no withdrawals from her bank, no pinging of her cell phone by towers. She had left her life, then left...everything else.

Mariah printed out the articles on Bethany Curtis and pinned them in an empty corner of Mom's corkboard. She placed the photo of Bethany Curtis next to Mom's.

The names.

The short time span between their disappearances.

The proximity of their homes, their lives.

The surprising lack of evidence in both cases. As if care was taken.

Despite their differences, there were these similarities.

And she had nothing else. She literally had no other clues to follow as a thread. This was it. Her other option was to chase shadows in the mall, humiliate herself in front of her father and the police.

And then she made up her mind. She had to know. The time span, the similarity of the names, no trail for either of them...this was a hunger suddenly, a need to know that gnawed at her. She would find the pattern, if it was there.

And if there was any way to make the connection back to her mother.

She emailed Reveal: Hi, Chad. Read your post about my mom and Beth Curtis. Want to meet me for a drink tonight? I wonder if you're right about patterns.

Reveal's answer came faster than she thought it would: I sure would.

Meeting him was defying Dad. So she wouldn't tell Dad.

4

MARIAH ASKED REVEAL if they could meet for a margarita at a Lakehaven Tex-Mex restaurant in a busy shopping center off Loop 360, and Reveal agreed. When she came downstairs, she found her father asleep in his recliner, a large wineglass empty and a half-empty bottle of merlot next to it, the TV streaming a British crime drama. He'd turned on the subtitles because he sometimes had trouble with the accents, and he kept the television volume turned down at night. Sometimes when she found him this way she would stop and be sure he was still breathing. She knew he had sleeping pills in the house, and sometimes she was afraid he'd swallow them with the nightly wine and leave all this care behind. It was her greatest fear. His chest rose and fell. She watched him sleep for a moment. He wanted to fix everything for her. But she needed to do this, to at least try. She put the wine in the fridge, tucked a blanket around him, turned off the television, and left him a note propped against the wineglass: *Meeting a friend over at La Luna. I need a little bit of normal, and I'll be very careful with your car. Thanks for understanding, Dad. I love you so much. I'll be home soon.*

She took the keys to his Lexus and drove to the restaurant. Reveal was already seated on the restaurant's patio, a beer in hand. He stood and waved at her.

The restaurant wasn't busy with the dinner rush past. It was humid and there was only one other customer on the patio, a young woman sitting alone by the railing, reading a thick book, sipping a margarita. It looked good, and Mariah wanted one, the sharp taste of the lime, the dulling of the tequila.

Reveal's real name was Chad Chang, but he insisted on people calling him by his stage name. He had been a couple of years ahead of Mariah at Lakehaven High School, and they'd known each other, but had gotten better acquainted since her mother's vanishment. He had written about the case a few times, without pointing the expected finger of guilt at her father. He'd studied psychology at Trinity University in San Antonio. While there, he started a podcast about true crime, and it had exploded in surprising popularity. He focused on talking about crimes both past and present for a young, hip audience. His advertisers on his podcast included publishers, fashion designers, and car companies. Tonight he was dressed in jeans and an Astros jersey, wearing gleaming sunglasses despite the fact that it was evening.

"The drinks are on me," he said.

The waiter came to their table and she ordered a margarita. "Thanks. I figured you're broke after buying those sunglasses."

He took them off with a shrug. "I got great news. I got a Hollywood producer interested in my podcasts. They asked me to pitch a series to the basic cable networks. Me, hosting a show on true crime cases. With a celebrity panel to discuss. It could be huge for me."

"That's wonderful, Chad—Reveal." She reminded herself he really preferred his blogging name.

"So I got out to LA for the first meeting, and I felt so not-a-celebrity. I'm just a Lakehaven kid. I felt I needed the sunglasses to look cool, like a prop during the pitch."

"Did it work?" He hadn't said the deal was in place.

He put the glasses down next to his beer. "Freddy—that's the producer—he's getting back to me."

That didn't sound promising, but she smiled encouragingly. "I hope it works out for you."

"Any news on your mom?"

"I want to talk to you about what you wrote regarding my mom and Beth Curtis."

"So, um, what I wrote was more a thinking aloud than a theory about your mom's case."

"Bethany"—it was easier to avoid confusion talking about the two Beths to use Curtis's full name—"Curtis left her husband. What if my mom did the same?"

Reveal frowned. "Have there been new developments?"

She didn't want to confess about today's mall incident. She had to be careful with him; he was a friend, but a friend whose main goal was to grow his name as a chronicler of crime. "No, I would have told you that immediately. But if I could find a pattern linking the cases..."

Then she noticed what was happening at the patio railing.

Reveal realized Mariah wasn't looking at him. He turned around. A young man with a weasel's smile had stopped at the patio's fence along the shopping center walkway and was trying to chat up the solitary young woman, who was trying to focus on her book.

"That a good book?" he asked. "You could turn my pages."

The young woman didn't answer, but she fidgeted in the seat, eyes on the page.

"Question is why a fine young babe like you needs to fill her time reading when I'm right here, ready to buy you a drink."

"I'm not interested, thanks," the young woman said. "I have a boyfriend."

"Yet here you are alone."

"No, thanks."

The jerk took immediate offense. "Listen, you think you too good for me? You're not."

"Excuse me," Mariah said. She stood and walked over to the table.

"Mariah..." Reveal started to say, but he kept his seat.

"Please, I'm just trying to read in peace," the young woman said to the jerk. An angry edge in her voice now. "Go away, I'm not interested."

"Listen, books make you into a snotty bitch, from what I can see," the jerk said.

"Hey," Mariah said, now standing at the woman's table, across from the jerk. She was tall, but not quite as tall as he was. "She said she's not interested. Move along."

The jerk smiled. Then he laughed. Mariah watched him study and gauge her and could imagine his thoughts. Here was this tall, solid, mouthy annoyance, dressed in black slacks, black mock turtleneck, even a black barrette holding back her hair. "Listen, was I talking to your ugly face? Is this patio bitch central? Because all of you need to..."

At the word *need* he jabbed a finger at Mariah, and a sudden sharp rage rose in her chest. Her hand lashed out and caught one of his fingers and wrenched it. The jerk's mouth opened in pain; he tried to pull the hand back, but with the table between them Mariah had the leverage.

"Another millimeter, genius, and it breaks," she said gently. "Step back and walk away. And consider how you talk to women. I mean, has this idiotic banter ever worked once for you? Ever?"

"You whore..." and he tried to yank his hand back.

The snap of the breaking bone was loud. They stared at each other and she released his hand. He gasped. The reader stared at them both, pushing away from the table.

"I'm sorry," Mariah said. "I didn't mean..."

The jerk cradled the broken finger against his chest, too surprised to cuss or yell, and he staggered away toward the parking lot.

"You did that," Mariah called to his back. She felt sick. A wild tremble ran along her bones. *I didn't mean to, I didn't mean to.* But it felt good.

"Mariah!" Reveal yelled. "What the hell?"

"I didn't mean to," she said quietly. They all watched the jerk get into his car and drive off.

"I feel a little sick," Mariah said, and she sat down. Didn't mean to. But it happened.

"Thanks," the woman with the book said, in a shocked voice. She couldn't quite look at them, and she quickly put some cash on the table, even though her bill hadn't been brought.

"You're welcome. Is that book any good? My book club picked

it for next month." This was a lie, but Mariah realized she'd stunned them with a moment of violence and she was trying to look like a person who would belong to a book club instead of someone who snapped the fingers of strangers. "I'm Mariah. I'm sorry about that..."

"No, thank you, Mariah, I appreciate your help...and it's a very good read," the young woman murmured. She got up and hurried off the patio, heading toward the parking lot, clutching her thick book.

"OK then," Mariah sat back down across from Reveal, who stared at her.

"Mariah, have you lost your mind? You actually broke his finger...that was both awful and awesome." For a horrible moment she thought he was going to pick up his phone and take a snapshot of her.

"It was an accident." She cleared her throat. Would the jerk call the police? She couldn't talk to the Lakehaven police twice in a day. He looked humiliated, so she hoped he wouldn't come back with the cops. She took a long sip of her margarita. She kept screwing up. Badly. She had to get ahold of herself. Hallucinations, rage—she needed focus. Clarity. Purpose.

"Um, when I go back to LA, will you be my bodyguard?" Now Reveal was trying to joke, put her at ease. She probably looked like she was about to cry or vomit.

She made herself smile, very slightly, at his joke. "So, do you have a contact with Bethany Curtis's family?" Mariah asked.

"Her husband, Jake, made a fortune in software. It wouldn't surprise me if a lot of people approached him with information or tips, looking for a payout. He communicated with me by email, but just once, and very briefly. Her mother, Sharon, was more forthcoming when I talked to her. I asked her to be interviewed on the show, said it might help find Bethany, but she said it was too upsetting." Her own father had appeared on Reveal's show, begging for information on his wife's whereabouts, but it had produced no solid tips and a number of hurtful online comments suggesting that Craig had killed his wife and disposed of the body.

Her father did no further podcast appearances. "I'd try her mother first."

"Can I pick your brain? You theorized that there could be a"—she couldn't bring herself to say *killer*—"perpetrator who targeted women with a certain name? I mean, you know about criminal psychology and all that profiling stuff."

Reveal leaned back. "He couldn't be like Ted Bundy or Kenneth McDuff, looking for victims at random. This would be planned. I don't mean to upset you…"

"It's OK," she quickly said. "We're just talking." She cleared her throat. "What if he was a guy who had a hatred for a woman named Beth and took out his anger on other women named Beth?"

"You mean like the victims are a substitute for a Beth in his life? He targets them because they have her name, or they remind him of her in some way."

"Yes."

Reveal considered as the waiter stopped by to see if they needed anything. They waited for the waiter, surprised, to scoop up the cash from the reader's table and leave.

Reveal took a long sip of his beer. "I've not heard of any other women named Beth going missing in Austin."

"I feel like it's worth exploring," she said. "I mean, the timing, their names." She looked at him, hope in her eyes for an answer. "I'm willing to take that chance, to waste time on it if it's nothing." *And,* she thought, *to take the risk of the danger if this leads to my mom's killer.* But she kept that to herself.

Reveal drank down more of the margarita. "All right. I want a promise from you."

"What?"

"First, be careful. Second, whatever you find you share with me. I want the exclusive if there is something to this. I gave you this lead."

"All right." That seemed fair.

"Because something like this…well, there's lots of cases I look at. This would be decidedly different, if there was a connection." He stopped, stared down at his food.

"What, Chad?"

He didn't correct her on using his real name. "Mariah, I know how I sound. I can get so technical about crime that I come across as unfeeling. I know every person I have profiled had a story. Had a life they loved. Had a life worth fighting for. Had people who loved them, cared about them, miss them every day. I may have the douchebag sunglasses, but I'm not a total jerk. It's not always a good idea to go poking around in cold cases. Sometimes the people involved get angry. They feel threatened. Like you're accusing them."

She closed her eyes. "I just want to know the truth so badly."

Reveal cleared his throat, took another sip of beer. He was trying to sound extra tough, Mariah thought, probably because he'd kept his seat while she'd confronted the jerk. He took a deep breath. "So, here's an even scarier prospect: you could be sticking your nose into an unrelated case where someone who's gotten away with killing Bethany Curtis might not take at all kindly to you asking questions. Putting yourself in real danger for something that has nothing to do with your mom."

It was a sobering thought. "You report on these crimes, but you have no idea what it's like to actually live through one...everyone telling you how you should feel. How you should move on." Mariah clenched the end of the table. "You can't move on. It's like being stuck. It makes me so angry. I hurt that man, but I didn't mean to hurt him...I can't go on this way. So, if this is a nothing thread, fine, maybe I can help someone else if I can't help my mom."

"I won't underestimate your resolve. I loved your toughness with that creep. I couldn't go get involved and get punched, not with a producer meeting coming up this week."

"Of course not," she said, her voice neutral.

"You're right. I don't know what it's like. But you know I run a support group for those with missing relatives. You should come. Two nights from now, at the Episcopal church over off Old Travis."

What didn't he do? Support groups, podcasts, maybe a television show. It all made her dizzy. "I might," she said, although she couldn't imagine getting up and talking about her mom in front of strangers.

Reveal smiled. "It might help with your anger."

"Finding what happened to my mom is the cure I need," she said. She felt the resolve in her voice. She'd stopped that guy; she didn't know her own strength. She could learn it. She could do this.

He raised his beer toward her and put the fancy sunglasses back on his face. "Then here's to your cure. There's no cure like the truth."

5

MARIAH'S PHONE RANG as she got behind the wheel of her car. She stared for a moment at the number.

Lakehaven Police.

She had them in her phone's contacts list—and answered, a chill settling into her chest. Wouldn't they just come to the restaurant to arrest her for breaking the jerk's finger? She watched Reveal, her one remaining witness to the incident, get into his car and drive off from the parking lot before she answered. It wasn't even self-defense. The jerk had just *pointed* at her.

"This is Mariah."

"Mariah. Hello. This is Dennis Broussard." Lakehaven's police chief. Her father's nemesis.

"Hi," she said.

"I just wanted to check on you and see that you were okay."

"I'm fine," she said, keeping her voice neutral.

"I'm concerned for you."

"I'm so sorry. I really am."

"I'm just glad you're all right."

She didn't know what to say. "Thank you for calling. I have to go now."

"Mariah, is there anything you want to tell me? As a friend of your mom's?"

You're no friend, she thought. "No. I made a mistake today, and I'm sorry."

"I'm worried about why you have all this gear in your trunk."

"I don't have to explain that to you."

"Is it for self-defense? Are you afraid?"

"No," she said.

"All right," he said mildly. "But I am concerned about you. If I can help you, I will."

Help pin my mother's disappearance on my father, she thought. No thanks.

"Really, I'm okay, and I'll pay for the damage to your police car. I'll make it right."

"We're insured. Again, my concern is for you."

"If you're so concerned, let me ask you this. You think my dad killed my mom. If I could prove to you that he didn't, that there was another theory that was workable, would you follow it up?"

"Of course," he said. "But investigating a crime isn't your job."

"But it is yours, and you haven't found my mom."

"I promise you we will. But I want you to stay clear of the investigation, Mariah. I want you to be safe. And if you ever don't feel safe living at your father's house, I want you to know you can come to us here at the police department."

"Why wouldn't I feel safe? He's my dad."

"I think your hallucination today was a response to something traumatic you saw. Maybe the day your mom vanished." Broussard said nothing more, waiting for her to speak.

"You're not a psychologist."

"No. But if you're protecting your father, you are carrying such a heavy load. An unfair load. If he was the one who hurt your mother. You're protecting him but betraying her."

"I don't need your psychobabble, and I'm perfectly safe with my father. Good night." She hung up, her anger a hard knot in her chest. Broussard, trying to be her friend while trying to prove her father was a monster. The accident had given Broussard a reason to insinuate himself back into her life. Pretending to care while he failed to do his job.

Why not start following the Beth Curtis thread this very moment? She didn't feel like going home, and Broussard's call made her feel like she needed to take action, now. Prove him wrong. She opened the browser on her smartphone.

She did an internet search on Jake Curtis. He had a Faceplace page—and she and he had one mutual friend, Rob Radlon, a high school classmate of Mariah's. She checked her friend's page and it said Rob worked for DataMarvel, the company that had bought Jake Curtis's company. She hadn't really stayed in close touch with Rob, but he might be useful.

She checked Jake Curtis's statuses. He didn't post often, and she understood that—when you had a loved one missing, you didn't much feel like talking about seeing a movie or snapping pictures of your dinner at the cool new restaurant or sharing a cat video. He did write statuses about technical issues in the public eye, or about having had a nice weekend of reading or fishing. It struck her those were solitary activities. There was a link to a page about Bethany—she followed it. FIND BETHANY was the page's name, but it was weirdly inactive. A few postings from people who sounded like armchair detectives, contemplating where she might have gone or what her fate had been. She went farther down the page. The original page had been started by Bethany's mother, Sharon—postings nearly every day, pleas for her daughter to return or for whoever had taken Bethany to let her go, rewards for information. And then Sharon had fallen silent. Perhaps exhausted for asking and never getting an answer that helped? Jake would "like" statuses and ask occasionally for help in finding his wife—"I just want to be sure she's OK, don't care about anything else"—but also had not posted in a while.

She went back to Jake's main page. He had "liked" other pages related to other local software companies, his alma mater's football team, a couple of TV shows. And Reveal's Faceplace page. Among Jake's likes was a bar just north of Lakehaven, off Loop 360—the weekly trivia game night was a favorite. That was tonight. Maybe he was there. She looked him up on the property tax database and found his residence, not far from that bar, in a high-end neighborhood on the edge of Lakehaven.

Her phone rang. CHAD, said the screen. She answered it.

"It's Reveal. Someone followed me from the restaurant."

"What?"

"A dark car followed me. I noticed it, started taking a couple of turns I never take to get home. Car stuck with me. Hard to hide on a quiet Lakehaven street." Chad, she knew, lived at his parents' house still, to save money.

"The guy," she said, "with the broken finger?"

"Maybe he wants his revenge on me, not you. A guy who won't punch a girl will beat the crap out of her male friend."

She thought he was overreacting. "Is the car still following you?"

"No."

"What was it?"

"Dark-colored SUV. I think a Toyota."

She had seen the man with the broken finger head toward the parking lot...but what kind of car had he gotten into? She had been in shock at what she'd done and couldn't remember. It was a dark car, yes? Her eyes had been on him, embarrassed and angry, and clutching his hand to his chest. What if he'd pretended to leave, then followed Reveal?

No, she thought. Wouldn't he have gone straight to an emergency room? But maybe not. An angry, bitter, hyper-entitled man might think more of revenge than medical attention. And a guy like that would never want to admit: a woman broke my finger.

But why follow Reveal rather than her?

"Are you OK?" she asked Reveal.

"Yes, but it was unnerving."

"I'm sure it was." She kept her voice steady. "Do you want to call the police?"

"No," he said after a moment, perhaps embarrassed at how scared he'd sounded. "I'm fine. As long as he doesn't know where I live. He wasn't still following me when I got home."

If she turned herself into the police, told them what had happened, they could check the emergency rooms and find the guy, and learn his name...and ask him if he had followed Reveal. But if she confessed to assault, or whatever the charge would be,

Broussard might lock her up now. On top of the car issue. She decided to say nothing.

"I'll talk to you tomorrow, then," she said.

She drove to the bar near Jake Curtis's house: an Irish-themed pub, with Guinness and Harp on tap and a menu of select Irish whiskeys. It was surprisingly crowded on a weeknight; she wouldn't have thought trivia to be such a draw. At one of the side bars, she noticed tables with four teams of four playing a trivia game among much laughing, yelling, and drinking. She spotted Jake Curtis at one of the tables, sitting quietly, volunteering an answer when it was his turn but not being loud or obnoxious. She settled on an empty stool at the bar, ordered a pint of lager, and watched, trying not to be obvious. But she quickly realized the rest of the bar was watching, so it was fine.

On the final round, Jake Curtis won it for his team by knowing that the eighth president of the United States was Martin Van Buren. The team cheered and toasted each other. Mariah sipped her pint and watched, pretending to be bemused along with the others at the bar. The competitors broke up into smaller groups, some leaving, some staying to celebrate their minor victory. Jake and a man and a woman, the latter two clearly a couple, took positions along the bar, ordering ales, stretching their legs. The woman was standing next to Mariah and was a little drunk.

"Martin Van Buren," the woman said. "Greatest of presidents that I never heard of."

"You never heard of him?" Jake Curtis said. He was a handsome guy in an everyday way, nice features, around six feet, reddish-blond hair, a slight scattering of freckles. His voice was low and quiet.

"I hated history," the woman said.

"Then you're doomed to repeat it," her partner said with a laugh.

"Ugh, I hate focusing on people who are dead and gone," the woman said, then seemed to feel that her words were ill-chosen. She took refuge in a quick sip of her ale. Jake Curtis's face betrayed nothing.

But the silence stretched into ten awkward seconds and Mariah broke it by saying, loud enough where they couldn't ignore her, "Martin Van Buren was the first and only president who spoke English as a second language."

Jake gave her a small, cautious smile, and the woman blinked at her and said, "Really? What was his first?"

"Dutch," Mariah said.

"Immigrants can't become president," the woman said. "At least not now. Like Arnold Schwarzenegger."

"He was born here. But he spoke Dutch first and at home with his family," Mariah said.

"Oh, you need to be on our trivia team," the woman said. Then she seemed to ponder. "I just wonder what are the odds that we'll get another Martin Van Buren question. It seems low."

"Time to go home, presidential scholar," the partner said. He nodded at Mariah, thanked Jake for the win, and helped his partner head for the exit. There was that awkward moment between Jake and Mariah—did he stay and talk to her, did he escape the bar with his friends, did he go socialize with his remaining teammate? She thought, *You have no idea how much you and I have in common.* This might be her one chance to talk to him.

He didn't walk away. "It's always nice to meet the one other member of the Martin Van Buren fan club."

She smiled. "I remembered that factoid from Disney World. The Hall of Presidents. That he grew up speaking Dutch. It stuck in my mind."

"Good to know amusement parks are educational," he laughed. "I'm Jake." He offered his hand and she shook it.

"I'm Mariah," she said. She guessed he was in his early thirties.

She expected him to ask her what she did for a living—guys were always overly interested in that—but instead he said, "I don't actually like trivia that much."

"Really? You seemed very good at it. So were your friends."

"I like hanging out with them a lot more than answering trivia," he said. "We've been through a lot together. They've...been there for me."

I understand, she wanted to say. Her friends hadn't, not as much as she hoped. But most of her close friends had gone off to college in other states, and she'd been a bit of a loner at UT. "Well, then, you found a nice way to repay the friendship, crowning them champions here at the pub."

"They'll owe me forever. I guess you're here because ESPN forgot to broadcast the competition?"

She nodded and he laughed.

I broke a guy's finger tonight. I read about your missing wife. You don't seem in mourning. But then neither do I. You have to stumble on while life happens around you. You have to find your way.

He didn't look like a guy who'd killed his wife. She told herself that was a stupid, dangerous thought. She could be sitting next to a killer. Then she thought, *That's what people said about Dad. It was unfair to him and it could be unfair to this man.*

"Well, we never had a cheerleader before," he said.

"Wrong. I didn't cheer. I was more of an ombudsman, waiting to correct someone."

"You mean if I'd answered wrong, you would have thrown me under the bus?"

"Yes, and then backed up," she said.

He smiled at her teasing. "I know Steve—he owns the pub—wants to expand trivia to another night. You should form a team."

"I'm not much of a team player," she said. She was so unused to making small talk. How did she get him to talk about his wife? Surely other strangers had tried. Curious people. True crime nuts. People who'd read about him in the news websites or newspapers and were thoughtless in broaching the subject. She didn't want to treat him the way she'd been treated. Like an object of curiosity, or pity, or disdain. *How can you defend your father?* a total stranger had once asked her in front of the dairy section. She had put back her yogurt, like she didn't have a right to it, and stumbled out of the store. Later she wished she'd opened the yogurt, poured it on the man's head, and then slammed a gallon container of milk into his face. Sometimes her rage left her shaken. She couldn't let her grief control her life. She had to get back to the Mariah she was before Mom vanished.

She glanced down at his hand and saw... he still wore his wedding ring. She couldn't ask the obvious: oh, a wife?

"Have you been in Austin long?" he asked. In a city full of new arrivals, it wasn't an unusual question.

"My whole life."

"Wow, the rare native," he said. "I'm from Albany."

"I grew up in Lakehaven."

"Ah, rich kid."

For some reason that bothered her. "Not everyone there is rich. My parents wanted me to go to school there. I think they bought the cheapest house they could find."

"I bet it's not cheap now," he said. "Smart investment on their part. Both the home and your education."

"Yes, what with my wide-ranging Martin Van Buren expertise to pay the bills."

He smiled at her. He had a nice smile. She had hardly dated since Mom died—her disappearance had commandeered so much of Mariah's life. There had been a boyfriend for a while, a nice guy she'd met at UT, but after Mom disappeared and he didn't seem to know how to do much other than pat her on the shoulder and tell her everything would be all right, she grew to loathe the sight of him. And his bland reassurances. No, it would not be all right. Her mother was *gone*. And for some reason new guys didn't come around after your mom disappears—not any worthwhile guys. A few that thought they could take advantage of her emotional vulnerability. There were always those types, and she shoved them away from her life with the force of her fury.

She kept the smile in place. "I design websites and phone apps. You've made me realize there's an app market for half-forgotten presidents."

"I work in tech, too," he said, without elaborating that he had been a founder of a publicly offered company who then sold it to an even bigger company.

"It takes over your life," she said. "I mean, when things are going well."

"Jake?" a woman's voice, lilting, cutting through the hubbub of the pub. Behind them stood a very attractive woman, dark-haired, well dressed in expensive jeans and a designer top of gray and red. "You done with your trivia game?" She gave Mariah a neutral look.

"Yes," he said. "Mariah, it was nice to meet you. Think about what I said about the new trivia teams."

"I will. Nice to meet you, too," she said, feeling her opportunity slipping away, watching him get up and go to a corner table with the woman and sit and start to talk.

She was confused. He still wore his wedding ring, even though his wife had run to Houston. Maybe he wanted Bethany back. Maybe he wore it because it made him look less guilty if he'd found her and killed her for leaving him. Maybe he didn't love her still, but he wore it out of respect. But what she hadn't expected was a woman who said his name with a proprietary air and whisked him away. He hadn't introduced Mariah, which she thought he would have if this woman was a girlfriend, just to signal to her that their idle chatter had been harmless.

She sipped at her pint. Another guy tried to chat her up and buy her a second pint, and she brushed him off, and twice she saw Jake Curtis look at her from across the room. She quit glancing at him; she was being too obvious.

Who was he, under the smile and the success?

I understand you better than she does, Mariah thought. *Better than anyone else in the bar does.*

She left and realized she'd had too much to drink on top of too little food. She could not risk a drunk driving incident and another encounter with the Lakehaven police tonight. She stood alone in the parking lot, under the bright light of the bar entrance, and summoned a rideshare car, which would arrive in three minutes. While she waited, she glanced around, uneasy, thinking of the guy with the broken finger. No one else in the lot.

The rideshare car arrived, and she got in. He pulled onto Old Travis, the main thoroughfare through Lakehaven. She was thankful the driver wasn't talkative; she thought about how to make another approach toward Jake. Trivia night would give her another reason. She heard the driver make a noise of irritation, and when she glanced up she saw bright headlights in the rearview mirror.

"This dude is right on my tail," the driver said.

She whirled, blinking in the bright bath of the headlights. A car, close up behind her. She stared into the lights and the driver had to have seen her, and then the car veered away. She saw a blur of dark-painted SUV and then it was gone.

"Jeez," the driver said. "What was his problem?"

Me, Mariah thought, thinking of Reveal. But how could anyone have known where I was going after the bar? She didn't know. She hadn't told anyone. So if someone had followed Reveal and given up, had someone then followed her? Could that person have returned to La Luna and spotted her leaving after her internet searches and chat with Broussard? Reveal didn't live that far from the restaurant. She trembled.

She had stirred a secret. She had poked the truth, just barely, and this had happened.

You also thought you saw Mom today. You're overreacting. Don't lose your grip on reality.

The driver drove along the dark of Bobtail Drive and pulled up to her house. It was dark, the one light on in the porch, Dad leaving it on for her.

It had once been the happiest of homes, now it was a prison. She wanted out. The house was always dark, even with the lights on. Haunted, but not by a ghost who trod on the stairs or watched the living. The truth would be a light. She had this one connection, and maybe it was enough. She would only know if she tried.

6

Craig Dunning woke up, the taste of wine sour in his mouth, feeling groggy and undone. He kicked free of the tangled blanket, got up from the recliner, and called out for Mariah. No answer. He stumbled to the garage, his heart sinking. His Lexus was gone.

She was gone.

He went back into the den and found her note, saying she was going to meet a friend at La Luna. A friend. She didn't really have friends anymore. He was her only friend. Beth had loved that restaurant. He felt a pang every time he drove past it, the ache of a familiar place where they had known happiness.

So, what was she really doing?

He checked her computer. He knew her password, and she hadn't changed it. He opened the browser. She hadn't erased her history.

He read her search results on her mother's name.

He read the podcast post from Reveal.

He opened her Messages app and saw her texts asking Reveal for a meeting and him agreeing immediately.

His chest tightened. She was looking for an explanation. *No.*

He shut her laptop. He glanced up at the pictures on her wall. Her playing basketball for Lakehaven, at parties with friends, standing next to him, leaning against his shoulder. A life, once rich and promising, now a pale shadow of what was and what could have been.

He had to fix this.

The phone rang. The house phone, which hardly anyone other

than telemarketers called. He answered the extension in her room, hoping it was Mariah, hoping she hadn't been in another accident, hoping she wasn't in trouble.

"Hello?"

Silence. Five seconds. Ten seconds.

"Hello?" he said again, bracing himself.

More silence. He could hear the soft hiss of breath, muffled.

He hung up. Nearly instantly the phone rang again. He answered it. "Hello?"

Silence with its cruel emptiness. His daughter, chasing shadows, leaving him at night, and now this. They started with the phone calls, and they would quickly progress to spray paint and stones thrown against doors and walls and dog feces flung on the porch, and something bent in him. "Stop it," he said. "What's wrong with you? Why would you torture a grieving family? Have you nothing better to do?"

He didn't hang up; he listened to the quiet. "How do you live with yourself?" the voice asked. Soft, quiet, male, a baritone, hushed just above a whisper.

"Who is this?"

"I know what happened."

Four words that detonated like a bomb in his brain. "What... what do you think you know?"

"So many secrets. Should I tell the last secret you know?" The voice low, mocking, chilling him to the bone. "I know what happened. Leave town for good. Do it quickly."

Craig sputtered. This was different from the usual prankster. "Who is this? What do you think you know?"

Then the quiet not of breathing, but of a disconnected line.

He looked at the caller ID on the cordless phone's base. The number was unfamiliar. He wrote it down, did an internet search. No result. A burner phone, bought for one use and then tossed? He wrote down the number on a paper pad, to have a record of it. He tried to dial the caller back. Six rings and then he was disconnected.

Craig didn't know what to do. He went back downstairs and poured himself another large glass of merlot and his hand trembled as he drank it. *I know what happened.* No harasser had ever quite chosen those words before. Normally it was just incoherent rage and threats and anger. This was different. Frightening in a way the other calls had not been. Eerie. Calm.

Two problems now. Mariah digging into the past and this harasser.

How did he get Mariah to finally stop looking and just...accept that Beth was gone?

He sat back down in the recliner. It was the only new piece of furniture in the house. When she was here, Beth wouldn't have let him buy a recliner; she said they were for old people. He bought one in the weeks after she vanished, because he spent so many sleepless nights trying to numb himself with late night television. A policeman had followed him to the furniture store, as the blame had begun to build up against him. He'd made his purchase and then gone home, and the next day the Lakehaven paper had a piece about him, about him "returning to normal life," which made him sound heartless and eager to move past his wife's vanishing, when all he'd done was buy a recliner so he could sleep well in his own home. Because he shouldn't want to sleep. He should spend every spare second looking for his wife. Or grieving for her. That was the public's view, and the phone calls had taken a sharp rise following the recliner purchase.

But it was like having a bed in the den, and it was so nice to sink into the solitary hush of sleep whenever he felt tired. He didn't like sleeping in the bed, with her empty half of the mattress barren and haunted, the sheets like an unused shroud. And he was so tired. For a man who rarely left the house, he stumbled about in a continual exhaustion. Always waiting, always watching.

He texted his daughter.

I'm worried, please come home, he wrote.

Within seconds she answered him: I'm just one minute from the house. In an Uber car, don't freak. All is fine. Just too much to drink.

If she had too much to drink, why couldn't Reveal have brought her home? Had she gone somewhere else?

He put on his fake smile, to reassure her that all was okay. He had to stop her. If the caller was serious...he had to prevent his own daughter from looking for the truth.

No matter the cost.

7

MARIAH GOT UP at seven a.m., dry-mouthed and hazy from the margarita and the lager. Her father was asleep, in his bed. He'd hardly talked to her last night when she returned, as though lost in thought, but she had been relieved to avoid conversation. Now she downed a hot cup of coffee and a croissant, then showered and dressed. She left a note on the kitchen table: "Off to retrieve your car and then try and drum up some new business since I have my car repairs to pay for... might be late. Don't worry about me, I'm fine." *It is an excellent lie*, she thought.

She had called a ride service and was opening the front door to wait outside when Craig said behind her, "Where are you going, Mariah?"

"I left you a note." The lie, easy as breathing. "Is it okay if I use your car today? You weren't going anywhere?"

"I'm not going anywhere," Craig said, as if it were a sad realization of his life. "And I have your mother's car if I need it." Parked, as always, in the garage. It had barely been driven since the police had returned it to them weeks after Mom vanished. Sometimes he started it up, just to make sure the battery worked. Those times Mariah made sure the garage door was open. She didn't want him tempted to sit behind the wheel in a closed garage, the carbon monoxide easing him out of this world.

"I've got leads on some new clients and I set up meetings. I've got to figure out how to pay to get my car fixed, right?"

"I'll pay for the car damage."

"She was my hallucination, Dad. My responsibility."

He seemed stunned at her word choice. "Mariah."

"You're right. She wouldn't run from me. So, she's gone, and I chased after someone else. I've had way too much time on my hands to think about Mom. I need to work. I need to... fill my days."

"I'm so sorry." Craig gave her an awkward hug, which she returned. "I just want you to be safe. I couldn't protect your mom, but I can protect you."

"You'll never lose me," she said, tears coming now, her face pressed to his shoulder.

"I know," he said. "We're a team, right? Right?"

She had told Jake she wasn't a team player. That couldn't be true with her and Dad. They were all they had.

They held each other in their mutual grief, and she could sense her father holding back his tears out of a misguided sense that he shouldn't cry in front of her. Then she went outside as the rideshare car arrived to take her back to the bar to get his car. Dad stood on the porch, sad in jeans and sweatshirt, watching her leave.

She had looked up Sharon Blevins's address on the property tax website for Travis County and had copied it into the notes app in her phone. She would only have one chance with this woman. The grieving had no patience with strangers, trying to pull thoughts and emotions from them. If she played this wrong, she'd get a door permanently slammed in her face.

8

THE DOG'S NAME was Leo, and Craig had told Beth, "Leo is a feline name, you know, like Leo the lion. Leonine. It's totally a *cat* name."

"It's perfect for *this* dog," Beth answered, and she had been right: jolly, sloppy, happy Leo, a Cardigan Welsh Corgi. Craig had never much liked the dog—he disliked when Leo felt ignored and would sit at his feet and bark at him, or when Mariah was younger, he would try to herd her and her friends running and playing in the backyard, like they were sheep on a Welsh mountain—but now he could not bear the thought of not having Leo around when Beth had been so devoted to him. Sometimes, after all these months, Leo would go to the front door and lie down around the time Beth usually arrived home, patient, waiting, hopeful for her light step, for the sound of her voice. Then Craig would sit next to Leo and scratch the dog's ears and belly and try not to cry.

Leo still had to be walked. It was a moment of normalcy in Craig's day, strolling along the sidewalk, Leo investigating the fallen leaves, interesting smells, and unfailingly deciding to deposit his droppings on the one yard where a neighbor knelt twenty feet away, tending to a flower bed. And as the suspicions against Craig grew and darkened, he resolved that Leo would be walked, morning and afternoon. Someone who was a killer, after all, he thought, would not walk a dog. It was a way to show his neighbors that he was just like them. A regular guy, whose wife happened to be missing and who had endured multiple interrogations by the police.

He found his University of Texas ball cap, hooked the leash up to Leo's collar, tied a waste bag to the leash's handle so he wouldn't need to dig in his pockets if Leo conducted necessary business, and set out. He saw parents with elementary school–aged kids, waiting for the Lakehaven ISD buses. One nodded at him. The others ignored him. Did their parents tell them something? *Stay away from Mr. Dunning. He's a bad man. He made his wife disappear.* Surely not. Kids were just ruder these days. That was it. Leo strained at the leash, angling toward the kids—to him they were a herd that needed herding. Craig gently pulled him back.

Leo barked once, at the bus, just to assert himself and sauntered proudly on.

Cars passed, people who could cope going to their jobs. Seniors driving to campus. Stay-at-home parents heading to the grocery or the gym or the preschool.

He walked past house after house of his neighbors and imagined the whispers within:

No way Craig did it.

Craig is absolutely guilty.

Mariah hasn't been right since her mother vanished.

I feel so bad for them.

He killed Beth, and that weirdo daughter's covering for him.

People found him guilty with no evidence, no trial. Totally awful.

He did it. It's always the husband. Always.

Remember when Mariah was fun? And so smart. She goes around town looking like a ghost. This has destroyed them both. They wouldn't be this way if they were guilty. I know what guilty looks like.

Did one of them call me last night? Craig wondered.

He turned back onto Bobtail Drive, his own house seven away from the corner. Leo completed his morning rituals, Craig tidied up after him, and they walked back down to their house.

Later he would decide that the rock would have been less scary if thrown through the window. He had had that happen before, twice after Beth vanished and the police had said he was under suspicion.

But now, the shape just sat at the top of his driveway, wrapped in festive paper, tied with a ribbon of green silk. For one moment he stared for several long seconds. He glanced around. No one else on the street. Leo sniffed at the package and turned away, bored.

Take it inside or open it up here? Craig knelt by the package, probed it with his fingers. It felt like rock underneath the wrapping paper, not a box, not soft. He didn't want it in the house. He unwrapped it. It was a gray rock. One side of the thick, heavy wrapping paper was illustrated with cartoon balloons and fireworks exploding. The other side was marked with dotted lines, in a graph, to make it easier to cut and measure for gift-wrapping.

In block printing on the other side of the paper it said, IT'S TIME FOR YOU TO GO.

Carefully he put the paper down. He picked up the rock, studied it for a few long moments. He set the rock down. He stood and glanced around, not expecting to see anyone, but how helpful it would have been to see a neighbor's face close to a window, peering out to study his reaction to this generous gift.

Leo sniffed at the unwrapped rock. Craig pulled out his phone and with a shaking hand, started to dial the police. Then he stopped.

I know what happened. The caller last night, now the rock... he needed to think.

Craig took Leo inside, along with the paper. He got Leo fresh water in his bowl and a treat. Then he went back and collected the rock and brought it inside.

He put paper and rock on the dining room table, where he and Beth and Mariah had spent their Thanksgivings and Christmases and Easters. Now when the holidays came he and Mariah just ate in the kitchen; it was easier when it was the two of them. Like Beth, being their third, had simply filled the room with the force of her love and personality.

The rock. He looked at it very carefully. For stains, for marks. Nothing. It was just a rock.

But of course, it wasn't.

If he called the police, what would they do? Dust the rock and paper for prints? Who was dumb enough to leave prints?

He had received two threats in twelve hours. One threat that someone knew what had happened to his wife, one to leave. Getting two like this told him some tormentor was waging a whole new war against him. Why now, after the abuse directed at him had quieted for months? He knew his neighbors wanted him gone. They wanted normalcy back, a nice family living next door, someone you could invite to the caroling party or the neighborhood barbecue or ask to pick up your mail when you were gone. He'd gotten offers before to sell, but his home had the best view on the hill of the surrounding countryside, and it was where he and Beth had made their lives, for better or for worse. He wasn't going to leave his home. He wasn't going to do that to Mariah. This house was, he decided, Fortress Dunning.

The police didn't want to help him. They never had. He thought of their patronizing smiles yesterday, the loathing they'd shown toward him, the suspect who'd supposedly evaded justice.

How would the police view this? Suddenly he knew that they would read it to reopen an investigation, suspect him further, accuse him of planting the rock and the note. Maybe this wasn't a coincidence in light of Mariah's accident.

Maybe this was the sort of stunt Broussard would pull. Maybe the enemy was right in front of him. If he couldn't convict Craig, he could make his life miserable. He could get him out of Lakehaven, where Craig wasn't a reminder of a failure of justice.

He hid the rock and the paper in a cabinet above the oven, and he sat down to drink coffee and think through the problem. Leo sat at his feet, hoping for another treat.

He felt the hate rise in him against anyone who would hurt him or his daughter.

I need to draw you out, he thought. *Get you to show yourself. Then I can deal with you. You want to play a game with me? I'll end the game. I'll end you. I'll find a way.*

9

Mariah parked her father's car in front of the neat little house in an older neighborhood in north Austin. It was a ranch style from the 1960s, well maintained, the garden beds neat, the lawn trimmed, brick painted gray. She got out and approached the door, her heart high in her throat. Then she noticed the yellow ribbon tied around the oaks in the front yard, a thin, faded strip. There was another yellow ribbon tied around the front door handle.

Hope, still here. Waiting. Waiting for Bethany to come home.

A small wooden cross, carved with Celtic curves, was mounted on the front door. She rang the doorbell. Silence. And then the door opened, and an eye peered at her in the crack before opening more. A woman younger than she expected, a shot of gray streaking her blond hair, bright green eyes narrowed in suspicion, paired with an incongruous smile on her face. "Yes?"

"Mrs. Blevins?" Mariah found her voice.

"Yes?"

"My name is Mariah Dunning. I wondered if I might talk to you about your daughter Beth's case."

"I don't talk to the press, young lady."

"I'm not the press, ma'am."

"Then I don't talk to the idly curious, either. Good day." Sharon Blevins started to shut the door.

"My mother went missing about six months after your daughter did. Her name was Beth, too, and I'm wondering if there could be a connection."

The closing door stopped. The woman stared at her. "I'm sorry?"

Mariah repeated herself. "Similar name. Just vanished."

"It must just be a coincidence." Her voice sounded strained. Mariah could see the broken strain in her eyes, like her father's. Maybe like her own. She forced herself to hold the woman's gaze. "I'm sorry for your...situation." Sharon Blevins was, Mariah thought, being careful not to say *loss*. "But what would one have to do with the other?"

"Two Beths, vanished so soon near each other? Without a trace? What does it hurt to compare notes?"

For a moment Sharon didn't speak; her mouth just moved. She began to pray, softly. "Oh Lord, hear our prayer, hear our prayers for answers to thy mysteries..."

Prayer made Mariah uneasy. She'd never been very religious—her family went to services at Christmas and Easter, and not otherwise. The other Episcopalians would kneel and cross themselves and go up to the priests for communion, and the Dunnings stayed seated, as if glued to the pew, Mom once saying, "I'm not really into the aerobics of all that. I just want to hear the music and the message, and hope it's all positive." When her mom vanished people would tell Mariah, "I'm praying for you," and part of her wanted to say, *What do you think that will accomplish? If God let this happen, do you think you praying will change his mind? Are you saying prayers to make you feel better, like "Thank you, God, for not taking my loved one"?* But always she said thank you; it was the polite response, and she was too exhausted for theological discussions. And she learned quickly, no one wanted to see her anger. They only wanted her mournful.

"I'm sorry to have intruded, ma'am," Mariah said. She turned away.

"Wait. Stop," Sharon Blevins said. "All right. Come in for a minute." Her voice wavered. "Like you said, what's the harm?"

10

THE BLEVINS HOUSE was as tidy on the inside as the yard and trim were on the outside. Sharon led her back to a den. Multiple ornate silver crosses lined the wall, along with a framed pair of Bible verses about kindness and forgiveness written in beautiful, readable calligraphy. Sharon wore a long-sleeved cream-colored blouse and navy slacks. She wore complete makeup, and Mariah wondered if she was keeping Sharon from heading to her job. "Let me just save my work." She vanished into a room down the hallway. Mariah could hear the clicking of a computer keyboard. Sharon returned. "Sorry. OK. You want a cup of coffee? I just made a fresh pot."

"Yes ma'am. Thank you."

"Let me get that for us both, and then we talk." She went into a small kitchen. Mariah didn't sit; she wandered to the fireplace, where the mantel displayed a long row of framed photos. Pictures of Bethany Blevins Curtis. Pictures of Sharon, all recent ones with her daughter. No baby pictures, no childhood photos. There was no picture of a father. The biggest picture was of Bethany in a college graduation robe. She had longer hair and a broad, warm smile. Dark hair, green eyes. She looked like her mother. No picture of Bethany with Jake.

Mariah turned away from the pictures as Sharon came back into the den, carrying coffee cups and sugar and a carton of half-and-half on an old but colorful patchwork tray. She set it down on the coffee table.

"Thank you, this is kind of you," Mariah said. "What a cute tray." She hoped this qualified as good small talk.

"I don't have a lot of call to use it, since I don't have a lot of company, other than church friends. And I don't always answer the door if I don't know who it is. For a while there were reporters. Or just crackpots with theories about the case." She poured coffee for them both. "One man showed up with an easel full of charts to try and tell me aliens had abducted my daughter."

"That same guy came to our door. He's harmless," Mariah said. "But I'm sorry you had to deal with that."

"Last year I got both a phone call and an email from a reporter on the anniversary. That was hard."

"Us, too. They knocked on the door. They emailed, they called."

"I'm sorry about your mama disappearing," Sharon said as Mariah sipped at her coffee. She had a raspy voice, tinged with a Southern drawl. "But I think this really might be coincidence. Jake, my son-in-law, I think he was behind my Bethany's disappearance."

"So, she went by Bethany?"

"When she was little"—she cleared her throat—"she was Beth, but in high school and beyond she was Bethany. She liked the full name."

Mariah felt uncomfortable sitting on the edge of the couch. She had thought her theory would be welcomed by a woman without hope... maybe it would lead to an answer. She didn't realize that it might compete with a theory held dear by a grieving mother: that Jake Curtis had done away with her daughter.

Sharon sipped her coffee, slowly. "You think what links them is their name? I mean, Beth is a pretty common name."

"I thought maybe if we compared notes that we might find something linking your Beth and mine. If there was something to be found."

"But Jake..."

"You seem very sure he is responsible for your daughter's disappearance."

"I am."

"But he's not in jail, right? He was never arrested?" She felt a sting of anger. The husband was always blamed. She understood why, but she didn't like the way Lakehaven had turned against her father. It never ceased to upset her.

"No." Sharon Blevins set the coffee cup down. "Jake's rich now. He's clever. He got rid of her right before he made all his money. That's what bothers me. He could have just divorced her if he was greedy."

"Rich *now*?" She pretended not to know.

"Jake started a software company. He was going to take it public—you know, sell the shares on the stock market. The stock went on sale several weeks after Bethany vanished. There had been talk that he'd cancel the initial public offering, but he refused to, even with my daughter missing. He made a mint. Then the company got bought by another software company for fifty million and he made even more."

She took another sip of coffee; her slurp was loud and angry. She put down the coffee cup, and Mariah noticed her manicure was perfect, nails painted a light sky blue. "Bethany supported him with her work when he stayed at home and started writing those computer programs that turned into his company's software. Then he got some initial angel investors, he started to grow it. Long hours, hard on both of them, all his extra money poured into the company. And I'm supposed to believe she takes off, right before he's going to be a millionaire? Now, I don't care about worldly goods, but she does. I mean, not in a bad way." She looked toward heaven. "God forgive me. You know I love you, honey."

Mariah shifted against the edge of the couch. She wasn't comfortable with talking to the dead. *No*, she thought, *you prefer to imagine them in food courts.*

"You think Jake did something to her because he was about to be wealthy? Wouldn't that endanger his taking his company public?"

"Money makes some people cruel and thoughtless. It made people feel sorry for him because he made it look like she left him."

"Maybe you could tell me about that day. I know how painful it is." And she saw Sharon look at her, as if measuring if she could comprehend the pain, and deciding that a girl whose mother had disappeared might have an inkling of what that pain was like.

"It's a punishment, I think," Sharon said suddenly. "Something we did before catches up to us. Our lives...the way we live them..." Tears came to her eyes.

"I never did anything to deserve losing my mom this way," Mariah said, keeping her voice steady. "Neither did my mom."

"God sees all. Knows all. In our hearts." Sharon wiped away tears. Mariah knew she should offer the woman her hand, some comfort, but she was so bad at this. So she stared down at the coffee for a moment, then brought her gaze up to meet Sharon's.

"Then God should punish me, not my mom," Mariah said.

"If only it worked that way. I'm sorry. I don't know you and I can't judge you." Implying, Mariah thought, that judgment might come with acquaintance. Sharon took a deep breath and her tone was calmer. "There's no club for us, is there? No prayer meetings. No AA."

"A guy I know, a crime podcaster, he runs a support group in Lakehaven for families dealing with this."

"That Asian boy?"

"His name is Chad. Yes. It meets tomorrow night. I might go." A sudden impulse took her. "You should come with me."

"I couldn't. It would do me no good. Because I know Jake did it, and all those other folks in that group, they don't have any answers. Just a big mystery. I have answers. But no one who matters believes them. Except God. He knows the evil in Jake's heart."

"That day. What happened?" It would be a starting point at least.

"Bethany and Jake came over for dinner the night before—September third. I made her favorite. Lasagna and a salad. Soccer was on some cable sports channel I didn't even know that I got, and Jake watched that. Soccer, it's so boring. Bethany and I were in the kitchen and she told me, in a whisper, she was thinking of leaving Jake."

"Did she say why?"

"No." She paused. "For a moment, I was shocked, and then I was so mad at her. Why would she tell me when we couldn't talk about it, with Jake there? And right before his company was going public and they'd be rich? It was like she had dropped a bomb. My hands were shaking. I had my issues with Jake, but marriage is a serious commitment, and I never thought...well, I didn't think he'd beat on her or bullied her, or cheated on her. I didn't have any reason to believe. I thought, well, he's worked long hours on this startup, and she's a young wife, and perhaps she's not being patient and seeing that soon he'd have much more time for her. Bethany could be impulsive." Sharon took a deep, fortifying breath. "So she whispers to me she's leaving him, and I knew no details. And she promised me we'd just talk later. She asked, though, if she could stay with me, and I said of course. I would have thought she'd stay in the house and make him leave, but I think she just wanted to be at home with me."

"How did she seem? Anxious, scared?"

"Uneasy. Not scared. Like she was taking a big step, but she was OK with it."

Mariah pressed on, just trying to get a picture of those final hours. "So you all had dinner."

Her earlier reluctance to talk had faded, and Mariah guessed she didn't get to talk about this aspect of the case often. "Yes. Jake was checking his email on his iPhone all through dinner, which I hate, and Bethany was quiet. They seemed fine and I thought, Jake doesn't know. He doesn't know she's leaving him. So I thought I'd make it easier for him when the hammer falls. I said nice things about Jake. Complimented his work ethic while he let my lasagna get cold on the plate what with his email and texting, and he just said, 'uh-huh, uh-huh, thanks, Sharon,' Said how proud I was of him, building that company from a dream and a loan. Thought Bethany might see she ought to slow down and not be rash, take a deep breath. It didn't work. I tried to keep the conversation lively.

But she was jumpy and he was distracted, and they didn't stay long after dinner. When she hugged me goodbye she told me she'd explain it in a day or so and not to worry. I thought I should tell Andy. That if she needed to break the news to Jake that Andy should be there." Her words had come out in a torrent and she pressed the back of her hand to her mouth.

"Andy?"

"Andrew Candolet. He's a family friend. He and Bethany went to school and worked together." She knotted her fingers together in her lap.

Mariah filed the name away in her head. "You thought Jake might take the news badly."

"I thought he would be dignified, but you never know how a man takes the news his wife is leaving him..." She shook her head and took a long sip of coffee. "What if, what if, what if. You can kill yourself playing that game." Now her voice shook.

"So what happened the next day?"

"According to Jake, at breakfast, she told him that she was leaving him. He said he was stunned, but he asked her not to go, and she said she was moving out. She left, with a small bag packed. He then went to work, like it was a normal day. We know from witnesses and video that Bethany went to their bank and withdrew a few hundred in cash—not really enough to last long. Then we don't know where she was, but a couple of hours later she booked a Southwest flight online and got a last-minute ticket to Houston Hobby." That was the smaller, regional airport for Houston. "Then the security cameras picked her up in Hobby and she vanished. Didn't rent a car. Didn't call a taxi or a rideshare on her phone. Never checked into a hotel." She ran her palms along her legs, steadied them in her lap. "She never used her credit cards. Never called me or Andy. She would have let me know she was OK." She was on the edge of tears. Mariah watched her. She knew she should offer her hand to the woman or put a comforting arm around her, but instead she stared at her own hands, clenched together. The only comfort, for real, after all this time, was the truth.

"Why Houston? Did she have friends there?"

"A few, from her college days, but none of them said they'd heard from her or seen her. They have no reason to lie."

Unless Bethany asked them to. People could always find a reason to lie. "Are you from there? Or any other family?"

"No, no," Sharon said.

"Could Jake have followed her to Houston and killed her?"

"I think maybe she knew something shady about his business. So, she decided at the last minute to run and hide down there, and soon enough he found her. He never said she told him she was going to Houston, but maybe she did. Or she used their credit card after she said she was leaving him and he was watching the activity. Maybe for Jake it was as easy as hiring someone to watch the airport, email a picture of her, and just wait for her to show up. He didn't report her missing until the next day. He said she told him she wanted the divorce right before he left for work, and I can't believe he went ahead and went to his office, but he did. But he excused himself after about an hour. He said he was so stunned he didn't know what to do. These engineer types, I will never get them. He says, he *claims* that he drove over to Marble Falls." This was a town about forty minutes from Austin, in the hill country. "His family had a lake house there, and he said he went and sat by the lake and thought about how to get her to change her mind, be a better husband to her. The next morning, he called here, looking for her, and that was when...we realized no one had heard from her. I didn't know where she was."

"You weren't surprised when she didn't show up at your house that day?"

"I assumed that whole day she hadn't told him yet. Or she'd had second thoughts after our family dinner." The regret in her voice rang like a chime. "About lunchtime I called her on her cell and she didn't answer. The voicemail was left about the time her flight was leaving, so she would have had her phone in airplane mode. When she didn't call back, I thought maybe she had changed her mind, or she couldn't talk...I was trying not to interfere. Stay out of her business. Be a good mother." Her voice broke again. "I shouldn't have let her out of my sight. Should have been with her when she told him, gone with her, insisted on it, moved her things to our house. But no. I stayed out of it." She wiped the back of her hand across her eyes.

Silence in the den, except for the ticking of an old clock on the mantel, surrounded by the pictures of the lost Bethany. "So, you don't know why she went to Houston?"

Now she was quiet, for twenty long seconds, as if she'd said too much. Mariah got the sense that she didn't talk much about this, and that words and ideas were boiling to the surface. "Obviously it had to be to get away from him. She told me that she felt life had gone sour for her in the past few months. Lots of things going wrong. She'd lost her job over some silliness, she'd lost her friends." Sharon hugged herself, rubbed her arms as if cold.

"Lost her job and her friends? How?"

"Her friends got tired of her never calling them back, and there was a misunderstanding at work. She wouldn't say what." Sharon was lying, Mariah thought. She didn't trust Mariah enough to give her a clear answer. Mariah didn't push it. "She clearly felt her life had gone wrong. Maybe she just wanted a fresh start. Is that a terrible thing to say? I don't know what was in her head. If she'd gone to church with me, this wouldn't have ever happened. She would have stuck out the marriage."

"Did you think Jake was behind this...losing her friends? Was he isolating her?"

"He wasn't paying enough attention to her to isolate her. It was just...a bad streak. We all get a bad streak now and then. That's why we need the Lord, to steady us on our journey."

"Did you go to Houston to look for her?"

For a moment Sharon Blevins paled. "No. No. Jake did, I'm sure for show, and the police down there tried their best. I don't...I don't care for Houston. I'm not one for travel." At this she got up and walked to the photos of her daughter sitting on the fireplace mantel, reaching out to touch one.

And Mariah, perhaps unfairly, thought, *How could you not go look for her? What's the matter with you?*

She wondered if she should tell Sharon she'd met Jake. Quiet, charming, assured...but all that could be a lie. This woman knew him, far better than she did. But this woman was also blinded by grief, one that seemed stronger than Jake's. But how Jake had managed all these various criminal machinations to eliminate his wife had not been explained.

"Was Jake abusive? Controlling?" Mariah asked.

"If he was, she didn't tell me," Sharon said. "I never saw a bruise. But he's very smart. He could have undercut her in many ways."

"Could she have had a boyfriend in Houston? Would she have told you if there was another man?" She felt a flush of shame asking this question, and she wasn't sure why, the words sudden and sharp in her mind.

"If she did, she wouldn't tell me. I wouldn't approve. I mean, not while she was still married." She smoothed her palms along her legs. "I don't mean to sound harsh. I wish she had told me. She could have."

"Perhaps she didn't want to upset you." Or be judged.

"The police didn't find any evidence she'd been having an affair."

"There are two hours where she's unaccounted for."

"Yes."

"Where do you think she was? She gets cash, she's leaving her husband—why doesn't she leave then? There are flights to Houston every hour. Why does she wait?"

"I don't know!" Sharon said, her voice a sudden, jagged scream. "I don't know!"

11

CRAIG GOT INTO the shower, where he did his best thinking. OK, what was he going to do when he found the person tormenting him? Ask them to stop? Shame them? Scare them so badly they never looked his or Mariah's way again?

Hurt them?

As he toweled off, his house phone rang. He went into his bedroom and picked up the cordless, not recognizing the number, but hitting Answer.

"I thought you should know, sir, that your wife was taken by aliens," a woman's voice said, breathy and soft-pitched.

"Aliens. You mean aliens from another world."

"Yes, Mr. Dunning."

"I haven't gotten that one in a while," he said. "What a refreshing theory. Thanks for sharing it with me and making a joke of my grief." He kept his voice steady.

"It's true. I saw her taken."

For a moment the words were a knife in his heart, his brain. "Who is this?"

"A golden beam of light lifted her from her car and into the saucer."

"Saucers don't seem the most aerodynamically smart choice for spacecraft," he said, and the woman, in her soft, polite voice, directed him to commit a physically impossible act and hung up.

He put the phone down. There hadn't been a prank call for weeks. Now the note and the rock, and now this. Something had happened. Something had shifted. He could dismiss the deranged caller much more easily than the rock with the message. That scared him. It promised that the conversation hadn't ended yet.

The phone rang again. He almost didn't answer, but he did when he saw LAKEHAVEN PD on the screen.

"Craig? This is Dennis Broussard. I'd like you to stop by today and talk to us."

"About what? I don't know if my lawyer will be available on such short notice."

"You don't need a lawyer, Craig. This is about your daughter."

The fist that formed around his heart whenever he talked to the police tightened. "About what?"

"It would be better in person. Could you stop by in, say, an hour?" Like Chief Broussard knew Craig wasn't busy, just sitting in his own house, watching what was left of his life tick away. "I just would like to talk to you."

"Yes," Craig Dunning heard himself say. "I'll be there in an hour." He hung up. Leo put his head against Craig's leg, anxious to be petted. Craig wanted to tell him it would be okay. But he didn't know.

12

I'M SORRY. I'M so sorry," Mariah said.

Sharon took a deep breath. "I just... I just wish I knew the answers."

"I pushed you. I shouldn't have."

"I should be tougher," Sharon said. "Some days I am. Others, I'm not." She tried a smile.

Mariah refilled Sharon's coffee cup, added cream and sugar; she'd noticed how Sharon fixed her own coffee before. Sharon nodded her thanks and took the mug into her hands.

"I'm fine," Sharon said. "OK. To answer your question on where she was, I think maybe those hours, she was with Jake. Maybe they talked. Maybe he begged her to stay. Maybe she thought of giving him another chance but she didn't. And so she left and it ate at him and then he waited for her to get to Houston, so he'd have an alibi, and he got someone to"—she could hardly form the words—"take her."

"Do you think he knows criminals who would commit a kidnapping on short notice?" She tried to keep her tone... well, not incredulous.

She shrugged off this bit of logic. "I don't know that he doesn't."

It wasn't an answer. The silence between them grew.

"Tell me about her and Jake." Mariah was starting to see the folly of thinking this case had anything to do with her mother.

These lives had never intersected. But now she wanted to know. This was still a tragedy parallel to her own.

Sharon set down the half-full coffee mug. "From the start: Bethany was crazy about Jake. I couldn't quite see what the attraction was. He was nice-looking, sure, and he had a real good job. Computer security. But quiet. Too quiet, for me." She risked a smile. "Not quiet like a strong and silent type, like her daddy. But quiet like a dirty secret." For a moment she stopped and took a deep breath. "Jake would sit here and smile at me, and I could tell I wasn't good enough for him. I guess because he had advanced degrees and I don't. Or maybe it's a matter of having faith. I never tried to preach at him or convert him. I never looked down on him. Sometimes he acted like he was rescuing Bethany from a sorry life, which wasn't true." She stopped, bit at her lip. "But Bethany had her cap set for him, and she loved him. I gritted my teeth and thought at the least they'd make cute grandbabies, so I could tolerate him having an ego." She leaned forward. "You know, Andy Candolet took Jake aside before the wedding and said if Jake ever hurt her, there'd be hell to pay from all of Bethany's friends. And you know what Jake said?"

Sharon Blevins waited for the reaction, so Mariah said, "No, what?"

"He told Andy that Bethany could take care of herself and it was sexist for him to stand up for her. Honestly!"

Mariah had no answer to this collision of values. "May I ask where Bethany's father is?"

Sharon's mouth made a tight line. "He's deceased. He died when Bethany was a teenager."

"I'm sorry."

"We've managed. But I think Bethany didn't have the best judgment when it came to men. She saw every man as tragic, when they're just weak." She dabbed a napkin at her eyes, briefly.

Mariah wondered if there was something tragic, then, about Mr. Blevins. But Sharon's face was a closed book, so she shifted subjects. "When she told you she was leaving Jake, that was the first sign of trouble? No earlier warnings?"

"Bethany *seemed* happy with him." Sharon finished her coffee.

"Feels like most of us *seem* to be happy, most of the time. We're seeming rather than being." She set the mug down with a hard click. "Does this help you with your mama's case? I don't see how it could." It was only now that Sharon seemed to remember why she was telling her sad story to Mariah.

"My mother doesn't seem to connect to your daughter. Other than her name." She considered. "And that Jake works in software. My mother was a sales rep for a small software company."

The flimsiest of links. The software industry in Austin employed thousands of people.

A phone rang in the distance. In the office. "Excuse me, I need to get that. Different ring tones for different clients, and that's a lady who won't wait."

Sharon got up and went into another room down the hall. Mariah stood, stretched. She wandered to the bookshelf, where there were photos of a younger Bethany and school yearbooks on the shelf. And a bound memory book. She pulled it free, hearing Sharon telling the client to let her check something. She went through the pages. Picture after picture where Bethany was with two other kids. The same boy, the same girl. The boy had dark hair, glasses, and a sly grin and the girl, prone to smiles, was always hugging on Bethany. Some of the older pictures had careful notes on the back. Andy and Julie and me, July Fourth party. Julie and me, Christmas caroling party. Andy, football camp drop-off. Maybe they could tell her something.

She glanced in the senior yearbook. A long statement of friendship on the first signature page, a place of yearbook honor. Julie Santos. She flipped through the senior pictures and found Andy Candolet. Yes, that was the boy Sharon had mentioned. Something familiar about him; her throat went dry. The name or his face? She wasn't sure. He was handsome, and she thought maybe he reminded her of an actor she'd seen. Then she made sure Julie Santos was the girl in the photos. Yes.

She replaced the books and went back and sat down on the couch with her phone, still hearing Sharon talking on the phone, calmly explaining a flight schedule she'd set up.

On Faceplace, on the FIND BETHANY page, she found Andy Candolet and Julie Santos as administrators. That took her to each of their individual pages. Julie worked as a fitness trainer at a local gym, closer to Lakehaven. Andy worked in security for a transportation company called Ahoy. Yes, she remembered that from the news accounts. Bethany had worked at Ahoy until a month before she vanished. She closed the browser on her phone as Sharon returned, blinking, trying to smile.

"I'm so sorry."

Mariah stood. "I'm sorry to have kept you from your work. Thank you...for your time. I'm sorry to have brought all this pain up for you again."

"It's not always painful to talk about my girl." Now Sharon seemed reluctant for her to leave. "I kept her room, mostly, as it was. I use it as my office now. Would you like to see it? I know it's weird that I use her desk, but it means I spend my days in a place she loved."

"I totally understand." In some ways Sharon made her think of her father, Craig: lost, unmoored, dealing with an endless grief. But Sharon hadn't been suspected of being her Beth's killer. That was one key difference.

Mariah followed Sharon down the hall to the room she'd seen Sharon duck into earlier. More crosses on the wall, a Bible quote framed: *And when he comes home, he calls together his friends and his neighbors, saying to them, Rejoice with me, for I have found my sheep that was lost.*

Mariah walked around the room. There was a daybed with pillows in there, a desk, and a small filing cabinet. The desktop was organized with file folders of different colors: red, orange, blue. Papers and notes and an airline ticket receipt carefully laid out next to the computer. A color-coded calendar app filled most of the screen.

"You look very organized," Mariah said. "My own desk is a mess."

"I'm a VPA," Sharon said. "A virtual personal assistant. I keep the schedules for some self-employed folks who need help but not a full-time assistant. I handle their appointments, arrange their hotels and flights, order online supplies for them and have them shipped, help them edit or put together their presentations, do additional research, whatever else they need when they need it...I can do all that remotely. I work for a few people in Dallas and a friend of my brother's up in Little Rock and another half-dozen here in Austin." She tried a brave smile. "I can work from her room."

Not from home. From *her* room. It made Mariah a little dizzy.

She noticed a sticky note on the monitor. "Oh, I do that too with my passwords."

"That's Bethany's. It was on her computer monitor when she was a student. I told her it was bad security but...I couldn't bear to throw it out." Sharon's voice cracked.

Mariah leaned forward and saw the password: spiker44. In loopy handwriting that was presumably Bethany's, and Mariah understood why her mother had kept the sticky note.

"That was her number in volleyball," Sharon said. Mariah nodded, politely, feeling a shift in her chest.

Sharon had created her bubbles: home and church, and this job she could do from her computer. In her missing daughter's bedroom. Like Mariah's web and app business. Minimal human interaction. Sharon was a mirror for Mariah's own life, and the thought jolted her.

Mariah studied the pictures on the wall. Mostly of Bethany. Pretty, smiling, with no idea that one day she would be taken from the world and leave broken lives and grief and unanswered questions behind.

"You would have liked Bethany," Sharon said quietly, tracking Mariah's gaze across the pictures. "Everyone did."

You tended to remember only the best of the missing, Mariah thought. "If we could find something that truly connected them..."

"Otherwise you think there's someone out there looking for women named Beth. What would be the motive? I thought serial killers"—it took effort for Sharon to say the words—"picked out victims at random. How would he even know their names if they were strangers to him?"

"Then they weren't," Mariah said simply.

"But don't serial killers have a type? Like Ted Bundy liked girls with dark hair parted in the middle." Sharon cleared her throat. "Bethany read a lot of true crime and talked about what she learned in them."

Mariah took a risk. She turned to Sharon and sat on the daybed, and Sharon sat down at her desk chair. "If someone targeted Beths, there would be ways to find them. Maybe he just spotted them somewhere where they had name tags on. A conference. A meeting, a happy hour, a fundraiser. They both could have been at a software event here, Bethany there with Jake, my mom there for her job."

"But it's crazy to kill someone based on their name." Sharon pressed her hand to her mouth and her hand trembled. "I gave my girl that name. I chose Bethany. It's a place in the Bible. Is this my fault?"

"Oh, no, you mustn't think that way." Mariah was horrified. "Listen to me, Mrs. Blevins. It's just a theory. Nothing more. The motivation might be he hates a Beth from his own life." Mariah wished Reveal was here so he could explain it better.

"It seems like a lot of work," Sharon said. Now her voice was steady.

She thought of an even simpler way. "Are you on Faceplace?"

"Yes. Well, not often. I don't need to know everyone's business or how great their lives are."

"But that is what they post, isn't it? Details of their lives, under their real names. If you wanted to find a whole bunch of Beths—or any other name—you could search on social media. You could narrow it down by geography. By interests. The website just thinks you're looking for a special friend. It doesn't seem suspicious."

Sharon was pale. She closed her eyes for a moment.

"But...my daughter went to Houston on that day, and only Jake could have known. It was out of the ordinary. No one knew she did it. She didn't post on Faceplace, 'Hey, I've taken off to

Houston.' She didn't even make the reservation until a couple of hours before the flight. I just don't see how she could have been targeted this way by a stranger. Bethany didn't go off with strange men." Sharon looked offended at the idea.

"But you clearly didn't know what she would do. She did several actions that were out of character. Leave her husband. Go to Houston. Not contact you."

Sharon seemed angry now, her mouth setting in a frown, and Mariah realized she'd overstepped. "I just mean, Bethany surprised you."

"Could this theory work with what happened with your mom? What was her last day like?" Sharon asked.

Mariah took a deep breath. "We don't have her on videotape, except at Starbucks, getting a morning coffee. She went to work at her office. She made phone calls to prospects, went to a meeting with the sales department. She had sales appointments that afternoon in north Austin, so she was going to be out of the office. At lunch she left—sometimes she ate lunch at home; her office was only ten minutes away—but she didn't have lunch plans with anyone, she didn't go to the gym, and she completely vanished. I was home sick, and she'd called me to see if I needed anything, and I told her I just wanted to sleep." She cleared her throat. "Her car was parked by some vacant land we own; she might have driven out there on her lunch. She didn't empty a bank account. She just disappeared." She swallowed. "My mom and I were close. I mean, yeah, we fought some, but we confided in each other. She didn't tell me she was unhappy. And even if she left, she wouldn't let me think she was dead. Not in a million years." *Not even after that fight. Not even then.*

Sharon started to say something more, then stopped. But she put her hand on Mariah's knee, the way a mom would to a daughter, and suddenly Mariah realized they'd each lost what the other was—mother and daughter. A longing, one she hadn't known in a long time, coursed in her guts.

She let herself take Sharon's hand and for a long moment they sat there, hand in hand. Mariah thought, *She wants to help you, yet she doesn't. She's reluctant. Most mothers would pursue any thread about their missing daughters. She hesitated. Why?*

You could be sticking your nose into a murder that has nothing to do with your mother, Reveal had warned her.

Sharon stood. "I have to get to work. Will you let me know if you find out anything?"

"Of course. How about if I call you later?"

Sharon nodded, grateful.

* * *

Sharon watched Mariah drive away, from the window. She felt sick. Why? Why now, what would possess a person? She had never understood the need of others to interfere in private lives. To come, to ask questions, to judge. Always, to judge. She realized she was shivering. She went and poured herself a glass of ice water and gulped it down. It didn't calm her. Oh, she hated them. Hated people like this Mariah person. People who dug into what wasn't their concern. And she was dangerous, because she thought she had a good reason. A valid reason.

What would she do if Mariah came back? She should have slammed the door in her face. She should have refused to speak to her. But it was important to know what this young woman knew. To know, so she could deal with her.

This young woman would be back. Sharon knew the type. She went to the dresser in her bedroom. The bedroom was sparse. There were no pictures of Bethany in here; she couldn't bear to feel Bethany's eyes on her here. She stared at herself in the mirror. She had been so young once, ripe with Bethany, married, knowing she would have a wonderful life. She had been very confident of that. She had done everything right. Nothing but good choices and right turns, but then you made one bad choice, one left turn, and that perfect world came undone, more fragile than you ever thought.

She had hidden the gun underneath a set of T-shirts, folded, that her husband had worn. Everything else of Hal's was gone, but she had kept these. They were good for hiding the gun. The pistol seemed like it was less hers, and more his, if it was hidden this way.

She checked the gun. It needed cleaning. It had not been loaded in a long time. The loaded gun was too much temptation. She got the oil and a rag and she cleaned the gun now, and then she loaded it, carefully, thinking, *You won't have to use it. You won't need it. There's nothing for this snoop to find, nothing for her to know. The police found nothing. No one will ever find anything.*

She realized she was crying as she prepared the gun, and she stopped, and then sobs racked her, sobs for her lost daughter, for her lost life, for every left turn she had made. She let the tears come, molten and welcome, and she felt an exhaustion when she was done. Then she just felt the coldness in her chest, the sense of doing what was necessary, like she had done before.

She finished cleaning the gun, loaded it, and then looked for the best place in the house to keep it. The couch. No, Mariah sat on the couch when she'd come before; it would be natural for her to sit there again. OK. The armchair by the couch, where Sharon had sat. She carefully wedged the gun into place, hidden by the cushion. She sat carefully. She moved the gun to the right side, because she was right-handed and it was less visible to anyone sitting on the couch.

Please don't come back here, Sharon thought. *Take pity on a grieving mother. Don't come back. Go away, go find your mother. Leave me and my daughter out of it.*

Then she decided she couldn't just wait and hope that Mariah Dunning didn't come back or gave up. She would have to take action into her own hands.

Sharon sat down at her computer and started to delve into Mariah's online life. She needed to know her enemy in case she needed to make her into a friend.

13

LAKEHAVEN'S POLICE STATION was not large. It did not need to be. There was a chief, and a staff of eight officers, two corporals, a sergeant, a detective, and an administrative assistant. Before Beth went missing Craig had only known Broussard's name; now he knew them all. Craig drove his wife's car, a red Mercedes—he thought for certain that would spark commentary—and parked by a police car. It had been so long since it was driven he was grateful the battery had started.

He sat in the small lobby and waited. The assistant looked at him, and he knew she knew who he was. So did the officers who arrived and left, coming off duty and going on patrol duty. He sat there and took their stares. It was as if he was the sole criminal mastermind in Lakehaven, mocking them with his presence.

The chief came out. He was a small, spare man with horn-rimmed glasses. Lakehaven's one detective, Carmen Ames, stood with Broussard.

"Chief. Ms. Ames." Craig was determined to be civil, be calm.

"If you'd come back to an interview room with us, sir," Detective Ames said.

Craig followed her. They sat down in a small room with a rectangular table. He had been questioned in this same room before. At least four times. "Is there a problem?"

"No, sir, but we wanted to talk to you about Mariah and the car crash."

"My insurance will pay for the damage, I said that already."

"Yes, sir, that's not our concern today." Carmen Ames produced a DVD, with the name Beth written across it, in a plastic case. He stared at it. "This item was found in a permitted search of your daughter's car, in the glove compartment."

"What is it?"

"It's a DVD. But it's password-protected."

"Why did you try to play it?" He kept his voice relaxed.

Ames and Broussard glanced at each other.

"I found the DVD," Carmen Ames said. "It was stuffed in the glove compartment, under the owner's manual for the car, and two years of expired insurance cards, and a first aid kit, and a worn paperback book. Maybe Mariah knew it was there; maybe Mariah didn't know it was there. The DVD has your wife's name, Beth, written across the front." As if Craig hadn't noticed that immediately. And they both looked at him, as if a reaction might flash in neon across his face.

"And you said it's password-protected?" Craig forced his voice toward total calm. He folded his hands in his lap. The picture of unconcern.

"Yes. It could contain photos, files, documents, we don't know."

"It's probably something from her work. She worked for a software company."

"Why is it in your daughter's car, then?" Dennis Broussard seemed determined to keep his voice equally clear, but the barest hint of a smile on his face said, *I'm closing in on you.*

"How odd," Craig said. "I can't think of a reason."

"Do you know the password?" Ames said. "Or any likely password she might have used?"

"No." He looked at Broussard. "I mean, you could try my name or my daughter's or our dog's name."

"It's just a very unusual item to find. We called her employer. They said they don't normally give out secured discs to their salespeople. Product demos are done online."

"It could be something as innocent as family pictures."

"It could be, but again, why is it in Mariah's car?"

"I'm sorry, Dennis," Craig said. "I don't have an explanation." He said nothing more. He'd learned long ago that if he volunteered information, they would seek to fashion it into a noose with which to hang him.

Silence in the room.

"OK," Craig said. "You've shown my wife's property to me, is there anything else?"

Broussard drummed fingers against the table. "Have you received any communications from your wife, or regarding your wife, since we last spoke?"

Here it is, Craig thought. "Define communication."

The silence was loud and thunderous. "Has someone contacted you regarding her?"

"I received a prank phone call saying that she was abducted by aliens. Probably the twentieth I've gotten along those lines since she vanished." He did not mention the other call, the more frightening one. "And someone left a rock in my driveway today."

"A rock. Why a rock?"

"I don't know. An implied threat. I've had seven rocks tossed through my front window. You've never found the culprits."

"Anything with the rock?" Broussard asked.

"A note."

"You really make me pull it out of you, Craig," Broussard said. He shook his head. "What note?"

"It told me that it was time for me to leave Lakehaven."

"Was there a specific threat if you didn't?" Ames asked.

"No. It's all bluster. But I am tired of it."

"I'd like to see this note."

"I'll send you a photo," he said.

"Where's the physical note?"

"I thought Mariah would find it upsetting," he said. "I destroyed it." The lie felt just fine on his lips. He had no intention of giving this to the police and letting them make no headway. He'd put it to better use when he found whoever was tormenting him.

"That was evidence."

"There's no evidence against me in my wife's disappearance, but still you think I did it. It's sad how you can't solve the biggest case in years in this town." He watched their faces for a reaction to his prodding.

Dennis Broussard said, "It's unfathomable to me how you think this is some kind of game."

"This is my life. My child's life. You're the one who treats it like a mental exercise."

"How's Mariah?" Ames asked.

"She's coping."

"She engaged in a reckless car chase," Ames said.

"She was certain she saw her mom."

"She had a trunk full of weapons and gear. She claimed to have an alternate theory of the crime when I spoke to her last night. Is she actually making inquiries? Because I would consider that most unhelpful. Perhaps even interference with the case."

Craig didn't know that Broussard had talked to Mariah; he felt angry that she hadn't told him. But he felt sure this was an empty threat. "It's all for show. She doesn't have a lead. She wouldn't know how to track it." He hoped Broussard or Ames wouldn't do an internet search and find Reveal's blog. "It makes her feel... like she has some sort of sense of control. That she can find her mother. Even if she can't. She needs to feel like she can do something to help. Do you understand that?"

"Does she often hallucinate?" Broussard asked. "Is she on medications, or other drugs?"

"Just Xanax. Five milligrams. To help her with her anxiety when needed, but she hasn't taken it in a while. I wouldn't call yesterday a hallucination. More mistaken identity, driven by hope. See, we still have hope, and hope is cruel in its own way."

"Let's go back to this DVD. A glove compartment," Broussard said, "is a really good place to hide stuff for a few days. No one ever looks in there unless they have to. Maybe Beth wanted to hide this from you, so she slips it into her daughter's car. And then something happened to her before she could retrieve it."

Carmen Ames spoke slowly. "Suspicion rises. Arguments escalate. Accidents happen. Then you feel caught, don't you, Craig?

Caught in a moment's heat, a moment's terrible decision. You're a big strong guy, former football player. A shove, a blow aimed at the throat, maybe, it's over. Or you get so mad you close your hands around her throat..."

"Did you rehearse these lines first? I didn't kill my wife," Craig said. "I've heard all this before." He stood. "Please let our insurance agent know what the estimate is for damage to the police car. I appreciate you not making our situation worse by filing charges against my daughter. She's had a difficult time."

"We reserve the right to change our mind," Broussard said. "On filing charges against Mariah. She had this evidence as well in her car; not coming forward with it could be seen as an interference in the investigation. We're not returning the DVD to you."

Craig sat back down, his legs feeling weak. He saw it now; this was leverage. "What do you want from me?"

"Have you thought about the strain you are putting on your daughter?" Broussard asked.

They thought Mariah was cracking because she was living with him. That his guilt was affecting her, that she suspected him as her mother's killer, and that the tension between loyalty to her father and to her mother's memory were undoing her. He could see this theory in their faces. The car accident was a new chapter for them. An opening. The next page. If only he'd stopped her at the mall. If only, if only.

"If someone knows about a crime and conceals it," Broussard said, "that person is an accessory."

They were going to charge Mariah as an accessory. To get him to confess, or to tell what he knew. "My daughter is not your pawn, Broussard." Craig stood. "Unless you're arresting me, I have nothing to say. Except this: you laughed at my daughter for saying she was looking herself for the perp. You have time to laugh, but not time to find my wife."

"Think about what we said, Craig," Broussard said. "And for once in your misbegotten life, think about someone other than yourself. Think about Mariah. You are seeing your daughter, a wonderful, smart girl I know you love, dissolve before your eyes.

You could stop it. You could set yourself free from that little prison you've made in your home."

"You never even tried to find someone else as a suspect, Dennis."

"You know, if Beth had vanished downtown, or at a shopping center, I would have thought it much more likely someone grabbed her. Maybe a random killer. But she just went to your lot, where no one ever is, where the only person with a reason to go there...is you."

"A transient..."

"We don't really have those in Lakehaven. Not for long."

"Someone with a grudge against her..."

"But everyone loved Beth."

"Someone who noticed her and followed her..."

"That would be very hard to confirm, and we just have no evidence this was a stranger abduction."

"And no evidence it wasn't." Craig looked at Ames. "Did you know your boss used to cheat off my papers in chemistry and math? He's never taken the hard road to an answer."

"That's not true, and I've also never fallen for a misleading story," Broussard said.

"Goodbye." Craig got up and left, thinking the whole time that he would feel suddenly strong hands on his shoulders, wrenching his wrists into the cuffs. But no. He walked out of the police station into the sunshine. They were willing to use Mariah against him, so certain were they.

He got into Beth's car and drove home, forcing himself toward calm, forcing himself to think.

Where had this passworded DVD come from, and what did it mean?

The calls. The rock. The threats. And now this.

He had to find and stop his tormentor. For Mariah's sake.

14

AFTER LEAVING SHARON'S, Mariah had sent Julie Santos a message via Faceplace, explaining that she was looking into Bethany's disappearance for a connection to her mother's and providing Julie with her phone number. Julie had called back quickly and seemed willing to help. Julie agreed to talk to Mariah but asked if they could meet at the gym. Her voice was chirpy, energetic.

"You got workout clothes?" Julie asked. "I've got a free period, and if people see me working out with a client, or someone they think is a client, I often will get stopped and get another booking. And I can't just stand around and talk while I'm at work."

Mariah's workouts tended to consist of running alone, sparring with a partner in martial arts, shooting baskets, and infrequent yoga, but she lied and said yes. Julie told her to meet her at a gym nearby in an hour. She hurried to a store, bought an outfit, tore off the tags, and changed clothes.

The front desk summoned Julie when Mariah arrived and asked for her. Julie was small, with thick dark hair, a sharp gaze, and a mouth that kept turning into a knowing smile, like she'd seen it all, heard it all. Her workout clothes were a lot more fashionable than Mariah's quick purchases.

The high school friend, Mariah thought: always an interesting view into a person's choices. That friend could be your greatest defender, ally, or critic.

"Working out all day must be exhausting," Mariah said, wishing this woman had been willing to meet for coffee instead. She felt weird and awkward trying to question Julie during physical effort.

"You mispronounced energizing," Julie said, with a laugh. Then she got serious. "This way," she said, like she was giving a tour. "Here, my son's in the daycare. Let me peek in on him, and then we'll find a place to talk."

They stopped at a nice daycare room, with windows where parents could watch, with a half-dozen small children inside.

"That's my son, Grant," she said, with pride, pointing at a three-year-old boy playing trucks with a little girl. "That's my heart."

"He's adorable," Mariah said and meant it.

"Bethany named him." Her voice grew quiet. "I mean, she suggested the name to me. I was a single mom, the dad wasn't around and wasn't going to be, and I wanted a short, simple strong name, and Bethany suggested it. She said a grant was like a gift, and that's how I had to view him." She fell silent, watching her boy.

Mariah felt a pang. Remembered Mom dropping her off at daycare, at a sitter's, telling her, "I'll be back soon, you be a good girl. No, you be the *best* girl."

"You mind riding stationary bikes? I thought it would be easier to chat," Julie said.

And sit, Mariah thought. "Sounds great."

They found bikes that gave them a view of both the TV screen—turned to a news channel, reporting on a plane crash in Pakistan and a bribery scandal involving a former member of Congress—and of the weight room. Mariah watched Julie set up her bike and did the same, optimistically pressing the controls to match so they'd be breathless and resting at the same time. They started pedaling.

"You said you've talked with Sharon. How is she?" Julie asked.

"Grieving."

"Well, it's what she does best." Julie glanced at Mariah. "That poor woman has just sunk herself into her misery. Maybe I'd do the same if Grant were taken from me. I cannot imagine." She sighed, frowned for a moment at the readout.

"I hope you never find out," Mariah said.

"I don't mean to be judgmental. But Bethany would have never wanted her mother to turn her life into a prison. Sharon rarely leaves her house. She's way into her church, and I'm sure they're supportive, but the last time I talked to her it turned into this mishmash of guilt and redemption and blame. There is no comforting her. She doesn't want it. I swear sometimes she acts like she deserves having lost Bethany. I don't think she's really mentally well."

"She said Bethany's life had gone sour in the months before she vanished." She kept pace with Julie, who was clearly competitive and glancing over at Mariah's workout readout. Julie went faster. Mariah didn't.

"The months before Bethany vanished, everything went wrong. Messes and strains like you can't believe. It really was not a shock she might leave for greener pastures..." Her voice suddenly shifted into encouragement. "Now, there you go! Shift to higher effort, see how the readout gives you the target heart rate? Excellent! You got it, girl!"

Mariah followed along, noticing a woman watching them for a few moments, then wandering off toward the weight room.

"Sorry. She's my boss. I'm a little behind on my quota this month. I upsell services. You know, more personal training, yoga classes, spa treatments, and so on." She shrugged. "I'd rather just train people, but it's part of the game."

Are you trying to sell me services while we talk about your dead friend? For a moment she couldn't look at Julie. "What messes? What strains?"

Julie slowed her pedaling pace back to Mariah's. "Someone bought sex toys using Bethany's name and credit card and shipped them to her coworkers at Ahoy, with typed gift notes inside from her. It was an absolute mess. She nearly got fired, but she convinced them it wasn't a bad joke but someone targeting her. Obviously, that's not how an ordinary thief would use her credit card number."

"Someone wanted to make her look bad to her employer."

"Then she apparently went on a spending spree with her replacement cards. She was buying all this stuff, from luxury stores, right, and she claimed she hadn't ordered it, but I don't think Jake and her mother believed her. I thought she was after his attention. He was never at home, working constantly. She said she didn't want the stuff, but I know some of it she kept. Jake told Sharon he found it later, stashed under her bed—high-end sweaters, jewelry, an expensive watch. Weird that she didn't take it with her."

Mariah waited.

"Then the drinking started. She said she was bored, she was lonely, because Jake was putting in so many hours at the startup and she was all stressed about this credit card drama. She was out with a new friend, and she said someone must have spiked their drinks. Bethany had a bad reaction to it, and she freaked out, hallucinating, and started throwing bottles at people in the bar parking lot. She nearly got arrested. I mean, Sharon and Jake both about *died*. You'd think she'd ease up, but she didn't. Got mad because they didn't believe her, tried to get her help. She drank even more, got messed up even more. There was nearly an arrest, her acting violent in the house with Jake, breaking stuff. Jake told Sharon he'd found prescription pills in her car trunk, not even made out to her, to someone else. She said they weren't hers, she hadn't taken any pills, but c'mon, they were right there in her car. She stopped eating and drinking for a while, said someone was trying to poison her, that's where the pills came from. It was crazy. She's telling me all this, and I'm all, 'Sure, Beth, whatever.' At least once Jake had to call the police."

"Who could have poisoned her?"

"No one. The idea is ridiculous. She was losing her grip."

"Well, who would have access to her food and water? Her husband. Maybe her mom. Maybe someone she worked with. Maybe a trusted friend."

"Listen. No one was trying to dope Bethany. She was doping herself." Julie sped up on the bike. "Oh, it gets worse. She lost her job. There was a question of her having...um, *borrowed* some funds from Ahoy. Andy—that's who got her the job—he stood up for her, but they still let her go. Quietly, without pressing charges."

This Bethany—troubled, accused of crimes—was not like the Bethany Sharon had described.

"I'd like more details about that. Would Andy talk to me?"

"He doesn't like to talk about her. They were close, once, before she married." She cleared her throat. "Andy and I are a couple now. It's a little weird. We were friends as kids. But kids grow up, don't they?" She gave a soft, awkward laugh.

"I'm just looking to see if there's a connection to my mom's disappearance. There are several similarities." This was a stretch, but she didn't offer details. "My mom was Beth Dunning. Ever hear her name?"

"No, I'm sorry." Julie looked right back at her and then at her digital readout. She brushed back a lank of dark hair from her face, behind her ears. "I'm sorry for your loss. If I vanished, I hope Grant would come looking for me."

"It seems like Bethany really had a run of bad luck." *And that you don't care. Why is that? You're supposed to be her friend.*

"The pills that were in her car were the explanation. She was a prescription drug addict, buying on the black market—I think that's how her credit cards got compromised. I think she took that money to Houston to get away from her messes, and she probably overdosed down there."

"Her body would have been found, though."

"Maybe. Maybe not."

"Do you remember the name on the pill bottle?"

"No. Most of the label was torn off. Like I said, probably stolen and resold. Or some friend we don't know about gave it to her." She didn't look at Mariah.

"Did she tell you she was leaving Jake?"

"No. But we weren't confiding in each other so much then."

"Any reason?"

"Andy and I were dating, and we were her two oldest friends. Normally you'd be happy for two friends falling in love. She was horrible. She tried to warn me off him in the vaguest, most passive-aggressive way possible. Which, hello, she had a husband." Her voice went dark.

This was a fractured friendship, then. "So, she never mentioned specific problems with Jake?"

"Nope. And she would have told me anything that huge, I think. Even though our lives had gone in different directions and hers was a train wreck. I feel bad I didn't do more to help her. But she changed, not me."

"What did you think of Jake?"

"On paper, Jake is wonderful. Cute, super smart, very ambitious, sweet natured, a good guy but not a doormat. She was crazy about him."

Mariah thought this a pretty fair description. "On paper. You didn't like him."

Now she looked at her. "Life is short. Both my parents died young, and they spent a lot of their time working, away from me and my sister, away from each other. I want to be a priority to my guy. I don't want a job or a company to matter more than I or our kids do."

"And the startup company mattered more to Jake than Bethany mattered to him."

"Yes. It did. Maybe that's why she was unhappy. Maybe that's why she self-destructed. Ugh, that was a choice she made."

"Sharon thinks Jake killed her."

Now Julie gazed directly at her. "I've never bought into the whole Jake did it thing. She had been drunk and on pills and violent; he could have divorced her easily. But he was still in love with her, and they were about to become rich. That's exactly when you *don't* kill your spouse."

Or maybe that's when you're starting the exciting new chapter in your life and that's when you shed the druggie spouse, Mariah thought. *What if she wouldn't go quietly? What if they argued and he got violent and then he shoved her and she fell and hit her head or he closed his hands around her throat...* She pushed the thought away, nausea roiling her gut for a moment. How horrible that would be.

"But Jake's the easiest person to blame, so she does. I mean, she doesn't go around saying this to newspapers. Just to her friends. And to me and Andy. I can see why she'd fault a husband."

She glanced down. "Sharon's husband...he killed himself. Bethany was fifteen."

"Why did he...?"

"Her dad was an alcoholic, and I guess that was a secret. Growing up, I never saw him drinking in the house. Not once. Then one day Beth's at school, Sharon at her job, and Mr. Blevins stays home sick from work and he downs a fifth of whiskey and a ton of pills and he's dead. Bethany and Andy found him, sitting in his recliner. He had a good job as an account manager for an ad agency. People always say it's a shock, but really, it was."

"Why did he?"

"Andy said there was a note, but it just said that he was sorry. Bethany said later her mom told her he'd been a drunk years ago when Bethany was little, and he'd gone back to it. So, he hadn't been drinking but he'd started again. Depression, I guess. Did you notice there's not a picture of him in that house? Not a single one?"

"I did notice."

"Yes, suicide is awful. But they erased him from the family, in a way, don't you think? And he left them some money, too. Oh, boy, the computer's going to make us climb. Don't worry if you can't keep up with me." Julie steadied her breathing. "I always think, blood will tell. There's all sorts of great stuff and bad stuff in our genes. Maybe Bethany had too much of her father in her. Is any of this helpful to you with your mom's case? Because otherwise, it feels like gossiping about my dead friend, and I'm not about that."

"You think Bethany's dead."

"She wouldn't let her mom worry. So, yes."

"You never know what people will do," Mariah said. "Maybe she was tired of you all. No offense."

Now Julie looked at her, surprised at the bite in her comment. "Well, maybe she was. That cuts both ways."

"You said the night she claimed her drink got spiked, she was out with a new friend. Who?"

Julie made a face. "She had a new friend named Lizbeth."

Lizbeth. Another Beth name. Mariah stopped pedaling. "Lizbeth who?"

"I never knew her last name. Bethany had an interest in writing, you know, like writing a book, and she started going to some critique group at one of the libraries where they had authors come speak and had lectures on how to get started in writing, and they'd bring work to get it critiqued. I think Lizbeth also joined. I didn't like her. I felt she was one of those types who latches on to a person and doesn't let go. But they were writing buddies and would go off in the evenings to bars together. I guess it filled the empty hours with Jake working on his company so much. Once Bethany couldn't go to lunch with me because she had to work on her pages to take to the critique group."

Lizbeth. "Sharon didn't mention Lizbeth. Or an interest in writing."

"I don't think Sharon knew about that friendship. Because I don't think Sharon wanted Bethany writing. You know, drawing on family stuff for inspiration. My goodness, look at that guy over in the weight room. I might have to ride an extra few miles just to keep the view."

Mariah didn't look because she didn't care. She was silent, thinking, sweating. "How could I reach Lizbeth?"

Now Julie gave her a long look. "What for? They didn't know each other that long, and Lizbeth didn't even come to the service honoring Bethany. We didn't want to call it a memorial, because what if she wasn't dead, so Sharon called it a gathering, which just sounds so odd to me. But some of the writing group members were there. They call themselves the Pen Pushers or something like that." She shrugged, mopped at her forehead with her towel, watched the guy in the weight room.

Julie was bored now. Mariah had seen it before. Bethany was from the past, and Julie was all about the future. People would ask Mariah how she was coping, how she was doing, and five seconds later their eyes were leaving her face, glancing elsewhere, waiting for her to be done. No one really wanted to know. They just wanted you to say, "I'm fine, thanks."

"So, you didn't hang out with her and Lizbeth together?"

"No. I only met her once or twice, running into them at Starbucks or the wine bar near our house, and it was clear that Lizbeth felt three was a crowd. You know how some women can be about their friends."

"Thank you, you've been very helpful. I really appreciate it." Mariah got off the bicycle, feeling like she'd stumbled into a dark room. Now she had more questions than answers.

"I can comp this workout, but if you'll fill out the survey, I'll get some extra points," Julie said as Mariah walked away. "And you have to get your guest pass stamped when you leave!" Julie called to her back.

Another Beth name, Mariah thought, heading toward the door. It couldn't be. It couldn't. Just when she'd decided there could be no connection...this. This oddity.

She glanced back at Julie, who wasn't watching her but was now chatting with the weight room guy. It just seemed like Julie had abandoned a friend quickly when things went wrong. Mariah knew what that was like, to be abandoned by friends because they didn't feel comfortable around her grief, or they didn't know what to say to her and, worse, wouldn't try to learn, or they thought her dad was guilty and didn't want to be around him.

Who was this Lizbeth?

15

Chad—er, Reveal—was sweating. He was glad he was alone. He had the speaker on his smartphone, running his damp hands along his jeans.

He had not tried so hard to be cool since middle school.

"So, Chad," the television producer said through the speakerphone, "we really adore the podcast, we embrace your energy, we love your voice. Very distinct. So distinct. Charmingly distinct."

Distinct, Chad decided, was good. "Thank you."

"We did decide, you know, just to be sure, to bring in some other hosting candidates..."

His hands froze on his jeans mid-swipe. "I thought I was it."

"Oh, sure, absolutely, you're in our top three. Along with Brian from Crimeathon and Louisa from CrimeCentral. But we think you're just so great."

He knew Brian and Louisa both; they did excellent work and probably had more followers than he did. And Louisa had a book deal, just announced last week, so she'd have all the heat. That was unfair. Who still read books? He had felt on top of the world ten minutes ago, now his stomach was wrenching in panic. He'd thought in the earlier conversation that this was a lock, a done deal. Even if the producer hadn't said this is a done deal. It had been all in his tone of voice: Chad was their guy. "I see. All right. What do I need to do to seal the deal with you, Freddy?" He hated begging, asking for this, but he didn't know what else to say.

"Well, I think we have to look at how in depth you go into cases. How far you're willing to push."

He swallowed past the lump that had formed in his throat. "I have an active case now. It's incredible. I've been followed by a suspicious car after meeting with a crime victim." Silence greeted this announcement, so he upped the stakes. "And I've been contacted by someone involved in the case who wants to meet with me and only me." Well, that was technically one way to describe Mariah. "So I think I'm really on to something distinctively hot."

"Chad, er, Reveal, that's great. Tell me more."

"I'll save it for our meeting," Chad said. "I think you'll be impressed. This is a family crime, and there's a key family member who'll only talk to me. Because of who I am. Because I am trusted. Because I get results." Sweat poured down his back as he counted off these bullet points. *Please*, he thought, *please*. He could get Mariah to tell him what she'd discovered. She kept hinting. He could tease them enough even if there wasn't a real tie between the Beths. Maybe even get Mariah to come to California with him. He'd ask his parents to fly her out. He would guess the other candidates weren't bringing a crime victim with them as an actual prop. *Contributor*, he mentally amended. "This case has everything. Gorgeous girl"—well, some people thought Mariah was pretty—"family tragedy, money, prestige, a town turning against a suspect, and an unexpected twist." That was if the crimes against the Beths were connected. He'd convinced Mariah with a casual blog post; think what he could sell when he put his mind to the problem.

"I'll look forward to our meeting, then, Reveal."

Chad thought it was a good sign the producer hadn't stumbled over his adopted name. He thanked him and hung up. Now he had to just get Mariah to share everything she knew.

He'd helped her by pointing out one possible solution to her mother's case—that it was tied to Bethany Curtis's, the wife of a famous software mogul.

He had all the elements for a great television show pitch; now it was Mariah's turn to help him.

16

MARIAH, SITTING BEHIND the wheel of her car, searched on her phone for writers groups in Austin. Not surprisingly for a creative city, she found several that met at local coffee shops or public library branches. There wasn't a group called Pen Pushers and Mariah's heart sank: either Julie misremembered the name, or they'd disbanded in the time since Bethany's disappearance.

Like Pen Pushers, but not quite? Mariah searched again, found one called Pushy Pens: We WILL Get Published! which met weekly at...an undisclosed location.

Seriously? she thought. One had to apply to join, with sample work of three chapters. Every member was expected to bring ten new pages, each week, for critique. They had done this to keep the group's membership "serious, small, and focused." There was a contact Gmail account for Yvette Suarez, the club's current chair.

On her phone, Mariah wrote Suarez an email, slightly bending the truth that she was helping the Blevins family on leads connected to the Bethany Curtis disappearance and was trying to reach a member of the group, Lizbeth, who had been a friend of Bethany's. She included her number and asked Suarez to call her back.

After her workout, she needed a shower. Then she'd see this Andy, both school friend and coworker, at Ahoy Transportation.

Her phone rang. The Lakehaven Police Department on the screen. She answered. "Hello?"

"Hi, Mariah. This is Dennis Broussard. We finished processing your car. Would you like to pick up your gear? Your father's having your car towed to a body shop."

"All right. I can come by now."

"Great, because I want to show you something that we found."

* * *

Mariah stared at the DVD in its case, with her mother's name written on it in black ink.

"Have you seen this before?" Broussard asked.

"No," she said.

"It was in your glove compartment. You didn't put it there?"

Her gaze met Broussard's. "No, I've not seen it before. Is it music?"

"We don't think it's just music, Mariah. It asks for a password. Do you know why your mom would have a password-protected DVD?"

"No."

"Do you know what the password might be?"

She shook her head.

"Think, Mariah. You might have seen this before but not remembered."

She bit at her lip. "Unless it came from her work. But I never saw her carting around DVDs. I really don't remember having seen this one."

"Why would it be in your car?"

"I don't know. Do I need a lawyer here?"

"If you want one, of course, but I'm not arresting you and you're not under suspicion of interfering with an investigation. But this was in your car, and it has to be there for a reason."

"I don't know." Her voice rose slightly.

"Did your mother ever use your car?"

"I had my car at UT. Well, at my apartment."

"Did your parents have a spare set of keys?"

"Yes," she said after a moment.

"Could your mother have hidden this here so no one, like your father, would find it. Probably he wouldn't think to look there."

She said nothing to this.

"Your mom's car was a red Mercedes, yes?" Broussard asked.

"Yes. She called it Baby. She bought it with commissions. She was very proud of it. Can you break the password?"

"We'll try."

"If it's in my car, it's my property...I could try and break it. I have a degree in computer science."

"I understand that, but with your mom's name on it, it could be evidence."

"She loved showtunes," Mariah said. "It's probably just a CD full of cheesy showtunes." She wiped a tear from her eye.

"You miss her."

"Yes. Of course."

"It must be so hard, living with your dad," Broussard said. "You love him. You want to be loyal to him."

"He didn't hurt my mom."

"Have there been any women in his life, Mariah, since she vanished? Maybe a woman you thought he knew before? It's not disloyal to say. Be loyal to your mom."

"I'm loyal to both of them," she said, her voice rising. "He didn't have an affair. And if he did, he still would never hurt her."

"When you saw her, it means you think she could be out there. Letting you wonder if she's alive or not."

"Maybe. Or maybe there's a whole other explanation."

"You say that like you mean something. Your father said you weren't really trying to"—he did air quotes—"*investigate* her case."

She bit at her lip again. "You wouldn't listen anyway."

"All I want is to find your mom and bring whoever...took...her to justice. Is there something you want to tell me?"

"When I have some proof. Because then I can go to the press, too, and then you can't ignore me or try to make it about my dad again."

"Mariah..."

"You can think I'm crazy, but as long as I'm not breaking the law, you can't stop me."

"Has Craig told you that someone has threatened him? Trying to get him to move out of Lakehaven?"

She absorbed this. "No."

"He might not want you to know. He might try to shield you. But you're an adult, and I'm telling you."

"Are you going to give me back my stuff now?"

"Yes. It's boxed up for you. Except the DVD. That's part of our investigation."

Mariah studied his calm expression. "I know what you think of me. I'm not crazy."

"I don't think you're crazy. I think you're deeply traumatized."

She didn't answer him, she stared at the table.

"I don't think that day is a haze to you because of medications and fever. Did you see your father kill her? Did you block it out? Is that why you're protecting him?" His whisper was like a knife. "You don't have to live like this, Mariah. Tell me what happened and free yourself."

She stood. "When I prove to you my father is innocent," Mariah said, "I hope you'll remember our conversation and be embarrassed." She left with as much dignity as she could muster.

* * *

She put the four guns, the Taser, the laptop, and the telescoping baton into the trunk of her father's car. She was trembling. Someone threatening Dad. She was going to go home and see if he mentioned this to her. Maybe she should take one of the guns into the house and load it and have it ready in case someone was after her father.

But she was wondering, *Why didn't Dad tell me about the threat?*

17

MARIAH HAD GONE home, showered, and changed into fresh clothes. Craig was in his office; she could hear the quiet sound of Miles Davis playing on his stereo; that meant he was working. Today the Miles album was *Sketches of Spain*, warm, soothing, playful.

She knocked on the door. "Come in," he said.

She stepped inside. His computer screen was between her and the door, so she couldn't see what he was working on. He was dressed though, in jeans and a nice shirt, which was unusual when he didn't leave the house. He silenced the music.

"I got my gear back from Broussard. He said someone has threatened us."

"Just me. You weren't threatened. It's nothing."

"Dad. Of course it's not nothing."

"This happens every few months," he said. "It comes and it goes and I wait it out."

"You can't keep this from me."

"There's nothing to keep. How did your sales calls go?"

It sounded at first like something he would have said to Mom, when she came back home from a long day. Dad was often fixing dinner when Mom got home, a glass of wine already poured for her. He joked that she'd had to deal with people all day and he'd had to deal with spreadsheets, so he'd had it easier. "I like people," Mom would say. "More than you do." And Dad would say, "Well, I like you, though," and Mom would laugh and say, "Oh yes you do."

She felt sometimes that if Broussard and whoever was sending her father threats could have seen her parents for just five minutes of their life together, they would know her father was innocent.

Instead she pretended she wasn't lying to him. "They were fine. I need to go to another meeting. Not sure when I'll be back."

"I saw you in the driveway. You came home in workout clothes."

"One of my meetings was with a gym manager. All sorts of needed phone apps in fitness and healthcare."

He watched her and he, she guessed, decided to believe her. "All right then."

"The police found some DVD they can't open in my car with Mom's name on it," she said.

"I know. They asked me about it."

"What's on it?"

"I don't know. It's probably something left over from her work. They'll crack it open and it will be nothing and they'll be embarrassed." His voice was firm.

"Dad. Are you sure?"

"I don't know what it is, Mariah, I promise you."

"They want us turned against each other," she said.

"Yes," he said. "And that can't happen."

"Do you want any lunch?"

"No. I ate already."

"All right." She closed the door.

She went to the kitchen, ate a quick sandwich, and decided to change her approach when she went to talk to Andy Candolet. She really would treat it as a business call. And she tried a series of searches on Lizbeth while she ate: looking for her on the FIND BETHANY page, on Bethany's Faceplace page. Nothing.

She needed the woman's last name.

If Ahoy and the writing group turned into dead ends, she'd call it quits, but an unappealing thought had crept into her mind: two missing Beths. What if she couldn't find this Lizbeth? Would she be the third?

* * *

There were a number of big trucking and transportation companies south of downtown Austin; they brought goods from the ports of Houston and New Orleans. She turned in at the entrance for Ahoy Transportation. She saw several eighteen wheelers and a bevy of smaller trucks, all with a smiling cartoon anchor painted on the side. AHOY FOR SHIPPING, the motto read beneath. She parked in a long line of cars in a spot marked for visitors and went into the main office.

Behind the reception desk sat a woman in her seventies, frowning, reading a *People* magazine. She studied Mariah with bright eyes and a piercing gaze, seeming to take in and analyze her clothes and her nervousness and her face with a single sweep.

"Help you?" she croaked, as if she couldn't be more disinterested.

"Hi. I was looking for Andy Candolet, if he's in."

The woman turned a page of *People* and said, "He might be. He might not be. Did you have an appointment?"

"I did not, but I'd be happy to make one."

"What you selling?"

For a moment she thought she'd try to say she was a friend of Julie's, but that would be a lie, and she'd decided to treat this like an actual business call. "I'm an app and website developer."

"I'm sure that means something to somebody. Call and make an appointment."

This woman took being a gatekeeper seriously. Mariah set her mouth in a determined line and put on her most professional tone. "I do web design and interfaces for mobile apps. When the big national rideshare services were temporarily banned in Austin, I wrote the web interfaces for the local companies that tried to replace them. I'm used to designing apps that include security, transportation, and scheduling, and I'm cheaper than the big firms." She just needed to get past this woman. "If I can just have five minutes with him..." She handed the woman a business card with MARIAH DUNNING APP DESIGNS on it.

"That is one hundred percent fascinating," the old woman said. "Let me see if Andy's available to get as excited as I am." She raised a phone, punched a button and spoke quietly, reading Mariah's name off her card, and glanced again at Mariah. She hung up. "He said give him just a few minutes."

"I appreciate your kindness. May I ask you what you transport here?"

"How I love lunch hour and covering the desk," the woman said. "It lets me interact with the public." She put down her *People* magazine. "We move whatever needs moving, sweetheart. It tends to be lots of produce, and then consumer goods from the factories down in Mexico, and what gets shipped in from the coast." She raised an eyebrow. "You don't research your possible clients?" But to Mariah's surprise, she softened the rebuke with a little half-smile.

Mariah forced a sheepish look onto her face. "You're right, I should have. I apologize to you and to the editors of *People*."

To her surprise the old woman laughed. For one moment. Then the steely gaze returned.

And then a man entered the reception area from a hallway behind the woman. Mariah's first thought was he looked like he could audition for Clark Kent. Tall, broad shouldered, athletic build, with dark hair, blue eyes, and very old-fashioned black-framed glasses. He wore a white polo with the smiling Ahoy anchor logo on it and navy slacks. He gave Mariah a shaky smile and said, "Mariah Dunning? Andy Candolet. Sorry, it's a crazy day, but I can give you ten minutes." He seemed to study her face for a moment. He took Mariah's business card from the woman, who had jabbed it at him as if it were radioactive. He pocketed it.

"Have we met before?" Mariah asked. His searching look and his slight air of nervousness made her ask.

"No, I don't think so," he said, smile suddenly bright. "Let's go talk."

"Thank you for your help," Mariah said to the old woman.

"Highlight of my day," she answered, flipping a page.

Mariah followed Andy to another office module in an opposite corner of the transportation bay. His office was cluttered: stacks of files on his desk, the corkboard behind him filled with pictures of Ahoy employees at gatherings, a number of "certificates of accomplishment" that looked like they'd come from the laser printer, a whole set of lanyards and credentials she recognized as from corporate conferences, hanging like little banners.

Lots of photos of himself, posing with people Mariah guessed were clients or customers or vendors, always smiling.

"My aunt Claudette dislikes working the reception desk," he said with an easy grin as they sat down. "But she owns the company, so we must suffer her charms."

"But she's so good at it," Mariah said, and he laughed. "I understand you run security around here." She was trying to place why his face had engendered a reaction in her the first time she'd seen it in the photo. She was sure she'd never met him; she would have remembered, she thought. But there was something... his name or his face.

"Yes."

For a moment she nearly said, "I worked out with your girlfriend a couple of hours ago," but she thought if he didn't know of her immediate interest in Bethany she might learn more. He hadn't reacted to her name. Julie, busy with her clients, must not have called him yet and told him about meeting Mariah.

"What's your specialty with apps?" he asked.

Fine. Keep it businesslike. "Well, I can code for RFID-compliant tracking," she said. She knew a little about transport apps, just from having read, but she wasn't confident she could fake her way through this whole interview. "I'll be honest, I'm not as experienced, but I'm cheap and I'd do the work at a very attractive price."

"We're a good-size company, Ms. Dunning. We don't normally hire freelancers for mission-critical work." He said this without malice. Behind the glasses his eyes were very blue.

"Of course. I was also thinking your drivers might like an app completely customized for them. One that took data from map, truck stop, and traffic apps and presented them exactly the data they need, when they need it." She lowered her voice. "It could also report back to you. Where they're stopping, how often they're stopping, if they make an unscheduled stop or route change. Is theft a problem with your shipments?"

"Not generally," he said. "I turn thieves over to Aunt Claudette."

She laughed then got serious. "Or one that could be modified for internal security. If you have problems with internal accounting, or embezzlement." This is what Julie said Bethany had been accused of here. He didn't react or blink.

"You got a portfolio?" Andy asked.

"Online."

"Show me," he said, "come around here."

But he didn't really scoot his chair that far from the keyboard. She bent close to the keyboard, aware of his physical proximity, ignoring it.

She typed in her website, going to her work samples page. "As you can see, I've done a number of websites for service-oriented industries. I can build both front and back end, and I can tie into whatever database or mobile apps you use." She stepped back from the computer and let him look at the portfolio. This was dumb. This wouldn't work. But he clicked through, taking several minutes to look at her designs and her work.

He leaned back and he said, "Here's the challenge for you. Your stuff looks really glossy. The people I work with don't care about gloss. They just want to know when their product arrives or when it reaches a certain stage or why their trucker is behind schedule. They want data, plainly presented."

"I can write simple interfaces. I pretty much accommodate whatever style the customer wants."

"Can you now?" he said. His smile broadened in confidence, and she braced herself for the flirting to start. Sometimes it did when she went cold-calling for business, and she'd gotten good at eviscerating such expectations. "Well, I'll tell you, the vendor I've worked with the past two years is good, but they have been painfully slow on updates. So, I'm open-minded to working with you."

"Give me a chance to show you what I can do."

"OK. I have another appointment in ten minutes, but I would like to talk to you some more about this, especially that customized app you mentioned. Because this app you wrote here"—he pointed at one of the samples on the screen—"I could see us adapting something like this..."

She was listening but then everything changed. Because of the big corkboard display behind him, full of photos and banners. She cast her eye quickly over it and saw something that made her stop. Made her think. She'd been collecting possible clues like shells on the beach, but now they needed to be threaded into a necklace. Tied. And she saw one way.

He was one of those guys who kept the name tags and lanyards from his conference travels. They were all stuck on the corkboard wall behind him, in among the pictures of himself with his customers. The corkboard was probably there as insulation from the outside noise, the rumble of arriving and departing trucks. But she could see several of the lanyards in a clump, with Austin WebCon on the badge. It was a huge software conference in Austin, attracting thousands, joined with a music and a film festival. The last five years, according to the badges, he had been there.

WebCon. Her mother went every year. Had Bethany gone as well if Andy Candolet did? Had Jake Curtis, as an entrepreneur?

Andy was still talking. "Are you calling on all the transport companies?"

"No, just you so far." Then she went for it. "I got a business card a few years ago from someone here at Ahoy, at WebCon in Austin. Do you ever go?"

"Oh, sure, every year. It's a blast. And exhausting."

"I'm trying to remember the name on the card...maybe... Beth? Bethany?"

The smile wavered, barely, and then he let it vanish. "Bethany Curtis. Yeah, she used to work for us."

"Oh, yes, that's it. I lost the card and didn't remember the person's name, just the company. Ahoy. I mean, it's so friendly and easy to remember."

He seemed to study her for an extra moment, as if trying to

divine if she had an agenda. She wondered if the press or the curious had contacted him much in the days after Bethany vanished. "Yeah, well, I'm the person to talk to, not anyone else. I'm happy to entertain a bid. We could talk about it over drinks. Tonight, maybe? I know a good place near here."

His hand moved to the small of her back. His smile went slightly crooked. It was confident; he knew he was good-looking. But he'd been so professional a few moments before, it was as if he'd given in to impulse. She made the words come out of her mouth while she thought about breaking his fingers. "I have some other calls to make. Maybe we could start with that custom app. Give me an idea of the scope of work, and I could work up a bid before we have drinks." She moved away, escaped his touch. He didn't reach again, still smiling as if thinking, *No harm, no foul.*

"I could make some notes on the scope of work this afternoon and email them to you," he said. His voice still pleasant, neutral.

"Great."

"Thanks for stopping by." Neither offered a hand to shake.

"I'll text you about meeting." His phone rang but he moved to escort her out, to put his hand again on the small of her back again, and she hurried ahead of him, saying, "That's fine, I can see myself out. I'll talk to you soon."

He nodded and answered the phone, his mild gaze still on her.

She closed his office door behind her, feeling sour and angry. She hurried out to the reception area, and his aunt Claudette glanced up at her, having moved on from *People* to *Us*. "So nice of your nephew Andy to talk to me," Mariah said, hoping there was no sarcasm in her voice.

"Grand-nephew. He's a bore, but I have to be nice. He'll pick out my nursing home."

"I remember why I knew this company name. I met someone who used to work here. Bethany Curtis."

Claudette stared. "Did you now?"

"I take it she doesn't work here anymore."

"Our poor Bethany. She's dead. I mean. We think she's dead."

"How awful. What happened?" Mariah feigned shock.

"She took off to Houston and disappeared a year and a half ago. No one has heard from her." Claudette's voice went low. "That girl is dead, if you ask me."

"Did you know her well?"

Claudette stared at her for five seconds, then said, "Do we ever truly know another person?"

"I guess not," Mariah said. "It was nice to meet you."

"Was it? Bye now."

Mariah felt dizzy. She turned and walked out into the sunlight. Got into her car, revved the air conditioning to blow on her face, to calm her thoughts. She looked up at the front window of the building. Claudette, on the phone, standing and watching her.

Telling someone on the phone her license number.

She could see the old woman's lips reading it off, T-L-J-6-9-0-7, her gaze right on Mariah's—well, her dad's—car.

Startled, she started up the car and backed out, driving faster than she should, nearly colliding with a truck turning in. She roared off down the road, saw a diner with half-empty lot, wheeled in hard and parked.

Andy was at the same conference. Same as Bethany, same as her mother. He handled security for an interstate transportation concern; her mother sold network security software to corporate clients. It wasn't beyond the pale that they could have met at WebCon. It could mean nothing. But it was the only thread, the only possibility.

Her phone rang. Sharon Blevins. They'd exchanged contact info on their phones before she'd left today.

After exchanging hellos, Sharon said, "Julie said you talked to her. She called me."

"I did. And I just talked to Andy, but I didn't tell him that I knew you, and I think I found a connection to my mom's case. A thread to follow. It's not much. But do you know if Bethany ever went to a conference here in Austin called WebCon?"

"That's the big one downtown every spring? Yes. She did. She complained about the crowds. She went with Andy, and Jake had to go, too, for his company."

Thousands of people were there. Maybe they never met. But maybe they did. A pattern, waiting for her, waiting to be found. "Thank you, we'll talk soon."

She called her dad. "A couple of years ago, do you remember if Mom went to WebCon, you know, that really big conference downtown?"

"Um…I think she did. She worked the booth for Acrys Networks at a bunch of trade shows. Why?"

"A prospective client I met with today thought maybe he'd met her there. Asked me if we were related."

"Oh. OK. It's awkward when people ask about the case."

"I just wondered."

"Her office would know. I had my own responsibilities then. My own client meetings. I didn't always pay attention to her schedule." He sounded exhausted.

"Are you OK?"

"Yes. Are you going to ask me this every time we talk?"

"Possibly."

"All right, sweetheart." Something in his voice. Something scared her. The thought of him being attacked. That could not happen. She had to protect him.

"I'll be home later," she said.

18

WITH MARIAH GONE, Craig finished installing the second small motion-activated camera, tucked in a corner of the garage. One camera faced the driveway, another the front door. Both could film at night. If the note leaver returned, Craig wanted to be able to see him or her.

And do what in response? Well, it depended.

Stranger? Report to police.

Neighbor? Well, it might be fun to post the video to the neighborhood's Faceplace page. Humiliate the tormentor. It would send a message to the neighborhood as well. If it was local kids, then he'd send it to both the police and the parents.

He had thought of doing this when the harassment first started, after it became clear there were no suspects but him...but he hadn't. He knew it would have won him no friends. He bore it. He endured it, for Mariah's sake.

In the days after Beth disappeared, friends and neighbors had brought food, sat with him, held his hand, brought comfort and prayers...until the police made it clear he was under suspicion.

He had been out of his office, with no alibi, during the time Beth vanished.

He said he'd been at home, but he had no way to prove that. Partners at major accounting practices did not usually come home for midday lunch and a nap, even if not feeling well, even if he had said he might have caught a bug from his daughter, who was already home sick and bedridden, down with fever and dulled with medicine.

And what an inconvenience to do it on the day his wife vanished. You never knew what small-seeming choice in your life could have a massive ripple effect.

People were still mostly kind, but mostly to Mariah. More than once, parents of her friends said something along the lines of *Perhaps it would be better if Mariah came and stayed with us*, like what he needed after losing his wife was for his daughter to be taken away. Mariah deeply resented these offers. He considered them in silence, because he didn't want to be arrested in front of Mariah, if the unimaginable moment came. He could not trust that Dennis would not work in his final, most awful humiliation.

The crime scene techs had scoured the Dunning house for signs of blood, of violence. None. Beth's red Mercedes, the preciously named Baby, parked by the empty lot, was scoured and eventually returned to him. Nothing. The land where they planned to build their house was searched. Nothing. So, the whispers began. Craig Dunning was either incredibly careful or entirely innocent.

But there were those unaccounted hours. The constant thorn of doubt.

The friendships melted into awkward puddles. He could count on both hands the number of friends he still had who he could count upon, who were unshaken in their belief in his innocence.

"You shouldn't have come home for lunch," one of his friends told him. "How different your life would be."

He went inside, called an eager Leo to him, hooked the leash on his collar. Leo danced in excitement. He walked Leo again. Usually he watched Leo, to make sure he didn't hoover up any bugs or earthworms or acorns (Leo was not discerning). He headed down the gently sloping hill, let his gaze drift from house to house to house as they walked by them all, wondering what secrets they hid. What accusations against him.

And he played a little game with himself.

So let's say someone had decided to play with his head. To start the cycle of accusation again. Why? Why now? Who benefited?

Leo stopped to snuffle at a dense bush in a yard; Craig eased him away. He felt the weight of a stare on him and glanced backward.

Half a block down was a man in a light jacket and fedora hat pulled low, walking, but his smartphone up. Taking a picture or a video, aimed at Craig's house at the crest of the hill. Craig glanced away, pretending not to have noticed.

Craig didn't recognize him. Perhaps a new neighbor.

He walked on. Leo spotted the man and barked twice in warning. Craig pulled him away from the yard and they resumed their walk, more slowly, the man on the opposite side of the street, one hand in his coat pocket, the other still holding the smartphone. Ignoring Craig.

But maybe recording me. And definitely taking pictures of my house. The angle was right.

Craig kept walking. He had been filmed several times on phones: people would post the videos to true crime sites, to local news sites, to social media pages. Sometimes the captions were over the top. Here walks suspected murderer Craig Dunning, having evaded somehow the long arm of the law. He wondered what the man would do if he stopped, turned, and waved.

So he did.

He was raising his hand to wave and the man stopped, for just a second, then went on, hurrying past him on the other side of the street. Walking at a much faster clip than Craig could manage with the elderly Leo.

He was watching me, Craig thought, wondering if he sounded paranoid yet. *I don't know him, but he knows who I am, because of his reaction.* Both kept walking, the man studying his phone. Separated by the street, on opposite sides.

Craig glanced at him. Not a neighbor. Not a face he'd seen before, even of the new people moving into the new McMansions that were rising on the bones of the old Bobtail Drive houses.

They walked past two new houses coming up, the man slowing, glancing over for a moment at the construction. Craig felt his own phone buzz in his pocket, but he didn't look at it. He kept his eyes on the merry Leo and then on the fedora man.

The street made a winding circle. Craig stopped. The man in the fedora kept walking.

"Hello," Craig said as the man passed him. Leo sniffed at the grass.

The man nodded. The man kept walking. He didn't glance over again at Craig. He was focused on his phone.

I don't know you but here you are. Where do you live? He watched the man get thirty feet ahead of him and then he thought, *Screw this.* Now walking Leo again, moving past the turn to his own house, the man now forty feet ahead of him, fifty feet. The man in the fedora was increasing his pace.

Leo stopped to attend to his bodily needs, and Craig wanted to hurry him along, but Leo didn't take long. The man hurried out of sight on another side road. Craig didn't bother to clean up after Leo and he hurried forward, a protesting Leo dragging him a bit. Down the side road, the man reached a silver SUV and got into it.

He's not from here. He's not a neighbor, Craig thought.

The car rocketed off. The license plate was smeared with mud. Unreadable. But there was a Lakehaven High sticker on the back though: a trumpet with the name Sean underneath it.

The trumpet meant a kid in band, right?

The car turned, was gone.

Leo panted, unused to the suddenness of dashing down the road. *So, maybe just a guy out for a walk. But what guy walks in a neighborhood where he doesn't live? Why is he taking pictures of my house? Because I put up the security cameras? And he was a Lakehaven dad. How many Seans could there be in the band?*

He turned back to walk home. The neighbor whose yard Leo had used as a bathroom was standing outside, frowning, watching Craig return.

"Well, I hope you went and got a bag," the neighbor said, an always annoyed man who Craig privately thought of as Tracksuit Guy.

"Sorry. Sorry...I was..." *What did you say? Sorry, I was chasing my tormentor?*

"No bag?" He gestured at Leo's mess.

"I'll go home and get one."

"You know," Tracksuit Guy said, "you're as awful as they say!" And he turned around and went inside.

Craig stood on the sidewalk, Leo snuffling in the grass. Because being delayed in tidying up after your dog was the same as killing your wife. He stood there, for a long moment, the breeze on his face, watching the neighbor watch him from his own front window. Then he turned and walked home and got a bag and came back and cleaned up after Leo and went home again.

Here for a reason. This man was here for a reason. I'm ready this time. I'm ready.

The cameras were in place. He walked next door and knocked on the door. After a few moments his immediate neighbor, Kumar Rajanathan, answered. Kumar and his family had been cool to Craig since Beth vanished, but not overtly unfriendly. He had two children, one in college, one a senior at Lakehaven.

"Hi, Kumar, sorry to bother you. I have an unusual request."

"Yes?" Kumar didn't seem to want to open the door wider. His smile was vague, hopeful that maybe Craig just wanted sugar or butter and nothing more.

"There has been a teenager coming around late at night, trying to frighten me and Mariah," he lied. "Standing at our windows, peering in."

"I haven't seen him," Kumar said immediately. "You should call the police, Craig. They're here to protect everyone." The implicit *even you* need not be said.

"I don't want to make a big deal. Kids make bad decisions. Except yours, of course." He tried a neighborly smile.

Kumar's mouth flexed in answer, but there was no warmth to it.

"I just wondered if I could borrow Anya's yearbook. Look through it, see if I can identify the boy that way. I can call his parents, and we don't have to get the police involved."

Kumar seemed to hesitate.

"I'm pretty sure if I call the police then the press will pick it up that I'm once again being harassed, and the kid will just get unwanted attention and more trouble. And I hope he won't be peeking into your windows. Anya's window." He let that little bomb drop.

"Hold on." Kumar returned a few moments later with a thick Lakehaven yearbook. "Here you go."

"I'll return it promptly."

"Is this why you were installing the cameras?"

They're always watching you. The murderer next door. "Yes, I'm afraid so."

"I understand. I hope...the problem is quickly and amiably resolved."

"Thanks, Kumar. How are the kids?"

"They're great, thank you." Parental pride melted the frost slightly. "Siddharth is doing well at Vanderbilt, and Anya has been accepted at Rice."

"Oh, that's wonderful. Mariah and I would love to have you and Sonia and Anya over for dinner. It's been too long." He couldn't believe the words spilling from his mouth. *An invitation. Are you insane?* But the man had spoken to him, offered him the yearbook. It had been so long for any kind of normalcy. "I'm a great cook."

"Perhaps. Let me check with Sonia. It's so kind of you to offer. But, you know, we are moving soon."

"Oh. I didn't ever see a for sale sign in your yard. Congratulations."

"Ah, no, we did not need to put it on the market. It sold before that was necessary."

"Well," Craig didn't know what to say. "We'll miss you."

Kumar could not bring himself to say the same. "Take care. You can leave the yearbook on the porch when you're done." Kumar couldn't close the door quite fast enough.

"I'll bring this back," Craig said to the closed door. He had forgotten himself, forgotten his place in this world. His face was aflame with shame and amazement at his own stupidity. No, they weren't coming to dinner, not in a million years. They were selling their home, hoping to escape his proximity. He walked back to the house, the yearbook under his arm. Did shame ever have an expiration date?

Who needs them, he thought. No one. Not him. Not when he had a daughter to protect.

Craig sat down at the table with a legal pad and a pencil, and began to page through the yearbook, looking for the band section, looking for names.

19

MARIAH HAD DECIDED she needed to go to her mother's former employer, Acrys Networks, to see if they had a record of whether or not she'd attended WebCon. One thin thread, but it was all she had. She wasn't sure she'd talk to Andy again if she didn't have to. She didn't want to design an app for him while dodging his hands. She decided to swing by Sharon's house first to tell her what she had learned and to ask a few more questions. She'd gotten two text messages from Sharon, asking how the talk with Andy had gone. Anxious.

Mariah parked in front of the Blevins house. She walked to Sharon's front door and noticed it was ajar. Her heart rose into her throat; Sharon did not seem the type to leave open doors. She knocked, called out "Mrs. Blevins?" and got no answer. She pushed open the door and it stopped halfway, hitting a weight. She peered around the door. Sharon lay on the tile floor of the entryway, collapsed.

Mariah knelt by her. She was still breathing, her eyelids fluttering.

"Mrs. Blevins!"

Sharon opened her eyes, trying to focus. "Oh...oh...Bethany?"

"No, it's Mariah Dunning. I'm calling an ambulance for you..."

Sharon's eyes focused; she grabbed Mariah's hand. "No, no, no...Mariah...oh, I got dizzy...no ambulance. Please. Ambulances are so expensive. I promise, I'm OK."

Mariah relented, because Sharon was already climbing to her feet, holding on to Mariah. "OK." Mariah brought Sharon to the couch. She arranged a pillow under her head, got her a glass of water.

"Thank you," Sharon said after sipping. "I'm fine. Thank you."

"What happened?"

"I guess I fainted. Just a lot on my mind today. I forgot to eat or drink water. I forgot some medicine I have to take. For my anxieties."

"I still think I should call an ambulance. Or take you to an urgent care clinic."

"Really, honey, I'm fine. I'm fine." Her gaze seemed steadier.

"Well, then you need to eat, let me fix you something."

"Oh, goodness, don't go to trouble, Mariah."

"It's no trouble. You just take it easy." In the kitchen she found eggs, Swiss cheese, mushrooms, a fresh bell pepper. She made omelets, and toasted sourdough bread in the oven. She made two cups of hot herbal tea, brought it all to the table, and helped Sharon walk in and sit.

"Oh, this is so lovely. Thank you."

"Of course. This is my fault. I've upset your day."

"It's not your fault." Sharon steadied her voice. "Sometimes the grief just hits you so hard."

"Yes. It does."

Sharon said a quick grace, Mariah politely keeping her head bowed, and then they ate in companionable silence. "This is wonderful, thank you. How...how was Julie? You didn't say much about your talk with her."

"She was all right." Mariah decided to choose her words carefully, so as to not further upset Sharon. "She said Bethany had gone through a very rough time."

Sharon frowned. "If she'd kept her life in order, prayed more, gone to church with me...she would have stayed in the guardrails, made better choices."

She's dead most likely, so what good is parsing her choices? Mariah thought. "Drinking, embezzlement, it's a lot of symptoms, but what did you think was the key problem?"

"She was lonely. Jake worked too much. She got involved with the wrong people."

"She mentioned a new friend named Lizbeth who she went drinking with a lot."

"Yes. I never met her. Bethany had no reason to ever bring her around me, although it would be nice to meet her friends. But once I saw Bethany eating lunch at a restaurant, when I'd gone there with a church friend. I went over to say hi. I thought she was alone, but she wasn't, Lizbeth was there…but Lizbeth never came back to the table. She'd gone to the ladies' room and then she'd left Bethany with the check. Anyone who is spending that much time in the ladies' room and walks a check…she has problems." Sharon lowered her voice. "Drugs, I think."

"Bethany never said that?"

"Oh, she wouldn't. But there had to be a reason I never got to meet Lizbeth."

"I understand there were pills in her car that weren't Bethany's."

Her face flushed with embarrassment. "Yes. Anxiety meds, painkillers. I think those all came from this Lizbeth. She gave them to Bethany."

"Could Lizbeth have drugged her?"

"Why would she? There would be no point. I mean, this Lizbeth might have given my girl drugs…oh, this idea Bethany got that someone was poisoning her? It's silly. If she had drugs in her system, Bethany put them there." She cleared her throat. "That's hard for me to say, I hope you know. It was a way for her to dodge personal responsibility."

"Julie is worried about you."

Sharon made a noise. "I'm sure she's not." She put a hand over her eyes. "Julie's always been best at taking care of Julie."

"I don't think you should be left alone tonight. Is there a friend I could call? Or a relative? Or even Julie? I'm sure she'd come."

"Really, no. Bethany was my only family that was left. I'll be fine."

"What about a church friend?"

"You know…I never talk about Bethany at church. That's my

refuge from thinking about it or talking about it...and I'd like to keep it that way. I don't want to have to explain why I forgot to eat."

Mariah felt terrible. "Then...would you let me stay? Just for tonight. I'd feel better if you weren't alone, in case you faint again."

"Mariah. That is kind of you."

"I don't want it to be weird, I know we've just met..."

"But you feel like we know each other. From what we've lost."

Slowly Mariah nodded. "Yes. Is that odd?"

"Similarity of experience." Sharon closed her hand over Mariah's. "I read about it in a book. Why don't you stay, if it puts your mind at ease? I'd...I'd welcome the company."

"It would. Thank you."

Mariah cleared up the plates and suggested that Sharon go watch TV or read and relax. In the kitchen she texted Julie: Hey it's Mariah Dunning. Mrs. Blevins fainted at her house today, I found her, she's OK but she was groggy and refused to see a doctor. I'm staying with her tonight just to be sure she doesn't get worse. Would you check in on her tomorrow, at least a phone call? Thank you.

She had just finished loading the dishwasher when Julie texted back: Sure, sorry to hear, sweet of you to stay. We'll swing by, maybe we can talk her into a doctor visit.

We. That probably meant her and Andy.

She then texted her dad: I'm staying with a friend tonight, she's sick and I want to be sure she's OK. All right?

Craig texted back: Who's your friend?

She wanted to say *I don't owe you an explanation*, but instead she gently bent the truth: A woman who's helped me, a colleague, she doesn't have anyone else to help her. But I want to know you're okay alone at the house.

Craig wrote back: I'm fine. I love you.

Mariah sent him back a heart emoji and trembled a little at the lie.

* * *

Craig frowned at his laptop screen, rereading the messages. Mariah sometimes used subcontractors on her website work. He knew he should be glad she had a friend who would count on her for help. Unless this was all a lie.

He went to a website. His car—the one she was using—had a beacon that could tell you where it was on a map. He pinged the car; it was in a north Austin neighborhood, not terribly far from Anderson High School and Spicewood Springs Road.

He wondered who this woman colleague was.

He had gone through the band members photos in the yearbook—he discovered they were helpfully broken out by instrument. The trumpets had, annoyingly, three Seans. He had written down their names, searched for them on social media and on the news site at the Lakehaven papers. He had also looked at their surnames and not found them in his neighborhood directory, at least from two years ago. He'd need to find their addresses and see if the car he'd spotted matched one. He felt foolish; this was probably a useless lead, and here he was wasting time on it.

He opened a window on the computer that gave him the front door camera's view. Then the one for the driveway. A man, wearing a baseball cap, his dog idling on the corner of the lawn, perhaps contemplating leaving a souvenir. Downstairs he heard Leo bark.

The same man from before, with the fedora and the dark glasses? It was hard to tell, with a baseball cap turned down low. The man pulled on the dog's leash and kept walking.

You can't see an enemy everywhere you look, he thought. But he pressed the keyboard command that snapped a picture from the camera and saved it to his drive. If he couldn't see the man's face, he could see the dog. He'd know the dog if he saw it again.

He wanted to take Leo for a walk himself. But not here on the streets of the neighborhood. He had had enough of his neighbors.

She's not home tonight. You could go. There's no one to ask where you've been.

He went, feeling like an addict going in search of his fix, hating himself, wishing he had more self-control. Craig Dunning put Leo on a leash, put him into the car, and headed out into the night.

20

Bethany left these clothes here when she moved out." Sharon held the long-sleeved T-shirt and pajama pants, imprinted with roses and thorns, out to her. "You're taller than she is, but it's not like we're going to the grocery or anything."

"No, it's fine," Mariah said, thinking, *They're just clothes.* The idea now of staying in Bethany's old room felt overwhelming. And now wearing her clothes. She forced a smile to her face. No, this isn't super weird at all.

Sharon insisted she had had to go arrange a complicated series of flights for a client who was demonstrating a new food product to buyers across the country, so she sat in front of the computer in Bethany's old room. She seemed recovered from her fainting spell, but she also seemed hyper, as if trying to convince Mariah she was really all right when she wasn't.

Mariah didn't feel like watching TV. She went to the small, built-in bookshelf in the den to browse. A bookshelf was always an interesting glance into a person's heart and head.

There were a few Bibles, not surprisingly, and a smattering of books by a married couple who were famous television preachers. The few novels on the shelf were picks from years ago on a popular talk show's book club, and there was an entire shelf of more self-help books.

Her phone pinged. A text, from a number she didn't recognize:

Sorry about our misunderstanding this afternoon. Look forward to reviewing your portfolio in my office, or in yours, wherever's convenient.

It had to be Andy. Misunderstanding? That sounded like he was making an excuse for his bad behavior. She decided not to answer—if he felt bad, let him stew for a bit.

She paged through the self-help volumes, wondering if she'd find a moment's inspiration in them. The books were older, the edges of the pages showing their age, passages highlighted in fading yellow, scribbled notes in the margins in pencil. *Try to remember to move forward. Be a better person. You can't undo the past. Undo* was underlined three times. This was an older person's handwriting. The book opened to where a piece of paper lay. A bookstore's yellowing sales slip was in the pages, apparently used as a bookmark. It had a date on it. The book had been bought over twenty years ago, at a bookstore in Houston.

Also at the page that she had opened, bookmarked, was a photo. Of a young girl, three or four years old, pale brown hair, a wide smile, dimples, pleased to be photographed, holding a kitten. Bethany as a little girl? But it was a newspaper clipping photo, yellowing and brittle with age, not a personal photograph. Just the photo, carefully scissored out, no caption.

Mariah shut the books, suddenly feeling like a trespasser. She put the books back and knelt to the bottom shelf. There was a small library of true crime books. A couple of classics by Ann Rule on high-profile murders. An account of a famous actor involved in a car accident that had killed a young woman and his attempts to cover his involvement. A book about the Zodiac Killer; another book about a nurse who had killed patients, young and old, in a hospital. The books, like the self-help titles, were worn, thumbed, tagged with notes and highlights.

She started paging through the book about the reckless actor: blue sticky notes included questions such as *How did he think he could get away with it?* and *Everyone around him enabled this.* Like the loopy handwriting on Bethany's sticky note, stuck to her monitor and preserved by her mother. Bethany kept showing new sides of herself: the unhappy wife, the partying young woman, the accused thief, the aspiring writer, the fleeing spouse, now someone interested in researching true crime.

Mariah sat on the floor by the bookcase, her back against the couch. The house was quiet. She called her father. She needed to hear his voice.

"Dad."

She could hear the car engine when he answered. He was driving, and he wasn't supposed to answer his phone then, even hands-free. She hated that.

"Yes, honey?"

"Where are you?"

A pause. "Going to the grocery store for some ice cream."

"Two outings in two days. Wow."

"I used to have a normal life, Mariah. Can I try to have a normal one again?"

"Sure, Dad. I'm all for that."

"How's your friend?"

"Better."

"Don't you need pajamas or a toothbrush?"

"I'm taken care of."

"If you're seeing someone you could tell me. I would approve."

"It's so not that, Dad. I would tell you. No guy wants to date me. I have more baggage than...an extremely rich person who travels with a lot of luggage. I don't even know who that would be."

Her father laughed, once. It was rare. "Tell me what kind of ice cream you want for when you get home tomorrow."

"Butter pecan." It had been Mom's favorite, too, and her eyes felt warm. "What would you do—hypothetically—if I found evidence that tied Mom to another criminal case?"

Five seconds of awkward silence. "What kind of case?"

"Hypothetically, someone who disappeared under similar circumstances."

"What?" His voice rose. "An abandoned car? No trace?"

"I'm just saying, Daddy. Calm down." She tucked her knees up under her chin. She faced the window looking out onto the front yard.

And there stood Andy and Julie, getting out of a car.

"Sharon?" she called. "You have company." She put her face back to the phone. "Dad, I have to go. I'll talk to you later."

"What crime—" he said before she cut off the call.

The doorbell rang.

Sharon answered it.

"Mrs. Blevins? Andy and I are just checking up on you. Mariah Dunning texted me..."

"Oh, how sweet, but y'all don't need to fuss." Sharon brought them inside, Julie giving her a hug, Andy locking his gaze on Mariah for a moment and then greeting Sharon, who accepted his hug and then stepped away.

"Mariah, this is my boyfriend, Andy Candolet. He grew up with Bethany, too."

I'm sorry for our misunderstanding this afternoon. The asking her out for a drink. The hand on the small of her back. Andy kept his smile in place, like he knew she wouldn't blow the whistle on him.

She could play this either way. Accuse him, and maybe alienate them both, or pretend he hadn't been a jerk. Their gaze locked, and on his side, she thought she saw a pleading in his eyes. He knew he'd been a bad boy.

"It's nice to meet you, Andy," Mariah said, evenly. "I'm Mariah Dunning."

"Nice to meet you, too." His voice was bright, friendly, but his smile was tight.

Sharon stared at Julie and Andy. "I didn't know y'all were dating."

"Yeah, I meant to tell you." Julie squeezed Andy's hand. "Not weird, right? We've known each other forever."

"We're worried about you, though, Mrs. B," Andy said. "Can we talk?"

"Y'all come in, sure, have some cake..." Sharon said. "And just when did y'all start dating?" She sounded a bit peevish, the older person cut out from the news of the young.

"Oh, several months ago," Julie said, like it was no big thing. "We're living together now, too."

"Oh." Sharon didn't seem to know what to say for a moment. "Well, isn't that sweet."

"We were just concerned about you. Mariah said you'd fainted."

"I'm fine, Mariah's been so sweet, but really I'm okay. Company does me good." She managed to say it like it wasn't an admission of loneliness. She headed into the kitchen, Julie following her. Andy and Mariah stayed in the den. They heard the clatter of plates, the two women talking, Julie continuing to ask if she was all right.

Mariah glanced at Andy. "Wow, and you invited me for drinks," she whispered.

"For a business reason."

"And then had to touch the small of my back."

"I'm sorry, I was trying to steer you back to your seat."

"I don't require steering. You knew you misbehaved. Texting me about a 'misunderstanding' of some sort."

"I didn't know you knew Julie. She's very jealous. Really, I did just mean drinks to talk over the proposal."

She didn't believe him. "I just met Julie, and I'm not going to interfere in her business. But you don't need to be touching me. Ever."

"I won't and I'm sorry." Then he couldn't help himself. "And you didn't tell me you were there to ask about Bethany's case." As though she had been unfair to him.

"It was half the reason. I do really need the freelance job."

He took a deep breath. "Fine. Let's start again. As potential colleagues."

"If you hit on me again, I'll tell her."

"I sent you the wrong message, and it won't happen again." He straightened his glasses. "Let me try to make it up to you. Maybe Julie and I can help you. What's your mom's name?" Andy asked.

"Beth Dunning."

He blinked twice, then shook his head. "Sorry, I don't know her." Andy got louder. "Mrs. B, you need anything?" he called to her in a hearty voice. "I'm at your service."

"No, I'm fine," Sharon answered in a small voice. They could hear her and Julie talking, in soft tones.

"I want to talk about Bethany, too. This embezzlement she was accused of."

"That was settled, and I can't really discuss it. She took off and told nobody, and nobody's seen her since."

"Still, your insights would be valuable. And I did you a favor."

"I know you have a good reason for this, but it's upsetting Mrs. B deeply. She fainted because of you."

"If that was true she wouldn't have asked me to stay. I'm not upsetting her. I'm giving her hope of an answer."

She turned without another word to him and went into the kitchen and smiled at Julie and Sharon, who had gone silent when she came into the kitchen.

Mariah felt eyes on her. She glanced over, saw Andy lounging at the kitchen door, watching her, his amiable smile back in place. He really thought a charm offensive would work on her. Now Julie, almost seeming to study Mariah. Now Sharon, turning with the plates of cake, tired, worn by the unexpected company.

What is going on here? Mariah thought. They're locked together, she thought. Because of Bethany vanishing. It changed them all. The way Mom leaving changed me.

Julie didn't want any lemon cake, so Andy gobbled down the slice Sharon had cut for him. "I can come stay with you, Mrs. B," Julie said, "if you need me to. I'm sure Mariah has her own life to get back to."

Not really, Mariah thought.

"Thank you. Mariah and I are talking. It's helpful. Someone else who's gone through the same ordeal in having a family member vanish."

Julie shrugged, dragged fingers through her dark hair. "I'm glad you two have found each other."

"Since there's no connection between your mom's case and Bethany's, though— " Andy began and Sharon interrupted: "So what if there's not? Talking to Mariah is a comfort to me."

"We're glad, then." Julie attempted a smile.

"We should go, babe," Andy said, all business. "Mrs. B, please call us if you need us. And I'll give you a call to check up on you.

Nice to meet you, Mariah. We should talk about you writing some apps for Ahoy."

He established the potential for a business relationship very smoothly, in case Julie asked what they'd talked about in the den. Julie gave Sharon a hug; Andy reached for a hug from Sharon as well, then nodded at Mariah. They left. Sharon didn't stand at the front door waving them off. She shut the door as soon as they were gone and leaned against it.

"Are you all right?" Mariah asked.

"They're reminders of the past. Of Bethany. Do you ever feel you're spending your whole life looking backwards because of your mom? Never forward?"

"Sometimes."

"But everyone thinks you should be ruled by tragedy. Like you don't have a right to think about anything else, even for a minute. If you do, well then you didn't love your daughter. Or your mom. I'm so tired of the judgment."

Mariah said, "I hope I haven't judged you."

"Oh, no, sweetheart. You sure you don't want cake?"

Now it seemed rude to refuse, so Mariah nodded and now Sharon carefully cut another slice and put it on the plate. "You seemed surprised that Julie and Andy were dating."

"I haven't seen them both together since the gathering to honor Bethany," she said. "Sometimes I see Julie at the grocery. We talk for a minute, but she hadn't mentioned dating Andy." She cleared her throat and sat. "I...I shouldn't tell you this."

"What?"

"Andy didn't take it well when Bethany married Jake. He loathed Jake. Bethany said he tried to tell her Jake was no good for her. Now, Bethany and Andy hadn't ever dated. They hung out together in high school, saw each other some at college. She'd say, 'I love Andy like a brother.' What do they call it...friendzone? When one wants to be just friends but the other wants more?" There was an odd little tremble in her voice.

"I guess," Mariah said. She hated that term, thought it always put the blame on the woman for not wanting the relationship to change.

"She'd say she loved him like a brother, and it was like a sting was stuck in his smile. He doesn't like hearing no. But when she wanted a new job, he got it for her. I think so she would be around him all day, away from Jake. Like he was trying his luck. If he'd been some random guy at work, she would have told him to shut up and leave her alone. But this was an old friend. He..." Sharon paused. "He'd been there for her in the past. When her daddy died." The last words were nearly a whisper. "He was here a lot then."

"He flirted with me at his office. He had no idea I knew you or Julie." He'd done more than flirt, but she decided to play it down, for now.

"Did he now? Of course he did." Her mouth wavered slightly and she shook her head. "Usually he's such a Boy Scout type. Until he's not. There are impulse control issues there."

"He apologized to me."

"Because Julie was here. Honestly, she should know better."

"More like you said. He tried his luck, he lost, he shrugged it off."

Sharon put a cover over the lemon cake and leaned against the counter. "Sometimes Bethany's friends aren't a comfort but a trial. I'm sorry."

"You have nothing to apologize for."

"I'm tired."

"Of course. Why don't you get to bed?"

Sharon nodded and checked the front door lock again. "I'm glad you're here, Mariah. It helps to talk with you." For a moment Mariah thought Sharon was going to embrace her, but she didn't. Sharon fiddled with her hands as if unsure where to place them. Finally, she just folded them together.

Something's wrong, Mariah thought. Julie and Andy here upset her. Why?

Mariah nodded. "I'm a light sleeper. You let me know if you need me in the night."

"I will. Good night." Sharon went into her bedroom and shut the door. Mariah stood in the den, surrounded by the photos of the missing Bethany, feeling the guilt and tension in the air like it was a shifting mist.

21

THE LOT WAS dark, no streetlights, only a distant gleam from a house at the end of the street, and a cloud-choked moon. There should have been a warmly lit house here, a place to welcome home Mariah, and her family if she'd ever chosen to have one, and a place where Craig and Beth could sit on the porch and sip wine and watch the sunset over the hills.

There was only an emptiness: the breeze, the quiet, the absence of her. This land, where Beth had gone missing, felt like a jagged rip in the universe, a place with both answers and questions. He hated it here now—he would never build a house here, and he knew everyone wondered why he hadn't sold the land—but he felt drawn here. He sometimes worried if he didn't sell it that something would happen to him and Mariah would build her own home here. And that must never be.

You haven't sold the land because someone will find her body there, won't they? Broussard had said to him a few months ago. But they'd looked for her body and they hadn't found it. Not a hint of her.

Craig parked Beth's car, took a deep breath, and eased Leo out on his leash. The stars were a reckless spill across the velvet surface of the night. He turned on his flashlight, played it along the jumble of pale limestone rocks that lay scattered and prevalent along this edge of the property. He stared for a moment at the rocks. Had the one left on his driveway come from here? Was someone being doubly cruel? He had no way to know.

Leo pulled hard against his leash, eager to explore.

Every day he missed Beth so badly it was a physical pain and ache. He ambled along the high grass, careful to watch for snakes or anthills, and stopped at the point where he and Beth had imagined the house rising when they sketched their dream on cocktail napkins. He closed his eyes against the steady, damp breeze while Leo snuffed and sighed, breathing in the night.

Beth. Beth. I'm sorry. I'm so sorry.

This land was where he went to remember Beth as he loved her because there was no tombstone for her, no resting place marked with dignity. He used to sing Kiss's ballad "Beth" to her, as an annoyance or as an apology, and sometimes here he wanted to hum it, but he couldn't get past a few measures of the melody without his throat closing.

The light flashed on his face and stayed there. Leo, useless, decided to bark now.

"Craig." The light lowered and then he could see the visitor's face.

"Dennis. You're trespassing, but I forgive you."

"Why are you out here?"

"Why do I have to explain myself to you on my own property? Why are you here?"

"Because I wanted to look around. Maybe I'll notice something I didn't notice before. Are you going to complain about me trespassing?"

"No."

"Are you here to grieve?"

There was a tone in his voice Craig didn't like.

"I like coming here to think," Craig said. "I feel she's close."

"I feel she's close, too. You didn't have long to get rid of the body. I suspect she's near here." Broussard shuffled his feet. "Do you ever hope I'll forget, or just let it go?"

"No. I want you to find out who took her," Craig said. Leo barked once, twice.

"Wouldn't it just be easier to confess? Than to carry around the heaviest secret imaginable?"

"You're still mad," Craig said.

"You refused to answer every question put to you after your statement. Why?"

"I had already answered them, and I operated under this delusion you'd go find whoever took her."

"You called her at work that day to demand to know if she was having an affair. People heard you arguing with her on the phone."

Craig shook his head. "Discussing, not arguing. But what's the point of nuance with you, Dennis? You're still mad. About her and me. You should have married your grudge. That's been your companion for thirty years."

The silence was long. Craig realized, suddenly, as Dennis lowered the light from his face, that Dennis was wearing his sidearm. They had never been alone like this together since Beth vanished. *He could shoot you out here.* No witnesses. He'd be investigating his own crime. He'd walk. *Craig tried to grab my gun, you see. I feared for my life.* Dread, hot and bright, rose in his chest. "I should go. My daughter is expecting me."

"I think we need to talk about your daughter," Dennis said quietly.

"My daughter is not your concern."

"She is protecting you. She had that DVD, Craig. Maybe she found it. Maybe she couldn't bear to part with it since it has her mom's name on it. She's protecting you, but she can't do that forever. At some point she'll crack. At some point she'll get mad at you and she'll tell me what she knows. Save her from that decision. Save her from the agony. Confess."

"Arrest me if you're so sure," Craig said. Leo whined. "Or shoot me. Just don't shoot my dog."

"You're so ready to think the worst of me," Dennis said. "Projection is an ugly thing. Aren't you going to ask me why I'm out here?"

"There's nothing to see."

"Is there?"

Craig felt cold.

"Because I wanted to give you a chance. Because I don't want to arrest you in front of your daughter."

"I didn't...I don't understand..."

Dennis Broussard looked at him for a long moment, and then he knelt and scratched Leo's huge pointed ears. Leo's treacherous tail wagged in awful joy.

He's bluffing.

"The very day after that DVD turns up, you start squawking about being harassed again," Broussard said. "Is that for Mariah's benefit? So you're the victim again?"

"I'm gathering information on who the culprit is."

"Like your daughter, huh. The two investigators. You both look foolish."

Like he knew something. That was why he was out here. Or he was trying to spook Craig, scare him into a dangerous reaction. He must be bluffing.

Or he's behind the harassment. The thought unnerved Craig.

"What is it? What?" he asked.

"Good night, Craig. Good night, Leo." Dennis Broussard walked away from them, into the darkness.

Leo barked once in farewell, while Craig felt frozen to the stony ground.

* * *

Craig's hands were still shaking when he started to turn into the driveway.

Then he saw the rock. A new one. He slammed on the brakes before he could hit it.

He drove around it, slowly, wondering *What if it's not a rock but something worse?* and parked in the garage, got Leo settled in the house. He didn't want Leo to get hurt.

He went back outside with a flashlight. He unwrapped the rock. It was the same wrapping paper from this morning. The rock was a bit smaller, pale limestone. The message read, IT'S TIME FOR YOU TO GO.

The same line as the first message. Then it was written:

I COULD LAND ON SOMEONE'S CAR WHEN SOMEONE DRIVES UNDER THE LAKEHAVEN BRIDGE. DON'T CALL THE COPS, I'LL KNOW IF YOU DO. JUST SELL YR HOUSE AND GO.

The Lakehaven bridge was a nickname for an old residential street overpass on the edge of Austin and the suburb, and Mariah drove under that bridge often. He stared at the words, and he felt a rage and a fear begin to war in his blood. But he kept his face still. Calm. Because his own cameras were recording him right now. And when he showed this film to Broussard, he wanted to show his calm. Not his rage.

He folded up the paper, went to his computer, and started up the video feed. The porch video feed was fine. He backed it up, didn't see anyone, but it didn't have a view of the driveway, only the walkway up to the house. The camera above the garage was dark. He backed up the recording. Still dark, and then it was clear. And then he saw a hand, holding a paint can, and then the screen filled with black. He went outside. The garage camera's lens had been sprayed with paint.

All right. Someone had spotted the cameras. His neighbor Kumar had noticed him installing them; maybe his tormentor was watching as well. The man in the fedora or the man walking his dog. He had the Sean-the-trumpet-player angle to follow further. He had to chase that down. He had nothing else.

Because now the tormentor had threatened Mariah. Craig didn't drive enough these days and not under that bridge on his way to the grocery or the bank, about the only places he ever went. This rock, as threat, was meant for her. It was fearmongering, he suspected. How would anyone know when he or Mariah was driving under a bridge? They were just trying to panic him.

Unless…it was Broussard who made this threat. He could have watched Craig leave, put the rock here, and then followed him to the lot. That made terrible sense. And could the police track where you were, through your phone?

He could not let Broussard, or anyone else, do this to him and Mariah.

This was his duty as a father, he felt. He had moved past a regard for law and order long ago—that was for people with normal, untouched lives. He felt sometimes that he lived in an unseen wilderness, hidden under the suburban quiet, a place where laws and norms no longer interested or protected him.

Don't call the cops, I'll know if you do. He weighed his options. Broussard wouldn't want him to call the cops, most of all. He had to find these people and put an end to their threats. If something happened to him... and Mariah was left alone with this monster watching her... well, he couldn't allow that.

He went to the window and looked out through the small gap in the curtains. Wouldn't they be watching to see his reaction? Gauge his next step?

He couldn't remember the last time these curtains were open. He yanked them apart, the rings rattling on the rod, every light on in the room behind him.

He raised his middle finger to the neighborhood, held his hand up high.

Then he checked on the napping Leo and drove to a home supplies store and found a FOR SALE BY OWNER sign. He bought it, and then bought a prepaid phone that came with a voicemail capability. He wrote the burner phone's number on the blank space on the for sale sign. This way, he figured, he could see who all contacted him about the house and not tie up his own phone with responding to people to whom he had no intention of selling his house.

Good enough. All he had to do was buy a couple of days of confusion.

He went and stuck the for sale sign in his front yard.

See? I'm doing what you told me to do.

It was going to make so many people happy, him leaving.

It would buy him precious time while he hunted his enemy.

22

MARIAH COULDN'T SLEEP, her mind crowded with thoughts of Bethany and Sharon and her own mother and Julie and Andy. She sat up in the dark, turned on the light, wishing she had a book to read. There was a bookshelf in Bethany's old room as well. A few novels, another Bible.

And journals. She took one down, glanced through it. It was a series of writing exercises—prompts of a sort. "Describe a character without having her look in a mirror. Write a scene where two characters speak and we know nothing about them—only dialogue, no description. Write a scene where a character dies."

And under each prompt was the same florid handwriting she'd seen in the margins of the true crime books. Bethany's. She wished the book critique group leader, Yvette Suarez, would call her back. She thought writing was so personal—maybe it would show her some aspect of Bethany that was relevant to what had happened to her.

There were more journals. Some were college workbooks, others were older, from teenage years. Not diaries, exactly, but thoughts of a young woman who wanted to make art. Who wanted to tell stories.

She slowly turned the pages thinking, *Forgive me, Bethany, for prying*. Surely Sharon had read these, trying to find some lost scrap of her daughter, hold on to her as if she were still here. Or maybe seeing these words was too painful. Pages were filled with notes for stories, book ideas, episodes for favorite television shows, random wisps of thought that Bethany wanted to build into something bigger. But nothing that seemed to relate specifically to her disappearance.

The last journal was the oldest, and surprisingly wasn't full, as though it had been started and then stopped. The penmanship tight and narrow, as though she were gripping her pen in a fury.

So the doctor said I should write in here about Dad. I don't know what to say. Who was Hal Blevins, really? I don't know that I know. He left us. Why do I have to do this? A page a day, the doctor said. Mama's not writing a page a day, she's praying and praying and there is no answer to the question, Why did he do this?

Well, no answer she wants to tell me.

The entries were like that: short, brief, dodging a truth, a prescription, a bitter pill barely choked down.

School has been hard since he killed himself. People don't know what to say to me because I found him. I saw what no child is supposed to see. I can't even talk to Mom about that. She says, closed book, closed book, it's all over now. How does she think this? Julie and Andy are no help to me. Julie makes it about her—how does she manage that, we end up talking about our friendship rather than my dad—and Andy tried to kiss me, what's wrong with him? Now of all times? He said he was trying to comfort me. My dad's dead, I don't want a make-out session. He is the walking example of what not to do. And I like Andy but not that way. He comes over to help Mom like mowing the yard or fixing the ceiling fan and that was Dad's job and I'm not ready for someone else to do it. I have too much to figure out. Dad had no reason to do this, none. Why did he? What broke him?

Mom knows. She won't say. I know she knows. She hides it all under her faith. My faith is supposed to be about strength but hers is about... camouflage.

Bethany's father Hal was a suicide. Julie told her that at the gym. But his death still seemed to have come as a surprise—so perhaps he had not been chronically depressed. She had feared for her own father's life in the days following her mom's disappearance. She paged through the journal. The entries petered out with a final sentence, written alone on one page:

There are no answers.

That couldn't be true. She would not accept that. There had to be. The answers were just waiting to be found.

So Bethany had wanted to write, maybe starting when her father killed himself, and she had developed an appreciation for true crime, where there were usually twisted reasons for the cruelty of the human heart.

And that led to a terrible, awful thought: *Was her own father's death a crime? Had she discovered something about it that wasn't a suicide?*

Mariah turned the page and found more photos of the young girl she'd seen in the newspaper clipping. Taped to the page, four of them. One like the newspaper picture she'd seen, two more from a party in a backyard, a birthday cake behind her, the girl maybe three or four, laughing, hands on knees. The cake was a mermaid, all purple and aqua frosting. One of the other pictures looked like a professional snapshot, the kind parents bought in different sizes from wallet to framed eight by ten. She dug her thumbnail under the photo and pried it loose from the tape. She studied the girl's face and then turned it over: *Penny, 4, Holy I.* written in large letters in smeared red ink.

Who was Penny? She had thought at first the girl in the picture might have been Bethany.

After a moment, and feeling like she shouldn't, she slipped the old photo into her pocket. She left the others untouched.

She turned to the last page in the journal. There, taped to the inside cover, were chits. One week. One month. One year. Five years, ten years. Sobriety chits. She ran a finger along the numbers on the chit. A man who had drunk himself to death with bourbon and pills had been sober for a long time. What had changed in this house?

Sharon would know. Had Bethany learned it?

And had any of this somehow connected to her mother?

She turned out the light and crawled into the missing woman's childhood bed, pulling the covers over her head.

23

SHARON AWOKE IN the darkness. She listened to the quiet and could hear the softest sound of snoring from the room down the hall. Bethany used to snore in that room, too, loud enough for Sharon to hear, and she would stop when Sharon would tiptoe in and gently touch her shoulder. It used to irritate Sharon, and now what she wouldn't give to have her daughter home, under her roof, snoring at double the volume.

She got up.

She went to the chair where she had hidden the gun. She couldn't have removed it after Mariah found her in her faint, not without Mariah seeing, but it was shoved so far down in the pillows that Mariah hadn't noticed.

In the dark, Sharon held the gun for a moment, then stuffed it back deep into the gap between the chair's frame and the seat cushion. She listened in the silence, and the sound she missed most of all was that of her daughter, lost in sleep.

* * *

Mariah had the dream again. Of course it wasn't the same dream every time, but the elements remained constant. Her mother, pleading, frightened, confused. Mariah, standing near her, powerless, frozen. Wind in her eyes. The world smearing, and something walking toward them...faceless, enraged, out of focus, but here to take Beth from them.

Mom's kidnapper. Mom's killer.

The shadow, brought to life.

The changeling, the boogey man, the monster exposed from a fairy tale.

"Where is she?" she asked the shadow.

He pointed toward her. Past her, behind her. If she turned around she would see a truth too horrible to imagine. She was terrified to look.

"Where is she?" she asked again.

Again, he pointed.

"Let this go, baby. Don't look," Mom said, her voice going from roar to whisper in Mariah's ear.

Mariah turned—slowly, feeling the weight of the world pressing on her, crushing her—but she had to see.

Turn and see who was behind her...see and know the truth...

And she awoke, screaming, a face inches from hers.

Sharon Blevins was leaning over her. "Honey. Are you OK? You cried out in your sleep."

At first she didn't know who Sharon was, where she was, and then it came back to her in a rush. "Fine," Mariah managed. "Sorry I woke you up. I'm supposed to be taking care of you."

Sharon sat on the edge of the bed. "I was already awake. I don't sleep that well anyway most nights. I understand the bad dreams. We talked a lot today about troubling things."

"It was just a bad dream." She dragged her hand across the saliva on her chin, feeling a hot shame. "About my mom. Trying to find her."

"All my dreams about Bethany are good," Sharon said. "She's here and she's happy and we're happy and nobody feels bad or guilty about anything. It's like an old television show."

Mariah wished her dreams were like that. She thought maybe she could get Sharon talking. "Julie mentioned Bethany wanted to be a writer."

Sharon shrugged. "Oh, that was just something she said now and then. I don't see why so many people want to write. Not everything needs to be written down. There's too much to read anyway."

She didn't want her to write, Mariah thought. *There are secrets in this house, and her daughter would have written about them.* "Did you not approve?" She kept her tone relaxed and neutral.

"Not to write about family stuff. That's private. It could be hurtful. I think she should have written children's books. Cheerful stuff, you know?"

"Was she going to write about her father?"

"Oh," Sharon said in a small voice. "I guess Julie or Andy told you he passed...by his own hand." The last four words felt like little jabs. Recriminations that Mariah had raised the topic.

"Yes. And that Bethany found him."

"You know, people can overcome things." The words came out in a rush, a flood. "Through kindness. Through prayer. Through...whatever centers your soul. For me it's the Bible, and for others, it's whatever. Bethany wasn't permanently damaged by what her father did. I'm sure she wasn't."

"I'm so sorry. It must have been so terrible for you both."

"I'm sorry I couldn't be of more help to him. See it coming. Spared my daughter the whole ordeal."

What about your ordeal? Or his? She didn't even say she'd wished she'd saved her husband, Mariah thought. She tested the water. "There was no doubt it was suicide?"

Sharon's eyes went frosty. "What do you mean, dear?"

"It might have been an accident? He didn't realize what he was doing?"

"Oh." She blinked. "I thought you were suggesting the unthinkable." Steel now, under the sugared tone.

"Oh, no," Mariah said. "I didn't mean that."

"No one would have wanted to hurt Hal. No one. We had a good, quiet life. He shouldn't have done it where Bethany would find him. I think he thought I would. He could have gone off somewhere, let a stranger or the police find him. It would have been better."

"Of course." Mariah didn't know what to say. "Did you have any other children?" she asked. Maybe Penny was a sibling.

"No, Bethany was our only blessing. Why?"

"I just wondered."

Sharon seemed to study her face and Mariah realized she'd made a mistake with this woman. Two hard comments in a row, and Sharon was now suspicious of her. She decided to lob Sharon's favorite target.

"Tomorrow I'm going to see if I can meet with Jake."

"I want you to be careful." Now Sharon took Mariah's hand into her small, dry palm. "I want you to call me and let me know you're OK after you see him."

"You really hate him."

She lowered her gaze for a moment. "If he didn't kill her, he drove her away. He drove her to whatever fate she met. So yes, I hate him." Sharon cleared her throat. "Do you want some hot milk to help you sleep?"

"You got anything stronger?" Mariah asked, before realizing she shouldn't.

Sharon's hand tensed in hers. "I don't keep liquor in this house."

She was embarrassed. "I think I can fall asleep now. I'm sorry I was a bother."

"You remind me of her. Of my girl. The stubbornness." She reached out and touched Mariah's cheek. "I feel God brought you to me for a reason. I know that sounds like a bad country song. I just wish…I just wish this hadn't happened to us. To our families."

And she started, quietly, to cry then, and Mariah didn't know what to do, but she put her arms around Sharon and held her until the weeping stopped. Her own face burned with unshed tears. The dream thing pointing past her, her turning to see what was there and always waking with a scream and never knowing who stood behind her. She wanted to cry, too, but she didn't.

Sharon wiped at her eyes and got up, trying to smile.

"Mariah," Sharon said. "Tomorrow you'll face evil when you see Jake. Be strong. Know that I stand with you."

Jake, smiling and laughing at trivia night. A nice guy. Or pure evil.

From a woman who didn't seem that sorry her husband was dead.

Mariah slid farther down into the sheets. From the door, Sharon smiled at her and turned off the lights.

24

THE NEXT MORNING, Mariah got up and had coffee with a subdued Sharon. Mariah's clothes were clean since Sharon had done her laundry for her last night, so she didn't need to run home to change. She showered and brushed her teeth with the fresh toothbrush Sharon had given her last night.

"I want you to be careful around Jake," Sharon said. She seemed genuinely unsettled at the idea of Mariah seeing him.

"I will. I know he's into trivia game night at a local bar; I saw that on his Faceplace page...I thought that might be a good place to talk to him. People would be around, since you're worried."

"Well," Sharon said, with a small smile that wasn't entirely happy. "Aren't you the clever girl? Will you let me know what happens? Have some more coffee."

* * *

Mariah drove down from north Austin, along Loop 360, to her mother's old office in a building on the cliffs above the ribbon of Lake Austin. It was strange to be here; she had not come here since the company had asked Craig to come gather Beth's belongings after she had been missing for three months—"You understand, Craig, we're all holding out hope, but we're a growing company and we need the space"—and so she and her dad had driven in complete silence up here, and they had cleaned out Mom's office: photos of their family on vacation at Disney World, of a trip to Hawaii, of Mariah graduating from Lakehaven High School and posing in front of DKR Memorial Stadium before a Longhorns football game. A wedding picture of Beth and Craig, looking gloriously happy in the summer sun. Her two plants she'd managed to not let die—someone had watered them since she vanished. A bunch of framed sales certificates on the wall. A mock hammer, made of rubber, from when she'd "put the hammer down" in sales meetings to keep the staff on topic. Together the two of them had boxed up that aspect of her life, her sales career, the job she loved, people drifting by, not knowing what to say except they were so sorry and everyone loved Beth and what can we do for you? Mariah trying and failing not to cry; Craig hardly even able to look at Mariah as he put these souvenirs of her work life into the plain cardboard box.

You're giving up on her. You think she's dead. Mariah had thought at them all, and the anger had burned bright inside of her.

Now she was back and she told the receptionist—who remembered her and came around the desk to give her a welcome hug—that she was here to see the CEO, Mike Alderson, but no, she didn't have an appointment. He had run a couple of different software companies in Lakehaven—much of the wealth in the suburb was tied to the technology industry—and had taken the CEO position at Acrys Networks after her mother had disappeared. She had not met him before. The receptionist said he was in a meeting, but she'd let him know Mariah was here. She sat down and felt tense every time someone walked by, bracing herself if they were going to say *Oh aren't you Beth's daughter, how are you, what are you doing here?* But no one spoke to her, and somehow that was worse. She told herself they were all new employees. It was clearly a growing company.

Alderson came out to the lobby twenty minutes later.

"Ms. Dunning. Hello." He offered her a hand to shake. "I'm Mike Alderson."

"Yes. I need to ask an unusual favor. You might know that my mother used to work here... well, what happened was..."

"I know about your mother and I'm so sorry. People here speak of her always with such high regard. Please come back to my office."

She followed Alderson to his office. He shut the door behind her.

"I've come to ask an unusual favor," she said. "I'd like a digitized scan of all the receipts from the last year of my mom's business travel. Especially any receipts from the WebCon conference that year, and the year before. Also, her emails."

He blinked. "May I ask why?"

Because my mother's missing and you should just give it to me, she thought, but instead she said, "I am pursuing a lead related to her disappearance."

The moment she said it she knew she'd made a mistake. His expression of concern went guarded.

He frowned slightly. "You are pursuing this? *You?*"

Like it couldn't be her business. "Me," she said, her voice firm.

"Not the police?"

"The police aren't doing as much as people assume," she said. "Nothing against them. But I am following up on a lead, and I have already told Lakehaven's chief of police I'm following up on this lead."

"A lead that you think is in her corporate emails."

"I'm trying to establish if she knew someone."

"What's their name?" he pressed.

"I don't want to make an accusation against someone. Are you going to give me her emails or not?" she asked, a bit too abruptly.

Alderson tapped his fingers along his desk. "I never knew your mother, but I know she was much loved here."

"Thank you." She could feel the blow-off beginning.

"That said, without a warrant, I'm not sure that I could release corporate records."

"They're just bar and restaurant receipts, and old emails," she said. "They're nothing secret. I'll sign any confidentiality agreement you could want."

"If you could tell me how you wanted to use them..."

"I want to establish if she had contact with another person." She wouldn't explain more than that.

"Is this about a coworker of hers?"

"No, it's not." She cleared her throat. "No one with ties to Acrys Networks. Please."

"Of course I want to help you. So let me consult with my lawyers..."

Something in her snapped. She recognized it, her temper surging at a slight provocation. "Fine," she said, getting out her phone. "Let me live-tweet that you are refusing to turn over nonconfidential records that could lead to my mother's kidnapper. Is your PR staff busy today? They will be. People get so frothy on the internet."

His polite smile vanished. "I won't be intimidated, Ms. Dunning, by some sort of social media threat."

"I won't be put off, Mr. Alderson. Do you have a mother?" And she could see the question was like a slap across his face. She didn't care. "Ask your lawyer, right now, please. Or, better yet, ask your staff if they would like to help catch the man who kidnapped Beth Dunning. I could just go down the hall and ask all the people who loved my mom as to whether you should help me."

His voice softened. "I cannot imagine how upset you are..."

"Please. Please help me. If you won't give them to me let me look through them. I'll sit in a corner and do it, nothing has to leave the office. Or put them on a copy-protected drive and I'll search it and I'll bring it back to you. I'm just trying to find my mother...find what happened to her."

"Did your father send you?" The question, asked gently, but sharp as a knife.

"Why?" she asked, her voice full of dread.

"He made the same request six months after your mom vanished. We knew he was a suspect, so we declined. But we did give them to the police. They never told us if they found anything; they never asked us further questions about her work contacts, so I assume they didn't." He was offering her this information as a truce, she saw. "So...they've already checked it. It's a dead end. I don't know what you think you'll find."

"My dad never told me he asked for her emails. He doesn't know that I'm here."

"Wait here, just one moment," he said, flustered. He left the office.

She waited. She felt cold. This was useless.

She waited for thirty minutes.

Mike Alderson came back in, with the Acrys chief information officer, a woman named Karen Sellers who had known her mother for years. Karen was holding a flash drive. "Hello, Mariah. Here's all your mom's receipts and emails. All of them. We still had a master file with all the scans and I just burned them for you."

"Thank you so much," Mariah said. "Thank you."

"I hope this helps you," Karen said. She put the drive into Mariah's palm.

"Yes, thank you." She folded her hands around the flash drive, like it was a precious treasure.

Mike Alderson nodded. "I wasn't trying to be difficult, Mariah. Karen told me it would be OK to trust you."

"I'm sorry I got upset. Thank you," she said. "Hey, since you're all in the same industry, do you know a man named Jake Curtis? He sold a company to DataMarvel."

She thought she saw Karen's mouth tighten slightly. "Yes, I've met him, haven't you, Mike?"

"Sure, I've met him."

"What's he like?" Mariah asked.

Karen folded her arms and glanced at Alderson. "Whoa. Stop. Is Jake Curtis somehow connected to your mom's disappearance?"

"Oh, no. Not at all. I just met him recently through my app design business." She hadn't thought this through, and suddenly words from her mother rang hard in her ear: no gossip network can compare with the Austin software community.

"Well, Jake's a very bright guy," Mike said. "He's overcome a lot. His wife vanished..." And then they both looked at her. Making the connection. Mariah said nothing.

"But it wasn't a kidnapping. Jake's wife left him, right?" Karen said.

Leave, Mariah thought. *Now. Before he worries helping me could backfire on him in this small world.* "Thank you for this." She shook their hands again and went out to the parking garage.

She was opening her car door when she heard footsteps behind her. Karen, breathless, hurrying across the garage. "Hey. I just wanted you to know...I think of your mom every day. *Every* day. We all miss her so much. I know it's nothing compared to what you and your dad feel, but she is missed here. Her smile, her intelligence, her kindness."

Mariah exhaled a long breath. "Thank you for telling me that."

"So. Jake Curtis," Karen said.

"What about him?"

"He's...did you really just ask because you casually met him? Not my business, I know..."

"We met once; he wouldn't remember me I'm sure," Mariah said.

"OK. We were going to do a partnership deal with them. This was a few months ago. And, um, given that his wife vanished, there was some reluctance with our team. I mean, I don't know how to say this and not hurt you."

"It's all right. Hurt me."

"Because the same things could be said about your dad."

"Just say what you want to say."

"I heard your mom and your dad arguing. Well, she told me it was your dad, and the police checked the phone records here, and the call came from his cell phone. He'd asked her if she was having an affair. This was the day she vanished."

"Did she tell you?"

"I walked into her office as she said, into the phone, 'No, Craig, I am not having an affair!'" Karen didn't seem to know where to put her hands. "She got off the phone and rolled her eyes at me, but she was shaken. I'm sorry."

"An argument doesn't mean anything."

"Oh, honey," Karen said. "I wish it didn't."

"So what does this have to do with Jake?"

"People didn't want to work with him because, well, what if it came out that he was involved in his wife's disappearance? I mean, no one wants to buy product from a guy who might have killed his wife, or had her killed."

"So, y'all didn't want to work with him."

"We knew there were potential risks. And we declined, after a lot of internal arguing." She swallowed. "A day after we told him no, the car of our COO was vandalized, all his tires slashed, mirrors broken. The next day, same thing to our then CEO's Porsche."

"And you thought Jake Curtis did this? It could have been another employee at his company."

"It seemed more than a coincidence. And he had the most at stake. Us working with him would have sent another message to software companies that we were confident in partnering with him, that he and his company weren't going anywhere. But we had no proof. But just know... I don't think he's a good guy."

The vandalism made her think of Bethany's misfortunes.

"Thanks for telling me, Karen."

"Sure. You mentioned you were doing app design?"

"I run a small web and app design firm. The firm is, well, me."

"I'm always looking for bright people"—*Oh no, oh no*—"and I know it would be strange to work where your mom did..."

"I don't think I could do that," Mariah said in a rush. She suddenly wanted to be in the car.

Karen gently took her hand. "I totally understand. But listen to me. We're moving to new offices next month. It wouldn't be like working in the same space where she did."

That wouldn't be bad. And she wouldn't have to *explain* so often. "Um, OK. Regular work is hard for me, what with taking care of my dad and such." Now she couldn't look at Karen. She felt a mix of terror and gratitude. It was like seeing a flicker of the life like she'd thought she'd have, before Mom eclipsed everything else.

"Mariah. I have no business to say this, but I will. You need to get on with your life."

"I hear you," Mariah said. She'd found this brief phrase to be very useful in ending conversations full of unsolicited advice.

"I'm just saying... you need to find a purpose for yourself

rather than proving everyone wrong about your dad, or finding out what happened to your mom. Not every mystery is solved."

Five words that felt like short, sharp jabs in her heart.

And then an image, like from her dream, Mom stepping back, receding from her, Mariah desperately holding on to her arms, trying to keep her close. Nausea swept over her, as it often did when she had this kind of conversation.

Mariah remembered how awkward it had seemed when she and her father came to collect her mother's belongings. That people had been kind to her, naturally, but had averted their gaze from her dad. She remembered Karen, saying, in a flat voice when she spoke to Craig, "I'm very sorry for your loss." Like she didn't mean it, but she couldn't not mean it. She thought it was grief. Now she realized that no one here had wanted her father around, even for the thirty minutes it had taken for them to collect her belongings, under the eye of a security officer.

"My mom... did she ever say anything else that made you think she was having an affair? Or that my dad was?"

Karen let ten seconds tick away. "Our offices are next to each other, and if one of us got really loud the other could hear... It didn't happen that often, and I think in the moment she had just forgotten." Karen swallowed, folded her arms over her chest. "I couldn't hear the first part of the conversation... I was concentrating on creating a slide presentation for a meeting. But then I heard her voice rise. She said, 'No, I'm not having an affair... no I wouldn't, you know I wouldn't... and then you are not going to drag our daughter into this. Fine. I'll talk to you later, when you've calmed down and you know this is ridiculous. I'll see you there.'"

Mariah listened to the wind rise. She stared at her feet. "You really remember those words."

"They kind of burned into my head once she vanished." She cleared her throat. "I knew things were rocky between them..."

"How? How would you know that?"

"Because she told me. About a month earlier. I went through a divorce a year before that. It happens a certain amount in the tech industry, with startups. The company takes over your life."

"That didn't happen with my mom."

"Honey, you were living on campus...you saw your folks every couple of weeks, not all the time. Isn't that true?"

Mariah nodded after a moment. "But Mom would have told me if they were splitting up."

"Only when that was a final decision. They may not have gotten there. Or she told him she'd had enough, she was leaving him..." Karen didn't finish the sentence.

"He didn't kill her. He couldn't have."

"OK, OK," Karen said. "I'm just telling you what I heard. And what I told the police."

"You couldn't have misheard."

"No, Mariah. I know what was said." Karen handed her a business card. "If there's anything more I can do to help you...with anything...please let me know. And think about what I said about the job."

She thought she would feel a hot bolt of hate for Karen, talking to the police about her father. But Karen had done what anyone would. Anyone. Mariah felt scared. Scared of what she was doing here.

Scared of what might be true.

"I will. Thank you." But she already knew she'd say no, as nice as it would be to work with Karen and the people at Acrys Networks. She would have no peace until she had answers.

* * *

Mariah got into the car. She tried to imagine her calm, gentle father calling his wife at work and yelling at her about an affair. Calling her office. And then the thought, like a blade through her thoughts: why? Why had he called *then*? At that time, which was not convenient, when his wife couldn't talk frankly to him. He must have found something. Learned something. Discovered something on that final day and called her because it could not wait. Why not?

I'll see you there. The lot? Had Mom agreed to meet Dad at the empty lot? Why talk there when they could talk at home, in relative privacy? Well, Mariah had been home that day, sick, a rotten late flu sweeping across campus, and Mom had told her the night before to come recuperate at home rather than stay alone at her apartment, and she had been bleary with fever and medication that reduced the world to a haze. She didn't even remember seeing her mother leave that morning; most likely Beth had peeked in on her in her room, saw her sleeping, and let her sleep rather than say that final goodbye. That haunted her... that her mother looked in on her, and left her asleep, because she must have been sure they would have ten thousand tomorrows.

But her parents had fought and argued. The police had asked her if her parents had argued. She told them no, it was a happy marriage, and yes she was busy with school and life but she was very close to both her parents. She would know. There had been rumors that they questioned her father over arguments. He never would discuss the questioning with her, even when she asked.

Why then? Why did he call her then?

She drove home. And stared at the for sale sign when she pulled into the driveway.

25

MARIAH BLINKED.

FOR SALE BY OWNER.

That...that couldn't be. She was seized with a sudden and strong desire to rip it from the lawn.

She parked and walked into the house.

"Dad?"

He was on his laptop, and he closed it as she approached.

"You can't sell our house!"

"It's not really for sale. I got another threat, another strong hint that we should move. So, I've decided to make them think we're moving. I won't be accepting any offers."

"You're playing games with these jerks," she said.

"I'm going to beat them at their own game," he said. "I know what I'm doing, so you don't have to worry."

"I just...I don't want to leave Mom's house. I really, really don't." The terror filled her. She had lost Mom. What would she do if she had to leave the house that held so many memories of her? This house had been the only home she'd ever known.

He stood up, closed his arms around her tense form. "I promise you, we're not selling. But no one can know that now."

"Another threat. Show it to me?"

"It's nothing. I'm handling it."

She stepped away from him. "Dad, I was already upset and this didn't help."

"What, sweetheart?"

"Did you really think Mom was having an affair? I mean, you called her and accused her at her office. I want to know why you thought she was seeing someone."

He let ten seconds tick by, a heavy silence between them. "I had my reasons," he said.

"Specifics."

"I was clearly wrong," he said. "The police looked at that possible aspect of the case and found nothing. She wasn't seeing anyone."

"They're human. They could have missed something. Maybe if she was seeing someone that person killed her."

"Mariah, look." He steadied his voice. "You have to know that I loved your mom more than life itself. I know that's a cliché; put it on a T-shirt and I'll wear it. We had a good marriage. But every marriage goes through ups and downs. I don't think she had an affair."

What wasn't he saying? Mariah said, "You think she was considering having an affair?"

"An affair takes some groundwork, if you don't want to get caught." He cleared his throat and took a deep breath. "I had one. Two years into our marriage, before you were born."

The strength faded from her muscles. She sat down in the armchair, quickly. It just wasn't possible. She opened and closed her mouth, silent. "You didn't," she finally said.

"Nothing I say is an excuse. It's just what happened. Your mom had had a miscarriage. A second one. We were both very depressed. She didn't want me to touch her. She didn't want me around." He cleared his throat again. "I had met a woman who worked at a client company. I didn't know how to help Beth or how to help myself, and this woman made her interest in me clear."

Mariah felt unsteady. She knew her father was considered a very handsome man, but it was one thing to say it and another thing to realize some woman who wasn't her mother had circled them in the wake of a tragedy, making herself available. Or that her father—*her father*—could have made such a choice in the face of her mother's pain.

"I knew I shouldn't, but I did. I didn't want you to ever know. Beth promised she would never tell."

"I don't even know you right now," Mariah's voice was brittle.

"I know you don't," he said. "I'm sorry."

"How long did it go on?"

"Not even two weeks. I realized...I wasn't suited for secrecy like that. It made me feel better exactly once, the first time, then an hour later the guilt was crushing me. I didn't love this woman, and I'd never love this woman." His voice wavered. "She was not someone I could have cared for. It was purely physical."

"Did Mom catch you?" She wasn't sure she could bear to hear an answer.

"I confessed to her after I'd broken it off. She cried. I cried. She asked me to move out. I did, for about three months. We went to see a therapist. Together, and alone. We worked out our issues. She asked me to move back into the house. We found our love again. And then...we got pregnant with you."

It was like there was a prequel to her life she never knew.

"So that was why you thought she was capable of having an affair...because you had."

He bit his lip. "She did not mention the past often. But if she did, she would tell me that I should know how it felt."

"I cannot believe you did that to her."

"I'm very sorry I did. She knew how sorry I was. She forgave me."

She's not here to say she forgave you, Mariah thought. *I don't know what she thought. I don't know what your marriage was. Clearly she took you back, but did they ever really love each other again the way they had before? Has my whole life been a carefully scripted play? A lie, designed to shield us all from unpleasantness? Was I the product of make-up sex?*

He took a deep breath. "And so my past behavior colored how the police viewed me."

"How did they even know?" she asked.

"You know she was friends with Dennis Broussard. In high school."

She felt her stomach twist. "I know he had a crush on her because you told me that."

"She was suspicious... that I was cheating... and she hired Dennis to follow me. He had left the Austin police force and was working temporarily as a private investigator, and then later he ended up joining the Lakehaven police department and he worked his way up there. But she went to him." His voice lowered. "He was her friend. A guy who already hated me. It was a risk. Dennis spotted me."

Her mother had hired a guy who was infatuated with her to prove her husband's infidelity. Her mind spun. They should have had a reality show. "But you told her before Dennis could?"

"Yes," he said. "He gave me twenty-four hours to come clean to Beth. Or he would. He thought for her it would be better coming from me. I told him I would. I couldn't go on this way. He told me he was in love with Beth. He always had been. I knew it. I knew he would be there for her if I wasn't. I knew I couldn't lose her."

She tried to imagine this conversation. Broussard and her father, unwittingly setting the course for the rest of their lives, and hers.

So maybe it wasn't guilt that drove him to confession. Maybe he knew he was about to be busted and he threw himself on Mom's mercy before Broussard, who was in love with her, could tell her. That Broussard had given him a chance... was a shock.

"I feel... I feel like I don't even know you, Dad." Her fingernails bit into her palms.

"I'm sorry. You weren't even born yet. I would have never..."

"What, you would have modified your bad behavior if I'd already existed?"

"Yes," he said evenly. "That's what many parents do. And if your mother hadn't forgiven me, there would be no you, Mariah. You and your mom were the greatest gifts I ever got. I would never... have hurt her, even if she was having an affair. Twenty years later is a long time for revenge. I wouldn't have threatened her, or left her, or... I would have done what she did for me. Forgiven her. But I would have wanted to know."

"Who do you think she was seeing?" Broussard, she thought. He wasn't married.

"I just had a general suspicion. I didn't have a name."

"Based on what? I want to know what evidence there was that made you doubt Mom this way."

"She was out late a lot. More than usual. There were phone calls here to the house, where the caller hung up."

Wouldn't a boyfriend have called her cell phone? Her mind was racing. She felt feverish.

"Is that it?"

"Yes. And she wasn't interested in me." His voice went to an embarrassed whisper. "I mean, physically. She always had been before. I mean, since you were born."

"Dad."

"Well, you asked." He looked miserable.

"So you called her at work? Why then? Why not wait for the privacy of home? What triggered that?"

"Triggered? Nothing. I just... I just couldn't wait. I wanted answers and I wanted them now." Her father's face was a careful study in control.

"That doesn't make sense."

He held up a hand. "I'm not an automaton, and neither are you," he said. "People do things that don't make sense all the time. You want a tidy explanation for everything. *Everything.* You..." He stopped, his voice strained. "There are no tidy explanations, sweetheart. I wish I hadn't made that call. I wish I hadn't accused her."

He clutched her hands in his. She could feel the sweat on her palms. Her father's mouth trembled.

"Mariah. What are you asking me now? Really?"

"I just want to know..." Her voice drifted off. A trunk full of weapons, a determination that led her to confront three strangers yesterday, but here was the truth, and she was scared to death of it. It was like the dream where she had to turn around to see the truth. She started hyperventilating. He eased her down into a chair, helped her calm down, whispering to her that everything would be okay. "Just tell me." Her hands trembled, but the worst of the panic faded. She could handle the truth now, she was sure of it.

"Are you thinking you're going to trip me up in a lie?" Craig gave a half-laugh, bitter, incredulous. He spoke with greater confidence. "Mariah. I have told you and the police all this. I went there. I knew that was where she went when she was upset, and if she was there we could talk. But she was gone. Her car was there but she wasn't. Then I called you. I thought you might have heard from her. You had not. You drove over, remember, although I told you not to because you were on meds and sick?"

Slowly she nodded. "I remember standing in the street. Her car parked there." But the rest of it...her father's phone call, Mariah driving to the lot, was a blur, milky, hidden. "We looked for her. On the lot, in the woods."

"Then we called her office. Then the police. It was too early for them to do anything like file a missing persons report." The words spilled out of him like a stream. "Even though her car was there. We came home and I put you back to bed and then I called the police again and that time I got ahold of Broussard."

She closed her eyes. She could remember stumbling around the empty land, calling for her mom, scared that Beth had wandered off or had fallen from one of the limestone cliffs to the unforgiving rocks and trees below, but the memory seemed like a dream, a haze, something too awful to be fully remembered, kept at arm's length. A fog she couldn't escape.

Was it all a haze because her father had done the unimaginable, like Broussard said, and she'd seen it?

The silence between them was like a wall; she wanted to turn away from him.

"You've never said you didn't do it," she said. "I've always defended you. Always."

"You never asked," he said, as if he thought now she would.

She bit into her lip, pressed fists to her eyes. She tasted her own blood, the barest tingle.

"I shouldn't have to say I didn't do it," he said. "Not to you." But now he looked at her, he pulled her hands gently away from her face. His face was inches from hers. "I didn't do it."

The clock on the wall ticked. They looked at each other. "I'm not sure what else to say," he said.

"Dad, I love you," she said. She controlled her voice. "Even if you had hurt her... I know it would have been an accident. I could forgive an accident."

He stared at her and then he looked away. "I would hope so," he said. "Are we done here? Have I said what you needed to hear?"

"Please don't be mean about this," she said. "Did you ask Acrys Networks for her emails and texts? Six months after she was gone?"

"Yes," he said.

"Why didn't you ever tell me?"

"Because I couldn't say to you then that I was trying to find out if she was having an affair. You didn't need to hear anything like that."

They had been such a team since Mom vanished, but she could feel them fracturing. The silence between them grew. "Maybe I should move out," she said quietly.

"No!" he said, suddenly, sharply. "I... I don't want you to move out."

"Dad..."

"I'm just not ready," he said. He turned away from her. "I'm sorry. I know I'm constraining your life."

She wanted to tell him that it was all right. That she didn't want to move out. Being out of the house held its own terrors. But that day would come, wouldn't it? She wasn't going to live at home the whole rest of her life. And if she found out the truth about what happened to her mother, then that would give her the permission to start her own life again.

"You're not, Dad. I'm sorry I accused you... I just..."

"We're never going to know what happened, unless something changes dramatically. Unless someone comes forward. Unless her... unless her body is found."

The hush between them thickened. She didn't know what to say.

"We just have to stick together," he said. He closed his hand around hers. "No matter what."

He had never said such a thing to her before today.

He's scared, she thought. *He's scared.* If he hurt Mom—and she could still hardly imagine it—he has been on borrowed time since that moment. And what if the time was running out?

What would you do if Dad was guilty? What? You have to face that. She pushed the thoughts away. "Swear to me you didn't hurt her."

"I didn't hurt her."

She closed her hand around his. Karen couldn't be right. She had to continue with her search. Find the pattern that gave a different answer.

And she hadn't told Dad she had the emails and the receipts: what Mom's company had refused to give him.

And she wouldn't. Not yet. She embraced him, and they held each other like the world was against them.

26

MARIAH DROVE TO a Starbucks in the Lakehaven Market shopping center and went inside. It wasn't busy, and she found a corner table with an open outlet and snagged a venti vanilla latte.

She could have done this at home, but she didn't want to be around her dad right now. He was her rock, and now she could see the cracks in him, the flaws. And she didn't want him to know she had Mom's emails. Not yet. She needed to do this alone.

She slid the Acrys Networks flash drive Karen had given her into her laptop's port. She opened the massive file with a text editor she used to write code.

She took a deep breath and searched for "Bethany Curtis."

Mariah made a noise in her throat. Over twenty threads of emails. She closed her eyes and took a deep breath.

Here it was. The link.

She read through the emails, slowly.

Beth Dunning: So fun to meet you at WebCon and have margaritas—I have pics! Maybe I should delete LOL. Take care and talk soon.

Bethany Curtis: You are a hoot girl! Yes, let's get together again soon—do you get an expense account? I'm kidding. OK I'm half kidding.

Beth: Well yes on the expense account but then you have to get Andy the Candy to place an order. Seriously though yes, let's meet up. Can your hubby join or do we do a girls night out?

Bethany: I'll see if I can get hubby to ignore his start up for an evening...what about yours?

Beth: Mine, no! he's so so boring. I can't inflict Captain Accountant on you.

Her mother *had* been at the same WebCon and *had* met Bethany there, trying to make a sale. This was it, proof of their connection. She shivered for a moment and reread the exchange.

Andy the Candy? With a jolt Mariah realized her mother meant Andy Candolet...who, after all, would have been in charge of security software purchases at Ahoy Transportation. Andy the Candy. She frowned at the idea of her mother talking that way about a guy only a few years older than Mariah. Or really, any guy other than her dad. And she didn't much like her mother describing her father as boring to a new friend. It made her feel cold inside. She read on:

Bethany: It's always a girls' night out with me! Until the husband gets that company launched IT'S TAKING FOREVAH

Beth: It was the same with me before Acrys went public—long long hours. I loved the excitement and vesting in stock but a lot of work and I know some marriages that didn't make it through or limped across the finish line...he'll do great and you're there to support and encourage him.

Bethany: Yeah I just wish he was here more. I miss him. And it feels like everything else is going wrong in my life these days. OK SORRY! Not complaining.

Beth: Let your hair down. He won't know.

Her mom, encouraging an unhappy wife to let her hair down.

But they knew each other. That was the key. The link. The hope for the truth, the pattern to take away suspicion off her father.

She read through the other emails: more plans made for margaritas, which happened but was cut short by Beth having a customer emergency so she had to leave early (apologized for in a subsequent email), mentions of a meeting, Beth asking Bethany to get her a sales meeting with Andy.

Then:

Bethany: You won't believe this, there's money missing at work and they accused me. I think Andy took the $$.

Beth: No way either you or The Candy took money from there.

Bethany: You don't know what he's capable of.

Beth: Your husband's about to make a fortune, why would you steal money now?

Bethany: I know but it looks bad for my job; Jake is going to be so upset.

Beth: You haven't told him?

Bethany: I just found out. I am surprised they didn't march me out the door but Andy stood up for me and said it was an accounting error or a mistaken transfer and we'd find it. I can't believe this on top of everything else: the stolen credit cards, the prank sex toys sent to the office here. My life is a train wreck.

No, I don't know your mom, Andy had said. Was that a lie? Her mother must have met him at least once; she'd used a nickname. Andy the Candy. It seemed so inappropriate and unlike her. But there it was, in glowing text.

Mariah had never thought of her mother having a social life as part of her sales job. She just assumed her mother called on customers, made her pitch, and came home. Had she ever asked about her mother's work? She hadn't. It put food on the table and helped put a roof over Mariah's head, and she'd never wondered much about the intricacies of it.

Beth emailed Bethany one more time about the embezzlement: Seriously did you get this worked out? Did they find the money?

Bethany: I cannot talk about this on email. I had to sign a confidentiality agreement.

Her mother left it alone. At least in email.

And then the next to final email, from Bethany to Beth: Have to cancel on the drinks, sorry, you know all the damage I'm dealing with. Would love to meet your daughter and hubby sometime.

Bethany knew I existed, Mariah thought. Mom talked about me to her. Of course Mom did. But she tried to remember if her mother had ever mentioned a particular friend she'd made at a conference or on a sales call. She didn't. Maybe Mom talked about it, and Mariah, busy with her own life, consumed by her own dramas, heard but didn't listen.

Was that why Andy's name seemed momentarily familiar?

She opened the final email exchange:

Beth: I'm glad you called. So, what are you going to do now that you know about your dad?

Bethany: I don't know. Long vacation? Some alone time. Think things through.

Beth: What can I do to help you?

Bethany: Keep it safe. And keep the margaritas cold for when life returns to normal. And say nothing. Just... say nothing.

Beth: All right. I'm here when you want to talk.

This was a week before Bethany took off for Houston.

Bethany's dad. What about him?

Keep *what* safe?

These two women had been friends of a sort, drinking buddies. And then closer, going into detail on their private lives.

Had her mother had an entirely parallel life she hadn't known about? That no one had known about? She could imagine Broussard trolling through her thousands of emails, looking for evidence against her father, or for a sign that there was a boyfriend or lover, and ignoring or speeding through the emails that were about female friendship or closing software deals. Had he even noticed she had exchanged emails with a woman who'd gone missing? But that was it. Bethany Curtis had been accused of a crime and had told her mother she was leaving her husband and flown to Houston and disappeared because she wanted to disappear. She wasn't considered a possible kidnapping victim like her mom was.

She searched for Candolet.

She found a single email to Andy. Great to meet you at WebCon at our booth. Would really like the chance to talk to you about how Acrys Networks can help address your security concerns. I'm enclosing some preliminary information and will follow up so I can better understand your needs.

Generic sales email. No cop searching her database would think this was odd or important. Maybe Andy and Mom had met, and he honestly didn't remember. But she was friends with Bethany. Did Bethany talk to Andy about Mom—try to help her win a deal at Ahoy? And the nickname...had it just been a flirty affectation, delivered from a distance? Maybe borrowed from Bethany or another woman?

She went through the receipt scans, checking during the four-day period that WebCon's interactive festival was held. Drinks receipt at Tequila Joe's. Margaritas. Scrawled on the top, in her mother's handwriting, was Ahoy Transportation.

So they knew each other, and they met more than once. They confided in each other. And then they both went missing. And so this couldn't have anything to do with her father, surely. She felt like she could breathe again.

She closed her laptop. She went back to her father's car. She opened the trunk, saw all the equipment she'd arrayed for when she found her mother's kidnappers. The police thought she was a joke. She wasn't.

But Mom had known something about Bethany's dad. Mom had been asked to keep something for Bethany. Heat and rage and a strange satisfaction all surged through her blood. She was going to find out the truth. It was in reach.

27

THE STARTUP JAKE Curtis had launched, TreyCord Systems, had later been bought by another local company called DataMarvel, headquartered in north Austin. Mariah drove east through Lakehaven, got onto the MoPac expressway, shot across Lady Bird Lake (a stretch of the Colorado River on the southern edge of downtown Austin), and up to north Austin. In one of the glassy cube buildings by the expressway she saw the DataMarvel logo, a bursting star. She pulled into DataMarvel's parking lot.

She orbited the lot, looking for a spot. She found one and parked in a visitor slot. Being closer to the building, she could see a security desk in the lobby. You couldn't just waltz in and get up to Jake Curtis's office.

Over the next ten minutes she sat thinking how she could approach him, considering and discarding approaches:

I'm not really into trivia like I said. I'm into what happened to your missing wife. I'm working with a noted crime blogger named Reveal...

Hi, your missing wife was sort-of friends with my missing mom. Money was involved. Secrets were shared. Do you know what those were...?

I know your mother-in-law, and she thinks you're a murderer...

I know something the police don't know about your wife's case...

It all sounded crazy. He'd slam a door in her face. She needed...

Andy Candolet. Walking out the front door, a briefcase in hand.

Andy was staring down at his phone, texting rapidly. Mariah got out of the car. He glanced up at her as he walked.

"Hi," she said. "What are you doing here?"

"I had an appointment," he said after a moment. Still staring at her. Then his smile came back.

"With Jake Curtis?"

"There are a few other companies in that building."

"Of course." *What a giant coincidence*, she wanted to say. One she didn't believe. And he didn't say no.

They were both silent, like two hunters who surprise each other in a field, neither wanting to turn a back or step away from their path. *He's lying to you, right to your face. What is going on with all these people tied to Bethany? What are they hiding?*

"I owe you specs for your bid," he said. "Sorry I haven't sent them. I've been busy and I'm sure you are, too."

"Are you really going to entertain a bid from me?" She immediately regretted the choice of verb.

"Yes, I said I would and I meant it. I know you've been busy helping Mrs. B. I didn't want to bug you. How is she?"

"Upset."

"I'll check on her later. I take it you're here to see Jake. I'm surprised he gave you an appointment."

"Well." She didn't elaborate.

"I think you should steer clear of him."

"Why?"

"I don't think you're going to get answers here. Jake doesn't remember much of the day Bethany left, he says. Every detail of that day when I heard she was missing is burned into my head. There's something wrong with that guy."

She decided to play a card. "I found an email from my mom to you. Do you not remember?"

"No," he said, uncertain, the smile gone. "I didn't know her."

"After you met her at WebCon."

"Oh. Well. After WebCon I probably got three hundred emails from vendors."

"She said you met there."

"'Met' probably meant she introduced herself and handed me a business card in the middle of their trade show booth. Repeat that three hundred times and you get my point."

"She and Bethany went out for drinks at least four times. Did Bethany ever mention her to you?"

"Not that I recall. I wasn't friends with most of Bethany's friends."

"She saw you, and I think it was more than that once. She had a nickname for you. Andy the Candy."

He blushed and frowned. "That is an old nickname an ex of mine called me that Bethany thought was hilarious. She used to tease me with it."

That made a weird kind of sense. Mariah felt her own face redden.

He let out an exasperated sigh. "I told you I didn't know your mom, that was the truth. Did I email her back?"

"No," she admitted.

"OK, Mariah. That's all there is to it, then. I wish I could help you."

"The money Bethany was accused of embezzling, tell me about that."

He laughed and shook his head. "You know I'm the security head for Ahoy, right? Do you think I hand out privileged information about corporate finances?"

"She was accused. The company said they dropped the charges. She quietly left. So, did Ahoy find their money? Or did you settle with her?"

"I can't talk about this stuff. It's confidential."

"You know Bethany thought *you* took it. She said so in an email to my mom."

He took a long, deep breath. "If I tell you what happened, please don't tell Mrs. B. Please. It would crush her."

She waited.

"I didn't take the money. It's ridiculous to think I'd steal from my own family. Bethany did. It was the first time she tried to leave Jake. My theory is she wanted cash, but she didn't want to touch their accounts, have him notice their money was gone. But then she decided not to leave him, and Claudette found the money was missing, and it was all terribly awkward. I nearly lost my job because I'd defended her. She agreed to resign and to return the money."

"And you don't want this known why?"

"Because I don't want Mrs. B to know her daughter's a thief. And I don't want Julie to know I risked my whole career to help Bethany. There. You got me."

"Claudette doesn't strike me as understanding. Why didn't she press charges?"

"She got her money back, and I begged her not to prosecute. End of story." Andy shook his head and moved his briefcase from one hand to another. "I like you. I want to be your friend. But this has nothing to do with your mom, and it's none of your business. Good luck. I have to go."

She watched him walk to his car—a nice BMW—and get inside without glancing back at her. She had picked up the thread but into something she didn't understand. This strange web of relationships between the people close to Bethany—her friends, her parents—and those on the periphery of her life: this Lizbeth, maybe Yvette Suarez.

And then she realized. He'd lied to her face. Right to her face.

After WebCon I probably got three hundred emails from vendors.

She said you met there.

"Met" probably meant she introduced herself and handed me a business card in the middle of their trade show booth. Repeat that three hundred times and you get my point.

She hadn't told him her mother was a software sales rep. Had she told Julie? She hadn't thought so. Maybe Julie had looked up her mother's case. Maybe he had, after last night. And yes, conferences were for meeting people. But he was so sure he hadn't.

Or maybe it was a slip. A mistake. A crack in his façade when confronted with the email.

As his BMW pulled out of the lot, she thought, *I'm going to crack you, too.*

She went into the lobby and approached the desk. "Hi. I'm here to see Jake Curtis at DataMarvel."

The security guard gave her a neutral look. "Your name?" He glanced at a screen, where there was apparently a list of expected visitors.

"Mariah Dunning, but I don't have an appointment, I won't be on your list. I have information about his wife, who went missing."

The guard looked at her. "Don't you people have anything better to do than bother a nice guy like Mr. Curtis?"

"I'm not a crank, sir."

"Get out of here," the guard said.

"Do people do that...show up offering him information?"

The guard frowned. "Yes, and always for a price. What are you charging?"

"Nothing. Because I actually do have information. May I leave a note for him with you then?"

"You can write a note and I will put it in an envelope with his name on it. Whether he opens it or puts it in the shredder is up to him."

She opened her purse, found her planner, tore out a blank page of lined paper. She went to a leather-covered bench, more for decoration than sitting, and she wrote on it: *My mom and your wife were friends and they've both gone missing. Within six months of each other. I don't think this could be a coincidence. Will you talk to me? I don't want anything from you except information that might help us find them both.* And after a moment she added: *We can always talk about Martin Van Buren if you prefer.* She wrote her phone number. She gave it to the guard.

He nodded and then she left.

She didn't notice the other car, the driver turning off a phone, pulling out after her, following her at a distance.

28

MARIAH DROVE SOUTH to the Starbucks in Lakehaven where she'd gone before to inspect the emails on the flash drive. The café was now crowded, nearly every table and chair full. She was standing in the line of people, half of whom seemed to be studying their phones, wishing that Jake would call her, when she heard the whisper: "That's her. With the dark hair. She covered up for her father killing her mom."

She could be very still. She could ignore it. She had ignored it before, usually when Dad was with her, and she'd see someone nearby saying, "Well, I guess she made her choice" or "She's protecting him." Usually a glare silenced the critic.

She turned. Two women, both in workout clothes, a bit back in the line, looking right at her, and then as she met their gaze one looked away in shame (hopefully). The other still stared at her, as if it was her right to challenge Mariah.

Mariah felt the rage, the devil she couldn't shake, rise in her.

"Do you have something to say to me?" Mariah said. The older man between them looked up from his phone, surprised, glanced around the café.

The first woman kept her glare on her. Mariah thought, *I'd bet you were a bully in school, and you still are one.*

"You'd think a daughter would want justice for her mother," the woman said.

"What do you know about anything?" Mariah said, her voice raising, the man between them getting a wide-eyed expression on his face. Mariah put her hand on his shoulder and eased him out of the way. He went.

"Celia, don't," the second woman said.

"You know what I mean," the first woman said, for a moment looking uncomfortable but unwilling suddenly to back down.

"Say it to my face," Mariah said, stepping closer to the woman.

One of the baristas had come down to where they stood at the counter, saying, "Hey folks, everything all right?" in a jovial voice.

"Say it to my face!" Mariah yelled. "Accuse my dad of murder while you're waiting on your latte. Do it!"

She felt a hand on her arm. She glanced.

Julie Santos.

"Let's go. Let's go," Julie said. Mariah felt Julie—who was smaller than her but strong—pulling her out of the line, past the two women, past the now-silent tables, out into the sunshine.

"Let go of me," Mariah said, hurrying past the outdoor tables, toward the other businesses in the shopping center.

Julie did. "Mariah."

"What the hell are you doing in there?" She'd now run into Andy and then Julie in an hour. Coincidence?

Or maybe they're watching you.

"I have a private workout client in Lakehaven. I'd just finished a session and was getting a chai," Julie said. "Never mind that. Are you OK?"

"Yes. Yes." She steadied her breathing. "I saw your boyfriend today at Jake Curtis's company. Are you two following me?"

"We have jobs. You think I take off from work to follow you around?"

"I told Sharon where I was going..."

"I haven't talked to Sharon today. I...I promise you we're not trying to follow you around." She lowered her voice, as if embarrassed to have to say the words.

Mariah bent over, hands on her knees, trying to calm herself. Like at the mall when she saw Mom. When she *thought* she saw Mom. She could not lose control.

But...was Julie already in the café when Mariah got there? Or maybe she had followed her...from Sharon's to home to Jake's office.

She thought of last night of the three of them, watching her, as if she had interrupted something secret and terrible between them all.

"Thank you for getting me out of there," Mariah said. "I just...when they talk about my dad that way...it's because he has no alibi for two hours when Mom vanished. I mean, other than me, and if he'd just been at his office, everyone would know he was innocent. But he wasn't. He wasn't. So...people think the most awful thing..." Panic clawed at her throat, her chest, her eyes.

Julie knelt by her, put an arm around her shoulder. "Do you want me to take you home?"

"No...no. Thank you. I'll be OK."

"Here. Let's walk." They strolled past the stores, down toward a park on the edge of the shopping center. Julie guided her to a bench and they sat.

"I don't want to leave you until I'm sure you're OK," Julie said.

"I'm fine." She was trying not to be suspicious; Julie was acting nicer than she had during their first meeting. "Can I ask you a couple of questions?"

"Sure," Julie said, but her voice was more neutral.

"Who is Penny?"

"Penny."

"I found pictures in a journal of Bethany's. Old photos of a little girl. From a newspaper, and one that was a personal photo. On the back of one the name Penny was written."

"I don't know a Penny."

"Maybe Bethany had a sister?"

"The Blevins moved here when Bethany was in preschool. That was where we met. She was an only child."

"Where did they move from?"

"Chicago."

"Not Houston?" She thought of the yellowing sales slip inside the self-help book, from a store in Houston.

"No. Did you ask Sharon any of this?"

"No. I didn't want her to know I'd gone through her daughter's books. But I wasn't snooping, I was looking for anything tied to my mom. They knew each other." She explained about the emails, watching Julie for a reaction. But Julie just frowned.

"Have you told this to Sharon?"

"No. Not yet."

"Maybe you shouldn't."

"Why not? She'll want to know."

Julie was silent for a moment, watching a pair of moms walk by, pushing strollers. "I think Sharon might know more about Bethany's disappearance than she says."

Stunned silence. "Why?"

"I got an email three days after Bethany went to Houston. From an account I didn't know. I didn't see it for a week until I was checking my spam folder for another email that had been put there." Julie leaned forward. "It just said, *I got to straighten out my life and make some amends. Don't tell my mom where I am, I'll call you tomorrow or next day. She'll go after my friend. You can't email me back and I don't want you to try.* Not signed. It came from an anonymous remailer service, and there wasn't a way to email her back."

"She must have known she'd already been traced to Houston."

"I don't know what she was thinking. And I thought her friend she meant was this Lizbeth person she was hanging with... what if the friend she meant was your mom?"

She'll go after my friend. Mariah tried not to let the words bounce around her head, to take on a darker meaning. "Did you tell this to the police? Or to anyone?"

"I went to Jake, and then we went to the police. But... they couldn't trace it because it was from an anonymous remailer, and anyway, they thought it might have been a fake. Jake and Sharon were getting prank emails and phone calls. Apparently that's common in a case like this. So they thought the email was sent by a prankster, or someone wanting attention, or... sent by Jake, to take the heat off him. To put suspicion on Sharon. They kept it quiet because... well, I guess they couldn't prove it was Bethany who sent it; remember, her disappearance wasn't considered a crime at that point. No one thought she'd been kidnapped. And if she's dead, she could have been killed any time after she left for Houston."

"Why would anyone suspect that Sharon hurt her daughter?"

Julie took in a long breath. "Jake always believed he was going to launch a successful company. He demanded a prenuptial agreement. I told her not to sign it, but she did, to make him happy. The prenup Bethany signed said if she and Jake divorced or she deserted him *before* his company went public, she got nothing. If after, she only got a quarter of his shares. And Bethany—she told me she'd promised her mom half her shares. For working so hard, doing so much for her after her dad died. Sharon stood to lose out on a few million dollars if Bethany couldn't stick out the marriage."

Whoa, Mariah thought. "And Bethany left him, even knowing it would mean millions to her mom." That felt like a punch. Mariah frowned.

"Sharon was so furious with her, until it became clear that Bethany had truly gone missing."

"But Sharon is her mother. She loves her."

"I know. You sound like Andy. But...I was her friend for a long time, and she was afraid of her mom. She...she once said, 'What if my dad didn't kill himself?' She whispered it. We were at her house. This was nearly a year after Hal Blevins died."

"She thought her mom killed her dad?"

"She never said it that specifically. I said to her, 'What do you mean?' And she said, 'There's just a terrible secret in that house, and I don't know what it is.'" Julie shivered in the sunlight. "Then she swore me to secrecy. What if she found out? If it was Bethany sending the email, why would she contact me and not her mom?"

"Why are you telling me this now?"

"Because she was once my friend. She and I, OK, we weren't as close as we had been. And I wonder, if Bethany came back but not to her husband, but to her mother...I think Sharon might have been really angry with her."

"You think she hurt her?"

"Maybe in a moment of rage. We've all been there. So much hurt, so much pain between them. I hate to say it of Mrs. B, but it's a possibility."

29

JULIE HAD GONE back to the gym. Mariah got in her car, her mind spinning with Julie's claims. Either Julie was telling the truth and was finally coming forward with information, or she was lying about Sharon Blevins.

But why would she lie? How would she gain? She couldn't, in any way Mariah could see.

She thought, *You are getting to them. You are upsetting them and they are talking. Keep at it.*

Mariah drove to Jake Curtis's address, a house off Old Travis Road, in an exclusive neighborhood. Lots of software execs lived in this area. Jake Curtis's home looked like a multimillion-dollar number. She drove up the cobblestone paved driveway to the Tuscan-style house. Stone exterior, tiled roof. It was lovely and huge.

He hadn't called her, but maybe he hadn't gotten her note. If what Julie said was true, then she had to speak to him. Find out what he knew about her mother's friendship with Bethany.

So. She'd wait here. He had to come home at some point.

She sat on the expansive front step. She opened up a browser on her phone and found Jake's Faceplace page. She remembered when she'd looked before at his social media presence she had a "friend" who had liked the page—a high school classmate who worked there. Rob Radlon. She called him.

"Rob Radlon."

"Rob, it's Mariah Dunning. Do you remember me?"

A pause. *Everyone remembers me*, she thought. "Hey, Mariah, of course."

"Great. Because I'm one of those people who only call when they need a favor."

He laughed, but then because it was Mariah, he stopped. She had noticed this, that people didn't like to laugh around her for long. Like it was an unkindness to remind her there was joy in the world. "How are you? How's your dad?"

Him asking the second question meant the world to her. Rob had been a choir friend, not a boy she knew well, but he had always seemed really decent. "He's okay. This never gets easier." She told herself it was acceptable to play on every sympathy he might have.

"I can't imagine. So, what's the favor?"

"I need you to get Jake Curtis to take my phone call."

"Um, why?"

"I can't go into details. Would you tell him it has to do with his wife's disappearance?"

Now the laugh was nervous. "Mariah, I can't talk to him about his vanished wife. He's my boss's boss's boss."

"Please."

"Why would you bother him?"

"Listen. His wife vanished. My mom vanished. They knew each other. I don't think this was widely known." She lowered her voice. "If I'm right, then you're the bright young software designer who brought me to his attention."

"His wife took off. She doesn't want to be found."

"OK, I left a note for him. Just tell him or his assistant that you knew me from school. That I'm not crazy. Please. Maybe that will be enough."

"I just don't think he wants to talk about his wife. To anyone."

"Tell him," she said, with a flash, "that I know what it's like. That I know what he's going through. Five minutes. That's all I ask."

"I'll try, Mariah." But she thought he would risk nothing. She couldn't blame him.

"Thanks, Rob. Let's have lunch soon. Regardless."

"Sounds good." He sounded a bit suspicious. He hung up.

She sat. She waited. She noticed the streets here, in the highest hills overlooking Lakehaven, were mostly cul-de-sacs, designed to give more privacy. She thought for a moment that if Andy or Julie were following her, it would be hard for them to not be noticed.

She wished she hadn't skipped lunch. She felt a little dizzy and dehydrated. After twenty minutes her phone pinged. It was a text from Rob Radlon: Try calling Jake Curtis now. I vouched for you, please don't mess up. You know I hope your mom is found.

She called DataMarvel and she asked for Jake.

Four rings. "Jake Curtis's office." A young man's voice, brisk.

"This is Mariah Dunning. Mr. Curtis is expecting my call."

"One moment."

Wow, the assistant didn't ask what this was about.

"Ms. Dunning. This is Jake Curtis." He sounded sterner than he had at trivia night. "I resent you intruding into my life. First the bar, now this? I am not interested in any pet theory of yours, and you are not to come around me again, or I'll get a restraining order."

"I am not any kind of danger to you," she said. "Your wife and my mother, Beth Dunning, knew each other socially, and they both disappeared within six months of each other. I think what happened to my mom is tied to what happened to your wife. This may be nothing, or it could be the key to everything."

"If you would like to contact the police, or my lawyers, with any information I'm sure they'd appreciate it."

She wondered how many crank calls he got, asking for money in exchange for hope. "I will do that, of course," she said. "But if we could talk face-to-face..."

"I'm sorry, I can't."

"I spent last night at your mother-in-law's. I slept in Bethany's old room."

"Oh," he said. Now, she supposed, she didn't sound like a typical information peddler.

"Sharon had a fainting spell while I was there, so I ended up staying the night as she refused an ambulance. She thinks you killed Bethany, but I think she's hiding something. And I've spoken, more than once, with Andy Candolet and Julie Santos about your wife's case. I'm not sure they've been completely honest with me." Make him think you're on his side. She decided not to mention she'd seen Andy at his office. "I don't want to talk about Sharon to the police or your lawyers. Not yet. I'm not throwing her under the bus because I don't know what to think. I'll talk, but only to you. I'm sitting on your front step. But if I'm being weird we can meet somewhere else. Or after work. Or at your favorite bar, even though it's not trivia night." She stopped, breathless.

Ten seconds ticked by. She thought, *He's going to call the police on me.* But he said, "Wait for me, Ms. Dunning. I'll be home soon."

He hung up. She sat and waited and wondered what she had unleashed.

She stood up, stretched. The other three houses on the cul-de-sac—the lots were so large, there were only three—had black metal fences enclosing them, but Jake's did not. The house was huge—she guessed it was six thousand square feet. For a man living alone, as far as she knew. He had done very, very well. Brick driveway, a stone mansion built in the Tuscan style, tiled roof. She wandered, trying not to look in the windows. She went around to the backyard: there was a large patio with a built-in outdoor kitchen, and an infinity pool. The site had a great view of the hills of Lakehaven stretching away in the distance, the mansions built in the past several years, the new school, a scattering of empty lots in smaller neighborhoods, the curve of Old Travis Road... the hills. A curve of road by an empty lot. Her gaze locked.

On the empty stretch of land, where once her mother's car had been found...

"We're not doing this now. You're not doing this." A voice behind her, clear and sharp, and before she could turn there was only blackness, nothingness swallowing her whole, and she fell into it.

30

GRASS, COOL AGAINST her face.

A hand on her shoulder.

"Are you all right?" A man's voice.

"Yes," she said, by default, but her voice sounded thick. She opened her eyes. Colors, coming into focus. "Where... where am I?"

"You're in my backyard. I'm calling for an ambulance."

"Am I hurt?" she said.

"I don't see any blood," he said. His face swam into focus. Jake Curtis. "What happened?"

"I was looking at your view... I heard a voice... then nothing. I don't remember. I don't want a doctor. Just... please... help me sit up."

He did. Details became clearer. His face, concerned but also a little wary.

"Are you drunk?" he asked.

"No. I guess I forgot to eat. I... I don't know what happened. Did I faint? Where's my phone?" She patted her jeans pocket.

"Here," he said, and went and picked up her phone, lying a short distance away on the grass.

"I don't... I don't remember if I put it back in my pocket after we talked. I walked around." Did someone take her phone from her and search it? Why? For her texts, her emails, her internet searches. All of it synced to her main computer. If they wanted it, why not steal it? Because a phone could be tracked.

"Here. It's here." He handed it back to her and she slipped it in her pocket. She could have dropped it, then staggered, blacked out. She couldn't remember.

Did someone attack me? She heard a voice. *Someone following me*, she thought. She let her gaze scan the hills again, and the dizziness came back in a rush.

"I am so sorry," she said. "Could I get a glass of water? The view is making me dizzy."

"Of course. I think you ought to get checked out."

She studied the grass. Maybe, if she had an arm flung out as she fell, the phone could have landed there. If not...someone had left it there.

Jake? He looked concerned, not guilty.

"Let's go inside," he said.

* * *

The house, vast and sparsely furnished, wasn't as tidy as Sharon's. She took in details as she walked through the entryway, the grand living area, the kitchen with a large informal dining nook. It looked like a person lived here alone. A pile of laundry was near one door, a haphazard stack of books on a coffee table. The furniture was expensive, but there wasn't enough of it, no art or photos on the walls, so the house looked half-finished. *Like his life*, she thought. Except, on the mantel, a wedding photo of Jake and Bethany, smiling, happy, unaware of approaching fate's heavy footsteps. An iPad, propped up for easy viewing, at one of the dining room table chairs. He probably surfed the web or watched Netflix while eating his solitary dinners. She could smell the faint funk of dishes in the sink that needed to be rinsed and put in the dishwasher.

"Pardon the mess," he said. "I don't have a lot of visitors. I've never quite settled into this house. Like it's a limbo and Bethany's going to come back and tell me to straighten it up. Stupid of me."

It was a naked thing to confess. "So if she returned and asked you would take her back? Even after all this?"

"I'm not a doormat," he said after a moment. "If she's still alive, she doesn't want me. I loved her, and I should have made sure she knew that. I wasn't a very good husband. I'd be better if she'd told me how unhappy she was." He stopped. "Sorry. That was more than you asked. I don't... I don't talk about this. I don't normally have people over here."

"We don't have a lot of company at our house, either." *Our houses are haunted,* she thought, *by people who might be ghosts.*

He said, "You want a water? Or a soda? I'd offer something stronger but that might be a mistake after fainting."

"Water, please, thank you."

He got her water, a cold bottle from a bar refrigerator. She gulped it down. She sat on the edge of a large leather sofa in his den. She tried to steady her nerves, but she felt an absolute humiliation. Here she had called, begged him to come talk to her, and then he'd found her passed out. He really would think she was unbalanced; he might call the police. She imagined Broussard showing up in a cop car and telling Jake all about her accident while hallucinating she'd seen her mother. Humiliating and crushing.

He sat down across from her on a leather ottoman. "You should go to a doctor. There's an urgent care place on Old Travis. I can drive you." His voice was neutral.

"I'm fine now, thank you." And she was. She touched the back of her head; no bruise. Her throat, in case an arm had closed around her and stopped her air: the same, no soreness. She thought of Sharon, half-conscious on her entryway floor. Maybe this is too much and we're just shutting off our brains. She shivered. "I thought I heard a voice behind me, but maybe it was the wind. Or my imagination."

"So. Not really into trivia, I take it." He didn't seem mad. "Poor Martin Van Buren, used and cast aside."

It was the slightest of thaws. "No."

"I think when you've gathered your strength you should go," he said. *Mind made up*, she thought.

"I think we should compare notes."

"I don't have notes," he said. "I'm not trying to figure it all out. That's for the police."

"How can you not want to know?" Her voice shook. She felt sick again.

He said, "Look, my wife left me. I don't know what happened to her after that. My mother-in-law blames me, thinks I somehow got to Houston, found her, and killed her because she left me. I lost a lot of friends over this. I'm entirely innocent. I'm not trying to solve this, I'm trying to keep it from... consuming me." He looked at her, as if surprised by the spill of words. "Is Sharon OK?"

"She's grieving. She's a little lost."

"I'm sure she had plenty to say about me."

Mariah nodded.

"See, lots of people walk away from a spouse. Who walks away from a parent who loves her? This has been the cruelest thing for Sharon."

"You feel bad for her?"

"Yes, of course. She needs someone to blame. I'm it. But she still..." He stopped. "Yes, I feel bad for her."

"Bethany ever mention my mother? Beth Dunning? They would get together at bars like Rancho's and Dos Amigos after work."

He shook his head. "She didn't. I was putting in such long hours—sometimes twenty a day—at the company. I ignored Bethany. I thought I was building a future for us, and instead I was driving her away." He stood. "I have a college friend who lives nearby who's a doctor. If you won't let me drive you to the ER, will you let her take a look at you? Please?"

She wondered if he were worried about liability. "I'm not going to sue you."

"I'm not going to keep talking to you unless she checks you out."

"All right," she said, because it was the only way to keep him talking, and he picked up the phone.

* * *

The doctor—her name was Hannah and she was polite and efficient and very pregnant—probed at a bump on the side of her head. It was a little tender.

"Someone hit me?" Mariah asked.

"I think you hit your head when you fell to the ground."

"She was on the edge of the rock garden," Jake said.

"That might be it. Or a sprinkler head. But you don't appear to have a concussion. I think you're going to have a headache for a few hours, but otherwise you're fine." She stood. "If you feel worse, call your doctor or go to urgent care."

"Thanks."

Jake walked her to the door, and Mariah could hear the softly spoken words: "That bump wasn't nearly enough for someone to have hit her. If she claims that, she's lying."

"I know." And then words she couldn't hear.

The answer stuck at her. She rubbed palms along her jeans.

After a few moments, Jake returned. "I'm sorry I can't help you."

"Your wife asked my mom for a favor. I'm wondering what it is." She showed him, on her phone, the pertinent email between her mom and Bethany. "What could Bethany have learned about her dad? And what is *it* my mom is supposed to keep safe?"

He took a deep breath and sipped at his water. "You know her dad killed himself."

"I know that was the story."

"The story? What, you think Sharon killed him and made it look like a suicide? Why would she? It made their lives so much harder."

"Bethany found out something about her dad, and she asked my mom to keep something for her. Then six months later my mom vanishes. That's the thread we need to find."

"Maybe she finds out her mom played a role in her dad's death. She freaks out. She can't be around her mom, so she leaves town. And then what?"

That really was a question.

Jake was still thinking aloud: "She could have trusted the wrong person in Houston. She was like a teenage runaway who gets in the wrong car. I . . . I can't stand talking about her like this. But . . ."

"And then what, this person finds out my mom has something related to the case? My mom would have come forward to the police if she had information."

He studied the email on her phone screen again. He rubbed at his face.

"Bethany asks her not to say anything. Maybe your mom just kept a promise. Maybe she didn't want to get involved. Maybe someone threatened your mom. Maybe your mom was in touch with Bethany when no one else was." He shrugged. "The what-ifs can kill you."

"I've found no evidence that they were in touch after Bethany went to Houston. And the only reason my mom wouldn't have come forward if Bethany was declared missing was that she knew she was OK. Or that disappearing was what Bethany wanted."

Jake rubbed his eyes.

"Look, you know what it's like to be wrongfully accused. Same with my dad. This has broken him. People have terrorized him. He's innocent, and I have to find out the truth so people will know he didn't do this."

Jake took a long breath. "Why didn't she trust me? I was her husband. If she found out something about her mom...why not tell me?"

"I don't know. What would you have done?"

"Told her we had to call the police."

"There's your answer. Maybe she didn't want to turn in her mother. Or it could have been something else. Something her father was involved in that she didn't want exposed."

"Bethany only spoke about her dad with affection," he said. Ten seconds ticked by. "But she rarely spoke about him."

"Andy came to see you today."

"How do you know that?"

She explained she'd seen Andy while she was dropping off the note. "But he dodged my question on if he was there to see you."

"Yes. He comes around once a month. He wants to work in a startup; he wants free of his aunt. He pesters me for a job. He thinks I owe him."

"Because your wife embezzled money and he kept her from being prosecuted."

"She didn't do that. Of course not," he scoffed. But he glanced away from her, got up, poured himself a glass of water at the den's bar.

"Who did the embezzling, then?"

"Might have been Andy. He'd have access to the accounts. And if he thought for a moment he could get away with it, he would."

"If he's her good friend, he doesn't frame Bethany for stealing."

"Good friend." He arched an eyebrow at her. "Andy is the center of his own universe. The rest of us are just orbiting around him. He knows how to use a friend, not be one."

That left her silent. Jake continued: "Andy could have taken that money. First, he'd have access for his job, and second, that's a family-run company, and their security's a bit lax—passwords on sticky notes on monitors. She had no reason to steal. That I know of," he said. "Or her friend Lizbeth. She left the company not long after Bethany did."

"Lizbeth?" Mariah asked. "Julie told me they were in a writing group together and had been hanging out a lot. I didn't know they worked together. Have you talked to her?"

"Maybe once since Bethany disappeared. She called me, just to say she was sorry and she hoped Bethany would turn up soon."

"Do you have a picture of her? Or did Bethany? Do you know her last name?"

"No. I met her only once or twice. I was busy." His voice went bitter. "Busy, busy, busy."

For a moment they were both silent in the huge, empty house.

"Would you let me look through your wife's papers here? Her computer?"

"She wiped her hard drive and her backup drive and drilled a hole in each before she left. Thorough."

Wow, Mariah thought. *She didn't want to leave a trace. She really was walking away from her life. What was she hiding? Or did the police think Jake had done it?*

"I can tell you that email she sent your mom was from an account I didn't know she had. It wasn't in her backup. I don't know if the police found it. They told me very little."

"Did you hire private investigators?"

"By the time I did, the trail had gone cold."

Mariah got up, despite her headache, and paced the floor. "Why then? Why at that time? Her life is falling apart, she gets accused of a theft, she learns something about her dad's suicide, she asks my mother for a favor, she vanishes. Right before you're going to have a big success, one she should stay here for. And then my mom's gone." Her voice shook. "All my family's suffering is because of Bethany, asking my mother to do something I'm guessing she never should have asked." She made her hands into fists and began to pound the pillows on the couch.

"Hey, hey, calm down."

"Don't tell me to calm down," she said, her voice ragged.

"OK, don't calm down," he said. "But I can tell you one thing. Bethany wouldn't have hurt anyone. Maybe your mother came across as a person she could trust."

"What would she have given her?" Ideas swam in her head: the money, papers, evidence about her father's death. Maybe the DVD? But then why password it—proof of a crime was useless if it couldn't be accessed. And it had her mother's name on it. She didn't even know where to start.

"I don't know." He frowned in thought. "You seem certain there's still someone who's a threat to anyone who digs into this," he said.

"Someone followed my friend Chad—he writes a true crime blog, and he was the first to notice that there were two Beths who had gone missing."

"Chad Chang? Dude calls himself Reveal?"

"Yes, you know him?"

"He was the most persistent requester of an interview." Something changed in his voice. "I always said no. You're a friend of his?"

"We went to high school together. He's not a bad guy, just ambitious."

"He gets web clicks off other peoples' pain. What, he sent you over here to get my wife's computer files?" His voice remained calm, but the annoyance was clear.

"No. No!" This was all going wrong. "Please. Because I found the email, I thought maybe your wife would have some emails with my mom, too. Maybe ones that got deleted on my mom's account. Or would tell us what she entrusted to my mom."

He unclenched his fists. "You could have faked that. I don't know you. You show up at the bar, you show up at my house, you pretend to have been attacked or passed out… " He stopped.

"It's not a lie that my mom is missing. I have no motive. I don't want anything from you except information. And Reveal didn't send me."

"All right," he said, calming down. But for a moment he'd scared her.

31

JAKE TOOK A CALMING BREATH. Mariah took one as well.

"Okay, Lizbeth you asked about. I'll have to go find Bethany's address book. Hold on a second." He vanished upstairs. Mariah went back to the window and looked out to see if anyone was there, watching. No Julie, no Andy. She stayed at the window for a moment longer, then went back to the couch.

He came down with a battered old address book made of faded red leather. "You said Bethany wiped her computer backups before she left. Was that something she knew how to do?" She wondered if her mother might have helped Bethany with that.

"She was tech savvy, yeah. And you can learn to do it with an online search. Any motivated person could manage it. When the police took her computer, I think they thought I'd done it." He cleared his throat. "So, I don't have her cell phone contacts list, but she also kept numbers in this." He handed it to her. She flipped through the pages and found it: Gonzales, Lizbeth. She called the number. She got an automated message—a voicemail but with a man's greeting. His voice was a little creaky; she thought he might be elderly. *We cannot come to the phone right now. Sorry, leave a message.* No name given.

"Hi," she said. "I'm trying to reach Lizbeth Gonzales. My name is Mariah Dunning. You can call me at 512-555-2390. This is in regard to a mutual friend, Bethany Curtis. Please, please return my call. Thank you." She hung up and Jake shrugged.

"Do you know anything about her?"

"No, I really don't. Do you think she matters? They hadn't been friends for long."

"Neither had my mom and Bethany, yet Bethany trusted my mom with something important."

He ran his hands through his hair in frustration. "When your wife leaves you like this, you realize that you didn't really know her. It tears you up, this person you spent your life with. And when she vanishes permanently, you think maybe you did know her. That she wasn't this stranger, and something happened that wasn't supposed to happen."

Mariah couldn't look at him; she didn't want to see his grief. She kept paging through the address book. Her mother wasn't listed.

"I don't talk a lot about this," he said suddenly, as if he hadn't said it before.

She looked up from the address book. His gaze on her was steady. "Do you talk about your mom with people?"

"No. It makes everyone uncomfortable. If I bring her up, or someone else brings her up, I lie. I had a client ask me once, just you know, making conversation over a working lunch, if my parents lived in town. What do you say? My mother went missing and my father was accused of having killed her and disposing of the body? And we had to endure that until the investigation against him was dropped for lack of evidence? I just say, yes, they're here and I change the subject. Doesn't it make dating hard?"

"I don't date," he said after a moment. "How can I? I don't know if my wife is still alive or not."

Here she had thought they would have so much in common, and she'd made a serious misstep. "Of course not. Yes. I understand."

"Did you know women wanted to date me, though? I would get emails." He shook his head. "I suppose they thought I was tragic. Or dangerous. It made zero sense to me." He took another sip of his water. "The police here suspected me, but not like Bethany's family does. Her taking the flight to Houston and being seen in the airport without me took the police pressure off me. But her case got shrugged off. Unhappy wife leaves town."

The silence stretched and finally she said, "What?"

He met her gaze. "I don't normally talk about Beth. I don't even know you. It's hard."

"I probably understand better than anyone you've met since she vanished," Mariah said evenly. He didn't answer, he drank his water, and she waited to see if he would say more.

"What no one wants to say is that Bethany wanted away from Sharon. Sharon hasn't been right since her husband killed himself. Which I get. It's hard. But marrying me...it didn't keep Sharon at bay. She used to invite herself over whenever she felt lonely. I mean, fine, OK, now and then. Not every other night when we're newlyweds. We'd go out with friends and her mother would text her, 'Why aren't you at home? I need you to go to the grocery.' And Bethany didn't like to say no to her. She was her mother; she felt she owed her everything." He ran the edge of his hand along his lip. "I was always second place. I'd told her this couldn't go on, I loved her, but she had to cut the apron strings. She wasn't willing to confront her mom. I guess it was why I threw myself into the startup world so hard, because her mom was always around, encroaching. And Andy..." He stopped. "Holy smoke, I just monologued." He shook his head with a half-smile. "I...I..."

"You haven't had anyone to talk to about all this," Mariah said quietly.

"I don't *need* to talk about it."

She let the silence fill the room, like a therapist might.

Jake broke the quiet. "You want to know what I think happened?"

She nodded, silent still.

"She hadn't had a great life since her dad died. Her two constants before me were her mother and Andy. Her mother hovered. Andy hovered. I could never figure out what his deal was. I think he couldn't accept she wasn't interested in him romantically. I loved her, and I think she loved me, but I was also her escape route. Except, I wasn't. Her mother was still here all the time, and then Bethany took a job working for Andy. She took off when she realized I wasn't an escape, maybe she went off with Andy's money, out of desperation. And I didn't chase her to Houston, but one of them might have. It could have gone wrong. But no one blames them. Everyone blames me. Suspects me."

"So Sharon had a motive. What about Andy?"

He took a deep breath. "I think Andy got obsessed with her when they worked together. I think she took that money from Ahoy, and Andy cleared her name because he was in love with her. I think if anyone lured her away, and if her new life in Houston went wrong, then it was him. The two of them. It's the simplest explanation, and I think it's the right one. But the police never looked hard at him."

She tried her own confessional: "People thought my dad had done away with my mom. I mean, my friends... their parents..." She stopped. "You see a side of people you never dream of when this happens. People abandoned every belief they'd held about him for years. It was like who he'd been meant nothing."

He nodded.

"You said you hired investigators. Did they check out Andy as a possibility?"

He nodded. "I aimed them squarely at Andy. They found nothing. I always wondered if his aunt—she owns Ahoy—"

"Yes, I've met Claudette."

"All the charm of a cobra. But she raised Andy, paid for his college. I could see her paying off my investigators to shield him. I hired two and both quit on me rather abruptly."

She thought of Claudette, reading off Mariah's license plate number to someone.

Jake continued: "When the police found out I'd hired private eyes it was politely suggested to me I was interfering in the investigation."

"Would you show me those files? In case something there relates to my mom?"

He nodded, and she thought, *If he'd done away with Bethany or my mom would he have hired investigators, would he share information?* It didn't make her fully trust him, but she almost breathed out a sigh of relief.

"I have the reports in my safe. I'll go get them."

He returned a few minutes later with a thin bound document from a company called Marston Investigations, with addresses in Austin, Dallas, and Houston. She paged through them. There were photos of Bethany in happier times, arm around Jake's neck, wedding picture, other photos from social events. A detailed tracking of her movements on that last day and details of her withdrawal of a few hundred dollars from her bank account, along with an interview with the teller who had waited on her. Then the details of her flight, a statement from the woman who sat next to her on the plane, a statement from the flight attendant who served her on the very short flight to Houston and hardly remembered her. She handed him back the reports. He took them and set them on the coffee table.

"If you were about to make a ton of money with your company, why would Bethany steal from Claudette and Andy? Why risk it?"

He shrugged. "Because there were no guarantees I would succeed...the company, the public stock offering, it could have all flopped."

"She couldn't wait a few months? Why risk losing so much leaving you then? I mean, why did she leave at all? For what reason?"

"I don't know why."

She felt a sharp, hot pang in her stomach, a bolt of pain in her head. "The answer is in front of us. Your wife and my mom knew each other. We just have to find out what they shared."

He was quiet, then he surprised her. "Are you hungry?" he asked. "I know it's early enough for a senior citizen discount, but I skipped lunch."

"I could, but then I have to go to a support meeting."

"Support meeting?"

"Reveal runs a discussion group of people who were affected by violent crime. I thought I'd try it." Reveal had texted her a reminder earlier today.

"He emailed me about that, too," Jake said, sounding doubtful, given his earlier castigation of Reveal. "But...if you want, we could go to that, too." He cleared his throat. "So dinner, yes?"

She nodded. He's lonely, she thought. Not an instant friendship, but an instant understanding. But not necessarily trust.

Because if she'd trusted him, she wouldn't have waited for him to have his back turned to tear a page from Bethany's address book and tuck it in her pocket.

Because of what she'd seen written there.

32

Craig Dunning waited. He watched. Cars drove by the house, slowing a bit to take in the for sale sign. He could almost imagine the relief of his neighbors. He tried to imagine that at least some of them wished him well with the sale.

The phone calls had started to come about the house. First four from real estate agents asking on behalf of their buyers, trying to set up chances to see the house, leaving messages on the burner phone. Calls from a couple of companies that specialized in teardowns, then putting up a much larger house on the same lot—he had seen their names on signs when the house across the street was a teardown and one downhill from his home, at the very end of Bobtail Drive. Then a call from two different buyers, calling him directly, and one call from a down-the-street neighbor who said, in a gruff voice that was a sorry attempt at a disguise, "Finally you're moving. Finally. I hope your house sells fast, murderer."

Craig didn't delete that message; he kept it. It would remind him what he was facing.

He got in his car and began to drive to a list of addresses he'd made. These were the three Seans who played trumpet in the Lakehaven High School band. He wanted to see if the car he'd spotted with the man taking his picture belonged to one of the players. That would tell him who this was.

The first Sean lived on the outskirts of Lakehaven, in an older neighborhood that featured lots of unfenced backyards, sloping lots, and streets without sidewalks. This neighborhood, Bonaventure, was an old one that hadn't been developed in one fell swoop like some of the other neighborhoods in Lakehaven. Here, from the 1960s onward, houses of all sorts: stone, brick, modern, ranch, and so on, had sprung up like strange, unrelated flowers. There was no homeowners association to enforce architectural consistency. He found the address along a side road, unpaved gravel, with a wood and metal fence surrounding the front yard and lots of brightly colored yard art made from metal and wood. There had been a time that artists flocked to this neighborhood, but it had gotten steadily more expensive as Austin had grown and as Lakehaven's school district reputation soared.

No sign of the car he'd seen—which was a silver SUV, he thought a Ford Explorer although he hadn't seen for sure. This was Sean Perez's house, a senior trumpet player. He stopped and got out of the car. He was unsure of what to do—go up and knock on the door and ask if someone from here drove a silver SUV and had been coming to his neighborhood for walks? He felt stupid. But none of the Seans lived close to his house, so if Sean's dad was the man who had been watching him, then why had he been in the neighborhood? Why had any of them?

He looked at the art: metal sunflowers, a painted windmill. He and Beth had walked through an art display like this once, at a museum fundraiser, full of primitive art. She had hidden behind one of the oversize sunflowers, peeking out, and he remembered with a jolt that she had been pregnant with Mariah then. Suddenly his chest ached.

I miss you, Beth, I miss you every day, and I don't know what to do to make this right. I'm scared. I can't do what I should do.

He stood, lost in thought, suddenly aware that the front door had opened. A woman peered out at him. "Can I help you?" she called.

"I was just admiring your art." He wondered how long he'd been standing there, thinking. Some days it felt like he was losing his mind.

She stared back at him. "Well, you've admired it. Move along." She had a phone in her hand and she raised it, like she was taking his picture.

Like husband, like wife? Why would these people have a grudge against him?

"I'm sorry," he called, with a wave. "I didn't mean to bother you."

He got back into his car, his face burning with shame, and drove off. He'd have to come back later, unless he found the silver car elsewhere.

* * *

The second address—Sean Wagner's—was in a neighborhood off Old Travis called Grand Creek, and while he didn't see a creek, the houses were certainly grand. These were all mansions, built in modern or Tuscan styles to complement the hilly limestone terrain of this part of Lakehaven. There were two cars parked in front, a sleek silver Porsche and a black Range Rover. No stickers on either car and no silver SUV. He thought, *These don't seem like the kind of folks who put a sticker on their ride that advertises their kids' name.* He drove by it three times, and the last time he did so he saw, past the iron fence, a woman getting into the Range Rover. She drove off. He left; he didn't want to be noticed again. Sean Wagner, he decided, wasn't his guy.

* * *

The third address was for a Sean Oberst, and there was something familiar about the boy's photo in the yearbook—something in his face Craig thought he had seen before. The house was modest, in an older section of town, near the old elementary that had once been the heart of Lakehaven.

No sign of the silver SUV, but there was a woman in the front yard, holding up paint samples next to the brick and studying them in the light.

He parked and rolled down his window. "Hello, excuse me, Mrs. Oberst?"

"No," she said. She took a few steps toward him. "Are you looking for her? She's not Mrs. Oberst anymore."

"Pardon me?"

"We bought this house from a woman who used to be Mrs. Oberst, but she remarried."

"Oh, I see. You don't happen to know where they moved, do you?"

Her smile stayed in place. "May I ask why you're looking for them?"

"My daughter has a class with Sean," he said vaguely. "Um, do you know Mrs. Oberst's name now? They're listed in the school directory at this address."

"It's Marshall," the woman said, after a moment. He thought he saw the barest flick of disapproval. "I'm not sure where their new house is."

"Thank you," he said, and he drove off. In the rearview mirror he could see the woman watching him, trying to decide if he was suspicious.

His phone rang. He hit the Speaker button.

"Craig. What are you doing?" Dennis Broussard's voice, tight, angry.

"What do you mean?"

"Woman on Granger Drive over in Bonaventure snaps a picture of you as you are standing and staring at her house. Sends it to us. I recognize it's you. What are you doing?"

"I was standing on a public street," he said. "I admired her yard art."

"You frightened her enough for her to take your picture."

"The art reminded me of Beth." His voice rose, and he choked it back to a normal volume.

"Listen to me. You can't do this."

Craig realized in his anger he'd missed his turn to get back onto Old Travis, the main thoroughfare that wound through Lakehaven. He got on the loop that would take him around Lakehaven.

"Craig. What. Are. You. Doing?"

I'm going the wrong way, Craig thought. He realized then that he was headed for the bridge where the note had threatened to drop a rock. He tensed.

It was just a stupid threat. He'd put up the for sale sign, they had no reason to doubt him now. Idle threat. Plus they couldn't know if he was there, or en route. His concern was ridiculous.

"Craig, are you there?"

On this stretch of the loop there was no immediate exit, no turnaround. A metal railing separated the highways. He had no place to go but under the bridge, driving his missing wife's car.

"I'm here. I'm sorry I scared her. It was nothing..."

It was nothing, I put the house up for sale, the tormentor is off the scent...

He went under the bridge.

See, everything is fine...

"Craig, this is a bad idea..."

He exited under the bridge and the back window exploded, glass shattering, the car veering, Craig fighting for control, swerving wildly, the car roaring toward the railing to the cliff below, his only thought *Mariah Mariah Mariah*, Broussard yelling his name.

33

I KNOW A good Tex-Mex place about ten minutes away. I'm not a great cook, so if you wouldn't mind talking over dinner..."

"Sounds good," she said. "And I need to text my dad and let him know where I am."

"Sure," Jake said. "Of course."

She texted Craig as Jake drove them in his Porsche: I'm fine. I'm going out to dinner with a friend. I'll check in again in a bit. Don't call, I won't answer. She decided not to mention her fainting spell in the yard. She still didn't understand what had happened, and she didn't want to worry him.

She could see the notification that the text had been delivered. But Dad didn't answer in his hovering way. Good. He was giving her needed space.

The restaurant on the border between Austin and Lakehaven was a big local chain she'd heard of but never patronized. Jake parked and they walked in, hearing the distant cry of sirens along the highway. *There must have been an accident to the west*, she thought. She and Dad didn't eat out much—they had both tired of the stares and the whispers and the inevitable empty chair that reminded them of Mom, who was always the most talkative when they were dining. The restaurant wasn't busy this early, except for a few tables of happy hour customers who looked to be far more cheerful than she and Jake felt. They were all having margaritas.

She decided if she had to question this man through dinner and then get through people talking about their feelings she could face it with tequila and Cointreau.

And she needed to call the phone number on the page she'd stolen from Bethany's address book.

The last number in the address book. Added at the end, without a name.

Who added someone to an address book and didn't write down the name? But it was a Houston area code, and Bethany had run to Houston. It was worth a try.

She ordered a top-shelf margarita, and he asked for a beer. When the chips and salsa came, he spoke. "I could see Bethany calling her mom after going to Houston and trying to explain. She would have felt guilty about walking away from her. Maybe she wanted to reassure them that she was OK, since she didn't want to have contact with me. Or she emailed Julie a second time, gave her more information. And then Andy following her to Houston and maybe it went bad." He looked at her. "Andy's alibi for that day she vanished is his aunt. And Julie might protect him. But I got the sense that Julie always resented that Andy paid so much attention to Bethany."

"He wasn't seen at work?"

"No. They were all out of town. All claimed to be at their place down on the Gulf, no phones, no internet. An hour from Houston. Andy runs security not just for that company, but he's like a bodyguard for his aunt. That family is crooked, if you ask me. I always wondered if they transported contraband."

"Any indications Bethany was having an affair?" She decided to be blunt.

"You really don't tiptoe around, do you."

"No."

"It's only fair, then, that you share with me about your mom. So, I answer your question and you answer mine. Since you want to find this pattern."

It was the first time he'd sounded like a tough-minded executive. For a moment she didn't speak. Then she said, "I don't have a nice, reassuring alternate explanation of 'Mom took off to start a new life.' My mom had no reason to vanish, and she's just gone. Without explanation." Except there was an explanation, the barest thread of one. That her mother had done a favor for Bethany Curtis, and it had caught up with her and gotten her kidnapped or killed.

Maybe by the man sitting across from her. He could be asking about her mother not from his own curiosity but to see what she knew—to protect himself. She reminded herself that he had more motive than anyone else. Maybe he didn't want to share his riches. Maybe he didn't want the embarrassment of a partner spiraling out of control. Maybe there is another secret here.

"OK. I'll go first," he said. "No, there were no indications Bethany was having an affair. I'd ignored her, for sure, and the marriage was under some strain, but I loved her and I believed she loved me. We'd had a miscarriage two years ago. We decided we wouldn't try again until I'd launched the business. So getting the business up and running took on a new urgency for me. The business took over every aspect of my life. And if she'd cheated, I think I might have understood, if not approved. But she filled the time with her own interests, like writing, and her work. And her friends that were happy to go party with her. I never much liked bars."

The story of the lost pregnancy jolted her; a parallel to what her father had told her. But Mariah said nothing, and he said, "Your mom. You were close?"

Mariah took a sip of her margarita. She hated talking about it, like words could re-create the horror and fear she'd felt. "Yes, but the day before we fought."

"Over?"

"I had been...inattentive to my grades."

"Her words or yours?"

"Hers. I was having a lot of fun. Not studying. It was unpleasant. I had gotten into a fight with another girl at a party. Over nothing, it was so stupid, it was so embarrassing."

"A physical fight?" he asked.

She felt shame redden her face. "I have a temper, and it got the best of me. Mom told me I was a disappointment." She put the straw back in her mouth, slugged frozen margarita down her throat. "I told her she was a crappy mother who was always gone and cared more about closing deals than time with me. Funny to think some of the times she was gone she was with your wife instead."

"You didn't mean that she was a bad mother."

Why are you doing this, Mom?

Words in her head. His voice cut through the whisper in her brain. "And that day?"

"It's kind of a haze. Some things I remember perfectly, and others are like they're on the other side of a grease-smeared window. Does that makes sense?"

"Perfect sense," he said. "It's the same for me. And no one believes it."

She stabbed the straw back into the margarita. "This is what my father told me: they had a normal morning, got up, breakfast together, both left for work. The night before she called me at my apartment down by UT to see if I was feeling better. I'd been sick, really sick, with a virus, but she assumed at first it was a hangover." Her voice broke for a minute. "I was crying, I was so sick with it. Fever, chills, that feeling when you might hallucinate at any minute. Mom felt terrible for not believing me at first and she told me to come home and let her take care of me. I remember saying 'Yes, please, can I come home?' I was taking painkillers for the aches. I was already on meds for anxiety because we'd been arguing. Probably overmedicated." She took a breath. "I hardly remember driving home, and it's only twenty minutes. I wish I hadn't been on the meds. Everything would be clearer, right?"

He nodded after a moment.

She continued: "I came home, went straight to bed, woke up early the next morning, took more meds because I still felt awful, and went back to sleep. My dad works downtown. He had the longer commute, so he tended to leave first in the morning. He did. He said he kissed her goodbye. We know the rest from her digital trail. And from witnesses. She stopped at a Starbucks for a latte, chatted with another mom she knew from volunteering at my old high school. She got to work at her normal time, around eight. She had a sales meeting at eight thirty with the VP of sales." Her voice wavered. "Nothing special, reviewing accounts, sales goals. She mentioned she'd called home later that morning, talked to me. I was at the house, in my old bed, sleeping. She offered to come home and fix me soup...I told her I could do it." She bit down on her own lip. "If I had said yes, let her mommy me, she would have come home and none of this would have happened, but I just wanted to sleep."

"You can't think that way," Jake said. "You cannot."

Revisiting that day was like walking over shards. She forced herself to continue. "Mom then responded to emails, she made some phone calls to prospects, setting up appointments for the next week when she was heading to Dallas. She went to another meeting on a new product plan. I've learned she had an argument with my dad on the phone, denying that she was having an affair—the company CIO told me this, and she made reference to meeting my dad somewhere. She told the sales team assistant that she was heading out for lunch, but she didn't mention going with anyone. Sometimes she came home for lunch. There wasn't a lunch appointment on her schedule. She got in her car and she left. I think everyone assumed she came home to check on me. But she didn't. The office missed her because she had one meeting that afternoon, and it wasn't like her to miss. I woke up when Dad got home. He wasn't feeling well either, but wasn't alarmed because Mom often worked late on proposals. He sat with me and rubbed my back; I slept a lot. When he hadn't heard from her he started to get worried. Called her boss, kept texting her phone. He went to look for her at an empty lot they own off Cliffside, because sometimes she went there to think, for the quiet. He came home and said she wasn't there, but her car was, and it scared me so bad. I was so sick, but I went back with him to look for her. Like maybe she was mad at him and was hiding in the woods, I remember thinking that. It was all sideways, like a dream. I was still so feverish Dad took me home and called the police and finally got the chief to listen to him, that something was wrong." She steadied her voice, but Jake had to lean forward to hear her words. "No sign of blood or struggle at the scene. We would have seen it. The area's wooded, with cliffs, and it was searched, thoroughly. The houses nearby, either no one was at home or no one heard anything suspicious. Major news coverage. Still no sign of her. Of course they suspected my dad."

She stopped and drank the margarita. "How about the day Bethany left you?"

"Bethany had been stressed out by the accusation at work, and she was drinking a lot more than she ever had before. Sometimes I'd come home late, and she wouldn't be there. She'd get back an hour later, drunk, having gone out clubbing with friends. Sometimes she'd take a rideshare home, and she could barely stand."

"She told Julie she thought someone had drugged her at least once."

"The fight at the bar. Yes. Lizbeth said there was a guy who might have slipped something into her drink. Lizbeth said she'd take better care of her, watch over her more. I thought this partying would all stop once I'd taken the company public. The pressure of launch would be off me, and I could take a step back. Then we could both catch our breath. And I thought she was numbing herself to the miscarriage.

"That morning she told me when I got back from my run that she was leaving me." He took a deep breath. "She didn't say the word *divorce*, just that we needed a break. I was stunned. I don't know how to describe it. It was like I'd just woken up from a long sleep and the world had changed. I had done all this for her, this company, to give her a great life, and she didn't want it. It was an awful, horrible realization that I'd done everything wrong. And how do you fix it when she's packed a bag and she's made up her mind? I didn't even know what to say. Usually I have a plan. A strategy. I had nothing."

"You can't live life according to a strategy."

"I know. She wouldn't discuss it. Our marriage was over, but no discussion. I felt like an anvil had hit me from the sky. She asked me to leave, so she could finish packing. She said she'd call me in a few days to let me know where she was. I left. I shouldn't have, but what was I going to do, stop her physically from leaving? Beg her to talk to me?" He shook his head. "I went to my office. I was like a robot. I tried to have a normal day. I literally couldn't function. After an hour I left."

"And went home."

"Yes. But she was already gone. The house was empty. I noticed she had taken a bag she took when she flew. So...I have an app on my phone that tells me when there's a credit card charge on my Visa, and I activated it. I thought, at least I'll know where she's going if she buys a ticket."

"Why wouldn't she just take her car somewhere?"

"Oh, because she said she was heading to the airport and she'd get a rideshare. She was leaving the car I'd bought her with me. But someone else must have taken her to the airport. There was no rideshare purchase on her credit card to the airport."

What if Mom took her? she thought. "Why fly to Houston? Why not drive? It's only three hours."

"I assumed she was going to fly on to somewhere else. Maybe she hadn't decided yet. Or take a shuttle from Hobby to Intercontinental." That was the larger airport in Houston. "You can get to anywhere in the world from Intercontinental."

Jake continued: "I couldn't stay in the house. Couldn't bear to be there with the memories of her. I have a place that belonged to my folks out in Marble Falls; I drove out there. In a daze. I honestly barely remember driving it. I got there. We always had food in the freezer, and a bunch of beers were left over from the last weekend we'd spent there. I opened up a beer and sat on the couch and I started drinking. I started making lists. Like what I could have done differently versus what I would do to win her back." He shook his head. "Lists. My wife left me and I made lists. Pathetic."

"Did you want her back?"

"Then? Of course," he said.

"Really? She had been accused of theft. That had to be embarrassing for you, maybe even bad for your prospects of launching the company."

"That never made it into the news. It was a non-event." His voice grew tight.

Had the threat of bad publicity given Andy some kind of control or leverage over both Bethany and Jake? "So you pounded beers."

"Yes. I got the alert that she'd charged a ticket to Houston on Southwest to the Visa card. I didn't know why she was going there. I tried to call her. She wouldn't answer. I left her voicemails. She never called back."

"Why Houston? Sharon seems clueless as to why she went there."

"Well, her friend Lizbeth was from there originally."

"She was?"

"Yeah. I thought they might have gone together. Maybe for a long girls' weekend, and all would be fine when she got back. But it was just the one ticket. And later when I talked to Lizbeth she said she hadn't seen her that day. She has no reason to lie."

"Did she go straight to the airport?"

He shook his head. "There were two hours between her leaving the bank and her showing up at the airport."

"You think she met someone?"

My mom, Mariah thought. Could she have met Bethany before Bethany went to Houston? Why?

"And so then, I got drunk at my grandparents' place. I tried to call her. Nothing, just voicemail. I kept drinking. I made a frozen pizza. I texted my assistant that I was going to be out the rest of the week, no explanation. I watched TCM"—she fought the urge to smile; it was her favorite channel, too—"and I went to sleep. I woke up, I tried to call Sharon, thinking maybe she's heard from Bethany or she knows why this has happened, there's no answer. I drank some more, I slept through the night." He cleared his throat. "The next day, I'm hungover as hell. Sharon called me back, tells me that she hasn't heard from Bethany but that Bethany told her she was leaving me. I raged at Sharon for not telling me, which was crazy, because of course her loyalty is to her daughter. She accused me of being a terrible husband. She'd never turned on me before; we always got along. That was over, this was clearly my fault and it would be forever."

"Sharon needed an explanation," Mariah said. "You're her pattern. You're her reason. So she hadn't heard from her?"

"She said she hadn't." Jake ran the back of his hand along his bottom lip, as though wiping his chin clean. "We weren't really, you know, worried yet."

"So what did you do?"

"I didn't want to see anyone. Explain to anyone that she'd left me. My phone was filling with messages from my investors, from my exec team, and I was deleting them all unheard. I couldn't even care. I went swimming in the lake, which was freezing. I watched stuff on Netflix. I drank beer. I waited for her to call me. After another day, and no word, I called Sharon again. Sharon said she hadn't heard a word from her. She was starting to panic."

"So did you call her friends?"

"I called Julie and Andy. Just begging them to tell me if they'd heard from her, if she was all right. Oh, Andy loved that. He loved me having to beg." A sour edge now in his voice. "Andy had the nerve to say to me, 'She stole money from me, and now she's gone.' And Julie..." He stopped, shook his head.

"What?"

His gaze met hers. "She told me that she thought Bethany had lost her mind. She kept saying what a great guy I was, Beth didn't deserve me, blah blah, did I need anything, did I want to have dinner so we could talk, all kind of weirdly coy, and I thought, what the hell, are you hitting on me two days after my wife's deserted me?" He shook his head; his face was pale. "I decided I had to be misreading her."

"What about Lizbeth?"

"I only met her twice. I thought she was kind of cool but weird. One time she had a blue wig, the other time white. Like white as snow. But...she was there for Bethany when I wasn't." Bitterness in his voice.

"And then Lizbeth dropped out of your life."

"She was never in mine. She was in Bethany's."

"And you didn't talk to my mother."

"I frankly didn't know your mother existed."

"And then the police started looking for your wife..."

"Well, after three days, really, maybe she's not going to call me, but when there was no contact with her mom, Sharon and I got frantic. Then they reviewed the security cameras. The cameras lost track of her in the airport. No camera caught her in a parking garage or at a car rental counter. The trail ran cold in Houston."

"So, someone picked her up. Or she changed her appearance."

"Why would she even care about the security cameras..." he started and then stopped. "You think she *planned* on vanishing into thin air."

"She might worry you would be looking for her."

"Sometimes I wondered if she really did take the money at Ahoy. And ran."

"You still wear your wedding ring," she said.

"Yeah."

"But you wouldn't take her back."

"Well, I'm pretty sure she no longer wants me, so that's a moot point. I don't want her. Not after what she did to me, her mother." He was taking up for Sharon, when Sharon always attacked him.

"That woman at the bar that met you on trivia night. Are you dating her?"

He glanced down at his plate, then back at her. "No. She's a friend. She might want to be more than that but...people don't understand what you've gone through. I can't just snap my fingers and be over what happened and ready to date. It's not like a normal breakup."

Mariah felt an odd sense of relief. She pushed the feeling away.

"So," Jake said. "What do we do?"

"We dig. We find what happened to them."

"Show the police that email."

"They're fixated on my dad. He and the Lakehaven chief have an unpleasant past. I need more proof."

He ate his last forkful of food, and verde sauce spilled on his shirt. "Excuse me," he said, and headed toward the restroom, dabbing at the stain.

Mariah pulled out the phone and the stolen page, and she dialed the unknown number from the address book.

Two rings, then an answer. A woman's voice. "Hello?"

"Hello?"

"Who's calling?"

"My name is Mariah Dunning. I'd like to know who this is."

"I don't know you. I'm not giving you my name."

"Please. I'm trying to find out how you are connected to Bethany Curtis. Your number was in her address book. What's your name?"

More ticks of silence. "Penny."

The name of the girl in the old photo. "Penny," Mariah repeated.

"Bethany called me once, but I don't really know her."

"Why did she call you?"

"Our families knew each other when I was a kid. She was writing something about her childhood. About her father. But I don't really remember them as family friends. And my parents have passed, so I really couldn't help her."

"This is a Houston number."

Another pause. "Oh, yes, I work and live in Houston."

"Is that where your families knew each other?"

"Yes," she said after a moment.

Sharon had lied to her. But Julie said she thought the Blevins family hailed from Chicago.

"I'm sorry, I couldn't help her, and I don't think I can really help you," Penny said.

Mariah didn't want her to hang up. "Her father killed himself."

"So she said. Like I said, though, I didn't remember much about them."

"Holy I. That was written on your picture I found."

"Oh. Well, Holy I was our school. Holy Innocents. But I only went to preschool with Bethany. They moved." Four beats of silence. "Where did you say this picture was?"

"Inside a book in Mrs. Blevins's house."

"How funny. I guess Mrs. Blevins is one for keeping old photos."

"It was a newspaper photo. You were maybe four. Why were you in the newspaper?"

More silence. "I won an art contest at the preschool. I think my picture was in the school paper. Back when they had school papers. I can't help you. Please don't call me again."

"Do you know where Bethany is? Did she come to Houston to see you?"

"No and no." She paused. "Look, she said she's writing a story or a novel or something that touched on suicide's effect on families. I think she was calling people from her father's past just to see what they could tell her. But I barely remember her dad, and like I said, my parents are gone. They could have helped her, but I couldn't. I'm sorry, I've got to go. Goodbye." Penny hung up.

On her phone Mariah searched for "Houston Holy Innocents." She clicked through. It was an Episcopal church and school in west Houston, close to the suburb of Katy. She went to its website. Nothing unusual. A big church.

She didn't know Penny's last name. She searched for "Hal Blevins Houston." She got a few hits, but nothing that seemed to match the situation—these were all men who were much older, weren't connected to Sharon or Bethany.

Jake came back to the table and she closed her phone.

"Hey, um, are Sharon and Bethany originally from Austin?"

"They've been here since Bethany was little. Before that they lived in Chicago."

"I found out they lived in Houston, too, when Bethany was little."

"Sharon told me specifically Bethany had no reason to go to Houston." His voice went quiet.

"That's a lie."

Her phone buzzed with a text. From Sharon. I thought about what you said and I think I'll go to that support group tonight. Maybe it will help me. Are you going?

She stared at the screen. What would happen if Sharon and Jake were face-to-face? What cracks might show?

"Anything important?" he asked.

"No," she said, slipping the phone back into her purse. "I think Reveal's meeting will be interesting, though."

34

The rock had blasted through the rear window. A second earlier and it would have crushed the roof and killed Craig. He was shaken but he was angry.

How? How did they know he was there? Somehow his location was traced. His phone. Or something in Beth's red Mercedes.

Somehow someone knew and was ready to strike at him. No more idle threats. They wanted him dead or scared and running. He was scared now. For himself, for his daughter.

"Who knew that you were driving that route?" Broussard asked. They sat in an examination room at an ER center in Lakehaven, where the ambulance had taken Craig to be checked. He was uninjured except for a few cuts from flying glass along his scalp.

But he couldn't stop shaking, trembling. He had nearly died. He couldn't die now and leave Mariah alone to face whoever was threatening them.

And really, who had a motive? Broussard did. Broussard hated him, blamed him, tried to turn Craig's own daughter against him. Broussard could have done this, with help. He kept his voice neutral.

"No one. I told no one. I didn't even plan to drive that way. I got distracted talking to you and missed my turn and just kept going because it's a pain to turn around when I could just loop back over to Old Travis."

"So someone was tracking you."

"Even if they were...how could they have gotten to the bridge so fast with a rock. This is crazy. It has to be random." He stared down at his lap. *Unless it was you, Dennis. Can't the police track people on their phones?* He had seen that on a television show. *All you need, Dennis, is one person helping you. Just one.*

"Well, there could have been two of them," Broussard said. "One in communication with the other, who is on the bridge. Someone could have been following you."

"On the off chance I drove that way? I don't get out of the house often. You know that."

"Maybe they thought you were Mariah."

"She never drives her mother's car. Neither do I."

"Why didn't you sell it?"

"Because it's Beth's car," he said, as if that explained it all.

"If they've been watching you, Craig, then maybe they knew what you were driving."

"And tracked me how?"

"Taped under the fender we found a very cheap phone. Someone could call the number and it would give off a signal that could be tracked with an app."

Craig pressed his palms to his eyes.

"You said someone left rocks in your driveway. With messages."

Craig lowered his hands from his face. "Yes."

"Were the rocks similar? Is this the same kind of rock?" He showed Craig a picture on the phone of the rock, lying in the backseat, the shattered rear window framing it.

"It's similar."

"Listen to me, Craig," Broussard said. "I am treating this as an attempted murder. You said you'd been threatened."

"They want me to move. Whoever it is. They just want me gone." He stared at Broussard. *You know what that's like, don't you? To want me gone. To want me dead.*

"We're trying to reach Mariah, but she's not answering her phone," Broussard said. "Where is she?"

"Off chasing down leads, like she said she would. It's delusional," he said.

"Tell her I want to talk to her. Now I have to go find who did this to you and how they did it."

Craig stood. "May I go?"

"Yes. I'll have one of my officers drive you home."

"No thanks. I'll try Mariah again, or call a rideshare." He had already decided he would call a car rental company. He wasn't going to be stuck at home. If it wasn't Broussard, then it was someone else, and he had to be able to find them.

"If this was not a random attack, then I want to be sure you're safe," Broussard said.

"Right. Of course." Craig got up and left without another word.

* * *

Broussard watched, from his window, as Craig waited in the parking lot. Five minutes later a rideshare sedan pulled up and he got in. Not Mariah.

So where was she?

He could sense the suspicion coming off Craig. He wanted to say, *If I wanted you dead, you would have been dead months ago.* It wouldn't have been helpful.

Carmen Ames, his department's detective, peered into the office. "The press is asking for a conference on the rock incident."

"Schedule it in an hour, please. I want to ask you something."

She stepped in and shut the door.

"Was this really an attack?" Broussard asked.

"What?"

"Mariah Dunning could have been on the bridge. She could have dropped the rock."

"It seems pretty unlikely they would stage this. He could have been killed. There was a phone taped under his fender."

"That could be a red herring they put there. But the two of them . . . it's very much them against the world. I can't imagine the pressures they're both under. So maybe they think it gets them sympathy. And misdirection, get us looking for someone out there who is targeting Craig rather than keeping our focus on him. If he draws Mariah into his cover-up, it binds her closer to him. He must be terrified that eventually she'll talk. I'm not sure that this whole thing about her mounting her own investigation isn't just a cover to protect her father. Or protect her image of him."

Carmen said, "She could have killed him, though."

"It's equally challenging that someone is tracking him to this degree," Broussard said. "Why? Let's say, as a hypothetical, our rock dropper is Beth's killer and Craig is innocent. Why even come back around for Craig? How is he a threat?"

"He knows something."

"What could keep him silent about his wife's case?" He shook his head. "If you'll go arrange the press conference, please."

She nodded and left.

Broussard sat down at his desk and opened up a window on his computer.

Two years ago, there had been a spate of rocks dropped from bridges onto Interstate 35 in the Austin area. A driver was killed, several terrible accidents resulted. The perpetrators—a group of kids—were finally caught, prosecuted, and convicted. Broussard had decided that this kind of random terrorizing wasn't going to happen in Lakehaven. So, he'd had cameras installed on the bridges in the city limits, including the one over the loop. He could remotely access the footage. He watched it, backing up the video feed to five minutes before the rock had crashed through the back of Craig's car.

The bridge was empty. Then movement. A tall figure, walking into view, with a coat on, and a hood pulled low over the face. He could see the shape of a mouth, not much more on the face. Carrying a rock in one hand, holding a phone in the other. Phone up so the screen could be watched. Glancing around. Arm extended from the bridge.

The rock dropped. The person ran off, eyes to the ground, avoiding the glance of the camera.

Mariah? He rewound and watched the recording again. He thought the person was about her height. But wouldn't Mariah have waited a moment to ensure her father was OK, if this was a stunt? The person had dropped the rock and hurried immediately away.

But the phone screen, being watched, as the rock was dropped. This wasn't random. This was someone tracking and targeting Craig.

And Craig wouldn't talk. Why?

He watched it a third time. Saw something. On the wrist of the rock dropper. He zoomed in. He could see a watchband on the wrist. Unusual pattern in it—the links forming a pattern of silver diamonds.

Broussard tried Mariah again. Still, there was no answer.

35

REVEAL'S SUPPORT MEETING was at an Episcopal church in the oldest part of Lakehaven, which dated back before Lakehaven was incorporated as a city. The church itself was small, pretty, stone, as if it had been dropped from an English village among the oaks and the hills.

"What have your dealings with Reveal been like?" he asked as he parked the car.

"I knew him, slightly, at school," she said. "Then he wrote about my mom's case." She glanced around the lot. She saw a few people walking into the church but didn't see Sharon. She felt guilty about this, but she wasn't going to warn them. She was going to lie and say the text hadn't come through. She saw she had some texts and missed calls but she turned off the muted phone.

"I still have reservations about Reveal, but I think this group might be a good idea. People who get it." He glanced at her.

"I hope it helps," she said.

* * *

Chad stopped them as they entered the room. He was in his white generic football jersey with REVEAL in black, the logo of the website on his chest, wearing white-framed glasses that made him look slightly ridiculous.

"You're here? Together?" He seemed weirdly pleased.

"Yes," Mariah said. "We thought we'd compare notes."

"Oh, this is fantastic. Because I want to highlight your cases on the show." He actually rubbed his hands together in glee and she reached out and stopped him.

"It's a done deal?" Mariah said at the same time Jake said, "Show?"

"We're so close. Hollywood close, which means hands just need to be shaken and it's done." He cleared his throat. "Jake, hi. We've never met, but of course I know who you are."

"Of course," Jake said, glancing at Mariah.

Chad continued: "I would love to be able to interview you on the show. Will you please consider it?"

"I don't know."

"Think of how wide an audience it could reach. Someone who might know what happened to your Beth. And your Beth, too, Mariah."

"I'll think about it," Jake said.

"Jake, will you go grab us seats," Mariah said. "I need to talk to Reveal for a minute."

Jake nodded and walked in.

"You got him to talk with you. That's excellent," Reveal said. He did a thumbs-up.

"Have you been followed again?" she asked.

"Maybe," he said. He peered at her over the top of the glasses.

"It was a yes or no question."

"I told the producers that I was hot on a couple of cases and that I'd been followed...as far as I know it's true. They are so excited. So, what have you found out?" A touch of greed was in his voice.

His attitude had changed since their dinner. If he hadn't talked about the TV show, she might have told him. But he would just take what she'd learned and turn it into part of his pitch. And this was her mother, and Sharon's daughter, and Jake's wife. It wasn't fuel for his career. "Not very much."

"Every detail matters to me, Mariah."

"I...I'm just talking to people." If she told him that the two

Beths did know each other and one had asked a mysterious favor of the other before vanishing, he'd run with the story. Because he would have been the first to ask about a connection, even if for the wrong reason. He had been ahead of the police. This new desperation to land this TV show was coming off him like heat with a fever. She would wait.

"You know, the whole reason you're talking to people is me," he said, a bit of iron in his voice. "I put the idea in your head that these cases could be connected, and I think you're holding back on me."

"I know. And I thank you, but I really don't have anything else to tell you. I promise I will."

"All right," he said. He put a smile on his face. "It's just going so well, Mariah, I want this so badly."

"I hope you get what you want, Chad." She gave him an awkward hug and went in to find a seat, feeling a sense of relief that Sharon hadn't shown up yet. There was enough drama as it was.

* * *

It was strange to think of a support group for people who had lost someone and never gotten an answer. It wasn't that common, surely? Yet there were nearly twenty people gathered in a circle at the meeting room. Mariah scanned their faces: a mother and a daughter (the resemblance was unmistakable), an older man in sunglasses and a battered cowboy hat, a heavyset man who looked like an ex–football player, a woman who wore a shirt that read REMEMBER ANNIE, a pair of women who held hands in solidarity, an elderly couple who looked crushed under their grief.

A club no one wanted to join.

Mariah sat next to Jake. He gave her an encouraging, brief smile.

Reveal stood at the edge of the circle. "I want to thank you all for coming. We're all here because you are dealing not only with a terrible loss but with the uncertainty of knowing what happened to your loved one. You are in the zone of the unsolved."

The zone of the unsolved? Mariah glanced around at the others.

They all watched Reveal, hanging on his words. She had never thought of her life in that way. Yes, it felt like a limbo, but you had to keep slogging through it. Who talked this way?

A guy pitching a TV show.

And that was when Sharon Blevins walked in. She was embarrassed to be late, Mariah could see, and she hurried to an empty chair on the circle, sitting as primly as in a pew, nearly directly across from Mariah. Her hair and her clothes were immaculately styled. She risked a quick smile at Mariah and then she saw Jake Curtis. The smile died.

Something came into her eyes that tightened the skin on Mariah's face. She heard a sound from Jake, something more than a sigh, less than a groan. She glanced at him; he wasn't looking at Sharon, but at the floor.

Mariah waited for Sharon to leave, to stand and point an accusing finger, anything. Instead she stayed in place, looking shaken, and her mouth trembled when she met Mariah's gaze—which was somehow worse.

Reveal, watching this all, cleared his throat and kept going. "I'm not a counselor, I'm a connector. I can't make you feel better, but I can make you feel less alone." She glanced up and his gaze was on her.

Mariah decided right then and there she would not speak. Surely he wouldn't call on people.

"Does anyone have any developments on their loved one's case?" Reveal asked.

She tensed, lest Jake raise his hand and talk about the connection between the cases, or Sharon rise to speak, but Sharon kept staring at Jake and Jake kept staring at the floor. She stared at his hand, resting on his leg. His wedding ring in place. She thought Sharon must see it, too.

One of the men—the one who looked like an ex–football player and wore a name tag that read BUDDY—raised his hand. "I went to a psychic," he said, sounding almost embarrassed. "I thought it would be dumb. I mean...if being psychic was true, wouldn't they all be rich from the stock market?"

There was, to Mariah's surprise, soft laughter. This didn't seem like a laughing crowd. After her mother had vanished people always looked at her oddly if she laughed, even if she smiled. As though she'd lost the right. As though she'd done something unnatural in showing an emotion other than confusion or grief. She remembered a dinner out with her father and them sharing a memory of her mother over the appetizers at Chili's, laughing because Mom would have laughed, retelling a story where Mom fell into the waters of the Florida keys trying to snag a fish, and people looking at them as if they had no freedom to smile. Like grief was a permafrost. She had started to raise a finger toward one table and Dad had caught her hand, closed it in his. They didn't go out to eat again for months, and they never went to that Chili's again.

She pulled her gaze up from the floor, studied the others while the big burly guy described his visit to the psychic. Sharon wasn't staring at Jake right now. She was dabbing tears from her eyes with a tissue.

"My name's Buddy. Well, my daughter Kimberly vanished ten years ago. She was working the graveyard shift at a convenience store near Buda"—this was a small town south of Austin—"and she disappeared during her shift, and no one's seen her since. And this psychic lady, she said that whoever took Kimberly was someone that she knew, at the least she'd met them. And I think maybe she's right. The police looked at her boyfriend, her ex-husband, her coworkers, but someone could have gotten obsessed with her, maybe a customer. Maybe a regular. It's a busy store. And Kim was friendly, that's why she was good at retail, she saw the best in people"—his voice wavered—"and she would have been friendly to someone who might have read it wrong, misunderstood friendliness for interest in him..."

He stopped. "But it's not like I can go back to the police with this. It's not new; it's not real. They still have her file open. Only because I keep calling." He stopped. "I thought the psychic could tell me where...she might be found." He was careful not to say *remains* or *body*. "She has to be somewhere. I need to know."

"Why did you give yourself false hope?" Jake asked. "I mean, seriously, a psychic?"

Mariah glanced up quickly at Jake, thinking his words unkind.

Buddy met his gaze. “Why not? I’ve tried everything else.”

“Our hope lies in science and forensics, not charlatans,” Jake said.

“This is Jake,” Reveal said. “His wife went missing.”

“Science and forensics have done nothing to find my daughter,” Sharon said, staring at her son-in-law. “I could unload science on him and he’d still lie.” She turned to Buddy, sitting next to her. “My daughter’s missing, too, and that’s her husband sitting there, and I think he’s responsible.”

Mariah could feel the anger spike in the room.

Reveal held up a hand. “Y’all. Mrs. Blevins, thank you for coming tonight. All are welcome. Mr. Curtis, I’m glad you’re both here. Obviously, disappearances can bring families closer in their grief, but they can also tear families apart.”

Mariah thought it sounded like a lead-in to a panel discussion. This was starting to go wrong.

“Where is she, Jake?” Sharon said.

“If I knew, I’d get her back here,” Jake said.

“You hid her real good when you got rid of her,” she said. She looked around the room and then she seemed to freeze for a moment, looking past Jake and Mariah, blinking, and then suddenly going quiet.

“I didn’t do anything to her,” Jake said. “I came here to try to come to peace with this, not be accused.” He stood.

“Mariah got you to come here, didn’t she? I warned you about him, Mariah, but I can see that was useless. Is she peddling this theory to you, that her mom’s and my girl’s vanishing are related? I’m sure you loved that. Anything to get you off the hook.”

“They knew each other,” Jake said. “Mariah has the proof. Yell at me all you want.” He looked at the group. “My wife and her mom were friends. We didn’t know, and they both went missing and yet she”—he pointed at Sharon—“still insists the bad guy must be me.”

“That’s huge news,” Reveal said into the shocked quiet. “I would have loved to have known this earlier.” He glared at Mariah. “Thank you for sharing, Jake.”

"Chad..." Mariah started to explain but he held up a hand.

Reveal said, "I did a podcast on Mariah's mom's case. Episode 89. The podcast for the case of Mrs. Curtis is Episode 75." She thought he added that for the group's benefit, in case any of them wanted to download them. He knew the number, off the top of his head. Mariah closed her eyes.

Sharon shook her head at Reveal. "You encouraged this theory. This is your fault."

"Mrs. Blevins, I only am trying to get to the truth."

"Truth? You picked up on a coincidence of names, and now you're giving the main suspect in my daughter's case a way to muddle the truth. So what if they knew each other? It doesn't prove a single thing. No. No. I thought this was going to help me tonight"—her voice broke—"and I thought this girl was on my side, and she's just a user like you." Sharon stood up, shaking. She looked again, over to the left, and Mariah saw she was looking at one of the men—an elderly man with a beard who wouldn't meet her gaze. "I can't do this. I hope you all find your loved ones. And I hope you never have anyone like these two in your lives."

"Mrs. Blevins, please wait. I want to talk to you..." Reveal said. "Please don't go."

"Talk to me about what? I have nothing to say."

Reveal seemed to realize he was making this plea in front of a crowd. "I would like to call you later. Please. It's pertinent to your daughter's case."

Sharon saw it. She almost laughed. "What? Why? To be on your television show? Oh, no. No. Not in a million years."

"They knew each other," he said. "It wasn't Jake."

"It still could have been him. Maybe he took your mother, too, Mariah." Her voice had turned into a hiss of darkness.

"I can't listen to her ravings," Jake said. "Excuse me." He got up and walked out of the parish hall.

"Sharon..." Mariah said. "All I am trying to do is to help you. Your daughter...this wasn't about her marriage."

"You can't let him fool you. He's smart. But you have to be smarter."

"The show," Reveal said, trying to get the conversation back in line, "it's going to be called *American Unsolved.* Each week another new unsolved case will be highlighted. I fly out next week to shoot the pilot."

The group applauded. Mariah kept her hands in her lap.

Reveal held out his hand. "Sharon, go out there with me. Please. Tell your story to the world. Help bring your daughter home."

She looked again at Mariah, at the bearded man, at Reveal, and she turned around and left without a word.

"So who wants to share next? Catherine?" Reveal asked, trying to sound calm, and a woman began to talk about the agony of her missing grown son, vanished in Holland, another soul trapped in the black void.

* * *

Mariah got to the parking lot in time to see Sharon bolting past Jake, who stood near his car, looking at his phone. Sharon stopped next to him. She slowly turned to Jake, as if she had gathered her courage.

"Where is she? Where is my girl?"

"I don't know. I wish I did."

Sharon slapped him. A hard blow across the face, then made her hand into a fist and drove it into his shoulder. He didn't move.

"Sharon, stop." Mariah caught her hand. "Bethany asked my mom to keep something for her before she left. I think it had to do with your husband's suicide," Mariah said, her voice low. She didn't want Reveal following them out in the lot and hearing this.

"What?" It was like the life went out of Sharon. She nearly sagged in Mariah's grip.

"What happened to your husband? Who is Penny? Did you come from Chicago or Houston?"

Sharon stared at her. Under the perfect makeup, the perfect hair, Mariah could see something break in her. Sharon, with great dignity, pulled herself free. "I don't know what delusion you have spun for yourself. But I called and talked to someone in Lakehaven, and they'd heard from a cop there you hallucinated seeing your mother. *Hallucinated.* At a mall. And you chased her and caused a car wreck. You're a menace. You've been covering for your father. You have to invent this story about my daughter so you can stand to live with your dad. I tried to help you. I felt sorry for you. I thought you understood. But you're like everyone else, wiping their feet on my daughter's memory. That she was a drunk or a thief or a bad wife when she wasn't."

"Sharon..."

"Don't ever come around again. I let you sleep in her bed."

Sharon walked to her car and got in and drove off. Jake stood beside her in silence. Mariah stepped away from him, her face in her hands.

* * *

The meeting broke up a few minutes later—the drama had ruined it. Mariah wanted to bolt, yet she wanted to talk to Reveal, to tell him she would update him tomorrow. Jake walked over to talk to Buddy (Mariah hoped it was to apologize), and Reveal hurried toward her as the group dispersed in the lot, shaking hands, giving pats on the back.

She looked for the bearded man. He was gone.

"That guy...the older guy, with the beard," she said to Reveal. "Where did he go?"

"He left by the other door, shortly after you did."

She hadn't seen his car leave, so he must have parked on the other side. "Who was he?"

"Don't know, had not seen him here before."

"Sharon seemed to have a reaction to him."

"Thanks for the Sharon warning," he said, anger in his voice. "I really needed to make the pitch to her and Jake separately. You ruined that."

"What's the matter with you?" She saw several of the attendees glance at them, uncomfortable.

"You made me a promise," he said. "To share what you found. And you didn't."

"I didn't have enough to share," she said and he laughed.

"Oh, please. That they knew each other? An actual link between the cases? What else haven't you told me?"

"I don't want a bunch of speculation...I just want the truth."

"Could be you don't like what you found. Maybe, until you share, I just have to start banging the drum that your dad's looking better for this crime." He said it like a threat.

"Mariah, let's go, please," Jake said, now standing next to her.

"Chad, you can't go after my dad," she said.

He turned and walked away.

"Let's go," Jake said again, easing her toward his car, Mariah aware of the gazes on her.

* * *

Jake and Mariah walked out to his Porsche and got in. He started the car but didn't shift gears.

"I want you to know I went and apologized to Buddy. I was thoughtless." Jake stared straight ahead. "I got a little engineer-ish on him."

"Well, a little, and I see your point. But I also see his. What is the harm?"

"Hope is the harm," he said. Now he looked at her.

"I think we're all beyond hope," she said.

"No, we're not," he said. "Hope just changes. You hope for answers because you know you're not getting your mom or your wife back." He cleared his throat. "When Reveal first approached me, I listened to a few of his podcasts. I heard him talk about unsolved disappearances from ten, twenty years ago...the parents died, the spouse died, without knowing what happened to their loved one. I don't think I could bear that. I need to know what happened to Bethany."

"I do, too," she said. "But I don't have a scapegoat like you do. I have no one to point a finger at." *Except my dad.* What if Chad decided to come after him, write about him? She felt sick.

"What if I'm wrong and Bethany's family is wrong?" he said. "What if we're all wrong? All that hate, for nothing."

"I dragged you to this, and I shouldn't have brought you. She told me she might come—at the restaurant. I should have warned you."

Jake studied her. "You're right, you should have, but it's all right. I'm not mad. I'm glad I've gotten to meet you."

She met his gaze and realized she didn't want to go home, to her father's thousand questions.

"Can we go back to your place and have a drink?" she asked.

36

THE RIDESHARE DRIVER brought Craig home, and thankfully there was no stone with another message in his driveway. But there was no sign of Mariah, either.

He went inside. In the kitchen he poured a glass of bourbon. He went into the den and sat in the dark in his recliner. He drank it, slowly, steadily, letting the smoky taste fill his mouth, thinking how good it was to be alive.

And then he heard a phone buzzing. A ringtone he didn't recognize. He saw the glow of a screen on the coffee table.

He had never seen this phone before. He got up and stood over it. Its small screen lit up with the word BLOCKED.

Someone had left a phone for him *in his house*.

He stared at it. It kept buzzing. He didn't move. Finally, he reached for it and answered it.

"Hello," he croaked.

The voice sounded masked, electronic in some way. "Craig. You made it home. That's nice."

"Who is this?"

"You put a sign out, yet you don't return calls from interested buyers. I think that sign is a fake. I think it shouldn't be. I think you are going to sell, cheaply and quickly. Take the hit. It's better than taking the rock."

"You... You cannot do this to me!" He didn't expect to say

those words, but there they were. "You attack me, you come into my home... how did you leave this phone here?"

"Craig. You have bigger concerns. You want to move out quickly. For your sake. And your daughter's."

"You stay away from Mariah."

"Fast. Cheap. Then leave." The line went dead.

He set the phone down. What about fingerprints? He could call Broussard. The person smart enough to break into his house or to get a key...

A key. Only he and Mariah had house keys.

The other house key had been with... Beth. In her purse. Vanished, with her.

A cold terror touched his spine, his chest. *No. No. No.*

He got up and checked all the doors. The back was unlocked. He snatched back his hand like the doorknob was hot.

They were in my house.

Why wouldn't Mariah answer her phone? Terror gripped him. He couldn't lose her, too.

37

MARIAH AND JAKE sat on his leather couch, the TV on, muted, playing TCM, which had on a Hitchcock film, *North by Northwest*. It was toward the end, Cary Grant dropping a note from the second floor of James Mason's totally cool house to Eva Marie Saint, trying to warn her from boarding a plane that she would be thrown out of during flight. Glasses of white wine were in front of both of them. Mariah thought she might be a little drunk. Her head no longer hurt. She shouldn't have drunk alcohol after fainting, but fainting seemed like such a dumb thing to do, something out of an old, problematic novel, a sign of weakness she didn't normally feel.

You've never fainted before, she thought, but then she saw her mother's face, shocked, surprised, swimming in fog, and then gone. She closed her eyes, opened them again, took another sip of wine.

Jake watched the movie, Cary Grant hurrying Eva Marie Saint toward Mount Rushmore. "So your dad was a suspect."

"Only because they always suspect the spouse." She thought his expression would change, but he only looked sad and aware. "No blood in his car, no sign of violence on him. No sign that he had done anything to her. No proof. But no proof doesn't mean innocence." Her voice went low.

His gaze widened. "You must have suspected your dad at some point. Even for a moment."

Mariah took a sip of the wine. Who else could she tell this to? No one. "I didn't think he could kill her. But there are accidents." The word felt funny in her mouth. "The marriage was kind of a mess in the past, and I didn't know that then, but now I do." She took another sip and let the wine soak her tongue, trying to think of how to say this and wondering what had made her say this to this man. "I thought maybe if they had a fight...if there was an accident..." She put down the wineglass, hand shaking, heart pounding. "But I know my dad. If he'd killed her, it would have been an accident, and he would have just laid down next to her. He would not have the coldness or the..." She searched for an appropriate word.

"Nerve."

"Yes. The nerve to dump the body, to lie to the police, to lie to me. I mean, this is a magnitude of lie I can hardly imagine. There would have to be a certain calculation and coolness. It's not a pretense Dad could manage."

Jake studied her. "It's hard to say that aloud."

"It's weird to have thought so much about murder while never having committed one," she said. She finished her wine and poured another glass. Why not? "I might be a little drunk. I've said too much. I should call a rideshare." She watched Cary Grant save Eva Marie Saint from falling off a president's sculpted face. She didn't reach for her phone. She didn't even feel like turning it on.

He stood to refill his own wineglass, and then he sat down next to her on the couch. A little closer this time. She thought, *Oh, OK, not really up for fending off a pass*, but then she decided she didn't mind. *Why should I mind?* she thought. When was the last time she'd gone on a date? This was one pathetic idea of a date and laughter, unexpected, nearly bubbled up in her chest. A few weeks after Mom vanished, a well-intentioned friend set her up with a coworker of hers, a perfectly nice guy. Completely ill at ease, she had felt like a drunk stumbling through a long evening. The guy had the decency to see how badly it was going and took her home early, at her request. He'd wished her luck. Luck. Like luck was how you got back on your feet, like that was how you lived with the sudden emptiness. Luck. Good fortune. Those were in decidedly short supply among the families of the missing.

But she decided it was fine if Jake sat close. He understood.

"I'm going to try and talk to Sharon tomorrow," she said.

"I'd leave that alone," he said.

"I know. But I won't. And I better make peace with Chad, too, or he'll write whatever he wants about my parents."

"He'll do that anyway," Jake said quietly. "I think Chad is a little blinded by ambition right now. He means well."

"It sucks not to be able to trust someone who's normally a friend," she said. "I mean, we're not close, but I don't talk about the case with anyone. He was the first. Then Sharon, then you..."

"People who have never experienced this think talking about it makes them understand it. Only living it makes you understand."

She surprised herself by putting her hand on the back of his neck. He looked at her, and she kissed him, gently, softly. He froze in surprise, for just a moment, as if he had forgotten what a kiss was, then he kissed her back. Her fingers tangled in his hair, she felt his palm lay along her jawline, gentle, a whispery touch.

The kiss broke. *What am I doing?* she thought.

"This isn't..." he started and she thought, *What's he going to say: Right? A good idea?* She didn't care. The loneliness swelled up in her, like a living thing fighting to breathe, and she kissed him again. He returned the kiss with equal fervor.

They broke apart. "I'm sorry," he said, like she was delicate china. Or didn't know her own mind.

"Don't be. Don't be sorry," she said, nearly in tears.

"I don't think..."

"So much thinking. Stop." She kissed him again, and he did stop saying the words she didn't want to hear, and shortly they stumbled down to the bedroom in the dark.

* * *

Mariah awoke in the night, and the first thought she had was wondering if this bed was Bethany's. She had slept in Bethany's old bed at Sharon's and now her marriage bed. Maybe Jake bought a new one when he moved here? The idea that she had slept in the missing woman's bed with the missing woman's husband should have bothered her. He had slid off the wedding ring when they reached the bed, like it was a chain he was slipping, just taking a moment to do that behind her head when he thought she couldn't see, and she had said nothing, then kissed him again. Was it better or worse that he'd taken it off?

She had never once wanted to sleep with a married man. She was sure that Jake had taken the side of the bed he was used to, and that must have been the side of the bed he slept on when Bethany was here. Couples had habits. She told herself to stop dwelling on this.

She hadn't been with a man since her mother vanished. She hadn't wanted to date. And she hadn't wanted to find a guy just for physical release.

Jake was asleep, curled in the sheets. Lightly snoring. She watched him for a moment and wondered, *Is this a good idea?* It was done. Move forward, whatever forward meant. She touched his arm and he stopped, immediately, still breathing heavily, deep in his dreams. She wanted to kiss him again, but she didn't want to wake him.

She felt a sick twinge of guilt, and then it went away, like cold rain blown by wind. It was there, and it was gone. Maybe he was a widower. She couldn't wish that to be true, but it might be. She got up and found her T-shirt and panties and slipped them on and walked quietly down the hall to the kitchen. She poured herself a tall glass of water, drank it down. She felt a little better. Not that she felt bad. She felt good. She wondered if he'd think she was easy. Maybe he wouldn't care. Maybe she wouldn't care if he cared. He might be the one who was easy. The first time had been awkward, perhaps ending a long drought for them both and each unsure, but the second time had been great and the third time...she smiled in the darkness.

I hope he didn't kill Bethany. I don't think he did.

She put the glass in the sink and tiptoed back to the bedroom. Jake was still asleep. He had his back to her and she curled into him, her forehead pressing against his back, and soon she slept.

38

THE MORNING AFTER didn't have to be awkward, but this one was likely to be. Probably, she thought, because of the assorted and heavy baggage they both had. She'd opened her eyes to hear the sound of the shower. It was six thirty according to his clock. She could smell coffee brewing.

He had laid out a yellow silk robe for her, across the bedspread by her feet. No doubt it was Bethany's. She was sure he was being practical, but she still felt a bit odd as she shrugged into his missing wife's robe. She wondered how she would have reacted if she'd ever seen some new woman wearing her mom's clothes. Probably would have torn the fabric off her back. And yet, she told herself, it was just a robe.

"Good morning," she said to the shower curtain. She made her voice strong, not wanting to sound weird or nervous. They were grown-ups.

"Hey, good morning. Coffee's brewing." He didn't peer out. His voice sounded a little hoarse.

"Do you want me to bring you a cup?" Well, she thought, that took three minutes to turn into little hausfrau, which was decidedly not her style.

"No, thank you, I'll get mine. You help yourself, though. I'll only be a minute."

She couldn't decide if it was a bad sign he didn't invite her to join him or at least stick his head around the shower curtain to speak to her. Or maybe he just had to get to work and another round of sex was what happened in a novel, not in real life. He was a techie, and they could be a bit distant. Or maybe he was having second thoughts. You might have been the first since she vanished. *You don't have to analyze everything*, she told herself. She went into the kitchen and poured coffee—he had set out half-and-half and sugar and packets of artificial sweetener, thoughtfully, so she took that as a good sign. He appeared in a few minutes, dressed for work, hair damp.

"Hi," he said, his smile broad.

"Hi. Look, I don't want this to be awkward..."

"I don't either." He kissed her, not the kind of lure you back to bed kiss but not a peck either, and she kissed back. When the kiss broke, their foreheads stayed pressed together. "I'm glad this happened. I don't have any regrets," he said.

"Me neither." She put her hand on his chest. "I mean, we're both dealing with a lot..."

"We're both surviving a lot," he said. "We're alive. We get to live."

"What a pair we make. Worst online dating profiles ever." And he laughed, and she laughed, and she thought *It's OK to laugh. It is.* She kissed him, and he kissed back.

"Breakfast is the only meal I'm good at cooking," he said. "What would you like?"

He made eggs with chives, bacon, and toasted English muffins. His coffee was strong, the way she liked it. They ate and she offered to clean, but he said no so she turned on her phone. Five text messages from Dad erupted on her screen. All variations of where are you? Are you OK? Please answer, Mariah, I'm a nervous wreck. Do I need to call the police? And then, finally, texting late last night: Someone tried to kill me and I need to know you're OK.

"Excuse me," she said. She hurried out onto the patio, the yellow robe fluttering around her. But looking out over the hills, like she had yesterday, a wave of nausea and blackness swept over her, and she stumbled back into the house. What was wrong with her?

Dad answered on the first ring. "Mariah."

"Dad, I'm so sorry...I had my phone turned off. What happened?" Her voice was hoarse.

He didn't even ask where she had spent the night. "Someone dropped a rock onto my car from the loop bridge."

She had to sit. "Oh, no. Are you all right?"

"Yes. I was driving Mom's car. It's wrecked."

"Oh, Dad, I am so sorry I wasn't there for you." Now Jake was watching her as he finished loading the dishwasher. "What do the police say? Who did this?"

"They don't know."

"Could it have been random?"

"I don't think so," he said, his voice quiet and thin. "Why didn't you come home?"

"I spent the night with a friend. And I'm coming home right now."

"Please do," he said.

She hung up, nearly bent over with shock.

"Is everything OK?" Jake asked. "Did something happen with your dad?"

"I have to go."

"What is it?"

"My dad...he needs me. I have to go." She hurried back toward the bedroom, in search of her clothes. *The one night you try to go back to normal, escape the cocoon of grief, and this happens...this happens...you will never have a life.*

"OK. So we should talk again about the case, depending on what you find?" Jake asked, following her, concern in his voice. "I'm working from home today, so call me on my cell."

She started to analyze what the words meant, if he was glad or relieved or sad, and then she thought, *It doesn't matter what he thinks. It happened, it might not happen again, it might. I can't deal with this on top of everything else.*

"Sure. I'll call you later," she said. She yanked on her jeans and her top, didn't bother with combing her hair.

"If I can help you, Mariah, I want to."

She nodded. She couldn't talk about this with him. She would lose it.

"Hey. Hey." He leaned close to her and hugged her, softly. "You're shivering." She let him hold her. It felt good.

"I hope your dad is OK," he said, into her hair.

"Thanks," she said. She broke away from him and nearly ran to the front door. "I'll talk to you later."

39

MARIAH HURRIED INTO her house. Her father sat in his recliner, in his blue jeans and a rumpled dress shirt. He had shaved badly, missing patches. He was drinking coffee. He looked at her with exhaustion.

"I didn't know where to look for you," he said in a monotone. "I didn't know where you had gone. You pick last night, of all nights, to turn off your phone." Now his voice shook.

"I'm so sorry," she said. "Are you all right?"

"It missed me by about a foot," he said. "And when I got home, someone had been inside the house. Left a burner phone, to call me and tell me to sell the house fast and get out."

She put her hands over her face in dismay. "How..."

"I want you to leave town," he said. "Go see your cousins in Dallas."

"I won't."

"You will. If I have to drag you onto a plane, you are leaving. I will not risk you, Mariah."

Now she looked at him. "Dad...I get why you're upset..."

"They can come for me. But you have to be safe. I should have taken you away from here long ago. But I didn't."

"Did you tell the police there was an intruder? Why don't they have someone here to guard the house?"

He laughed. "It could be Broussard. But I don't want them here around me. I have to be able...to do what I need to do. Take care of this problem."

That frightened her. "I am not leaving you."

"Go pack your bag. Now."

She knelt by him. "I am close to finding out what happened to Mom," she said, in a soft whisper. He shoved her away from him.

"Stop playing at detective. It's humiliating!"

"No, it's not!"

He stormed past her and marched up the stairs to her room. The room where she had grown up, the room where she had returned and cocooned herself against the world.

He went to her closet, yanked open the door.

"Dad..."

He pulled out the suitcase she kept on the top shelf. "Get packed." He grabbed an armful of clothes off the hangers, tossed them onto her bed. Then he stopped. He stared.

She stepped forward, took the suitcase from him. Saw what he saw.

He pulled the corkboard out from behind her clothes. With its pushpins and photos and maps, and colored yarn connecting the elements of her mother's case.

"I told you to get rid of this," he whispered.

"It's just a representation of Mom's case. Timelines. And pictures. And theories." Her voice trailed off.

"My name is on here. On an index card." He jabbed at it with his finger.

"You were a witness," she said. "Not...not as a suspect, Dad."

"This isn't healthy. This is something a detective assigned to the case has, not you."

"I've found out so much in the past couple of days...about her life, about her connections to Bethany Curtis."

"Paper and string and photos. It's all meaningless. And what are you going to do, Mariah? Write it up and give it to your gossipy friend who writes the true crime blog? The one who treated your mother's case like gossip for his listeners?" And Craig smashed his fist through the corkboard, through the map she'd printed of the streets and lots where Mom had vanished. He threw the corkboard to the floor, stepped on it, yanked the metal edge of it upward, ripping it. Pins and string fell to the floor. He tore it again as she screamed at him to stop.

A picture of her mother fluttered free.

"This stops right now," he said. "This obsession. Let her go. Say goodbye and let her go. She's gone. Gone."

Mariah was so upset the tears wouldn't come. "You can't do that..."

"Where were you last night? Who were you with?"

"That's not your business."

"Your sick friend again?"

"No," and now she felt defiant, fire blossoming in her chest. "I spent the night with Bethany Curtis's husband." Something shifted in his face, and she wished she could take the words back. He seemed almost staggered by her announcement. "Dad..."

His face had gone red; he fought to steady his breathing.

"I saw what Reveal wrote about the cases. The husband. He might have killed his wife and you...slept...with...him."

"Dad..."

His laughter was broken. "Did you get the clues you wanted? Did you interrogate him in the sheets?"

He had never spoken to her like this before. Or destroyed her property. He'd cheated on her mother. What was he truly capable of? She realized she didn't know her father, not this side of him. "Don't talk to me that way."

"Don't talk to me that way," he said back, mocking her, his voice nasal, but she was staring at him, and his lips and mouth hadn't moved. But she had heard it. In her mind. He opened his mouth to speak, saying her name, and she hit him. A hard slap, a shove and he sprawled back into the wall.

Then she hit him again as his hands came up to defend himself.

"You don't care, you don't care..." she began to scream.

"Mariah—"

"You don't care that we don't know. How can you not care? How..."

Because he knew. He knew. He knew what happened to Mom.

She stood and staggered away from him, the realization sharp and awful and life-changing.

He saw it in her face.

"Mariah!" he called to her.

She ran. She ran down and outside, past the for sale sign, leaned against the car, and then she got in and drove off.

He followed her out to the driveway. He was shaking. He realized his mouth was bleeding.

She'll come back, he told himself. *She'll come back when she calms down.*

He had to end this. Now.

40

MARIAH DROVE TO a nearby café. She took steadying breaths after she parked, feeling dizzy, the words echoing in her head.

It couldn't be that her father knew with certainty. Unless he had... There had been no confession made, this was all in her head. The solution involved Bethany Curtis and her secrets. That would explain the following, the messages, the attack on her father. She had stirred the nest of a murderer who'd gotten away with it. She was close to the pattern. She had to follow it.

Did you see your father kill her? Did you block it out? Is that why you're protecting him? Broussard's words rang harshly in her head.

How badly had she hurt her father? Shame welled up in her. She hadn't meant to shove him, but when he mocked her like that... she couldn't help it. It just happened. The girl she'd gotten into a fight with at a college party, which had so upset Mom, the man whose finger she'd broken at the restaurant. The rage could rise like a storm in her body. After what he'd already gone through, the shame burned like a fever. She had to get ahold of herself. Find the pattern, bring peace to their lives.

Mariah's phone pinged. It wasn't Dad calling, but an Austin number. "Hello?"

"Is this Mariah Dunning?"

"Yes."

"Hi, Ms. Dunning. This is Yvette Suarez. From the Pushy Pens writing group. You emailed me?" Her voice was soft, musical. "Sorry to be late getting back to you."

Mariah wiped her eyes, steadied her voice. "Thanks so much for returning my call."

"You were asking about Bethany Curtis?"

"Yes. I'm interested in what she was writing with your group."

"Um, well, I think that would be private. Are you some kind of reporter?"

"No, my mom was friends with Bethany. They've both gone missing—my mom six months after Bethany vanished. I'm trying to see if there's a connection. I've met with Bethany's mom and her friends."

"Have you talked to her husband?"

"Yes," she said. "I got the impression she didn't show him her writing. Can you at least tell me what she wrote about?"

"Why would that matter?" Yvette sounded impatient.

"I think her writing could have had clues in it to why she ran."

"It doesn't. She wrote a number of short stories about suburban life, and they were good, full of detail, but lacking in drama. She told us she had an interest in true crime. We all told her she needed to maybe combine her two interests. She said she took our advice and was writing a crime novel."

"What was it about?"

"She said it was about a suburban family dealing with the aftermath of a crime. A drunk driving accident, and how the various family members deal or don't deal with the loss."

A drunk. Like Bethany's father. "You read her manuscript?"

"Only the first twenty pages. It was very rough but had a lot of promise."

Mariah considered. "In this story, was there a suicide?" Penny had said that was Bethany's topic in their brief phone call—a family affected by suicide.

"It was hinted at," Yvette said slowly. "How did you know that?"

"Was the suicide a father figure?"

"Yes. The man who causes the accident. The manuscript opens with him considering suicide years later, and then goes back in time to the accident. She wanted to know what we thought of him as a character. He was compelling...but loathsome. We all said so."

Mariah found her voice. "Who gets killed?"

"A small child...that was where the sample ended."

Mariah closed her eyes. "Thank you. How did your critique group operate?"

"Everyone brings around ten pages each week, then we pass pages around and read them and mark up the manuscript with comments or questions. Then it goes back to the author. The author gets to ask three questions."

"Do you have any of the pages she wrote?"

"No, they all would have gone back to her so she'd have our comments right on the manuscript as she rewrote."

And where had those pages gone? Had she taken them with her? Or destroyed them like she had her computer files?

"Do you remember her three questions?"

"Um...usually they're about tone or character. I think she asked what we thought of the driver. We all hated him. We talked about that a lot, how hard it would be to make him likeable after what he'd done."

"Bethany's friend Julie told me about your group. She said Bethany had another friend there, Lizbeth Gonzales."

"Yes." Her voice was suddenly hesitant.

"Do you know how I'd find her? I have a phone number, but I'm not sure it's current or if she'll call back."

The pause became one of those awkward ones. "Sorry, I don't. Lizbeth wouldn't consistently bring pages to read. She was mostly talking about writing rather than producing pages. Always starting a new project, never sticking with one long. And then...well, she just didn't work out." A lingering tone on the last few words, as if a secret was being kept.

"What do you mean?"

"I don't want to say," although Yvette clearly did.

"I won't repeat it. I really need to find Lizbeth, and I don't know what kind of person I'm dealing with. Neither Bethany's other friends nor her mom seems to have known Lizbeth well."

"Well, Lizbeth brought her ten pages, and another writer recognized the work as having been taken from a published novel. A very popular one. She only changed the character names. Clear plagiarism. We went back and looked at what she'd written before, did some internet searches... everything she'd brought was copied, from books that weren't as well known. We had to ask her to leave the group. I mean, that's just... there's no excuse."

"Of course not."

"It was awkward. Lizbeth and Bethany were friends and had joined together. They were tight. But it was clear that Bethany was serious about her writing and Lizbeth wasn't. When Bethany brought these novel pages, we were all raving about them, and yet Bethany looked miserable and Lizbeth looked happy. It was so odd. That was the last meeting they both attended."

Then why join this kind of group, only for the most serious, and pull this inexcusable stunt?

"And then we had a get-together after Bethany's disappearance, I mean, beyond our regular meeting. I sent Lizbeth an email inviting her. She wrote me back, declining, she said she was too embarrassed to come given what had happened. I told her that didn't matter, we were all Bethany's friends and just wanted to be together. She still said no. I asked her if we could do anything to help her and she said no."

"You really didn't like Lizbeth."

"I didn't like how she was in the critiques. She would smile sometimes when we were hard on Bethany—all to help her make her work better—in a way that made me feel she enjoyed seeing Bethany stumble. And here she was, everything she brought was a lie... I didn't like her."

"And you haven't seen her since Bethany vanished?"

"I tried to call her, to see how she was doing, but her phone had been disconnected. I tried the email again and it bounced. The account had been deleted. Poof. She was a gone girl."

"Were any of the other members friends with Lizbeth?"

"No, not really, and after the plagiarism, I don't know that any of them saw her again."

Mariah steadied her voice. "Do you have a picture of Lizbeth?"

"Um, no. I don't. She liked to wear wigs, though. I mean, it was kind of showy. The wig was a bob, you know, the hair just down to her jawline. A blue one once, a purple one, a red one, styled the same, just different colors. But usually she was a blonde. She was one of those people who thought if she looked artistic, she would be... you know, without doing the hard work." Yvette Suarez scoffed.

"I really appreciate your time. Thank you."

* * *

Mariah went inside the café, got a cup of tea, and sat in the corner. She slid the flash drive with her mother's emails into the laptop port and opened up the computer again. She searched her mother's business emails for Lizbeth Gonzales. One result, but not an email. A text message, captured and filed. Karen must have included those as well.

Hey Beth this is Lizbeth I'm Bethany's friend her phones on its last bit of charge and she said she's running late so I'm texting you for her, I'm already at Tequila Joe's. Hey we're the Three Beths like the Three Musketeers or Charlie's Angels or something I'll order you and Beth platinum margaritas, the drinks are on me. Look forward to meeting you.

She read the text twice. During one of the times her mom and Bethany had gotten together for a drink, Lizbeth had met her mother.

What had her mother gotten involved in? The date was three months before Bethany left. What else had happened between these women?

41

After Mariah left, Craig had reserved a rental SUV, taken a rideshare service to go pick it up, and driven back toward home. The whole time, he kept the phone the intruder had left in his house on and in his jacket pocket.

He gathered himself. He had a purpose. He had to do this.

The media was at his house. Three local news vans—it had leaked out that he had been the car hit by the rock from the bridge. He should have realized this would reignite interest in his story and the press would again be torn between painting him as the grieving husband or the guilty suspect. He drove past the news vans, deciding not to turn in, and hoped they would be impatient, go chase another story soon enough. He knew their patterns. If they saw the for sale sign and he didn't answer the front door, they'd give up after a while, come back closer to the noon broadcast and the evening broadcast. He'd need to get the locks changed, given that someone had been in the house to leave the phone, but that could wait until the press left. No one would be walking into his home with them camped out in front.

He had a job to do.

In the old Lakehaven directory, Sean Oberst's mom was listed as Patrice. He'd searched the property records for Patrice Marshall—the name the new homeowner at the old Oberst address had given him—and gotten another hit in Lakehaven, with a Jeffrey and Patrice Marshall owning a property in one of the older neighborhoods, on Canyon Grove Avenue.

The house was big: a McMansion on a street that looked to be half older, original homes and half teardowns, replaced with limestone homes at double the square footage. A kid sat on the wraparound porch, typing on a tablet, in a rocking chair. Next door was a teardown in progress, a large two-story home well under construction. A sign indicated COMING SOON—ANOTHER MODERN MASTERPIECE BY PLATINUM DESIGNS.

Sean Oberst glanced up as Craig drove by, and Craig thought, *Oh, great, now if I drive by again I look like a predator.* But he turned around at the edge of the street and drove back by, thinking I can't worry what anyone thinks of me. I have to find this man.

Sean Oberst looked up as he parked and got out of the car. He was a tall kid, taller than Craig, probably a senior, with reddish hair and a scattering of faint freckles across his nose and cheeks. Craig was surprised he wasn't in school.

"Excuse me," Craig said. "Does your dad drive a silver SUV?"

"My dad lives in Houston now," the boy said. "Who are you?"

"Oh," he said. "Are you Sean?"

The boy didn't answer at first. Then he said, "My stepfather drives a silver SUV." He made stepfather sound like the squelch of a nice shoe in mud.

"Well, the other day, I scratched a silver SUV with a band sticker with the name Sean under it when I was parking. It was my fault, and I didn't leave a note, and I wanted to apologize. Another band parent said it might be your dad. I misunderstood that it was your stepfather."

"Jeffrey's a bad driver," the boy said. "He probably parked crooked."

"It was still my fault."

"He put my band sticker on the back of the car, even if I didn't want him to," Sean volunteered, still frowning.

"Could I talk to him?"

"Well, he's not here."

"Well, please tell him... what's his name?"

"Jeffrey. Jeffrey Marshall."

"Please tell him I'm sorry."

"He's not the kind of guy you need to apologize to," Sean said.

"Still."

"I won't see him for a few days. As soon as my mom gets home, we're driving to Dallas. For a funeral. Jeffrey's staying here, though. You want his cell phone number or his email?"

"You know, that's all right. I'll contact him later."

He nodded.

Craig drove off with a wave. *OK, Jeffrey, you'll be home alone, so I'll see you soon*, he thought.

42

MARIAH RANG THE doorbell of Reveal's house. She thought Reveal's parents would have already headed to work.

The door opened. Reveal was dressed in jeans and another basketball jersey, his hair spiked.

"I'm in trouble and I need a place to stay just for today," she said.

"You have some nerve."

"Chad, please..."

"Let me cut to the essentials. Surely you're here to tell me what's going on with this unexpectedly related case."

"I can't tell you."

"Take, take, take, Mariah. Time to give. I need details I can share. The whole story between you and Jake Curtis and Sharon Blevins. I am supposed to fly to LA for meetings on this show. This is my big chance, and you are screwing it up for me." Chad turned away from her.

"How am I affecting your chances?"

"I told the TV producer that I could break open a high-profile case."

"You shouldn't have said that."

"Well, I had to! It wasn't quite the sure deal they promised me. I found out they were talking to two other crime podcasters. And one has a book deal already. I'm trying to compete with that. I need something big to impress them." He lowered his voice. "I needed the support of Sharon, and that won't happen thanks to you. The only reason you're even on this trail for your mom is because I pointed something out to you. You owe me, Mariah."

"I don't know the truth yet."

"Forget the truth! I just need some suggestive details. Give me something I can spin a pitch around these two women."

These two women. Like they were his props. "I can't."

"You know, I kept my mouth shut for you when you assaulted that guy at the restaurant. How would that have looked after your little car chase, Mariah? Lakehaven white girl, endless second chances."

"You're from Lakehaven, too."

"How many Asian American men are hosting television shows, Mariah? Shall I wait while you count, or even think about it? Don't give me that. This is my big chance, my one chance probably, and you could boost me, but you won't." He crossed his arms. "I heard about the rock being dropped on your dad's car. Did you do it?"

She was shocked. "How...why would you think that?"

"I went over to the bridge when I heard about your dad. There's a small surveillance camera there. I think it's safe to assume Chief Broussard has a video of the person dropping the rock. Was it you?"

"No, of course not." Her voice went thin. "Maybe it was you?"

"What?" Reveal's voice rose with shock. "That's insane."

"I mean, you could really want to spice up your pitch to these producers. You have to make this case more interesting. I can't believe how desperate you're acting."

"Rethink your words," he said, his voice tight. "I would never risk another person's life."

"But you think my dad and I are capable of this. And you're mad at me, because I'm not lining up to help you make money on my family's misery."

"What?" He looked genuinely shocked.

"This isn't just a podcast or a story or a TV show to me. This is my mother!" She was nearly dizzy with rage. "And you're worried about . . . your ridiculous TV show, with your stupid bedazzled hat and your sunglasses and your nickname. Reveal! Why don't you call yourself Uncover or Disrobe?" The words out, ugly, before she could stop them. She took a deep breath. "Chad . . ."

His voice went flat. "Everything I tried to do was to help you. To give you some peace, I mean. I wanted closure for you, Mariah." Then his tone hardened. "Maybe you're lying about your mom and Bethany Curtis being connected. Maybe this is all a stunt to distract you from your father's guilt. Because you can't face that your father is a killer. I know it. Broussard knows it. Everyone but you knows it."

"Chad. I'm sorry. Please."

"Maybe that's what I'll pitch," he said. "Maybe that's the big case to work on. How your father could possibly still be free after what he did."

"Please don't."

"I don't have time to waste on you. I have to get ready for California, okay? I have to go."

The silence was like a weight.

"Good luck," she said. "I really do mean that. You're my friend, and I really do hope you get your show, but please, but you don't have to drag my dad through the dirt." Her voice broke with emotion. "Please."

He shut the door in her face.

43

Mariah hadn't known where else to go. She pulled into Jake's driveway, nearly veering onto the manicured grass. She hurried to the front door and rang the doorbell.

"Hey. What's the matter?" he said.

"My father threw me out," she said. "I don't need a place to stay, you don't need to worry, but I need a place where I can collect my thoughts and find a spot to stay and get my life in order."

"Why did he..."

"Someone has attacked my dad, trying to get him to leave Lakehaven, and he wants me to go hide in Dallas and I won't." She didn't want to say more.

"Mariah."

"What? I can't leave him."

"Of course not. We need to call the police."

"The police know already. I just have to figure out what to do. I didn't know where else to go."

"Of course, come in." He opened the door wide.

She followed him into the kitchen.

"Is your father all right?"

"Yes." Voice wavering, she told him about the rock. She didn't tell him about her fight with Dad, or that she had shoved her own father in a senseless moment. She was deeply ashamed.

"Wow," he said. "Mariah, maybe you both should get out of town for a while."

"He won't leave. He won't be chased off."

"Then... both of you, come and stay here."

"I can't convince him. I don't mean to disrupt your morning. Are you still working from home today?"

"I was, but there's been a crisis with a client, so I'm heading in for a couple of hours. Will you be all right here alone?"

"Yes."

"And you and your dad can stay here. If you need to."

"We also have an elderly Cardigan Welsh Corgi named Leo."

He smiled. "Leo, too. As long as he'll play with me."

Her heart shifted in her chest. This was all happening fast. "No, it's way too awkward. Thank you, though."

"Mariah. Regardless of what happened... what we're figuring out... I have this huge house. It doesn't mean we sleep together again if you're having regrets or if your dad stays here, too, obviously. I'll hire security."

"That's very kind. But I don't think that would be a good idea," she said.

"What, you're going to stay with Sharon? Or Reveal?" He raised an eyebrow.

"I don't know yet. I'll figure that out."

"Sure. Whatever you want. But you're welcome here." He slid her a piece of paper. "That has the garage door code on it, so you can leave if you need to and lock up."

"Thank you." She slipped it into her pocket. He went upstairs to finish getting ready for his day.

She set up her laptop at the quartz-topped breakfast bar in his large kitchen, thinking this is weird, so weird, but life has been weird for a while. Online she found a hotel, cheap, in south Austin, that would accept pets—she thought of Leo, and what would her dad do about him? If someone had come into their house, they couldn't leave Leo there. She made a reservation for herself. She felt a tug of regret in her chest. She'd rather stay with Jake. She knew that. But it was probably for the best to stay elsewhere.

Jake came downstairs. "Make yourself at home. If you're hungry, there's stuff in the fridge, and the pantry's in the mudroom."

He pointed toward a door. He kissed her, softly, before he left. For a moment she sat in the quiet of the house. *OK*, she thought, *he's gone. You could search the house.*

You can't do that, she told herself. *He's trusted you, trust him.*

Maybe it's dumb to trust me, she thought. *Maybe this is my one chance.*

She made herself focus on the laptop and what she needed to do.

She sent a text to Reveal, apologizing again, asking him to call her. She left the messages window open so she could see if he responded.

She tried to find details on the suicide of Hal Blevins. The newspaper accounts of the time were sparse. A police detective, Eben Garza, was quoted that it was clearly a finding of suicide. She internet-searched Garza and found him on Faceplace. He was retired now, and most of his photos showed him enjoying himself with three adorable grandchildren.

She sent Garza a friend request, with a note: I'd like to talk to you about Hal Blevins's suicide. Do you remember it? He left behind a wife and a daughter. The daughter found him. He overdosed on liquor and pills. I'm not a vulture or a ghoul, please call me.

She sent the message.

Then searched on Faceplace for Lizbeth Gonzales. There were a couple of them, neither in Texas, both older women. Not her Lizbeth.

Penny. She entered in Penny and the phone number she'd called into the search engine. No match.

Bits and pieces. A name of an old neighbor. A church in Houston. A story about a hit-and-run. A family who lied about where they lived. But none of it fit together.

She thought, and typed "Houston child hit-and-run." But… there were dozens of results, from this year and starting to go back. "Child hit by car" was its own tag category on one Houston news station's website. She started digging through them, hoping it wasn't a waste of time.

Her phone rang. "Mariah Dunning."

"Uh, hi, yeah. This is Eben Garza. You contacted me?"

"Yes, sir. Thank you for returning my call."

"I remember Mr. Blevins's case. Who are you, exactly?"

"A friend of the family."

"You know where Shreve Park is?"

"Yes." It was a park off Old Travis, in Austin.

"I'm heading there with my grandchildren, I'll be there in twenty minutes. If you want to talk, we can talk there. Otherwise, don't bother me again."

She said, "I'll be there."

44

THE PARK WAS on the south side of Austin, not far from the Lakehaven boundary. The swing sets and the playscape were new, the sunshine was bright and cheery, and at this time of day the park was busy with moms and little ones. She saw Eben Garza sitting on a bench, watching two little girls slide down a slide and run back up the steps with glee.

"Hi, Detective Garza, I'm Mariah Dunning."

"Hi. Just a minute." He got up and walked over to an older woman who was standing closer to the playscape, spoke to her, she nodded. He returned and sat down next to Mariah.

"My friend is a nanny for another family. She'll keep an eye on my granddaughters while we talk. But this time is precious to me, OK? Don't waste it." His tone wasn't unkind, but it was firm.

"Yes, sir. Hal Blevins."

"I remember. He took the overdose at home. His daughter and a friend, a boy, found him."

"Andy Candolet?"

"Yeah. Big kid. Looked like a young Clark Kent. I remember him, too."

"Was there anything suspicious about the death?"

He considered her. "How are you a friend of the family?"

She explained, without too much detail. "I wondered if there was an obvious reason for the suicide, or if it seemed like it could have been..."

"Murder. You can say it."

"Yes."

"It wasn't a murder. He left a note. No sign anyone had poured the pills or the liquor down his throat."

"What did the note say?"

"I don't remember the exact wording. Just that he was very sorry and that he loved his wife and daughter. It was short."

"I understand he was a recovering alcoholic. I found his sobriety chits taped in a journal."

"He laid out those sobriety chips on the coffee table."

She could imagine Bethany gathering them up, preserving them in her notebook. "Do you know many alcoholics that drink their way out?"

He shrugged. "The concern was where had he gotten all the pills. Because neither he nor his wife had a prescription for tranquilizers. We checked."

"Did Sharon know?"

"No. We found a guy he worked with who had a side business with black market painkillers. We think he supplied him. The guy denied it up and down. But we never found out for sure."

"He must have been drinking all day to have killed himself."

"It was more the pills. He took more than enough. He had maybe been dead an hour when his daughter got home from school, but she thought at first he was sick and just taking a nap—he had told them he was taking a sick day, and Mrs. Blevins had a job as an office manager downtown, so he was alone all day. He was in pajamas and robe. The suicide note was in the robe pocket. Along with the boarding pass."

"Boarding pass?"

"To Houston. He had booked himself on a flight for that night."

"Houston," she said slowly. "Why would he buy an airline ticket if he was going to kill himself?"

"I don't know. According to his wife—and she was hysterical—there was no reason for him to go to Houston. Unless he'd planned to go there and kill himself and changed his mind. The ticket was one-way, no return flight booked. He might as well have decided to end his life at home."

Pills that he shouldn't have had. A ticket that made no sense.

"How were Sharon and Bethany? I mean, obviously, this was horrifying."

Garza took a deep breath. "The daughter, she was devastated. She couldn't believe it. I mean, unless the suicidal person has attempted before or has a long history of depression...people generally can't believe they've done it." He cleared his throat, watching his granddaughters, then yelling, "Joanna, don't let Esme get too dirty, please! Her mom will yell at me! Thank you!" while Joanna waved him off with a flap of the hand. He continued: "Depression at that level is not normally a thing you can conceal, but I guess he managed. She seemed a sweet kid."

"And Sharon?"

Garza winced as Esme, hanging from the monkey bars, dropped to the soft ground. The girl giggled. "It's no one's finest hour. Sharon Blevins was mostly worried about her kid. She was afraid that he'd talked to her daughter before he died, she couldn't be convinced he was already dead when Bethany arrived...she kept asking Bethany, 'What did he say, what did he say?' I thought she meant he would have given a reason. Only after we found the ticket did I think maybe she meant something else." He watched his granddaughters chase each other, a smile touching his lips. "I thought really Mrs. Blevins wanted to protect her daughter. And I'm sure she did. But I think she was scared at first the dad told Bethany something else. Something Mrs. Blevins didn't want told. You know, like a confession. Sometimes people decide on suicide because they did something bad and don't want to face the consequences. I thought, given the mother's concern, maybe he had confessed a reason to the daughter, you know, in the days leading up to it."

"Did you ask Bethany?"

"I asked if she knew why her dad had done this. She said no. I believed her."

"And Sharon gave no explanation?"

"No. And in a way, I mean, she was upset, she was distraught, like you would expect, but I thought maybe she was…relieved."

"As if she was out of danger? Maybe he was abusive?"

"No signs of abuse on her, and when we asked if he'd ever hurt her, she got upset and said no, never."

"So, she was relieved for another reason."

"I would suppose." He shrugged. "He drank the booze, he took the pills. That was unusual; most men use a gun or a rope. But she said they'd never owned a gun. But I also took it that there was no alcohol normally in the house. He was recovering and she was religious, if I recall."

"Yes," she said, sounding flat. "So he had to stockpile the booze and the pills. He had to plan it."

"Unless he found a delivery service, yes."

Esme and her sister ran to their grandfather in the middle of the game of tag, tagged him, informed him that he was it. "Anything else? This is precious time to me with the girls."

"Was there any mention of a Penny? By Bethany or her mother?"

For a long moment it was as if Garza forgot the granddaughters who were waiting for him. "Not from them. On the note. He'd written it in pencil. And he'd tried to erase a line."

"Yes?"

"It said, 'I'm sorry about Penny.' He'd nearly erased it all. It was down by the bottom of the page. Like a postscript. I asked Mrs. Blevins what it meant. It's unusual to see erasure on a suicide note—usually they just start over and write a fresh one. It's the last communication they make to the world, so they want it to be neat and clear. I thought it odd. She said she didn't know. I assumed perhaps it was a girlfriend."

"And you didn't dig into it further?" she asked, blurting out the question before she thought.

"Welcome to the reality of police work. It was a suicide. There was absolutely no suspicion of murder. It's not the police's job to solve the mystery of that man's life. Just that no one else killed him."

"I understand. I think I know who Penny is."

"Who?"

"A woman in Houston. A neighbor of theirs. Her phone number was written in Bethany's address book. But Mrs. Blevins told people they moved here from Chicago, that they never lived in Houston."

"Maybe it was an affair?"

"I don't think so," she said. She felt cold. "Is there anything else you remember that was unusual? Was there any hint he'd been involved in a crime? Or maybe a hit-and-run?"

"None," he said. "Do you know of a crime?"

She shook her head.

Eben Garza studied her for a moment. "Well...did you know that Blevins was her name, not his?"

"What?"

"I talked to his employer, you know, just to see if he had said anything at work to indicate there was a problem, and he told me that Blevins was Sharon Blevins's maiden name and Hal took it later in life. His job experience before was all in Houston, and his name then was Hal Meadows."

"Meadows."

"Yeah. But Mrs. Blevins told me privately when I asked her about this that when he was a drunk, he cheated on her and she made him take her name as a condition of getting back together. He agreed. She said her daughter didn't know, only remembered Blevins as their name. I did call the last place he worked in Houston, and they confirmed they'd had to let him go. There had been an issue with drinking on the job and sleeping with a coworker. He had no criminal record."

She could see Sharon striking this bargain. "Meadows. All right. You wouldn't remember the name of that company would you?"

"No, sorry. Long time ago."

"Thank you for taking the time to talk to me."

His stern expression softened. "Are you all right? I feel like I gave you bad news."

I'm sorry about Penny.

"It's all right. I just appreciate this so much. Thank you."

She said goodbye to Garza, thanked him again, and sat for a moment, watching him go play with his giggling granddaughters.

Penny was tied to Hal's suicide. She opened her phone's browser and searched for "Hal Meadows Houston."

She found a few hits, some from recent years involving other men with the same name. Then she found one, from many years ago, a man with a slight resemblance to Bethany—he'd won an award from an advertising professional group. He stood awkwardly at a podium, accepting the award. Nothing else on him. He'd worked for an agency called Harper & Smythe. They'd shut down six years ago.

She searched for "Sharon Meadows." She found a wedding announcement between Sharon and Hal; they looked young, hopeful, and happy. Not much else, although Sharon had later won the award for Volunteer of the Year at Holy Innocents School.

"Bethany Meadows." Just a birth announcement.

She looked at the results of her earlier Houston hit-and-run search. Then she added another search term: "Penny."

She held her breath and waited.

Lots of results...but all with the word *Penny* marked out. A dead end.

So what was Hal sorry about with Penny?

She needed to talk again to Penny. And to Sharon.

45

HER MIND WAS full of what Sharon knew or what Sharon might know or what Sharon had hidden. So Mariah found herself driving to Sharon's house, unsure of what she would say but ready to confront her with her questions.

She seemed... relieved.

Mariah drove by Sharon's house. Andy's car was outside. Why was he here now? She drove past the house. Instinct took hold. She drove down the street, around the corner, and parked out of sight so Andy wouldn't see her car.

She walked to the front door, and she could hear the raised voices in violent argument. Sharon yelling at him, "This is all your fault!"

She didn't knock or ring the doorbell. Maybe it would be valuable to know what they were saying. And not have them know she heard.

She eased open the backyard gate and snuck close to the window of the breakfast nook. She could hear a distant murmur of voices. One man, one woman. She listened.

The words were quieter now, indistinct. She heard "I promised" and "Bethany" and "never again." Sharon's voice got louder. Then quiet.

Then they were in the kitchen. Mariah risked a quick look through the window. Sharon at the sink, filling a glass with water.

Andy in the doorway, still talking. She ducked down again before they could see her.

"Can't you find out what she knows?" he asked.

"I'll try."

"You don't want her digging too deep, Sharon."

"I know. I know." Her voice was soft. But sad.

What is this? Mariah wondered. Had the two of them conspired in Bethany's disappearance? She could not imagine it of Sharon, who had shown herself to be a devastated mother.

Mariah hunkered down on the grass, keeping her head close but beneath the window.

"You didn't have to talk to her when she showed up at your office," Sharon said.

"She's a Dunning. I had to know why she'd come to see me."

Hunkered down below the window, Mariah couldn't see Sharon's reaction.

"You're way more worried about yourself than worried about me," Sharon said.

"Well, this is your problem to solve. And I am worried about you, Sharon," he said, his voice softening. "You know I've always been there for you."

"You're here for me when you can have an advantage over me," Sharon said, her tone bitter. "I wonder what Julie would say."

"You won't say a word to Julie," Andy said. It was a sneer. "And you really will have nothing if this goes wrong. We're both stuck. Let's make the best of a bad situation. You don't want to mess up this arrangement for me and Julie."

"I thought you loved Julie. That's rich."

"I have a lot of love in me."

Something awful, taunting in his tone. Something was wrong here, Mariah thought, oh so wrong.

"Love for yourself," Sharon said. "I cannot keep doing this. Just go and let me figure out what to do."

Andy didn't answer. Silence. Silence. Then a gasp.

Mariah peered through the window.

Andy, one hand tangled in Sharon's hair, the other on the small of her back, holding her close. Kissing her deeply. Sharon, not moving, not fighting him, enduring it.

Then Sharon put her hand on the side of Andy's face. Like it was all right.

Mariah ducked back down, her breath gone, holding her gasp of shock inside her throat.

"You've got me good and woke up now," he said.

"Go. Not today. No."

"You miss me," he breathed. Sharon murmured something she couldn't hear.

He laughed. And he left.

* * *

Mariah crouched down on the grass. She waited and then looked again. She watched Sharon drink a glass of water and put the glass in the sink. And then Sharon gripped the edge of the sink and trembled.

Mariah moved back from the window. She counted to one hundred and eased herself out of the backyard. Andy's car was gone. She rang the doorbell.

* * *

Sharon walked slowly out of the kitchen. The careful web of her life seemed to be coming undone, falling apart, and she went to the armchair where she'd hidden the gun next to the seat cushion.

She had left it there, just in case. But Mariah wasn't coming back to this house unless Sharon called her and asked her to visit. She could have turned the gun on Andy., but she needed Andy. As much as she hated to admit it.

For a moment she thought of turning the gun on herself. End it all. But she was, at the same time, too scared and too hopeful that this would somehow get better.

Hal died in that chair. I should have thrown it out.

The doorbell rang. She peered through the peephole.

Mariah.

Sharon ran back to the armchair, made sure the gun was properly hidden, and then took a deep breath and went to the door.

* * *

Sharon opened the door, looking gaunt. "I told you not to come back here." But she didn't shut the door.

"What does he have on you? Andy?"

"What?" She took a step back.

"What does he have on you? That he can force himself on you like that in your own home. You can be rid of him. I'll help you."

Sharon looked at her in absolute shock. Her mouth moved but no words came. She moved into the den and sat in the armchair. "Can't you just leave us alone?"

That Sharon was sitting was a good idea, Mariah decided. She showed a willingness to talk. Mariah sat down across from Sharon on the couch.

"So many pieces, slowly falling into place." Mariah made her voice a whisper. "It's not hard to realize what the biggest leverage over you would be. Andy was here when Bethany found your husband dead. Does he know the truth about your husband?"

"Truth?"

"I called a number that was written down in some of Bethany's papers. A woman named Penny answered."

Sharon went pale. "You called Penny."

"So, let's see. Penny knew your family and lived in a city where you claim you never lived. You and your husband changed your name from Meadows—but to your maiden name. Probably much easier, right? Even though it's not that common. Penny was at Holy Innocents School with your daughter, right?"

Sharon didn't move, didn't react.

"Your husband wrote in his suicide note that he was sorry about Penny. What does that mean?"

"How do you know..."

"I talked to Penny. She said Bethany was writing something about Hal, but that Penny barely remembered you all as family friends. Why would Bethany call her? Why would he apologize for her? Did he do something to her? Hurt her?"

Sharon said nothing. Did not seem inclined to speak.

"And Bethany started writing a book. About a suicide driven by a cover-up over a child run down by a hit-and-run driver."

Sharon made a noise in her throat.

"You can trust me with what you know," Mariah said. "If it has nothing to do with my mom, I won't tell anyone. But if you don't tell me, I'll put Reveal on the trail of this story, and you know how hungry he is for a big story to tell. Talk or silence. Me or him."

"If I tell you, and you see this has nothing to do with your mom, will you stay silent?"

"You'll have to risk it. I won't make a promise to you just to break it, Sharon. But I will call Reveal if you don't tell me."

Sharon took a deep breath. "The only Penny I know," she said, "is dead."

* * *

Mariah let the words slide over her. "I talked to her."

"That's not possible." Sharon's hands were trembling.

"Who is she?"

Silence moved over them both like a wave. Sharon closed her eyes, opened them, seemed to fight for both breath and words. "She was a girl. Same age as Bethany. Not a neighbor. They lived a couple of miles away. We were casual friends with her parents; the girls were in preschool together. Hal worked with her mother."

"Your girls were at Holy Innocents in west Houston."

Sharon nodded.

"You said you came here from Chicago, not Houston."

"We went to Chicago for a couple months then moved to Austin. So that's not a lie. We just didn't talk about coming from Houston before that."

"What happened to Penny? What did your husband do?"

Sharon took a deep breath. Her hands, folded in her lap, went to her sides, as if she were bracing herself in the chair.

"Hal drank. He drank during the day sometimes, because he'd go on sales calls and have cocktails at lunch with a client and rather than go back to the office he'd come home and drink. So. He went to get Bethany after preschool. She'd gone home with Penny. He'd lost a big account that day and left work. He told them he was sick, but he was drunk. I didn't know." She steadied herself. "I'm not sure what happened, but Penny got out of the house and was in the street. Playing, I guess. Bethany was still inside. He ran Penny down. He didn't stop. He kept going. He left her in the street. In an insane, drunken panic." She took a deep breath, shuddering, as if fighting for control.

"And you did what?"

"I did what I had to do. Hal came home. And he told me what he'd done. I wanted to call the police, but he said we'd lose everything if I did. I was terrified. He cleaned the car, and then he stashed it at his uncle's house; his uncle had died recently, and no one was living there. I had to cover for him. We chose...that we would not say anything."

"You concealed this crime."

She nodded. It took her several seconds again to speak. "So while he started covering his tracks, I had to drive over and get Bethany while the police and ambulance were all there...pretend I'd been late to pick her up. I didn't have to see Mary—Penny's mother—the police had Bethany, who was hysterical." She pressed her hand to her chin. "Penny...didn't suffer. It was instantaneous." She said this almost as she was trying to reassure herself. "Mary didn't see Hal's car. No one did. No one knew who could have done it."

Mariah could hardly breathe.

"We were never suspected...I showed up to collect my daughter, as expected. This was my husband; it was an accident. My daughter couldn't lose her father. We couldn't bear to stay in Houston. We had to wait for the investigation to die down. We told people Bethany was so traumatized that we had to get her to someplace new, start again. People understood. Other mothers told me I was a good mom to do this for her." Her voice wavered again. "We went to Chicago, for a few months. I told Hal we couldn't live as we had before. He had to get sober. He wanted to change our names...he thought it would make us harder to find if anyone ever came looking for us. So he and Bethany took my maiden name of Blevins."

"Didn't Bethany ask why?"

"Bethany, she shut down. She saw that child's body in the street. She didn't speak for five days. We gave her new memories and she took them. We told her we were changing our names, and our cities, to put all the bad behind us. Kids accept a lot. She was ready for a new explanation. A new reality, the old one was unbearable."

Mariah suddenly felt a memory: wind on her face, sunlight in her eyes, an ache in her knees. She blinked it all away. *A new reality, the old one was unbearable.*

"There wasn't a news account of a hit-and-run involving a girl named Penny. I looked."

"Oh. Penny was a nickname. For the color of her hair. Her real name was Barbara. She was named for one of her grandmothers."

Mariah thought of the auburn hair in the news photo.

"And then we came here," Sharon said.

"So Penny was dead, Bethany was blissfully unaware, Hal was sober, and you had a new life."

"Yes. It was a closed book."

Closed book. She remembered Bethany's journal, quoting her mother using that phrase. "No justice for that child."

Sharon's fingers went white with gripping the armrests of the chair. "I was more interested in justice for my child. It wasn't her fault Hal was a drunk. Why should she suffer? He was sober now. He was a good man." She swallowed.

"So it was all perfect, and then he killed himself years later. Why?"

Sharon moved slightly in her chair. "The guilt ate at him."

"That's why he had books on dealing with guilt and used Penny's newspaper picture as a bookmark. And he suddenly couldn't take it anymore? After years of coping with it."

"I don't know. But I know you don't really cope. You endure it."

Don't you ask for my pity, Mariah thought. *Not after what you covered up.* "There had to be a trigger."

"Can't you just leave us alone? He's dead. There's your justice."

"Penny's dead, too. So why is someone pretending to be her when I call her?"

"I don't know."

"Bethany found out about this. How?"

"I don't know, but you cannot tell anyone. I think... maybe the woman who talked to you as Penny... is my daughter. Bethany's still alive."

The silence in the room grew huge.

"You know this how?"

"She found out about what happened with her father and Penny. I don't know how. There must have been someone who knew or learned about it. So she doesn't want to go to the police but she also doesn't want anything to do with me. She is angry with me; she keeps her distance."

"What about her marriage?"

"She wanted out. This was a way out."

"Yeah, she wanted to not be around when her husband made a fortune. And when you would have made a lot of money, too, with the stock she promised you. Funny how you never mentioned that to me. Maybe her taking off was a way to punish you, both emotionally and financially."

"I want you to leave. I'm telling you all this only because this has nothing to do with your mom."

"My mom knew Bethany'd found out the truth about her dad. That means I think you had a motive to hurt my mom, Sharon." Mariah's voice was like steel. "Get up."

Sharon stayed seated. She worked her hand into the cushion and she brought up the gun.

Mariah froze.

"I never met your mom, never hurt her, don't know anything about her," Sharon said. Her voice trembled. So did the gun. "I'm tired of people trying to ruin my life. My husband, my daughter."

"You killed your husband. Maybe his version of breaking after all those years was confessing, and you couldn't let that happen."

"I didn't!" she screamed. "I swear, I was at work. I have an alibi."

"He bought a plane ticket to go back to Houston. What, to go confess to the police? And you didn't know that he'd gone that far, and when he told you what he was going to do, you killed him. Did you hold that same gun on him and make him swallow those pills?"

"No, no, no, no, it wasn't like that. I didn't."

"A man who is going to kill himself doesn't buy an airline ticket, Sharon." Mariah kept her gaze on the gun. *If she somehow killed her husband, she won't hesitate to kill you.*

"He changed his mind. I swear it. He was going to go and confess, and then the thought of it must have crushed him and he took the easy way out. I know him like no one else ever did." Her voice broke into shards. She wept and Mariah stayed still. After a few moments Sharon regained some control, wiped the tears and the snot from her face.

"Why then? What happened?"

Sharon shrugged. "He couldn't live with it anymore."

Mariah watched the gun, still aimed at her. "Bethany wasn't running from Jake. She was running from *you*. She didn't tell Jake why to protect him from you. If he knows your secret, he's in danger. Is that it?"

Sharon didn't answer.

Mariah said, "Oh, I meant to ask. Who was the older man at Reveal's meeting you were staring at?"

Sharon blinked, wiped at her eyes with the back of her hand. "I don't know any of those people."

"You reacted to him."

"I was reacting to everyone!"

"I'll find him and I'll ask him. Unless you're going to kill me. It would be awkward though. Jake knows I'm here. My father knows I'm here." The last was a lie, but she had to keep her voice steady. "I am not interested in tearing down your life, but if Bethany is alive, then I need to talk to her about my mom." She felt a sting in her chest, between her shoulder blades. She felt the hot rage of tears unshed. She stood up. "Sharon, put the gun down and we'll forget this part of our talk, all right?"

The gun held steady. Mariah felt ice creep along her spine. She had never had a gun aimed at her before. She was unarmed, with a trunk full of weapons in her car, and she had the baton in her boot, but she thought words would be a better weapon. "If I can talk to Bethany, maybe I can talk her into coming home."

"She won't. She'd have to explain why. It means telling what her dad did."

"If she hasn't broken any laws, then there's no case. Jake just wants to know she's all right, and he wants to move on with his life. Let's all move forward. Put the gun down." She decided not to mention the embezzling; maybe that was what kept Bethany away. Maybe she had done it. But she would have to tell Mariah what she knew about her mother's involvement in this mess.

Slowly Sharon lowered the gun, tears in her eyes. "I haven't spoken of what happened with anyone since Hal died...I thought it was over. Then she found out, and she told me she knew, and she never even let me try to explain my side, why I did it to protect her...Please, don't tell..."

There was no excuse for what she and Hal had done. But Mariah forced her voice to be calm because she needed Sharon's cooperation. "I know you must miss Bethany so much. I know it must have been hard for you. But you must understand how much I miss my mom, right? Help me." Mariah leaned over and took the gun from Sharon's hands. Sharon didn't resist. Mariah unloaded it with care, including the round in the chamber. She put the gun and the ammo down on the coffee table. Her hands were shaking.

"I want you to understand that I'm not a bad person," Sharon said. "I'm a devoted mother. Devoted."

"I understand," Mariah lied, afraid if she said anything else Sharon would quit talking. "Is this what Andy has over you?"

"What do you mean?" Her voice had gone to a whisper.

"I saw him kiss you. And you kissed him back."

Her face contorted, and she looked away. "It was so hard after Hal died. Because I knew what had killed him and I couldn't say. I was terrified the police would make a connection back to our lives in Houston."

The words, so small, felt like a punch to Mariah's gut.

Sharon went on, not seeing the horror on Mariah's face: "But they only cared about being certain it was suicide and not about anything more. Andy was here all the time. She cleared her throat. "But it wasn't my fault. He preyed on me when I was really weak. And now, even when he's got Julie, he won't leave me alone. He takes any opportunity he sees. That's how he could turn on Bethany, even after they were close for so long."

Mariah asked, calmly, "Do you talk to her on the phone?"

"No. She doesn't want to talk to me because of what her father and I did. The cover-up."

"She blames you for the suicide."

Sharon ignored that. "She only communicates through email with me."

"Then how do you know it's her?"

"She called me the morning she left for Houston and told me it was the last time she could speak to me for a while and if I tried to find her that she'd tell the world what I'd done. I couldn't believe it. I thought she would protect me. But she said we'd only talk through email. That she had set up the Gmail account for me. When I signed in with the account name and password that she told me, I saw a message from her." Sharon's voice shook.

"Show me these emails."

Sharon got up, and Mariah followed her into the office. She brought up an email client and a listing of messages from an account, one that didn't use Bethany's name or initials. She scanned through them:

If you killed yourself like dad did, how would you do it?

You claim you miss me. I don't miss you. I miss Dad and I blame you for what happened. He wouldn't have tried to cover this up, this is all about you and your comforts and what people think of you. To you that was more important than what you did to that family. You said you did it for me. That's just to make yourself feel better.

If you and Dad had gone to prison you all might be out by now and everyone's lives wouldn't be ruined. Closure matters, Mom.

What would you do if I never came home? I can't bear to look at you. I can't decide what I want you to do, Mom? Die like Dad or forget about what you did. I honestly don't know. I am your only justice now.

"She's not well," Sharon said. "Clearly. I mean, to speak to me that way."

Mariah wondered. Bethany had every right to be angry. But what was she doing this for? What was she doing in Houston, period? How was she living and working? No trace of her. She'd have to be living under a new name, which was not easily done. She needed money, and so maybe the embezzlement was a real thing, and she had indeed stolen and was now living off that money. What did she hope to accomplish by tormenting her mother from a distance when she could simply tell the Houston police the truth? But she kept this to herself. Sharon had hope...and only hope. The cruelest drug of them all.

"How did she tell you she knew about Penny's death and your cover-up?"

"When she called me that morning."

"Did she say how she learned?"

"No."

"Does she know about you and Andy?"

"No. No. She couldn't."

"Is she in touch with Andy?"

"She doesn't tell me such things."

Mariah checked the last email. It had been sent a month ago. But then she opened the Sent folder and searched in there for her own name.

Nothing.

"You didn't email her about meeting me."

"I was afraid it would make her skittish. Make her scared, to know someone else was looking for her. She might stop talking to me." As if Bethany's notes, defiant and angry, were still treasured.

"Email her. Write what I say. And I'll get you free of Andy."

"How?"

"Just trust me."

"No."

"Do what I say, or I'll call the Houston police right now and tell them Hal killed Penny and that you covered it up. Like you said, even if they can't bring charges, your life is done."

She stared for a moment with the resentment of the powerless and put her hands back on the keyboard.

"Ask her: what did you give Beth Dunning?" She thought, *If this is Bethany, this ought to scare her into answering me. If it's not Bethany... then whoever is on the other side of that email message might be who killed my mother.*

Sharon obeyed. And hit Send. "She may not answer. She doesn't always. It drives me insane."

"Forward me her response." Mariah stood to leave.

"Where are you going?" Sharon called.

"Where did Andy say he was going when he left?"

"Back to his office. He said he would have to work late."

"If you talk to him again, you haven't heard from me. And if you don't do what I say, Sharon, you'll be the lead story in the news here and in Houston tonight."

"*You promised,*" Sharon's voice shook in rage.

"What, you want to hold me to telling the truth when your life has been a lie built on a dead child? Sorry. I lied. Oops."

Sharon started pleading. "Listen to me. If Bethany isn't alive, if she's not the person on the other end of the email, then I know Jake killed her. I have to find a way to prove it. I can't let him get away with it."

"Jake isn't your problem, Sharon. You just see if you get an answer from that email account."

Mariah walked out, the sunlight bright. She wondered if it was smart to leave the gun with Sharon; the woman might use it on herself. Mariah kept walking.

46

Reveal had loaded up the car for the drive to the airport. His parents were out, and he thought of all the times he'd spent watching television in the den, dreaming of being on the big screen, having something to say that people were desperate to hear and know. His parents had shaken their heads at him, but when he came back here, it would be with a television show. He could not allow himself to picture an alternate future.

He left a note for his parents: Off to airport, love you both, not sure what day I'll be back but will text you when I get to LA if there is time. Thanks for always believing in me. That was a touch of revisionist history, but he felt bighearted and generous.

He had just sent the text when his home phone rang. He answered it.

"I read what you wrote on your blog," the woman's voice said. "About Bethany Blevins. It's not true. There's not a connection between the Blevins case and the Dunning case."

"Who is this?"

"My name doesn't matter. But I knew Bethany."

"So how do you know there's no connection."

"Because I know what happened to Bethany."

This. This was the kind of moment he had waited for. Prepared for. He got crank calls and bad leads, but there was something in her voice: certainty. "You should tell me, and then we should go to the police," he said. It was important he never be seen as interfering with an investigation. An arrest would end everything for him with the producers.

"The police don't pay," she said, a touch of lightness in her voice.

"I'm sorry?"

"Your big announcement about television. That you're hosting a show..."

His stomach twisted. "Well, that was a preliminary announcement. We haven't sold it to a network yet."

"It wouldn't be preliminary if you had a knockout punch," the woman said. "If you solved the mystery of the disappearance of a software company millionaire's wife."

"And you want me to pay you for information." The crazies had come out.

"Just a small fee. In exchange for some evidence that would point to Bethany's killer."

"She's dead?"

It was as if she didn't hear the question. "And then you could take the evidence to the police. You yourself, brought to you as a result of your blog...and your TV show, *American Unsolved*. You could say it was anonymously brought to you. You go to the cops, you're a hero. And a TV star. What a start it would be for you."

He licked his lips. This was a risk, but it might seal the deal for the show. He did not think to wonder how this woman knew this news he hadn't shared yet on the blog. "I'm about to leave for LA," he said. "My flight's in three hours."

"So responsible, getting to the airport early. Meet me at this address on highway 71." She gave it to him, he wrote it down. "It's on the way to the airport, so you won't be late."

"How will I know you?"

"I'll know you, Reveal," she said, and she hung up.

47

MARIAH HAD STOPPED by the Starbucks to gather her courage to do what she must, and thought she'd sit in one of the big chairs to drink her pre-felony vanilla latte. She had only taken two sips when Dennis Broussard sat down across from her. He had a backpack on his shoulder, with a Lakehaven Police Department patch on it.

"Hey, Mariah," he said. "I saw you come in. May I join you?"

"This really is the doughnut shop of the twenty-first century." She kept her voice steady. Here she was considering breaking into a house, and a police chief wanted to talk to her. Maybe the universe was sending her a message.

"I thought we could talk. Informally."

"You can't really have an interrogation in Starbucks," she said.

"How are you?" he said.

She knew what this meant. Not how was work or how was her dating life but how was she coping with the loss that never left her? *Oh, and I'm thinking of breaking and entering into a dangerous guy's house and sitting here trying to work up my courage to commit a felony. I'm great.*

She answered, "I'm feeling so tired. My mom is still missing, and someone tried to hurt my dad. How are you?"

He seemed surprised by the question. "I'm angry about those same problems you have."

"I mean, here's the big case you could never crack, no matter how hard you looked at my dad. Doesn't that keep you up at night? That the one case you don't solve is the girl you wanted to date in high school?"

"I want you to know something." He took both her hands in his. "The first time I met your mother, it was the first day of school. Freshman year. I had just moved here. And you know what Lakehaven High School is like. So many kids here start in kindergarten, and so they're already old friends. It's a hard school to be a new kid."

She nodded. "I know."

"Now they do all these extra things to make a new kid feel welcome. Bend over backwards. Back in my day you were on your own." He took a long breath. "I tried to be funny, you know, the first day, tried to crack a joke with the most popular guy in class, and it was a mistake. A big one. He turned on me, decided I was going to be the butt of every joke because I'd presumed too much, crossed that social line. At the end of the first day I begged my parents to move us back to Baton Rouge. My dad told me to be a man, and my mom offered to call the boy's mother, and that would have made it all worse. The second day I walked toward that school like it was a prison. I think I'd slept an hour at most that whole night. I could see the guy who tormented me all that first day waiting for me by the flagpole. You feel like your life is over." He stopped for a moment, looked at the floor, then met Mariah's gaze again. "And suddenly, walking next to me is the most beautiful girl I've ever seen. The best smile. The kindest look. And she put an arm around me and said, 'You're Denny, right?'—I went by Denny then—and I could barely nod, thinking maybe she was going to tear me up, too, maybe humiliate me some way. Maybe she's the girlfriend of the mean kid."

"She wasn't," Mariah said.

"No, she wasn't," he said, with the first smile he'd ever offered her. "She said, 'My name's Beth, and I'm sorry you had a bad day yesterday. Today will be different.' And I said, 'No it won't,' and she said, 'Yes it will,' and she went up to that kid—his name was

Wade—and she said something to him I couldn't hear. Then she took my arm and smiled at everyone who'd gathered to see me beat up, and we walked into the school together. Wade didn't ever really bother me again. She told people that I was her cousin who had just moved here—why she did that I don't know—and she hadn't had a chance yesterday to introduce me around. We had four classes together, and she made sure we sat together in all of them. She'd noticed I was struggling that first day, she'd heard what happened to me, and she decided to help me."

"She could have just said you were a friend."

"I think she knew the blood claim gave me more protection," he said. "It took until end of freshman year for people to realize it wasn't true, but by then I was okay. I had friends. I'd found my place." He looked at Mariah. "She gave me a gift I could never repay. No one's ever been kinder to me in my time of need. Do you see why I can't let it go?" He cleared his throat. "She helped me when I needed help. She needs justice."

Maybe she did the same for Bethany. Mom, always trying to fix the trouble for someone else. "I'm glad she made it so you didn't sit alone in the cafeteria at lunch, but that doesn't mean my dad killed her."

"She liked your dad. Craig was impossibly good-looking. Football star and smart. It was so annoying. They were that perfect high school couple. I was just the guy with the wrong kind of face and the right kind of heart." His voice wavered. Then he pinched the bridge of his nose and closed his eyes for a moment.

"But still. She wasn't a case file. My dad wasn't just a suspect."

"Mariah, has it ever occurred to you that I am concerned for you and your father?"

"No, it really hasn't." She took a sip from her latte. "You've suggested to me, to my face, that my father is a killer and that I'm lying to protect him."

"I am concerned for you," Broussard said. "For what you're doing."

"You've always wanted to trap my dad," she said. She was trying not to shake, thinking of what Dad had said, of her shoving him into the wall after he destroyed her investigation board. Not give away her doubts.

He shook his head. "If your dad killed your mom, I know it had to have been an accident. I don't think he ever would have willingly hurt her. And maybe he panicked and covered it up."

She took another sip of her latte. "And I helped him?"

"Through silence. I know you love him very much."

"And now someone wants him dead," she said. "Doesn't that point to another culprit?"

"It might. It might be a vigilante who wants your father to face justice."

"Justice isn't a rock dropped from a bridge."

"I know. Did you see what happened with your mom?"

"What?" His sudden question felt like a punch.

"Your very muddled memory from that day... if you'd just been in bed, you wouldn't have a memory problem. You slept, you ate, you slept some more. That you don't remember suggests to me you saw something you'd rather forget."

"I didn't know you were a neurologist," she said, not looking at him.

"It's so unfair," he said. "You are forced to choose. You can't help your mom, but you can help your dad. The pressure to stay silent. To not remember what really happened."

She thought of the stray images that crept into her mind: Mom, her hands up, a voice yelling "We are not doing this!," the breeze on her face, a pain in her knees. "That DVD you found in my car."

"Yes?"

"What's on it? Will you tell me?"

"It's password protected. We haven't broken the password yet."

"If I can guess the password, will you let me watch it with you?"

He said nothing for a moment. Thinking. "It could be evidence. I think not."

"You were her friend. You helped her before. Let me see it, and I'll help you."

He studied her for a moment, then he pulled a laptop out of his backpack. He then pulled an evidence bag with a DVD inside it. "I was about to head down and see if a guy at the APD forensics lab could tell me how to break the password."

"Put it into your laptop," she said.

He stared at her. Weighing. He did. He clicked on the DVD's icon and a password prompt appeared. He put his fingers on the keyboard. Waiting.

"Penny," she said.

"As in penny for your thoughts?"

"Capitalize the P, like the girl's name."

He turned the screen so she could see it. He typed it. "Nope. Why Penny?"

She thought of the password on the sticky note on the old computer in Bethany's old room. The one Sharon couldn't bear to throw away, written in her daughter's handwriting.

"Try spiker44."

He typed.

A video started. Mariah felt her breath lock into her chest.

Darkness, then focus. Grainy with age—this hadn't been shot digitally, but transferred to disc later, Mariah realized.

A bedroom. A child's room: dolls on an unmade bed, a soccer ball, a child, maybe four. Mariah recognized Penny from the picture. Half her face was obscured by a bright pink feather boa. *Playing dress-up*, Mariah thought.

"Beth, we are going to be models," Penny announced, her words muffled slightly by the boa.

"You are," another girl's voice said.

"Yes, me first. Ask me questions like the lady on TV." Penny threw the boa over her shoulder dramatically.

"I don't want to play this," the other girl—Beth—said off-camera. "I want to go home."

"When they're done talking," Penny said. She whirled dramatically. "Hello, everyone, I'm so glad you're here to see my movie. I am the star."

"What is the name of your movie?" Beth asked.

"Princess Penny," Penny said.

A noise in the distance. The camera moved slightly in response, but Penny inserted herself in front of it, annoyed. "Hello, I'm the star."

"Yes," Beth said. "Do you have a boyfriend?"

"Many," Penny said. "They all love me." She started singing a song about love, making the words up as she whirled.

"Don't wake up the baby," Beth warned. "Can I set the camera down and be in the movie, too?"

"The baby won't wake up," Penny said. "And you need a costume and a boa, and I only have the one."

"Penny…"

"I need a runway like on TV," Penny said. "We can use the sidewalk. Or the street."

Mariah tensed. *Oh no, no, no.*

"I'm not supposed to go outside alone," the voice said.

"Not alone." Penny turned and walked out of the room. Beth, with the camera followed.

"What is this?" Broussard said. "Who are these girls?"

Penny went out the front door. In the background a baby began to cry. The camera didn't follow Penny outside.

"She's crying," the voice of Beth said. Penny didn't answer.

The camera—held by Bethany, Mariah thought—stopped, panned back. The sound of the slamming front door. The video showed the camera moving back through a hall, toward the hallway. Then through a door, where a crying infant lay in a crib.

"It's all right, baby," Beth's voice soothed. "It's all right." Her hand, touching the baby's head, trying to quiet it.

Then outside, a horrible thudding noise, the scream of brakes. A sound of nothing but wrongness. Then an engine, roaring, racing, gone.

The camera fixed on the baby, who had stopped crying, looking into the lens. Feet thundered on the stairs.

The camera moved back toward the front door.

"Penny! Penny!" A woman's voice screaming, then howling, horrifying, a grief that sliced the air.

Then the camera appeared to be carefully set down on a table. She left it running. It showed empty hallway, part of a den. Fifteen seconds. No words from Beth, and she wasn't in the shot. Then the sound of footsteps walking toward it. A man's voice. "Honey, what's happening?"

The last words heard on it were Beth's: "I'm sorry."

Then the man and the child, walking away into the camera's view again, the girl glancing back at it, only the back of the man visible, hurrying toward the screams outside, the two of them moving out of range of the camera's lens and gone.

The video ended.

Mariah was trembling.

"What is this? Who are these people? Did your mom film this?" Broussard asked.

"When she was four? No. But it is proof that my father didn't kill my mother."

"Mariah, tell me what this means?"

"I can't tell you yet. I don't have all the proof. But this is why she vanished."

"Now you're saying this video clears your father? How? Why does your mom have this? What is the screaming? Did something happen to that first girl? Was that the sound of a car hitting her?"

She wrenched her hands free of Broussard's grip. The rage that so often spiked in her heart nearly overwhelmed her; she wanted to hit him. Instead she fled the table, conscious of his stare upon her.

"Mariah!" he yelled. She ran to her car and got in.

Bethany had given Mariah's mother that video. Had Mom known the password or watched it? Or just kept it for safekeeping and it had ended up in Mariah's car? Had Mom hidden it there in case her own car was searched? Had someone come looking for it and hurt her mother to get it? In her car she tried Penny's number again. No answer. She had to take this fight to Andy.

Mariah wheeled out of the lot. She thought about what the video meant, and that she was close to the truth now. A terrible truth.

48

ANDY AND JULIE lived in a nicer neighborhood on the west side of town, off 2222, a road that curved and snaked through the rising hills. Mariah drove there, wondering how far she would go to find what she needed. The video—it tied her mother's fate even more tightly to what had happened to Bethany Curtis.

Andy knew about Hal's suicide. Andy was leveraging this knowledge to victimize Sharon. He was at the heart of this, somehow, and she had to know how.

Mariah parked down the street from Andy and Julie's house, opened the trunk. She had a set of lockpicks, and she stuck them in her pocket. A telescoping baton was already in her boot. She left behind a Taser and a pistol in the trunk. She had felt so tough buying the objects, filled with such purpose, watching the training videos (which now seemed ridiculously inadequate), and now she felt like a child caught at a game she shouldn't be playing.

Because now it mattered. It wasn't a game. And she didn't know what she was doing.

She shut the trunk and walked up to the door.

She tried the doorbell. No answer.

She went around to the back. The yard needed mowing, but the flower beds were neat and had been recently mulched. There was a swing set and a squadron of Star Wars action figures scattered across the yard. A paperback, open facedown on a chair. That froze her for a moment, because maybe Julie was at home and had just been outside reading and hadn't heard her knock. She went and knocked on the back door, boldly, a lie for Julie ready on her lips. But there was no answer. The book had just been forgotten in an earlier moment.

She studied the lock. She had her lock picks. But she started checking under the numerous potted plants, and she found a key under the fifth pot she searched. She slid it into the back door, turned it, and opened the door.

No sound of an alarm, but it could be silent. She walked quickly through the house, looking for an alarm pad. There wasn't one, and she was relieved to see that Julie and her kid weren't lying down for a nap. The house was empty.

There was a corner desk in the kitchen, a little nook with built-in drawers and a computer. She touched the keyboard and the computer awoke. It hadn't signed out the last user: Julie.

She scanned through her emails. There weren't many. Appointment requests from the gym for personal training, correspondence with clients, emails from the preschool her son attended.

Nothing from Sharon, nothing of interest. She checked the list of users. Andy didn't have an account on this machine.

She went to the browser. Her recent history was all higher-end shopping sites: furniture, clothing, shoes.

And a Google search on Mariah. Julie had visited several news accounts about Mom's disappearance. And a Faceplace page on Bethany. Mariah clicked on that, and it jumped to the main Faceplace login page, with Julie's email and password prefilled out—an option one could set so not to have to log in every time you visited the page.

She opened the FIND BETHANY page.

There were all the same postings Mariah had found before when she'd glanced at the page after reading Reveal's article. Nothing new. But as the page's administrator, there were postings and messages sent privately to Julie. Mostly from people who had gone to school with them, asking if there were any new leads, asking how Sharon was doing. Kind notes.

Then she saw the name on one of them: Penny Gladney. The profile picture was the same as the one she'd seen in Hal's book. The one from a newspaper.

The note, sent to Julie, said: I want her to suffer some more.

Nothing else. The note was dated a month ago. Julie had made no answer to it.

She clicked on the profile. Penny Gladney had just one Faceplace friend: Julie Santos. Penny had posted no statuses, no updates, liked no other posts by other people on the site. There were no pictures or biographical data.

OK, a full name. Penny Gladney. For a moment she thought of sending a note saying, "Is it you, Bethany, hiding behind a dead girl's name? Who are you really?" But then Julie would see it and know her account had been accessed.

Mariah logged out. Now she had a full name, and she was rattled that in all the drama she hadn't asked it of Sharon. Didn't matter now. If this was Bethany…she wanted her mother to suffer.

Quickly she searched for "Barbara Gladney," using the child's real first name. There it was. Years ago, run down in the street by a hit-and-run driver in a quiet neighborhood. No witnesses. No charges ever pressed against anyone. She had been playing outside her home. Her parents declined to be interviewed, except for a statement asking for anyone who knew anything to come forward. There was no mention of a suspect. Or a witness named Bethany Meadows, not by name. It simply said she had been playing with a friend. Of course another child's name would be kept out of the newspaper accounts.

No further news reports in the years that followed. An unsolved mystery.

Mariah cleared the search history and then went to their bedroom. The furniture, she'd noticed, was very high-end. Andy and Julie had spent money on this place. She searched their closets. Julie had nice clothes. Really nice clothes. A few still had the sales tags on them: three-hundred-dollar, four-hundred-dollar tops and pants and sweaters. Her shoe collection was large and high-end. Andy had nice suits and shirts as well. In a drawer she found multiple watches, including two Rolexes. In a box she found a nest of jewelry that looked expensive.

He worked for a family company. It must pay very well. Or...there was other money.

She went upstairs, to the little boy's room. More Star Wars stuff. She almost ignored the room, nothing to see, but she wanted to be thorough. She checked Grant's closet. He also had very nice clothes, lots of designer labels, considering he'd probably outgrow them every few months. She looked under his bed. Nothing but a suitcase with a cartoon character on the side...and a large duffel bag that appeared to be full. Next to it was the sleek briefcase she'd seen Andy carrying when he was leaving Jake's office.

She looked at it with a sense of dread. It didn't belong in a kid's room unless he'd decided to play, what, investment banker?

She tried to open the briefcase. Locked. She opened the duffel bag.

Neat piles of bills. All hundreds. There was room where a couple of bound clumps of cash had been removed.

Why? She counted one stack of bills, made a best guess at how much was in the duffel based on how many similar stacks there were. It was nearly twenty thousand dollars.

Andy and Julie had thousands and thousands in cash that they weren't keeping in a bank.

Was this the money Bethany had stolen from Ahoy? If so, then Bethany had never taken it to Houston. Then that meant what? They'd killed her for this money? How did it fit in?

She debated what to do for a moment. Take the money or leave it here? If she took it, then they'd know someone was on to them. But the money could be a bargaining chip—she could trade it for information. But then she thought, *You don't know what they're capable of. All Sharon has to do is tell Andy what you know, and he'll come after you. And if he has legitimate reason for this cash, then you've committed another felony.*

Choose.

She zipped the duffel bag closed, lifted it, and settled the strap on her shoulder.

She heard a car door slam and her blood turned to ice. She peered out the window, staying low, barely parting the curtain. Andy, parked down the street at the community mail stop. He would be here in moments. Why wasn't he at work? She watched him open his mailbox and pull out envelopes. Had Sharon called him? Told him about Mariah learning the truth? No. He didn't seem in any rush.

Carrying the bag of money, she hurried down the stairs and back out the back door, and froze in front of the row of potted plants. She replaced the key and moved the pot back into place. She heard the garage door powering up; he was driving into the house. The garage entrance into the kitchen was right by the windows she would have to cross—he might see her as he exited the garage.

She ran the other way. She started to climb over the fence, into a neighbor's yard, and a large, angry dog barked at her, leaping upward toward her. She ducked back down and went over the other side of the fence, awkwardly holding the duffel of cash. Quiet, empty, but now she was in a backyard of a house on the street parallel to where she had parked. She would have to hurry. She exited the yard, walked down the street, turned, and then turned left onto the street where Andy and Julie lived. He'd be in the house by now; he wouldn't see her. Her breath felt ragged in her chest.

Andy stood in the driveway, before the raised garage door, staring at her car parked two houses away. Now turning to watch her.

Oh, no.

She still held the duffel.

"Mariah?" he called slowly. "Are you looking for me?" he called. He started walking toward her. He must have noticed her car, started pulling into the garage, and then realized that the car was hers. Maybe he memorized her plates when he'd spotted her at Jake's office. She remembered Claudette, at the window, reading off the plates. Maybe even then he saw her as a threat. She felt sweaty and sick.

He saw the bag she was carrying... recognized it.

"What are you doing?" His voice hardened.

She pulled out her keys, aimed them at the trunk, it opened.

He was running toward her now.

She dropped her keys into her boot, pulling out the telescoping baton. With a flick it snapped free and he reached for her, trying to grab at the duffel.

She slammed the baton down on his arm, and he howled in shock and surprise.

"What the hell!" he yelled, taking a step back. "You're a damn thief," he said.

"Am I? Or are you? This money. Where does it come from?"

"That is none of your business," he said, gritting his teeth. She slammed the baton into his other arm. He cussed and staggered back.

She moved to the open trunk, eased the duffel into it, and pulled out one of her Glocks. This she aimed at him and his eyes went wide.

"Put that away!" he yelled.

"Is this the money Bethany took from your company?"

He stared.

"I am going to drive straight to the police and tell them I took this from you. I don't care. They won't press charges against me. They'll want to talk to you."

"It's not what you think. I didn't take the money from her." Now his words were a pleading rush.

"Did she give it to someone else? Like my mom? Did you take it from my mother?" Her voice rose, the gun unsteady in her hand. "Did you kill my mother for this money? Or for the video?"

"No! No, I don't know anything about your mom! Please, it's not what you think."

"Whose money is it, then?"

He tensed. She'd whipped both his arms, and he was in clear pain and couldn't grab at her. *You might have to shoot him*, she thought. She shut the trunk, with the money inside, and began to move toward the driver's door.

"I'll give you half of it," he said. "Just take it out of the trunk and leave and I won't call the police."

"I don't want it."

"Well, you're driving off with it!" he yelled.

"I guess I am," she said. She made her way to the driver's door. Got inside.

He charged at her. She slammed the door shut, hit the locks. "You don't know what you're doing," he said. "She'll kill you."

"Where do I find Bethany?"

He shook his head.

"I'll try another name. Where do I find Penny Gladney? Tell me and I'll give you back the money."

"Let me make a phone call," he said after a moment, gritting his teeth in pain. "Then I'll call you. Just don't go to the police, please, Mariah."

"Stay away from Sharon," she said after a moment. She'd decided what to do. "I know what you've done to her."

Something shifted in his face. He leaned back and tried to kick in the window. She hit the ignition button and powered the car away as he tried to make a second kick.

He screamed, "You don't know what you've done!"

She saw him watching her in the rearview mirror, standing in the street.

You don't know what you've done.

She was shaking as she turned south at the main road. But she knew what she was going to do.

49

IT WASN'T LUNCHTIME, but Andy's aunt Claudette was at the front desk. She was reading a new issue of *People*.

She glanced up as Mariah came into the office. "He's not here. You should call first."

"I know he's not here. I'm here to see you."

Claudette appeared unimpressed by this announcement. She wet her finger and turned the page, shook her head at the young actor pictured in the article. "You know who was handsome? Cary Grant. Sidney Poitier. Paul Newman. All these young guys look like they got over-polished." She made it sound like a bad word.

"Andy took the fifty thousand in cash from your company. Not Bethany. He did."

"That's quite an accusation." But it made her look up from the magazine.

"He framed Bethany for it when the embezzlement was discovered. But then he offered to settle with her, and promised you he'd pay back the money. Am I right?"

"What's your interest in all this?"

"It's a yes or no question, Claudette."

"It's Mrs. Candolet to you, dear."

"I'm sure the police will call you Mrs. Candolet as well, when I tell them you withheld critical information in the investigation."

"This is a family business. We don't have shareholders or investors. Our matters are private."

"I assume like most businesses you have bank loans," Mariah said. "Right? The bank might care about fifty thousand vanishing and not being reported to the police. It could make getting future financing difficult. There could be a concern that where one crime gets covered up, there could be more."

Five seconds ticked past. "What do you want?"

"I don't have to go to the police, or to anyone else. But I want to know the truth. If you lie to me, I'll burn Andy down, and I'll bet the fire will spread to this place."

Claudette put her hands on the desk, on each side of her magazine. The wry attitude was gone. She was all business. "All right. Bethany was working here. Andy got her the job. Then Lizbeth got a temp job here, and the two of them became instant friends. They went out together a lot, they talked about writing books, Bethany and Lizbeth joined some writing club. Whatever Bethany was interested in, Lizbeth liked, too."

"Lizbeth." That was right. She'd nearly forgotten. But she had only worked here for a few weeks. "That was during the embezzlement?"

"Yes. I thought at first Lizbeth had helped Bethany steal the money from the accounts. But she hadn't. It was Bethany who had logged in and accessed the account and moved the money into some falsified vendor. Those vendors didn't exist. It was an account set up by Bethany."

"That was your only evidence against her? Someone could have gotten her passwords. At home she left them on a sticky note on her monitor." She thought of that sentimental memento in Sharon's office.

"Andy's in charge of security, and I trusted him when he said she did it."

"Andy has a large amount of cash hidden in his house. I've seen it." She showed photos she'd taken of the opened, cash-filled duffel on her phone to Claudette, who blinked once but whose expression did not change. She didn't mention the cash was in her trunk. "Do you know why he has that much cash on hand?"

"I do not."

"And when you discovered your money was missing, you reacted how?"

"The last person who stole from me was in the hospital for a long time. Unfortunate accident in their car," Claudette said. "These coincidences are a part of life."

Mariah waited. *This woman's a seventy-five-year-old gangster*, she thought. *He's not supposed to have it. I can see it in her eyes.*

"Andy told me he would get the money back. From her husband. More than money. Some shares in his stock. I said no, I don't like the stock market. I've always preferred cash. But Jake Curtis has been paying us back, in cash, over the past several months."

Andy, going to Jake's office. Would he really give Andy cash there? Well, it was as good as any place.

"So Andy's brought the money to you?"

"Yes. In cash. In small amounts that wouldn't attract attention when deposited. We just added them to existing invoices. Banks look for large cash deposits. I don't want the attention."

"I think Andy's playing both you and Jake. He's told Jake that Jake owes more than what was stolen. And Andy's pocketing some of that money instead of giving it to you. To finance that lifestyle he and Julie like. Which is really dumb, but he seems to not think well about consequences."

The clicking of the old clock on the wall was loud. Claudette took a deep breath. "You've done your good deed for the day. Go. I'll deal with Andy."

"I want to know about Lizbeth Gonzales. She's the other side of this puzzle."

"What about her?"

"Do you have a picture of her? A file with her address?"

Claudette got up and went to a file cabinet in the corner behind the desk. She unlocked it and pulled out a file and opened it. Blinked. "There was a picture after we hired her. She had to have it for an ID card. It's gone." She pointed where a photo had been torn from a stapled job application.

"Do you have it on digital?"

Claudette went to the computer and typed. Something in her expression shifted. She looked up at Mariah. Her mouth narrowed. "The picture is gone."

Mariah leaned down to look.

Claudette's voice was steel. "She's been deleted from our records."

"Who could do that?"

"The network administrator. Or Andy."

Mariah looked at the application in the file, the one bit of evidence that Lizbeth had worked here. Her name was written as Jennifer Elizabeth Gonzales. There was a Social Security number, an address in Lakehaven. Her emergency contact was a man named Bill Gonzales, listed as her father. There was a Houston phone number for him. Houston, again. Mariah took a picture of the form.

"Andy deleted her. Why would he?" Mariah said.

Claudette shook her head.

"You and Andy both talked about Bethany's life spinning out of control. Credit card spending, drinking, this theft, inappropriate gifts sent to coworkers to embarrass her."

"Yes."

"Her life wasn't spinning until someone set it to spinning."

"You think it was Andy and Lizbeth?"

"Or just Lizbeth."

"Why? What motive would they have?"

"At first I thought it was just Andy. But why would he hide Lizbeth?"

Claudette looked at her, seemed to weigh what to say. "I thought the two of them might have been seeing each other."

"I thought he only had eyes for Julie." Mariah knew this was false, but she wanted to see Claudette's reaction.

"That boy has eyes," Claudette said, "for whatever gal looks back at him. Or for ones he can't have, like Bethany."

"How long after this embezzlement incident did Lizbeth stay?"

"A week after Bethany left, she gave two weeks' notice, but Andy just cut her free. Paid her for the time she didn't work, too. It annoyed me, but he said since she and Bethany were such friends, it was better if she was gone."

"Do you know anything about her? Her references?"

She waved her hand. "Andy checked all that, I didn't."

"She was here just long enough to help Bethany lose her job," Mariah said.

"I never thought of it that way, but yes." Claudette reached for the phone. "I think I'm gonna tell Andy he needs to get over here." Then she surprised Mariah with a knowing look. "Do you have this money? You took pictures of it. I bet you took it with you. For proof. So he couldn't hide it."

Mariah kept her voice steady. "It's in a safe place." The trunk of her car, which wasn't safe at all.

"Fine. You can leave the money with me. If it's not mine, he can pay me back with it." The anger was rising in Claudette's voice.

"I think I'll hold on to it for a while," Mariah said. "Until we've established where it came from."

They stared at each other. Mariah could tell Claudette wasn't used to being told no.

"He will be chasing you down, little girl. You going to call the police? I'll give you a cut of the money. I don't want this in the papers."

"If he killed my mother for it, I don't want a cut," she said.

"Now you listen to me. Andy is clearly a total mess, but he's not a murderer," she said.

"I could drive straight to the police with this. Even having entered his house. They put me in jail, I'm safe from you all. But then he has to explain this money. Either he stole it from you or from Bethany, but he's a thief, and I don't think you want him in jail. Talking to the police about what goes on here, what you might transport beyond legitimate freight. Trying to reduce his sentence."

"So what do you want?"

"I want you to call him and bring him here. Keep him busy."

"What are you going to do?"

"Have a talk with Julie."

Claudette's face made a little sneer.

"You don't like her?" Mariah asked.

"He could do better."

"She has expensive tastes. Maybe that's why he was stealing."

The sneer deepened, and Mariah knew it was the right card to play. "He's my heir, and if he's so dumb to risk inheriting this company to steal from me now just to keep that Julie in jewels, I'll cut him out. I'll find out whether he's lied to me or not. If there's a tie to your mama, I'll find it. But you don't go to the police. I help you, you help me."

Even with Andy possibly cheating her, she was trying to protect him. He was family. "We'll see," Mariah said. She walked out the door.

50

MARIAH DROVE BACK to Julie and Andy's house. Andy's car was gone, but Julie's was there. She thought this was the last action Andy would expect her to take. The money was still in the back of her car.

Mariah had on a jacket, and she had moved the baton to her waist, tucked in the small of her back. She didn't want to aim a gun at Julie. She didn't think it would be necessary.

Julie opened the door, shock on her face. "What?" She looked flustered.

"Where's Andy?"

"I can't talk right now," and she started to slam the door and Mariah put her foot and shoulder into it. She forced the door open and Julie backed into the small foyer.

"Mariah, what is your problem!"

"Why are you messaging on Faceplace with a dead girl?"

Julie went silent.

"Penny Gladney."

Her mouth narrowed. "I don't really know who that is."

"Penny Gladney is dead. Bethany's family is connected to her death. Someone is using her name. I think it could be Bethany."

"How do you know that?"

"It doesn't matter. If I think this relates to my mother's case, I'm going straight to the police. They will turn your and Andy's lives upside down, and I don't think you want that with thousands of dollars in unexplained cash in your house."

Julie's face paled. She took another step back.

"Mommy?" Her little boy, Grant, came into the den, holding a Star Wars figure.

"Sweetie, hi," Julie said, mom mode slipping into her voice. "What's the matter?"

"Can I have some juice?"

"Sure." She turned and went into the kitchen. Grant stared at Mariah like *Who are you?*

Mariah knelt down, feeling the baton shift in her back, wishing now she hadn't brought a weapon. There was a child here.

"I don't know who that is," she said, pointing at the action figure.

He explained who the action figure was, that he was going to be a Jedi warrior, and that he had several other action figures but sometimes he left them outside and Mom got mad because they were "spensive."

"Here's your apple juice, baby. Go back to your room and play, OK?" Julie handed him a juice box.

"Can she play with me?" He pointed at Mariah.

"Not right now. She's about to leave," Julie said.

Grant said, "Bye."

Mariah said, "Bye, sweetheart."

Grant went down the hall with his juice. He stopped at the stairs and waved a goodbye to Mariah. She waved back, and he went into his room and shut the door, as if he knew an adult argument was brewing.

"You are leaving now," Julie said in a hiss, "and don't bring your crazy self to my house again. I tried to help you, and this is the thanks I get?"

"I don't think you've wanted to help me as much as watch me and make sure I didn't find out anything about you all. The money. Where is it from?"

"What money are you talking about?"

"The duffel bag under your son's bed."

Five seconds and Julie kept the controlled expression on her face. "Claudette doesn't trust banks. We keep it for her."

"Under your own son's bed."

"A burglar wouldn't think to look under a kid's bed for money like that." Julie's voice was quiet.

"Don't protect Andy. He's not worth it. He was sleeping with Lizbeth Gonzales at work. He is involved with Sharon. I saw him kiss her in her house."

Julie laughed, disbelief contorting her face. "Andy. And Mrs. B. Sure. Right."

"He has been involved with her for a long time. Since he was a teenager."

Julie's eyes widened. Mariah knew she'd landed a punch. "He wasn't hanging out there in high school and later for Bethany. He was there for Sharon. I think maybe he blackmailed her into it. He knows something about Hal Blevins's suicide, and it was leverage over her."

"Get out of my house," Julie said. But Mariah could see something in her eye, the dawning of realization, of possibility. Julie averted her gaze to the floor, put the back of her hand against her mouth.

"Penny Gladney. Who's using her name? Is she Bethany?"

"I don't know for sure." Her voice lowered. She seemed shaken. She was flushed. "You cannot go to the police. You cannot. This is all Andy. It has nothing to do with me or Grant. You will ruin our lives."

She was scared of jail. Of being taken from her child. Mariah stared at her. "Bethany's life was ruined. You were supposed to be her best friend."

Julie bit her lip.

"Does this . . . Penny contact you in any other way?"

"She only communicates through the page. And not often. I don't know her. I just give the message to Andy."

"What kind of message?"

"She wants to know what Jake is doing, if he's paying back what Bethany stole. What Sharon is doing—if she's suffering, if she's miserable. Sometimes I see it's a message from her and Andy reads it, not me."

"Does she ask about anyone else?"

"No. Not to me."

"Contact her. Ask her where we can meet her."

Julie didn't move and Mariah took a step forward. "Now."

Julie turned and went to her computer. Went to the FIND BETHANY page. Wrote a message to Penny Gladney: I need to see you. Where can we meet?

The answer came back quickly: No way.

Julie wrote: There is a problem. I have to see you. Andy in trouble.

No answer for a minute, and then said: I'll contact you later. It's not safe right now.

Safe? Mariah wondered.

Julie wrote: No, now. NOW.

Silence.

Julie typed: Andy is in serious trouble. We have to talk face to face.

Silence.

"Tell me your login," Mariah said. Julie did. Mariah logged into Faceplace via her phone's browser as Julie, so she'd see the reply as soon as it came. "If you warn her, I will call the police and I'll make sure you and Andy are both arrested. If you stay on the sidelines, you'll be fine."

"Please think of my son, please, Mariah..."

"I don't want to separate you from your child. I know what that is like. Julie, you got into a bad situation. Get out of it. Andy is not worth this."

Julie pressed her fist against her mouth, and Mariah walked out the door.

Penny Gladney was just a name, a ghost from the past.

Maybe "Penny" was Bethany, hiding behind a name designed to punish her mother.

Or maybe she was the other ghost in the story: Lizbeth Gonzales, who Andy had conveniently made it hard to find, who withdrew from life after Bethany disappeared.

* * *

From her window, Julie watched Mariah heading to her car. She typed onto the laptop, still signed into Faceplace messaging with Penny Gladney: Penny. a woman named Mariah is looking for you. She made me write you.

I understand, the message came back.

She's logged in as me.

Understood, the reply came. Then that brief burst of messages winked from existence, gone, deleted on Penny's side while Mariah was not looking at her phone and starting up her car.

Julie watched Mariah drive off. Bethany had been a real disappointment as a friend, stealing that money and blaming Andy, the man Julie had always loved and finally won. Julie was all for women sticking together until she wasn't, and she wasn't about to tolerate someone hurting Andy. Bethany had screwed up her life. She wasn't going to drag Andy, and in turn Julie, down with her.

Julie went to go check on her little boy, hold him, sit with him on his bed and not think about the money. Andy would fix it. He always had.

51

THE WOMAN HAD suggested she and Reveal meet on the route he'd take to the airport. As beautiful a city as Austin was, the stretch of highway closer to the airport was full of mobile home dealers, warehouses, and industrial use. Reveal saw the sign for a company in one of the industrial parks that distributed light fixtures and it was the address she'd given him. He turned into the parking lot.

Reveal had plenty of time to make his flight, and if he told the producers in LA that he was breaking open a case that had stymied the police, they'd push back the meeting. He hoped. This was a gamble, and he felt that all his ambitions and dreams were hanging in the balance for the next ten minutes.

No cars in the back of the lot. That was odd. He went to the door; it was unlocked. Lights out. Fear crept up his spine, but ambition pushed him forward. "Hello? It's Reveal. I'm here."

A woman's voice: "Oh, hey, thanks for coming! I'm back here, sorry I forgot to turn the lights on. Just catching up on paperwork."

She sounded so casual. He could see a gleam of light back down the hallway, which ran parallel to the warehouse space.

"That's OK," he called back. He walked to the lit office.

Stopped in the doorway, stared. Blinked in surprise. Narrowed his gaze at the figure standing, waiting for him in the room.

It took him a moment, it was so unexpected.

"You," he said.

"Me."

And then jarring, sharp pain, again and again. He didn't know how long it lasted. He thought of his parents, and the team in Hollywood, and then Mariah. *Oh Mariah.* Then he felt the prick of a needle in his neck and all his ambitions and hopes and dreams fell into the darkness.

52

IS IT TRUE?" Claudette sat behind the desk when Andy walked in. He could hear laughter down the hallway, a dispatcher and a trucker in the break room.

He tried the smile that always worked. She didn't smile back.

"What... is what true, Aunt Claudette?"

"That you, not Bethany, embezzled the money from me."

"Of course it's not..."

She held up a hand before he could finish. "Don't finish a sentence that's a lie, boy. Not to me."

He stopped talking.

"Clever," she said. "You frame Bethany for the theft. You make a deal where we don't prosecute her and her husband, who doesn't want bad publicity before his company goes public, 'restores' the money to us in small cash increments that don't get noticed. Along with extra for you and Julie, as a handling fee, and for your silence. So, you pocket the first fifty thousand, and get the scared millionaire to repay even more for your silence, and only some of that cash has made it back to me and my company so far. Do I have it right?"

His mouth worked. "If you will let me explain, Aunt Claudette..."

"It's clever. It's actually cleverer than I gave you credit for. I know that scatterbrain Julie didn't come up with it. And you're not a planner, Andy. You're more a dumb opportunist. Maybe that little temp you were screwing, she might have the brains for this." Her tongue tented her cheek. "I could see the two of you cooking up a scheme. The problem is you've impacted me. You've dragged us into this and any police investigation. And you've made a crazy girl think we had something to do with her mama going missing." She gestured to the trucks outside. "And I really don't want the police sniffing around all my trucks, Andy."

"I've taken care of everything."

"If you had truly taken care, then I wouldn't have that crazy girl in here with pictures of cash in a duffel bag, what might be my money. You stole from me."

"I..."

"After all I've done for you. This burns, Andy, and I don't like feeling burned. I don't like the idea of handing over the company to you if you just create messes."

"There is no mess."

"There won't be." Her voice was ice. "You're going to fix this. Get rid of this Mariah. I don't want to ever see her here again. And whoever helped you steal this money, shut them up. I don't like loose ends. Avoiding them is how I've gotten to my ripe old age."

"Aunt Claudette..."

"Not your aunt. Not until you've made this right, Andrew. And neither is this company. For years I've watched you smile and charm your way through life. And be impulsive. I thought working here would settle you down. I was wrong. I've got a phone call into my lawyer to change the will, to strip you of this birthright if you don't straighten yourself up. This is a multimillion-dollar enterprise, and you've risked it for what? Quick cash to keep your limber girlfriend happy and live beyond your means. There's a reason I don't live in a vulgar style. I put the money back into the company, and I don't attract attention from the police or the authorities. Our...other clients admire that about me. Be like me. Not like Julie, not like you. It's time, boy, for you to grow up. Am I understood?"

He took a step toward, only wanting to plead his case. And then she raised the gun from under the desk.

"Aunt Claudette..."

"I don't know what you're capable of. Did you kill Bethany?"

"No...no, I wouldn't." He had gone pale.

"Do you know what happened to her?"

"I have a suspicion. But I don't know for sure," he said slowly.

She held up a hand. "I do not want to know. But I also do not want you being an accessory after the fact. So you need to clean up this mess so it can't ever be pointed back at us. Do you understand?"

Andy took another step forward. "I just want you to know I am so sorry..."

"Stop. Not another step. I don't want to hear your sweet words. They have ceased to work on me. I'll shoot you in the leg if you threaten me. And Carlos and Dave are down the hall, and I've told them already to be ready to beat the living tar out of you and put you in the hospital if you cross me. They're loyal to me, if my own nephew isn't."

"I would never," he said, his voice hoarse and broken.

"I'm glad. I don't want to shoot you. Now. Go fix your mess, and then we can talk again."

"Yes, ma'am," he said.

Andy turned and he left.

Claudette watched him. She put the gun back in the desk. She wiped away a tear that had formed in her eye. She opened up the new issue of *People* and tried her best to focus on the words. These actors today, all polish, no depth.

53

MARIAH CHECKED THE Faceplace page...still no answer from Penny Gladney. But now she had an address in Lakehaven that was tied to Lizbeth, thanks to the Ahoy Transportation file. She drove to the address for Bill Gonzales.

It was a large, older home, with a detached garage and what looked like an apartment above it. It was on a quiet side street, with many towering oaks. One house was being torn down and a McMansion rising in its stead—she parked close to it, where she could still see the Gonzales house. She went to the door and rang the doorbell. No answer.

She went back to her car. She could wait. She internet-searched Bill Gonzales. He owned a number of lighting fixture wholesalers, in Houston, Austin, and San Antonio. There wasn't much else about him. She guessed from the house that he'd done well for himself.

She realized she hadn't yet done an important task: checking her mother's calendar from September 4, the day that Bethany Curtis boarded a flight to Houston and vanished.

She slid the flash drive with her mom's records into the laptop and opened up her mother's calendar and email files.

On September 4, her mother had an eight a.m. sales meeting with a client at their office in Austin. Then she had a lunch meeting with a product team, and then other meetings at two and four, both in-house.

So she wasn't in her office that morning. She could have met Bethany.

She went to her mother's email, and searched on September 4. She had received four dozen emails in the course of the day. Mariah scanned through them. Most were internal to her company: a discussion on how to close a big deal that was looming, a product feature request.

There was no email from Bethany or from any suspicious account.

She searched the week before, the week after. It took a while. Salespeople got a lot of emails. Nothing.

She went to the Sent folder. Searched the same, nothing.

Then she saw the Drafts folder. Opened it up. Her mother was apparently a great one for starting emails and then saving them in case she needed them again as she redrafted her sales proposals, her responses to execs who wanted to know why sales numbers were down, and her diplomatically worded requests to the development staff to fix a bug or enhance a feature.

She started searching. On the morning of September 4, an email to a Gmail address with the letters *bbc* as part of the name:

Leave it for me in your mailbox. And I won't look at it. And I won't tell anyone. Where am I supposed to hide this? I hope you find what you're looking for. I'll stay quiet.

There wasn't an email that matched this in the Sent file or in the Archive file. Mom must have deleted those but forgotten about this one. And the police hadn't noticed this.

She sent a test email to the address. There was no bounceback. It was still out there. BBC. Bethany Blevins Curtis. The timestamp on the draft was at 9:05—she must have gotten out of her early client meeting and been getting ready to return to the office when Bethany emailed her.

Her mom didn't send another email until 12:12, telling someone she was stuck in a lunch meeting and would call them back shortly.

So she'd had time, during the same two-hour window where no one had seen Bethany Curtis. Maybe not enough time to take Bethany to the airport, but enough time to retrieve something Bethany left for her.

And Bethany had asked to see her. How had Jake or the police missed this in their search for Bethany? She'd had an email account no one knew about. Or it had been wiped by the time Bethany was gone—perhaps by Bethany herself, as part of wiping out her trail. Both the police reports and Jake said she'd erased her computers.

Or someone else had. Someone who wanted to hide what Bethany had learned.

The video. She felt sure that was what Bethany had given her mother. For safekeeping. And written her name on it so anyone who came looking for Bethany's evidence would not be suspicious and it would never be mistaken for a blank DVD if Bethany needed it returned. If Mariah or her father had stumbled on the DVD and tried to load it, Mom could have just said it was a confidential project for work.

And then maybe, somehow, someone had found this email on Bethany's side of the conversation and . . . a target had been painted on Mom's back.

Mariah felt sick. She fought down the surge of bile in her throat. Think. Stay calm.

She sat in the car and waited. She kept thinking someone would notice her loitering here, get suspicious, and call the Lakehaven police. Broussard knowing she was here was the last thing she needed. She kept checking the Faceplace page. No answer.

Night fell. A man came to the house. He parked in the garage, the door slid closed.

She waited a few minutes and then she knocked on the door. The man answered. Close up he was in his sixties, bleary-eyed. He had already put on sweatpants and a T-shirt. He wore a bathrobe and he held a drink in his hand.

It was the man from Reveal's missing persons support group. The one that had engendered a reaction from Sharon.

He stared at Mariah. *He recognizes me*, she thought.

"Hi, I was looking for Lizbeth Gonzales," she said.

"No one here by that name." He spoke slowly, carefully, keeping an iron grip on the door.

"Are you Bill Gonzales?"

"Who are you?"

"My name's Mariah. Lizbeth and I were in a writing group together." This was how she'd decided to play the angle. "Kind of like how you and I are in a support group together. Who are you missing?"

His mouth worked. "My daughter Lizbeth."

"Really?" Her stomach sunk. A third Beth, gone. "When did she vanish? Did you report that to the police?" Mariah crossed her arms.

"She takes off sometimes. For months. I...I get worried when I don't hear from her. I heard about that meeting..."

She didn't believe him now. "Where is she, Mr. Gonzales? Where?"

"I don't care for your tone." His voice wavered. "Now, leave, or I am going to call the police."

"Lizbeth might be in some trouble."

"What do you mean?"

She felt the sharp rise of her temper and she pushed the rage down. "Sir. Please. Just tell me where she is."

His gaze darkened. "Get off my property." He slammed the door in her face.

She walked off, but then quickly cut back, sticking to the shadows. There were windows along the front of the house. She could hear him pacing the floor. She risked a glance through the window, hiding in the space between the bushes and the window. She could see him, on a cordless phone, pacing, saying, "You need to call me. Don't come home. Just call first." He hung up.

So much for her being a third vanished Beth. Mariah ducked back. Listened. She heard footsteps, rattling of glass, a glug of something being poured. Bill Gonzales was probably right by the window. She tried not to breathe.

She heard the front door open. Bill came out onto the lawn, looking up and down the street, holding a drink, maybe looking to see if she was there.

The bushes hid her from his view, and he seemed more interested in the street, as if trying to see if she was sitting in a car.

Then he went back inside as his phone began to ring. He slammed the door.

"Some girl here asking questions," he said. "Looking for Lizbeth Gonzales." Silence while he listened. "Do what?" He listened again. "No. I won't."

He listened again, for what seemed a longer time. Mariah peered through the window again. She had the baton in her boot. But all the other weapons were in her trunk.

"I won't," he said again, but with a little less fire.

She waited.

"Fine, all right, stop yelling at me," he said. He hung up. Through the window Mariah watched him sigh and close his eyes in apparent frustration. Then he went upstairs. She waited. Bill Gonzales returned, dressed in jeans and a pullover, his hair combed a bit better. He went outside. She crept to the corner of the house and watched him pull out in his SUV.

She ran across the yards to her own car. He drove away from her, down the street. She followed, hanging back. He got onto the 360 Loop, headed south, then onto 71 east, heading toward the airport. Then past the airport, heading out of town toward Houston.

She grabbed her phone, called Jake's number, and hit the speaker.

"Hi," he said, and she didn't want to think how nice it was to hear his voice.

"Hey. I'm following Lizbeth's father. He lives here in town. I think he's driving to see her."

"Uh, all right."

"Why are you giving money to Andy?"

Silence. "You know."

"I found it."

"To pay off Bethany's . . . debt."

"She didn't steal the money from Ahoy. He's tricked you."

She waited; she could sense his frustration as he absorbed the news. "I knew that was a possibility, but I couldn't let anything derail the company going public."

"You let him shake you down." She couldn't keep the disappointment out of her voice.

"Yes. I couldn't take the risk. Not just for me. For all the people who worked to launch the company...for most of them, their stock options represented a lot of potential wealth. I couldn't let their hard work be ruined. I was willing to pay hush money."

"Penny Gladney. Does the name mean anything to you?"

"No."

"Lizbeth's father's name is Bill Gonzales. He lives on Whistledown Road in Lakehaven. I'm following him from his house; we're already east of town. Almost past Bastrop. He called Lizbeth and seemed to be in a panic."

"I'm calling the police."

"No, don't. I'll call you when I know more." She paused. "I'm glad of one thing. That I got to meet you. I'm grateful for that."

"Mariah..."

She disconnected the call, focusing on hanging close to Bill Gonzales. But not too close.

Mom, she thought. *These people drew you into their scheme, and something went wrong, and they killed you. I'm going to shove them out in the sunlight. I'm going to turn around, like in the dream, and see the monster that took you from me.*

* * *

"Mariah...Mariah!" he yelled. She had hung up. Jake pocketed his phone. He wanted to check Mariah's claim. He went online, finding the property tax records for a William Gonzales on Whistledown Road. He had bought the house four years ago. Jake wondered if he could find out anything at that house while Bill Gonzales was gone. It was a risk. But Mariah had said they were nearly to Bastrop, which was in Bastrop County, just east of Austin. Maybe he owned other property. He jumped to Bastrop County's property tax page and found another address owned by a William Gonzales. Off a rural road, not in Bastrop proper. The Google view showed mostly piney woods. This house was out in the middle of nowhere.

He grabbed his car keys and headed for the garage.

The doorbell rang.

He answered it.

Sharon stood there.

"Hello," he said, a bit surprised.

She produced a pistol from behind her back and aimed it at his chest. He froze. "Where's Mariah?" she demanded.

"She's not here. Sharon, put that away." He had never had a gun pointed at him in his life.

"Where is she?"

He kept his voice steady. "I have no idea."

"Liar. You were just yelling her name. I heard it through the front door. You know where she is, and you're going to take me to her." She gestured with the gun. "I've thought this through. I can't live like this. So. I'm going to fix all this."

He kept staring at her and she said, quietly but firmly, "Now, Jake."

54

W*HAT DOES THIS Jeffrey know?* Craig asked himself. *Why is he doing this? What does he hope to gain?*

How did he get into my house?

Does he have Beth's key? That was the thought he could not erase, that this man could have gotten Beth's key, the one she must have had on her when she vanished, and used it against him. The thought was like a little poisonous seed. Craig could never have brought himself to change the locks. It felt like an admission that Beth would never need to come home. And he was afraid of what changing the locks would say to Mariah. She was simultaneously steely and fragile. He felt he walked on constant eggshells in dealing with her.

And then he wondered if Jeffrey Marshall was connected to Broussard. Dennis was Craig's most determined enemy. He could survive the averted gazes or the glares or the people turning around in grocery aisles so they didn't have to come near him: the parents of kids who had started first grade with Mariah, the parents of the sports teams she'd played on, the parents who had worked backstage at the high school musicals. The vast parent network one forged when you went to a good school district and were in it for twelve years. They could hate him, but they couldn't really do much to him.

Broussard could. Broussard could hurt him and avenge Beth and every slight he'd suffered since Beth chose him all those years ago.

"It's OK," Beth said. Craig looked up from the screen where he was watching the security camera feed. Beth was there, yet not there—he knew that—close to him, as if she'd come to his office to sit and tell him he'd been working too hard and Mariah needed him and she needed him and all life and love was giving each other our precious attention... and there, in the last year of his wife's life, he had failed her completely.

"Beth, is it?" he whispered. His words barely more than breath.

"Just protect her... from whoever this is." Her voice, soft like a whisper. She used to whisper to him in bed. Her soft words were like a spell on him when he was young. He loved her beyond reason.

"Whoever this is," Craig repeated. "Do you know?" he whispered. "Is it you?" The question he dared not to ask.

But then she was gone, like she hadn't been there, and of course she hadn't. He blinked. So many movies and TV shows these days where the dead paid visits as mentors, prodding the characters into action or providing them with insights. Like being haunted was a great and helpful process. He closed his eyes and took a deep breath. She wasn't there, and she hadn't been there; he knew that. He just missed her more than he'd ever thought possible. She had emptied his heart. They were supposed to grow old together, stride together toward old age, learn from and comfort each other over the years. Beam at grandchildren, take pride in their daughter's work and happiness, grow wiser together. Lean on each other and love each other and never hurt each other again. But that was all gone. All that was left was Mariah.

"Just protect our daughter," he heard Beth's soft voice whisper.

He would.

* * *

Craig left the rock, wrapped in paper like the ones left for him before, out in his own driveway. Just in case. If he was being watched, him leaving a rock would be like lighting a signal. His watchers would wonder what he was he doing. He was counting on the weakness of human curiosity.

How would a guy who was used to leaving rocks react to seeing a rock left from him?

He'd written on the note that wrapped the rock: I will leave but I need a guarantee you never come after my daughter.

That, after all, had been what every message so far pointed at: a desire to see him and Mariah gone.

Would he take the bait? Would he come to watch?

In the dark, he waited.

Soon…

* * *

The camera picked up the note being removed from the rock, a shadowy figure kneeling. It also picked up, emerging from the shadows of the oaks across the street, a hurrying figure dressed in black sweater and jeans. A swing of a sock filled with sand, once, then twice, then the first shadow collapsing into the second. Then the quick shuffle of someone being dragged down the driveway and through the open door of the house with the for sale sign.

* * *

"Where am I?" the man said, his voice thick and slurring.

"To quote you, 'I know what happened. Should I tell the last secret you know?'" Craig said. A single small light, from a lamp on a table, was on in the room. The light was pale.

"Where…you…"

"You were leaving rocks in my driveway," Craig said. "And, I suspect, dropping them on my car."

"What did you do to me…I wasn't…"

"I have you on film in my front yard."

"It wasn't me…"

He produced the paper used to wrap the first rock. "I bet if I show this to the police, they're going to find you have very similar wrapping paper in your house."

Jeffrey bit his lip and took a deep breath.

"I have you on film, Jeffrey," Craig repeated. "Now. I could call the police."

The man blinked at him. "How do you know my name?"

"You were smart not to bring your wallet, but I spotted you following me. I figured it out from there." Best to leave his stepson Sean out of this. He was an innocent kid.

"Why were you even here, Jeffrey?" Craig asked, his voice quiet and reasonable.

"I was just coming here to make an offer on your house, but you've kidnapped me... you've assaulted me..."

"Or I could kill you." And then he let Jeffrey see the knife in his hand.

Jeffrey went silent. He began shivering.

"This is so silly." Jeffrey, his words slurring, tried to laugh. "I'll make a good offer on your house. We can all be happy..."

"An offer."

The man wouldn't meet his gaze. "We want you gone."

"Gone."

"Sell your house. Move out. Go live somewhere else. Get a new start."

What would you do to protect someone you love? That question always got asked—in books, in movies, like the decision was a struggle. It had never been a struggle for him. Anyone who came at Mariah was to be dealt with, no matter what. She had lost too much already. She could not lose more. *I would kill you and not blink. I would get rid of you and never worry for long about the loss your loved ones would feel, because my loved one is safe.* He told himself this was true. He thought he believed it. That for Mariah he could turn his heart to steel.

"This," Craig said slowly, "was all about scaring me and my daughter out of our home so you could buy my house on the cheap, do a teardown, and turn a tidy profit."

Jeffrey finally nodded. "I own Platinum Homes. I buy houses, do teardowns, build a new and modern house to replace these old smaller ones. Look, I won't tell the cops you attacked me... just sell me the house, I'll give you a cut of the profits, we'll both do well..."

"You have one right next to your own house you're redoing." He remembered the sign when he spoke to Sean. He leaned down to Jeffrey. "Your work is beautiful."

Jeffrey didn't speak.

"I can't imagine my little house was worth so much trouble to you."

"Your lot...you're the highest point along this road, the top of the hill, you have the best view in the neighborhood. I already have gotten agreements from the houses on each side of you to sell. I was going to tear down all three houses. I got a buyer from California who wants to build a gated home here, a huge mansion. If I don't get this property for him now, he'll look elsewhere. I needed you to sell fast and cheap, and if I came to you, you might have asked the same deal as the others. I thought...you would be more willing to go cheap, given your situation. You were the final piece of the deal I had to have." His voice broke. "Look, clearly I made a mistake, and I'm really sorry."

"And the rock you dropped on my car? I could have died."

"I made sure it wouldn't hit you." Jeffrey Marshall tried to sound convincing. "I was so careful..."

"And if I was dead, the cops here wouldn't care, and my daughter would sell to you?"

"I didn't try to kill you, I swear, just prompt you into action."

"You taped the cell phone under my wife's car."

Jeffrey had decided answering questions was the fastest way out of here. "Yes. It gave off a signal I could trace with an app on my phone. I'm remodeling another house right by the bridge. I got an alert you were headed that way in the app, and I picked up a rock and walked down there. No one saw me."

It was so shockingly *petty*. But that was the world now. But centered entirely on him being an outcast because of Beth's disappearance.

But he could have attacked Mariah. *Attacked my child.*

"How did you get in my house?" Craig made his tone light, as if they'd moved past the unpleasantness.

"You walk your dog around the same time every day. I watched you. Sometimes you don't lock the front door if you're taking a shorter walk. You walk him, and that gave me a few minutes to slip into your house and find your spare key ring and take an impression of the house key. I had one made." Jeffrey tried to smile. "Look, we have to come to an understanding. You can profit from this, all right? Sell me the house. It's got to be full of bad memories for you. You get out of this place where everyone hates you and you make some money and start over somewhere else, you and your daughter. Find a new home."

Craig's grip tightened around the knife. "Speaking of homes, I have an idea."

55

Andy pulled his car deep into the woods, off the road. He wanted to approach the house on foot, not be seen. He had a gun, loaded. He could put that gun on a truck to Arkansas or Louisiana or Utah tomorrow and never see it again. He had friends among the drivers, friends who'd long done him special favors.

You messed up. You got greedy, you got dumb, and you let it slip out of control. You let her run the show when you should have put a stop to it all. Aunt Claudette's right. Fix this. Andy approached the side of the house away from the porch. No sign of her. The garage was shut, but she was likely here. He could hear the soft sounds of music: Frank Sinatra playing. She loved Sinatra.

He entered the house without knocking. The door was locked, but he'd gotten an impression of her key once; he had thought it would be useful. He stood in the silence of the foyer, listening. He would get what he needed from her and then deal with her. She would just have to understand the arrangement had come to an end. He didn't want to spend his growing-old years with Julie looking over his shoulder.

He could hear the music, upstairs. Probably she was in the creepy room of hers, revisiting her life. Why do you have all this stuff up on the walls, he'd asked once, and she'd told him never to mention it again. He knew better.

He entered the room. Pictures of the people in his life, and people he didn't know, all pinned to the walls. The music came from a laptop. He stepped toward it and bent to look at the screen because there was a picture of him and Julie and Julie's little boy Grant and then he felt the needle slide into his neck. He whirled and that lunatic was behind him, smiling, and she'd pumped something into him and a wild panic clawed at him. He felt his muscles start to collapse, his strength, what kept him safe, fading. He wet his pants. He fell to his knees.

"What…what…" his lips felt thick, he could hardly move them.

She stepped back. "I thought you might turn on me. And I need you to do one more little thing for me, Andy. Right now I just need you to be still and keep breathing. For a while."

"Uh…la…ess…Beth…" he tried to say.

"I'm not her anymore," she said, and the blackness swarmed over him like a living thing, constricting, suffocating.

56

MARIAH DROVE EAST, letting Bill Gonzales stay a few cars ahead of her, going past Bastrop. In the moonlight as it broke through the clouds she could see the remains of the pine forests around the town that had been decimated in a fire years ago and were slowly growing back.

His car turned onto a side road. She had to follow him, but he'd likely notice her now. Fine. If he stopped, then she would stop him and force him to tell her where he was going.

She slowed onto the shoulder off the highway, waited for thirty seconds, then turned, letting him stay well ahead. But they were now the only two cars heading north. He slowed. She slowed. Then she had an idea, and she turned into the parking lot of a small café. He kept going.

She saw a text from Jake. Another address for Bill Gonzales, this one in Bastrop County. It saved her having to make the search she planned to make. She punched it into the maps app and drove off.

It didn't matter if she kept Bill in sight now. She knew where he was going.

But she didn't want to be too far behind. Just where he couldn't spot her.

She drove deeper into the piney woods.

The maps app put her onto a farm-to-market road off the main highway, then another one. The pine forests began, and not all the roads were paved. Mariah drove into a dark overhang created by the density of trees, the car jostling as she got closer.

She turned at a sharp bend in the road, and down the hill, she could see a house, aglow from a porch light. She killed her headlights. Two stories, wooden, a stone chimney. The landscaping needed attention: shrubs overgrown, weeds sprouting in the flower beds, the grass a bit high. But it didn't look abandoned.

Gonzales's car was parked to one side, next to a car that looked like Reveal's, which stunned her. Why was he here? What had he learned? There was a garage, but the door was closed.

She parked in the trees in the darkness. She opened the trunk, trying to shield the light with her body. She put a gun at the back of her waist, her telescoping police baton in her pocket, her knife in her boot. She gently shut the trunk. She cursed herself for not having thought to arm herself before she parked—they might have seen the trunk light. She could not make mistakes now. She walked toward the house, staying in the pines.

She risked moving down the long curve of driveway, in the open, and reached a shadowy corner out of the halo of porch light.

One lit window was close to the garage. She peered through. She could see Bill Gonzales alone in the kitchen, leaning against the refrigerator, rubbing his face, as if weary or sick. Then he walked out.

She heard the front door opening. She ducked around the edge of the house. He got into Reveal's car, started it, and drove away.

Why is he taking Reveal's car? she wondered. Fear was an icepick in her chest.

She listened. She didn't hear voices.

Had he locked the door behind him?

She gently tested the lock. It was open.

A trill of absolute terror ran up her spine. The truth was here. The not knowing…for so long…she took a silent breath and opened the door. A dim light came from the kitchen, left on by Bill Gonzales. She stepped inside and left the door open in case she had to run. She killed the porch light. If she had to run, she wanted the night to hide her.

She stood in a small foyer. A mirror hung by the door, an umbrella stand, a piece of art on a stairway leading to the second floor.

The air smelled a bit stale, and a bit coppery. Like blood. She told herself that was her imagination.

She walked from the foyer into a den, simply decorated with a leather couch, a basic coffee table. Some framed art hung on the walls—but they were all a child's paintings. Paper yellowing with age, the name JENNIFER carefully written in crayon in the corner of each one. A picture of a home, with a mom and a dad stick figures, with two smaller stick figures next to them: two girls with dresses and curly hair. Stick figures at the circus, with elephants and lions and clowns. At the ocean, on a mountain.

There was a single photo framed. Two girls. One of the girls was the same as the photo she'd found at Sharon's inside one of Hal Blevins's books. Same coppery hair, green eyes alight with joy. Penny? She held a baby, with a pink ribbon in her hair.

The final drawings, each a portrait, had labels: Mommy, Daddy, Penny, Jenny. Rhyming names.

Mariah walked deeper into the house, past the entrance to the kitchen, past the staircase. She reached a larger room, a bedroom but with no bed, and she stepped inside. It was dark, the windows shuttered and curtained, and in the pale glow of a weak lamp she saw Reveal, bound to a chair, head lolling toward his chest.

Mariah rushed toward him. He was breathing, but he'd been beaten nearly unconscious. She turned as she sensed someone behind her, someone who had been in the corner in the shadows.

The light switch flicked on.

"Hello," the woman said. "Again."

Mariah blinked at her.

Not Bethany.

It was the woman who had been reading the book, sitting on the patio at the Tex-Mex restaurant. Mariah had broken the jerk's finger who wouldn't leave her alone, the night she met to compare notes with Reveal.

What... what... had she been spying on us, listening to us talk about the case...

"Thanks again for standing up for me," the woman said.

"Are you Lizbeth?"

"Yes," she said, and then Mariah saw the gun in her hand.

57

THE CALL CAME into the Lakehaven police late, past midnight—a loud crashing noise reported from a house under construction on Canyon Grove Avenue. The responding unit investigated, then sent out for Dennis Broussard, because he had asked to be summoned any time there was a suspicious death. Lakehaven had a very low crime rate, and he was determined to keep it that way.

The house was one of those teardown-and-buildups that Broussard, as a longtime Lakehaven resident, hated. The walls were up, but the house was still unfinished. The sign out front read Platinum Homes—he'd seen others of their signs around. The officer led him into the partially finished house. The man's body lay at the foot of a long staircase, neck broken, a broken flashlight by him.

"We got an ID?" Broussard knelt by the body. The corpse was male, in his late forties, well groomed, broken eyeglasses.

"Yes, sir, the driver's license says Jeffrey Marshall. He lives next door."

"So he was trespassing?"

"Well, there's some business cards in his wallet, too, and he owns the company that's building this house. Same name on the card as the sign out front. I'm guessing he came over here to check something, and he fell down the stairs. His neck's broke."

"Why would he come over here in the middle of the night?"

"Must've heard a noise?" the officer suggested. "Maybe a thief? They'll steal copper out of these houses."

Broussard leaned down farther. He could see a watchband on the man's wrist, with a distinctive pattern. Like the silver diamond pattern on the video, on the wrist of the person who tried to kill Craig Dunning.

He took a deep breath. "Anyone at Marshall's house?"

"No, sir, no one responding. It was another neighbor that heard the crash and called, and then the unit was here in three minutes."

"Did they see anyone leaving the scene?"

"No, sir."

Broussard stood, feeling very tired. He pulled out his cell phone and dialed Craig's number, half wondering if he'd hear a ring in the nearby darkness, hiding. But there was nothing, and no answer from Craig.

Did you find the man who was after you, Craig? Did you find him before I did?

Broussard put the authority back into his voice. "OK, let's get this processed. I want this place gone over carefully. Find me any evidence that suggests this wasn't an accident."

58

LIZBETH?" MARIAH SAID AGAIN.

"Yes. Very slowly, turn around. Put your hands on your head."

Mariah did. Lizbeth relieved her of the baton and the gun tucked in the back of her jeans. But she didn't see the knife hidden in Mariah's boot. Mariah wasn't sure how quickly she could draw it before Lizbeth could shoot her.

"OK, turn back around," Lizbeth said.

Mariah obeyed. The gun held on her remained steady. They were both silent for a moment. Mariah couldn't stand the quiet, so she spoke, trying to fit the pieces together.

"Bill Gonzales isn't your father. He's your stepfather."

"Yes."

"Jennifer Elizabeth. Jenny and Penny. Penny Gladney was your sister. You were the baby crying in the background of the video."

The gun didn't waver. "Yes. Penny was my older sister."

"Your grudge is against the Blevins family."

"*Grudge* is such an inadequate word for all I've done." Her voice was very calm.

"Why is Reveal here? He hasn't hurt you."

"Lots of loose ends. Reveal, Andy, you. Fortunately we have a crime to discuss. A reason why Bethany and your mother got into trouble. Reveal's going to write an explanation on his blog. And I think he's more likely to do it with you here."

"Where is Bethany?" Her voice sounded small.

"Not far," Lizbeth said, her voice quiet and even.

I want her to suffer.

"*You* were behind derailing Bethany's life. Pretending to be her friend. Ruining her. The drugging her when she was drunk, the planting of the pills her mom found in her car, the pranks, the credit card abuse."

Lizbeth gave a tiny nod.

"Because Hal killed your sister. But Bethany was innocent of that. Why would you come after her?"

"None of them are innocent. Hal, Sharon, Bethany...your mom."

"My mother is here?" Mariah's voice rose. Nausea waved over her.

"She's not far from here," Lizbeth said, her voice still calm. Echoing what she'd said before about Bethany.

What did that mean? A cold fear knifed through Mariah. "Hal's already dead. What point is there?"

"Reveal?" Lizbeth called.

Reveal opened his swollen eyes. He focused on Mariah and mouthed the words: *I'm sorry.*

"Do you want me to tell you the story?" Lizbeth said to Reveal. "I've wanted to tell it for a while, and you have your pitch to finish."

Reveal nodded, very slowly. His mouth was gagged with cloth, his lips bloodied.

Mariah wanted to say, *Chad, there is no pitch. She's not letting us leave.* She could see Lizbeth forcing him to write a solution for his blog on the mystery of the Beths, then tragically killed...by Mariah. And Lizbeth, or Jenny, would melt into the shadows, vanish again, emerge elsewhere with a new name.

"Let's start with Hal," Lizbeth said.

"He killed himself out of guilt," Mariah said.

"Oh, there was guilt," she said. "He bought a ticket to Houston because he wanted to come see me."

"You?"

"Well, my mother had just killed herself a week before. He felt just a smidgen of guilt about that," Lizbeth said. "Penny's death destroyed my family. Her death was a never-ending ripple. Absence as presence." She swallowed. "My dad got cancer two years later, and he didn't want to fight it. He didn't have the will to live. Wouldn't even do chemo. Just let himself die."

"I saw the video. Your dad was on it."

Lizbeth's teeth touched her bottom lip. "You found the DVD."

"Yes."

"I began to believe Bethany had destroyed it after she stole it from me. She had every reason to. Where is it?"

"The police have it now."

Lizbeth let the silence fill the room for a moment. "My dad's not the man on the video. That was Hal Blevins."

But that couldn't be right, Mariah thought. Hal was driving the car that hit Penny. He was drunk behind a steering wheel, not inside the house. Mariah opened her mouth to speak, but Lizbeth went on.

"My dad couldn't summon the will to live, to fight, even for me and my mom. After the cancer killed him, she remarried."

"Bill Gonzales."

"Yes, and Bill tried and tried, but Mom was never happy. Ever. She killed herself over it, finally. Pills and booze. I found her dead. I was fourteen."

Mariah felt nausea climb up her throat. "I'm sorry..."

Lizbeth waved away her sympathy. "And I called Hal. Mother had found Hal and Sharon, a year before, but done nothing on it. She could prove nothing about their guilt, but she wrote out all her theories in her suicide note. I told Hal my mother and father were dead because of what he'd done."

"How did you know?"

"Something my parents said." She glanced over at Reveal. "Can you guess?"

Mariah said slowly, "Hal wasn't drunkenly driving over there to pick up Bethany. He had another reason. He got fired for sleeping with a coworker as well as drinking. Was your mom the coworker?"

"My mom is not to blame. Be very careful of what you say."

"I can't guess," Mariah said.

"Are you really scared of me? Because you're not thinking straight," Lizbeth said. "Hal wasn't driving."

Mariah's chest tightened. "Sharon was."

"Hal was *already* over there. He'd brought Bethany over for a playdate she didn't want. But he was really there to see my mom. They went upstairs—talking, or worse—while Bethany and Penny were playing. I was a baby, asleep in my crib. Foolish, stupid of them, but people having affairs whose families know each other can use their kids as camouflage. Bethany didn't keep Penny inside the house. Sharon raced over there in her car when she suspected where her daughter was, that her husband was using a playdate as a moment to be with my mother, and *she* hit Penny and just kept going. Like Penny was nothing. Maybe it was a revenge against my mother. Maybe it was an accident. None of it matters, because it's still her fault. I never knew every detail until my mother's suicide note. She laid it all out—the affair, her suspicion that it was Sharon driving like a maniac over there to catch them, Penny being run down, that worthless family leaving Houston a couple of months later to go off and have a normal life. To have what the Gladney family could never have again. But my mother had no proof, and she didn't want to go to the police. I kept her suicide note, and that way only I knew the truth of why everyone I loved was now dead."

"I'm so sorry," Mariah repeated, horrified. "Why didn't your mother tell anyone?"

"She didn't want to lose my dad. Or what was left of her life. Her job, her friends, her parents." Lizbeth shook her head. "What do you think everyone would have thought of her, if her child was dead because she was distracted by her married boyfriend? Her family? Her church? Society loves to hate on a wayward mother."

Mariah had no answer.

"So. Hal kept tabs on my mom through a friend back in Houston. He heard about her suicide. When I called him, he said he was going to come to Houston to see me—he'd bought a ticket. I guess to confess, like I already didn't know. But I could hear in his voice he couldn't face it. So I came on a bus to see him. I told him to stay home from work so we could talk, and I wouldn't tell the police what he and his wife had done. I brought my father's gun. I think that surprised him, but it showed him my maturity. My seriousness. We sat. We talked. And I think once he knew how our family was destroyed, totally destroyed, that he couldn't face living with Sharon anymore. They'd kept a terrible secret, the two of them together, and three people were dead from it." She glanced at Reveal. "Is that the right kind of tone for your podcast? Dramatic enough for you?"

"He killed himself," Mariah said in a whisper.

"I gave him a choice. Suicide, or I could shoot him and shoot his family when they came home. It was his fault his wife was rushing over to our house. He agreed. I think the years of the lies had broken him. He did it while I watched. I gave him the leftover pills my father had been given for his pain. He sat and ate them and drank a bottle of liquor I'd brought from my house and made me promise I would leave his family alone if he did this. He wrote a couple of drafts of his suicide note, and I sat with him while he died. I even held his hand, once he was unconscious. I'm not a monster. I'm a better person than he ever was."

What had Eben Garza said about Hal acquiring the booze and the pills? *He found a delivery service*. It had been Lizbeth, but she had brought the means with malice aforethought. Mariah couldn't speak. "How could you..."

"Am I really the one you want to judge in this little tragedy?" Lizbeth cleared her throat. "I stood in a neighbor's yard, behind a tree. Watched Bethany and Andy come home from school, watched Sharon arrive, watched the police arrive. Just a kid, watching all the excitement. Then I went to the bus station and went back to Houston."

"Who erased the line about Penny in his suicide note?"

"Sharon, probably. Erasing that line about my sister was all she could do, probably in a panic. She couldn't destroy the note. She needed the note to stop the investigation, make it just a plain suicide. But in the news report, there was nothing about his rough draft of his suicide note."

"Andy found the rough drafts of the suicide note. I'm guessing they explained more of what he and Sharon had done. Meant for Bethany. But Andy took them when they arrived on the scene and found Hal. He used them as leverage against Sharon, even if he didn't know who Penny was, that there was a secret Sharon didn't want known. To get her into bed, to do whatever he wanted her to do." Mariah shook her head. Andy, the endless opportunist.

Lizbeth shrugged. "Hal didn't bear all the guilt. But he destroyed my family with his lust, and he lived with a woman who was capable of running down a child and then covering up the crime, cool as could be. Veiled herself in faith and respectability." She cleared her throat. "But I killed him. Just by telling him that my parents were both dead because of him and Sharon." She smiled at Mariah, and Mariah felt dizzy, nauseous. "I killed him with a visit, smiling at him. What could I do if I really applied myself?" She gave the softest of laughs, and it felt like a knife blade on Mariah's skin.

Keep her talking, Mariah thought. "You had your revenge. Why did you need to come after Bethany?"

"Bethany wouldn't go outside with Penny. You saw the video she made. If she had, Sharon would have stopped."

"They were four... You can't blame a child for what her mother did."

"Oh, I disagree. Responsibility is responsibility," Lizbeth said. "It was all their fault. But I wanted to hurt Sharon, and the best way to hurt Sharon was to take her daughter away from her. Piece by piece, step by step. I just had to wait until I was old enough. And until Bethany was happy. I wanted her happy before I came after her."

"You need help, Lizbeth." Mariah took a step forward.

The gun centered on her. "Actually, I'm the healthy one here. I've dealt with my emotions. Not you or Reveal. And I don't think you should judge me. You've done worse." Her grin was back, slightly crooked.

Mariah didn't know what Lizbeth meant, but she stayed still. "So you came after Bethany."

"I thought it would be better to destroy her before I destroyed Sharon. So. I studied her life. For four months. Then I befriended Bethany. She had no idea who I was. She didn't remember much of that day. She'd blocked it out."

Mariah felt nausea twist her guts.

"And I made sure to steer clear of Sharon, in case she saw my mom or my sister in my face." Mariah thought of Sharon telling her about the time she'd seen Bethany eating lunch, and Lizbeth—the new friend—had ditched the table. "Bethany was lonely. She was bored. I followed her. She was interested in writing. She got a job. So I got interested in writing and got a job at her business. I recognized Andy as the boy who came home with her the day her dad died. Andy wasn't going to hire me, but I convinced him. Right there in his office, with the door locked." Her smile was cold and crooked. Her fingertip played along her lip. "He's not the sharpest pencil in the cup. I found out soon enough he needed money, constantly, for his Champagne tastes, and I thought of a way to get it. Because I couldn't have Bethany getting wealthy off Jake's company. That could have put her out of my reach. I had to hurt her, ruin her, before she was rich and could enjoy it."

"You embezzled the money," Mariah said.

"I don't dirty my hands. I planted that idea with Andy. If you make a man think it was his idea, he'll run with it."

"Then Andy stole the money."

"I helped him. Except I made sure the theft was discovered. I told him we had to blame Bethany. He went along with it. There's not too much to him, and then he was under my thumb. See, I knew I'd need a crime. One that Bethany's death and eventually Sharon's death could be tied to. Andy stealing that money was it. Money's such a good, simple motive for murder. Make it look like Bethany was in on the theft, ruin her life, and then after I've gotten rid of her, Andy has a motive to kill her, whenever I want to play that card. I had proof he committed the theft, but I could place it so it looked like Bethany had it and he'd killed her to keep her quiet. Then months later her mother could"—she air-quoted—"'find out,' and I'd get rid of her, and then Andy would be done as my useful idiot. Poor mom and daughter who found out about his embezzlement. And the police wouldn't look at any old crime, when they had a new, easy one to deliver simple answers."

Mariah stared at her. "That also set up the chance to take advantage of Jake. You knew Jake would be desperate to protect his reputation, to protect his precious company."

"So Andy could get money from both his awful aunt and the guy he hates most in the world. It made Andy feel so *big*." Her mouth wrinkled. "But most of the money came to me, or I'd tell on him to Claudette. Julie is expensive, so he had to get more and more from Jake to keep his cash flow going."

Past tense. "Where is Andy?"

She ignored the question. "I knew when Bill called that you'd follow him here," she said. "You're not the smart one here. I am."

"Andy is desperate right now because his aunt knows he took the money, not Bethany."

"Oh, he is," Lizbeth agreed. "I told him I'd get you here and then we'd strike a deal."

"A deal."

"I'll give you Andy. I think you'll want him. You need someone to blame."

"Blame."

"For your mom. I thought she might have my DVD of the video that Bethany had made that day. I had shown Bethany a copy, finally, when I told her the truth and told her that if she didn't do as I said I'd tell the police her mother had murdered my sister. There is no statute of limitations on that. But Bethany stole it and didn't have it among her things in Houston. I didn't know where she'd hidden it or if she gave it to someone." Her mouth worked. "The obvious choice was her own mother. But I couldn't reveal myself to Sharon. I had to wait to search her house when she wasn't there. Then Andy and Julie, or anyone else Bethany worked with, or her friends in the writing group. It took me weeks. I had to lay low, not look suspicious, and I avoided people. I thought maybe she'd destroyed the video; she had every reason to do so. I watched everyone who mattered to her. I searched their homes when they were gone. But then I realized your mother might have had it. She met us for drinks, once. Bethany invited her. It was the only time we socialized with a third person who I didn't know. I didn't think Bethany had confided in your mother, because Beth Dunning would have gone to the police. But then I realized she might have proof but not know it."

"Why?" Her voice was cold because she was starting to suspect the worst.

"I ordered Andy to get close to your mom, using their mutual worry about Bethany as a starting point. To find out if Beth Dunning had the video. Of course he had to go overboard and start sleeping with her. Sorry if that upsets you and your dad."

You aren't doing this to us, Mom. Who is this guy? Who is he? Dad says you're having an affair… You aren't breaking up our family.

We are not doing this right now. You're not doing this.

Words, as if rising from a dream.

"You're lying," Mariah said through gritted teeth.

"I mean, what else were you arguing with your mom about that day?"

"Arguing." Mariah repeated the word and it sounded like a question. "That day? How did you—"

They could hear the wind in the trees. A ghostly sound.

"I think, though, we need to bring all this to a close," Lizbeth said. "You and Reveal shouldn't have tried to link the cases. I had to follow him, follow you. I wanted to ruin Sharon without implicating myself, and you've taken that away from me. Everything gets taken from me."

"You can't kill us," Mariah said. "People know I've come here. You won't get away with it."

Lizbeth gestured her out of the room with the gun, forced her down the hall, upstairs, and into a second room.

Mariah gasped.

Andy lay on the floor, unconscious, breathing heavily. Sedated but alive.

Her gaze went across the rest of the room, stunned.

On its walls were photos, from the past and the present, maps, schedules, a snapshot, she realized as she studied it, of Bethany Blevins Curtis's life. Pictures of her and Jake out together. Of Jake leaving and entering his office. Of Bethany alone, writing in her journal in a coffee shop, typing on her laptop in a café, frowning at her words, having a lunch with her mother. Pictures of Bethany at a bar with Andy Candolet and other Ahoy coworkers. Her throat went dry: a picture of Bethany and Beth Dunning, both wearing conference tags for WebCon, laughing and holding margaritas.

Maybe the night they met, and *even then Lizbeth had been watching her*.

Mariah touched her mother's face.

Penciled schedules next to pictures, with notes: "Read Bethany's emails while she was connected to coffee shop server. She's lonely. Tired all the time. Wants to write, not really happy in her marriage but loyal to Jake. Seems protective of him. Her coworker Andy flirts with her and she ignores him, this angers him. Could be useful."

This was followed by several more reports.

HOW TO BE BETHANY'S FRIEND—A PLAN

1. Pretend to be a writer.

2. Be interested in true crime. Ha ha ha! She'll have no idea.

3. Avoid Sharon—cannot take chance she will recognize you.

4. A crime that serves as the reason for the crimes that follow. Andy? Embezzlement? Make him think it's his idea. Use the theft to make them all pay. Fear of this crime exposed is leverage you need.

5. Different colored wigs/contact lenses. If questioned why wigs tell Bethany you survived cancer. It will make you more sympathetic.

6. Step by step end her reasons to stay in Austin and then get her to Houston. This is the long game, the end game, and justice. Never waver. You take Bethany from them the way they took Penny from us.

You take Bethany from them the way they took Penny from us.

On another wall: pictures of Lizbeth Gonzales everywhere. Variations on her, like an artist studying her might make. Different hair colors. Different eye colors. Different makeup, different clothes. Frump Lizbeth. Hipster Lizbeth. Scholarly Lizbeth. Sultry Lizbeth. A woman of a dozen faces and looks.

A single picture of Beth, her mother. Under it, in thick black pen: WHAT DOES SHE KNOW?

Mariah repeated the words aloud, like they could mean something more than an awful dismissal of a life. Taped nearby were pictures of her mother and Andy together, at a café, at a hotel. Attention from a callow, attractive younger man, perhaps the antidote for an unhappy woman who had wondered if her husband would ever know what being cheated on felt like. Then more news clippings, pictures of Mariah and her father in the press scrum in the hectic days after Beth Dunning disappeared.

Then chillingly, handwritten, another list titled "What Beth said in her last days—asked for Mariah, would not say if she had the DVD, begged to go home."

The words, rattling and echoing in Mariah's head. She made a noise in her throat.

This room was like a madwoman's brain.

Turn. Turn and see the monster behind you.

"I'm a visual person," Lizbeth Gonzales said from behind her. "We believe what's in front of us."

Mariah managed to find her voice. "You're a monster."

"As are you." Lizbeth's voice, a quiet doom.

59

ANDY MADE A cough, moaned, fell back into a stupor.

"Do you want to kill him," Lizbeth said, "for what he did to your mom, to your family? I'll let you."

"For what?"

"Andy took advantage of your mother. That's what he did with Sharon. What he's done with Julie. Find a weakness, seek to fulfill it, get what he wants. Don't you hate him? He told me you beat him with a police baton." Her mouth crinkled again. "I bet that felt good."

Mariah said, "Did you drug him?"

"Animal tranquilizers. My stepfather keeps horses here. He does whatever I ask. He hates the Blevinses too, for what they did to my mother. I'm all he has, and he's all I've got. People will put up with a lot to not be alone." Lizbeth prodded Andy with his foot. "He wrecked your family, didn't he? Bad boy."

"Are you saying…are you…" Mariah could hardly look at Andy's big frame, sprawled on the floor. "Are you saying he killed my mom?" *To cover up their affair?* Bile rose in her throat.

Lizbeth touched Mariah's jawline. Gently. Like a friend. Mariah tried to think past the shock. Get your knife. Cut her. Hurt her. Run. Mariah forced herself to speak. "Or…are you saying Andy's like Hal? Andy knows who killed her and he protected whoever it was?"

"Your mom finally pillow-talked and told him Bethany had

given her something important to keep. Which is why I was following her..." Lizbeth said and then they heard the grind of gravel on the driveway. Lizbeth went to the window and glanced out. "Oh, thank you, karma. Sharon and Jake."

Mariah barely heard the words. She was going for the knife in her boot, yanking it free, lunging toward Lizbeth as she turned from the window. Jake. He'd come. She had no idea why he'd brought Sharon, but she couldn't let Lizbeth hurt Jake.

Mariah slashed at Lizbeth's gun hand. The blade caught in the fabric of Lizbeth's sleeve, scoring along the skin. Lizbeth was smaller, but she was strong and wiry and she knew how to fight. She hit Mariah, hard, twice in the nose and then the throat with the edge of her gun. Mariah staggered back, tears in her eyes, blood on her face. She swung the knife again and Lizbeth caught her arm, twisted it, made her drop the knife. It clattered to the floor.

"You slept with him. I'll let you say goodbye. Plus I want to give Sharon my best."

Lizbeth jabbed the gun into the side of Mariah's head, and using her like a shield, hurried down the stairs.

* * *

Sharon stared at the two of them. They had made it to the porch, Sharon with a gun leveled at Jake, when Lizbeth and Mariah stepped out, Lizbeth's gun on Mariah. Jake closed his eyes.

"I'm so sorry," Mariah said. "I shouldn't have told you where I was going."

"Hi, there, Mrs. Meadows," Lizbeth said, brightly. "Do you know me? I know you. I see you."

Sharon stared in shock.

"Do you see some of my mom in me, maybe?" Lizbeth said. "Or my sister?"

"You look like Penny Gladney," Sharon said. "The baby. Jenny." Her voice sounded like it was made of dust.

"Lizbeth Gonzales," Lizbeth said. "Your daughter's mystery BFF."

Sharon made a noise in her throat.

"My dad wouldn't fight his cancer. My mom killed herself. You mowed down my sister. It all comes back to you."

Sharon's voice shook. "Is Bethany..."

"Here. Waiting for you." Giving cruel hope.

"Sharon—" Mariah started, but Lizbeth didn't let her finish.

"Bethany's in a grave about two hundred yards away."

It was as if Sharon didn't understand. "She went to Houston."

"She did because I made her. She knew I could destroy you with a phone call. I wanted her to see the house where I used to live. My stepfather still owns it. I flew with her to Houston as Jenny Gladney—my first name. She was scared to death I was going to expose you as the murderer you are. I'd told her who Penny was, who I was, and that you had murdered my sister and that I would expose you and you'd spend the rest of your life in prison. I wrote up a chapter of a novel about the day you ran my sister down, changed all the names, made it so that the father was driving, and made her take it to that stupid writers' group. I listened to them critique it and watched her sweat. It gave her a taste of how you would be judged. She would have done anything to protect your worthless hide, Sharon, and to protect Jake. She did. That was why she left Jake and gave up a fortune. That was why I told her where there was a blind spot in the Houston airport cameras. We could vanish for a moment, change our looks, and walk out arm in arm. On the video, they would be looking for a woman walking alone."

Jake made a noise in his throat. Mariah tried to lock her gaze on him, give him strength.

Lizbeth continued: "I sent Bill to Reveal's group session, to see if he would talk about the case or if Mariah showed up. But he didn't realize Sharon would be there. You recognized him, I think, Sharon—he was a neighbor across the street before he married my mom. You knew the past was closing in on you. You could have confessed to those good people, but you can't, you won't take responsibility. Do you know what that has cost you? Your daughter."

"Lord, help me," Sharon said, a whisper. "Lord, forgive me. Forgive this girl."

Lizbeth's tone was a knife. "Forget your forgiveness. I took Bethany to our house. Where Penny died. Part of the penance. See what she remembered of that day. *Make* her remember. And do you know what your daughter said to me?"

Sharon could hardly look at her.

"She said she hardly remembered any of it, but being back in that house she remembered me, in my crib, crying. Crying so loud, because my mom was occupied with your cheating garbage husband because neither of them had a lick of self-control. She said it was an accident. Her, arguing with me, pleading to leave you alone. Saying she'd do whatever it took if I would leave you alone. Then she attacked me. She wanted to kill me there, in my own home, to protect her dear mother. Kill me, the last of my kind. I killed her on the spot for that. I strangled her dead."

Sharon screamed.

Lizbeth grimaced. "Oh, does that hurt? Poor you." Her words were a whip. "I found the email and the password she'd set up to communicate with you, written down on a card in her purse. So I didn't need her. As long as Andy was getting money from Jake to pay back a nonexistent debt, he was happy and quiet. As long as Jake wasn't enjoying his success and was under a cloud, he was happy."

Sharon sobbed, raging. "You killed my daughter." The gun shook.

"You killed my sister."

"Don't kill anyone else," Mariah said. Quietly but firmly.

"You have no room to talk," Lizbeth said. "You and your dad."

A coldness shifted in Mariah's chest. This woman was insane. She'd say anything.

"Sharon, I'll let them go if you'll come with me. I'll take you to her. But you have to put down the gun." Lizbeth's voice was soft and cajoling.

"What do you want to let us all go?" Jake said. "How much?"

"You, rich nerd, came so close to giving her a great life"—Lizbeth held up her fingers, a centimeter apart—"but I stopped you."

"You even tried to ruin Jake's deals," Mariah said, remembering

Karen's words. "When he met with my mom's company, you vandalized the cars when he didn't get a deal with them."

"I followed him. In the parking garage, he was walking to his car and I heard him calling his office and angrily telling them the deal was off. So I vandalized the cars, two days in a row, in the reserved exec spaces there to make Jake look bad. Why should he be happy?" Lizbeth said.

Jake snapped at Lizbeth. "You don't love your family. You never did. You saw them suffer, but you think you're owed something. Is money going to make it right? Fine. I'll give you all mine. Take it. I'll sign it over to you."

She laughed, keeping Mariah between them like she was a shield.

Mariah said, calmly, "She's going to kill us all and make it look like Andy did it. Sharon, shoot her."

The porch was silent. Sharon was crying, the gun she held now on Mariah steadying. Praying under her breath. Lizbeth aimed her own gun at Sharon.

Jake stepped in front of Sharon.

"Move!" Lizbeth yelled, as if she couldn't start shooting elsewhere. But he'd read her, her gaze fixed on the woman she blamed for everything wrong in her life.

"You killed my girl," Sharon said, trying to contain her rage.

"You're responsible for all of this," Lizbeth said. "What kind of person does what you did? You and Mariah, just the same, leave someone in the street..."

"Stop it!" Mariah screamed. Her mind swam with images, thoughts that made no sense. Her father's face. Her mother's voice. She wrenched her arm free of Lizbeth. She pulled away and fell off the porch.

"Like you're better! I followed her that day. I saw what happened!"

Leave someone in the street. I saw what happened. Words in the air, false words, they had to be false words.

Turn around and see the monster behind you. What if no one was there? What if the monster was herself?

Mariah jumped back onto the porch, reaching for Lizbeth,

grabbing at her arm. Sharon screamed and began firing wildly. Jake launched himself into Mariah and knocked her back off the porch into the dirt.

The two women, firing their guns, hate blinding and binding them.

Mariah screamed, and the birds exploded in flight from the trees.

60

THE POLICE FOUND the two bodies buried next to each other on the Bastrop land—Bethany Curtis and Beth Dunning. The investigation concluded that Lizbeth Gonzales had killed them both: Bethany for revenge and Beth in an attempt to get evidence left by Bethany. Presumably, this evidence was the DVD containing the video from the day Lizbeth's sister, Penny, died.

Bethany had been strangled; Beth had been killed by a blow to the back of her head.

Lakehaven had been wrong about Craig Dunning.

* * *

The news stations gave the story of the three Beths national coverage: the disturbed young woman who had orchestrated a horrifying revenge on the family that had wronged hers. Bill Gonzales, to avoid prison, confessed to his role in helping his adopted daughter with what he called "her project." Andy Candolet, in exchange for immunity, confessed to his part in the framing of Bethany Curtis for the embezzlement and the extortion against Jake Curtis. Julie quickly broke it off with Andy and moved to California with her son, Grant.

Reveal's producers flew out to the crime scene and to his hospital room in Austin, to hear his pitch. He got the deal. *American Unsolved* started streaming on a service a month later.

Sharon lived, a bullet striking her in the shoulder. Lizbeth died, a bullet piercing her throat, her hate finally dying with her. Sharon confessed to the cover-up that had lasted years and destroyed two families. She was taken back to Houston, but considering she had lost her husband and daughter in revenge, the prosecutor decided not to file charges. Her church in Austin closed ranks around her in support for the person she had become rather than the person she once was, and she mostly remained in her house—a prison of its own—until the media glare died down.

The death of Jeffrey Marshall was ruled an accident, a fall down the stairs, resulting in a broken neck and skull fracture.

Jeffrey Marshall might have thrown himself down the stairs—he had financial troubles. He might have slipped. Broussard wrestled with his conscience. There was no proof of Craig's involvement, he decided, and the file was closed.

And Sean Oberst, glad to be rid of a stepfather he didn't like and who was rough with his mother, never mentioned to his mother or to the police the man who came asking about his stepfather.

Lakehaven was forced to reevaluate its opinion of Craig Dunning when his wife's body was found. Neighbors who had not spoken to him showed up on the Dunning porch, bearing dinners and apologies. He accepted both. His accounting firm asked him to return to work at the office; his former clients clamored for his advice. *We were wrong*, they said in their roundabout way. *We're so sorry we judged you. Forgive us and let us feel good about ourselves again.* Craig smiled a lot and nodded and said thank you, all while wishing he was somewhere else, but Mariah needed this return to normalcy.

Mariah had gone to dinner with Jake—second time this week—and come home early and sat down on the couch with her father. TCM was on, but muted. It was another Hitchcock film, *Vertigo*, where identity and memory are intertwined—and where we see what we want to see, we are who we wish we could be. She left the film on mute.

Craig had decided he didn't need the recliner anymore and sold it, and he sat next to his daughter on the couch. Leo waddled in, sat close on the floor, imploring eyes locked on them to see if a treat was a possibility.

"Nice date?" he asked.

"Yes. Jake's a good guy. I don't know if it will go anywhere, but I enjoy his company."

"You don't look like you enjoy it."

"I don't have a right to enjoy it, Dad." The silence between them was awkward. "Karen offered me a job again at Mom's old company. It would be great. But I can't move forward with my life. I haven't told you something Lizbeth suggested to me."

"What?"

"Lizbeth kept hinting that I left Mom in the street. Why would she say that?"

His mouth twisted, and he took her hand in his. "Because she was insane."

"But everyone knows now Lizbeth killed her and buried her."

"Because it's a lie." He tightened his grip on her hands.

"She also said that Bethany's memory of Penny's death was suppressed by the trauma. I think mine was, too. Bits of it have come back." Now she looked at her father. "That day Mom vanished...I was sick. On medication. But I think...I found out about her and Andy. Somehow. I didn't like him from the first moment I met him, even before I had reason to."

"Mariah...."

"You accused her of having an affair. Lizbeth said he was sleeping with Mom." She asked the terrible question. "Did you know?"

He forced the words out like they were painful to speak. "Yes. I had followed her the evening before, seen her meet him. That was what we argued about. Beth and I agreed to meet at the lot. I wasn't feeling ill; it was just an excuse to leave work and not come back. But she didn't want to have this discussion at home, with you there sick."

"So I went with you to the lot? But I was sick." Mariah's voice was a whisper.

"I...I told you about the affair. About her and Andy Candolet. I wanted you on my side. And I thought if you knew, your mother would break it off. We would be back to being a family. I'm sorry."

"You are not dragging our daughter into this." Karen's quote of her mother's words on that overheard phone call at the office. He must have threatened, during that phone call, to tell me. And then he did.

"Lizbeth said she was following Mom, trying to see if she had the DVD Bethany had stolen from her. She was following her that day because Mom told Andy that Bethany had given her something. She kept hinting that she saw what happened." Mariah took a deep breath. "Tell me what happened."

He shook his head. Tears in his eyes.

"Dad. You have to tell me. We can't go on this way." *He's going to confess the most terrible thing*, she thought, *and I have to be here for him. We can't be like Sharon and Hal and hide this away. It destroys a person.*

"You were out of your mind with anger toward her. Especially after she had criticized your bad choices in school. The meds and the fever weren't helping. She tried to reason with you. She grabbed your arms; you pushed her; she fell. Hit her head on a rock. So much blood. I panicked. You lost your mind. I had to get you out of there. Your mind had shut down. I couldn't find a pulse for Beth; I thought she was dead. I panicked. I couldn't have you in trouble, not over a disagreement between her and me. I had dragged you there, and this was my fault. So I took you home, got you into bed. You just shut down. You believed you had killed her."

Mariah couldn't look at him. He cleared his throat. "I came back to get her, and her body was gone. The rock was gone. Someone had taken her body. Lizbeth, who was watching her." His voice shook. "I didn't know what to do. Had someone else found her body? If so, where were the police? They'd be treating it like a crime scene. I thought maybe in blind panic I had missed her pulse, she had crawled or wandered off. But the rock was gone as well, and the blood. Like she had never been there. If I told the truth, I destroyed your life."

Just like Sharon's reasoning. Mariah started shaking and couldn't stop.

"When I got home I waited for the police to call me, to say they'd found her. But they never did. You woke up and you acted as if it hadn't happened. As if you had no memory of the day. I thought at first you were faking, but you weren't. It was as if it hadn't happened." His voice broke again.

"Lizbeth said the same about Bethany." Mariah could barely manage the words, and they felt like a defense. If she didn't remember, then it didn't happen. "But I remember looking for her..."

"I told you we'd done that. I just kept telling you and finally you believed it, because you didn't want to think about the reality."

Mariah's mind felt like it was about to break.

"So I said nothing. I thought someone took her and was going to blackmail me. It never happened. She was just gone." Craig took her hand. "But I swear, I couldn't find a pulse."

"Lizbeth had a list. Of things Mom said in her 'last hours.' Lizbeth took her to that house, didn't she? Mom was still barely alive, horribly injured, and that woman tried to make her talk." Mariah's hands shaped into claws and she dragged them through her hair in rage at herself. "I killed her."

"No. No. What you said to me when you thought, a few days ago, that I'd killed her: *I could forgive an accident*. It was an accident. You didn't mean to hurt her. Never, ever."

Mariah made an indecipherable noise.

Craig's voice was cool, trying to calm her with her own words. "But listen to me. You know the police found Beth's DNA in that bedroom of Lizbeth's, with all the pictures. She was alive, for a while, and I think Lizbeth took her to question her. To find out what she knew. She took her to Bastrop and she died there in that bedroom—Lizbeth wouldn't have brought her into that house if she was already dead—and *you didn't kill her*. Do you understand me? Lizbeth killed her by not getting her medical attention. Or me, for not calling for the police and doing too much to shield you. But not you."

"I shoved her. It's my fault...it's my fault..."

"Listen to me," he said. "You hurt her. It was an accident. But the person who *killed* her is Lizbeth. I never could have dreamed that someone would take her."

"You were willing to bear all this guilt, Dad. You let Lakehaven hate you. You could have said something..."

"I had to protect you. Always protect you." He embraced her. "I'm so sorry. This is my fault, not yours. But I truly thought she was dead and you were so upset...I could only help you, in that moment. You, Mariah. We all make our choices, good and bad, and then we have to make the best of them. When it was clear you didn't remember, I had to make the best of it. To protect you."

Mariah closed her eyes.

She had loved her mother so much, and now the truth hadn't set her free; it had caged her. The fragments of memory made sense now: her mother's surprised face, the words *We are not doing this now*, which lit the fuse of the fatal argument about love and infidelity and a family in tatters, the sense of Mom pointing past her to the monster behind.

But Mom, that ghost in her broken memory, was pointing at her. The monster was her.

The time she'd imagined Jake killing Bethany, the loss of control, the violent shove—that had been an echo of her reality. Fainting at Jake's house when she saw the panorama of Lakehaven—including the lot where she'd so badly hurt her mother. Hearing those words again, *We are not doing this now*, an echo in her ear as the sight of the land and the road where her family had ended overwhelmed her.

"No, baby, you're safe," she heard her mom's voice say. "You're safe now. You're safe now." A kaleidoscope of memories: growing faint even at the sight of the land from the view on Jake's house, the remembered feeling of her mother's hands on shoulders before she pushed her: *Oh, Mom, I'm so sorry I'm so sorry please wake up Mommy please please I didn't mean it...*

EPILOGUE

EIGHT WEEKS LATER

MARIAH STOOD BY the empty lot. The memories had come back, slowly, like smoke rising into a room through door and window.

And she knew what she had to do. She waited.

She had fainted when she saw this lot, from Jake's house, for the first time since her mother vanished. She could not live this way.

Her father drove up in his car, dressed in a suit, as he'd returned to his regular work. He had been quiet for the past two months, seeing how she coped. Giving her space.

"Hi," he said. He hugged her, held her close. "Why are we here?"

He sounded a little afraid.

"Because I remember enough now to tell Broussard exactly what happened here. And I need to. But I can only do that if you're all right with it, Dad."

He said nothing. She thought of what all he had sacrificed for her: his reputation, his career, his peace of mind, all to protect her. She tried not to think too much of Jeffrey Marshall. But that had been ruled an accident, and he'd tried to hurt her father. So she could push those suspicions aside.

"I think you need to do what you need to do," he said quietly. "I left you out of the decisions for so long. You must decide now."

"What will happen to us?"

"He might arrest us both. You could be charged with assault or attempted murder. Me with obstructing justice. Or he might tell us to go home. I don't know. But I can face it with you."

"I need to tell the truth, Dad," she said. "All of it. I can't live with myself if I don't." She closed her hand around his. "But that means you tell, too. We can't make Sharon's mistake. And we can't say it was all Lizbeth."

He slowly nodded, as if he'd known this day would come. "Do you want me to call Dennis?"

Broussard's car approached them and parked, and Broussard got out. "I just asked him to meet us here," Mariah said.

Dad nodded.

"I think it will be a relief, Dad." What had Reveal said to her at their dinner: "There's no cure like the truth." He was right.

Craig closed his eyes for a moment, but Mariah took his hand, and they walked toward the police chief together.

"Hey," Broussard said.

"I know you loved Mom. You know we loved her," Mariah said.

Broussard nodded.

"Do you remember at the coffee shop when we looked at the DVD and you said if my dad killed my mom, you knew it had to have been an accident? That he never would have willingly hurt her. And maybe he panicked and covered it up, and I helped him?" Mariah took a deep breath. "Do you remember?"

Broussard nodded, looking at them both.

"You were right. But it was me that hurt her, and he protected me. I hurt her. I didn't mean to. Dad only tried to shield me. I didn't even remember that I had done it, and he got me away and Lizbeth took her." She extended her hands, as if for forgiveness, or handcuffs. "I don't know what to do to make it right with the world. Will you make it right? I can't be like Sharon and her husband. I can't live with the secret."

Broussard didn't move for a moment. Then he embraced Mariah, tucked her head into his shoulder. She sobbed against him as if the weight of the world were on her. He looked over her shoulder at Craig, who met his gaze in silence. Craig closed his eyes.

"What would your mother want to happen?" Broussard whispered to Mariah. "Do you think your mother would want you to suffer? To pay?"

"I don't know. I don't know."

"Your mama knows you never meant to hurt her. No matter what happened. I can tell you that."

Mariah shuddered in his embrace.

"She knows. She knows. That's what truly matters. She knows. She knows, baby girl. She knows."

Mariah sobbed. She tried to breathe. The breath came. Then the next one. And the next one.

Take her home, Broussard mouthed to Craig. *Take her home. It's going to be all right. Take her home.*

ACKNOWLEDGEMENTS

I was writing *The Three Beths* when our house burned down. It made for a challenging experience, to try to be creative during a time of displacement for me and my family, who were my primary concern. My thanks for those who helped me with this book are particularly heartfelt. Special thanks to Lindsey Rose (who patiently shepherded this book through this difficult time), Ben Sevier, Karen Kozstolnyik, Beth de Guzman, Matthew Ballast, Andy Dodds, Jordan Rubinstein, Joe Benincase, Flamur Tonuzi, Jeff Holt, Nidhi Pugalia, Lori Paximadis, Peter Ginsberg, Holly Frederick, Jonathan Lyons, Sarah Perillo, Madeline Tavis, Shirley Stewart, Eliane Benisti, and Chip Evans.

A special thanks to our many neighbors, family and friends, and kind strangers—here in Austin and from around the world—who responded with help, comfort, prayers, and aid to our family during this time.

Thanks as well to my fellow authors JT Ellison, Meg Gardiner, and Laura Benedict, who in the aftermath of the fire coordinated a book drive among authors and readers to help me rebuild my personal library. Their kindness, and the generosity of those who responded meant a great deal to me as I was writing this book. JT also kindly read an early draft of the book and provided thoughtful feedback, and Meg met me at our local coffee shop for writing sessions. Thank you all.

Thanks as well to Harlan Coben and Daniel Stashower, who were constant friends during the process of writing and rewriting this book and encouraged me over the rough patches.

As always, my deepest thanks to Leslie, Charles, and William for their love and support.

You will not find Lakehaven on a map. You also will not find "Faceplace" as a widely used social networking site.

Any errors or manipulations of fact for dramatic purposes are all on me.